DISTURBED

"Molly, I told you, if you'd just screen your calls—"

"Let me finish, Jeff," she insisted. "The woman left a message on Rachel's answering machine today. I heard it. She threatened Rachel. The same woman called Angela and Kay shortly before they were killed. I'm beginning to think Kay's death wasn't an accident. She could have been murdered. Have you stopped to consider all the deaths and accidents and tragedies this one little block has experienced lately? You should have heard Lynette last night accusing me of stirring up some kind of hornet's nest of bad luck for everyone here on Willow Tree Court."

"You can't take what she said seriously."

"I know it's not me or bad luck that's making all these horrible things happen lately. I think it's the work of this demented woman on the telephone—I think she may be responsible for everything from Erin's smashed pumpkin to Courtney's car wreck. I need to tell this to the police—before someone else is hurt or killed. . . ."

Books by Kevin O'Brien

ONLY SON

THE NEXT TO DIE

MAKE THEM CRY

WATCH THEM DIE

LEFT FOR DEAD

THE LAST VICTIM

KILLING SPREE

ONE LAST SCREAM

FINAL BREATH

VICIOUS

DISTURBED

Published by Kensington Publishing Corporation

DISTURBED

KEVIN O'BRIEN

PINNACLE BOOKS
Kensington Publishing Corp.
www.kensingtonbooks.com

PINNACLE BOOKS are published by

Kensington Publishing Corp.
119 West 40th Street
New York, NY 10018

All Kensington titles, imprints, and distributed lines are available at special quantity discounts for bulk purchases for sales promotions, premiums, fund-raising, educational, or institutional use. Special book excerpts or customized printings can also be created to fit specific needs. For details, write or phone the office of the Kensington special sales manager: Kensington Publishing Corp., 119 West 40th Street, New York, NY 10018, attn: Special Sales Department; phone 1-800-221-2647.

ISBN-13: 978-0-7860-2137-6
ISBN-10: 0-7860-2137-3

First printing: May 2011

10 9 8 7 6 5 4 3 2 1

Printed in the United States of America

*This book is for my friends Terry and Judine Brooks,
and John Saul and Mike Sack.
Thanks for twenty-five years of your generous support,
writing advice, and friendship.
You guys are the best.*

ACKNOWLEDGMENTS

A great big thank-you goes to my ever-patient, encouraging, intelligent editor and friend, John Scognamiglio, and the wonderful folks at Kensington Publishing—especially the magnetic and magnanimous Doug Mendini. I had a terrific time visiting with everyone at Kensington in May. You guys are the greatest!

Thanks also to my wonderful agents, Meg Ruley and Christina Hogrebe, and all the fantastic folks at Jane Rotrosen Agency, with a special nod to Peggy Gordijn for making sure my books go around the world.

Another huge thank-you to my writers' group pals, who weathered early drafts of this book and helped whip it into shape. John Flick, Cate Goethals, Soyon Im, David Massengill, and Garth Stein, you guys rule!

Many thanks to Garth and Seattle7Writers for all their support—what a great group of authors! I'm honored to be associated with them.

And don't even get me started on how much I love the people at Open Road Media. Thank you, guys!

I'm also grateful to all the cool folks at Levy Home Entertainment.

The list of friends who have encouraged me and pushed my books gets longer every year. Thanks to Nancy Abbe, Dan Annear and Chuck Rank, Pam Binder and the folks at PNWA, Marlys Bourm, Amanda Brooks, Kyle Bryan and Dan Monda, George Camper and Shane White, Barbara Riddle Cegielski, Jim and Barbara Church, Anna Cottle and

Mary Alice Kier, the terrific Tommy Dreiling, Paul Dwoskin and the gang at Broadway Video, Tom Goodwin, Dennis and Debbie Gotlieb, Cathy Johnson, Elizabeth Kinsella, David Korabik, Stafford Lombard, Roberta Miner, Jim Munchel, Meghan O'Neill, Midge Ortiz, Eva Marie Saint, those crazy kids at Seattle Mystery Bookshop, Jennie Shortridge, John Simmons, Dan, Doug and Ann Stutesman, George and Sheila Stydahar, Marc Von Borstel (who always makes me look good), and Michael Wells.

Finally, thanks again to my sensational sibs: Adele, Mary Lou, Cathy, Bill, and Joan. I love you guys like a brother.

PROLOGUE

Sitting at the wheel of his family station wagon, Ray Corson watched the gas gauge needle hover at empty. The red warning light flashed on, and he felt his stomach tighten.

He'd been driving for the last hour, making several loops around Seattle's Montlake neighborhood. Part of his route wound through the Arboretum along the edge of Lake Washington. But on this rainy April night, Ray couldn't see the water beyond all the shadowy trees. It was just murky blackness.

At a stoplight, he caught his reflection in the rearview mirror. People often mistook him for someone in his early thirties. At forty-two, Ray loved hearing that. His wavy brown hair hadn't yet turned gray. It helped that he stayed in shape running laps around the high school track every weeknight; or perhaps just being around all those teenagers kept him thinking young.

But Ray hadn't been to the school in months. He couldn't go back there.

That probably explained why the reflection in the rearview mirror was of someone who looked old, haggard—and frightened.

With a sigh, Ray leaned back and cracked the window a

bit. His three-year-old son had stepped on a half-full juice box in the backseat over a week ago, and the car still had the sickeningly sweet smell of Hawaiian Punch gone bad.

The light changed, and he drove on. The fresh air revitalized him, and he took a few deep, calming breaths. He was about to drive past the Arboretum's parking area again. The two light posts didn't quite illuminate the entire lot, which was about the size of a basketball court. Beyond it lay the woods and the lake. The lot was empty right now. No one in their right mind would be at the Arboretum on such a cold, crummy, wet night.

Still, Ray kept his eyes peeled for a parked car—or maybe the silhouette of a man at the edge of that lot.

He suddenly realized his car was veering off the road. Tires squeaked against the curb and gravel ricocheted against the station wagon's chassis. Startled, Ray twisted the wheel to one side and swerved back into his lane.

His heart was racing. "Chill out, for chrissakes," he muttered to himself. He'd thought by now he would be at peace with what was about to happen. But he was still scared.

Ray figured he was good for one more loop around the neighborhood before the station wagon would start to fail on him. He glanced in the rearview mirror at the parking lot again. Then he checked the clock on the dashboard: 12:49 A.M.

He needed to be back there eleven minutes from now.

It would be the end of so many of his problems—including the whole mess at James Monroe High School, where he'd been a guidance counselor. The tension and turmoil with Jenna would be in the past. Jenna and the kids would be covered financially. And maybe his runaway sixteen-year-old daughter would even come home once everything was over and done with.

Ray lowered the window farther and felt the cool rain on his face. He smelled the night air and gazed at the trees swaying along the roadside. All of his senses were suddenly heightened as he took his last loop around the area. Everything seemed so beautiful, each moment so precious. He started to cry; he couldn't help it.

Just as he'd figured, the station wagon began to sputter as he approached the small parking lot for the ninth time. Wiping the tears from his face, Ray steered into the lot, parked the car, and left the engine running.

The wipers squeaked against the windshield, and rain tapped on the car roof. Ray tipped his head back against the headrest of the driver's seat. He gazed over toward the shadowy edge of the lot. He couldn't see it now, but somewhere there in the darkness began a dirt trail. It wove through the trees and shrubs, down to the lake.

He remembered parking his beat-up red VW bug in this same spot on a warm May night nearly twenty years ago. He and Jenna had been sophomores at the University of Washington, out on their first date.

Ray had been admiring her from afar ever since freshman year, when he'd spotted her at a kegger, dancing with this nerdy guy who couldn't keep up with her. The long-haired, pretty brunette was so sexy and uninhibited. Every once in a while she whispered into her dance partner's ear, and Ray figured that guy was the luckiest son of a bitch at the party. Ray was so enamored of her that it took him a while to notice her dance partner had one of those shriveled arms resembling a bird wing. And yet he looked so damn happy. Ray kept thinking, *she could have any dude in the room, and she picked that guy.* It didn't make her a saint, but it certainly made her more interesting. For nine months, he looked for her in the cafeteria or at different parties. Unfortunately, when he spotted her on occasion, he never got up the nerve to talk with her. She was always surrounded by guys.

Then they'd ended up in the same English lit class, and he'd finally had an excuse to approach Jenna and ask her out on a date.

Ray paced himself when they split a bottle of red wine in her dorm room. He didn't want to get drunk and smash up his VW on their way to dinner. They ate at My Brother's Pizza in Wallingford. She loved that he had a car, and wanted to go for a drive afterward. While they aimlessly drove around Montlake, Madison Park, and Capitol Hill, Jenna talked and talked and talked. He loved listening to her, and he loved the subtle, flowery scent of her perfume in his car. At one point, she put her hand on his knee and confessed, "Ever since I first saw you in Converse's English lit class, I've thought you were super cute. . . ."

After that, Jenna could have said anything. He didn't care where they were going. He would have driven to the end of the earth with her if she wanted.

"Well, um, the feeling's mutual," Ray managed to reply. He tried to keep his eyes on the road. But her hand was still on his knee, and he felt his erection stirring.

It shrank a bit as Jenna told him about some of the other guys she'd been with—and how horrible they'd treated her. She'd even made a little doll resembling one guy who had really screwed her over, and she used to stick pins in it. She confessed that in high school she'd tried to kill herself twice—the first time with sleeping pills, and the second effort, with a razor blade. Both times she'd called a friend immediately after the final swallow or slash.

"Why did you do it?" Ray whispered, tightening his grip on the steering wheel.

"Call my friend?" she asked. "Or why did I try to kill myself?"

"Both."

She pulled away from him a bit. Jenna leaned her head against the half-open window and gazed out at the road. Her dark hair blew in the wind. "I guess it seemed like the only way I could take control of things, and—I don't know—get out. . . ."

"Get out of what?"

She shrugged. "Bad relationships, mostly—and other things, too."

"No guy's worth killing yourself over, Jenna," Ray murmured, glancing at her. "You must have figured that out. Is that why you called your friend?"

Still staring outside, she shook her head. "No, I just didn't want to die all alone." She let out a sad, little laugh. "But instead of coming over and keeping me company, my stupid friend called the police."

"Well, I for one am glad she did," Ray said.

Jenna was quiet for a moment. "You're right about the guys," she said at last. "Both those times, they were total jerks. They didn't really love me. They were just using me. You know, I'm a firm believer in karma. They'll get theirs—eventually. Time wounds all heels."

Ray managed to laugh. He didn't quite know what to think—or where this night would go. The gorgeous creature sitting across from him was pretty screwed up. But he liked her. She was vulnerable and sweet—and in need of someone to rescue her. Ray wanted to be that someone.

Jenna also had a hell of a lot more experience than him. Ray couldn't help feeling intimidated by that. If things got sexual later on—and he was hoping they would—then, she might find him pretty inept in the lovemaking department. He'd been so crazy about her for so long, he didn't want to disappoint her.

Jenna scooted over toward him again, and he breathed in the smell of her perfume. She nudged him. "Y'know, you're the first person I've told about my suicide attempts—at least, the first person here at the U." She rested her head on his shoulder, and fingered the buttons of his blue oxford shirt. "I meant it when I said that I can really talk to you, Ray. . . ."

She giggled. "God, I didn't mean to get so serious on you! We should do something fun. It's so beautiful and warm out. We should go swimming. . . ."

Eyes on the road, Ray thought for a moment. Back in September, he and two other guys from the dorm had gone skinny-dipping in the Arboretum late one warm Friday night. They'd had a blast. At the time, Ray kept thinking how sexy it would be to share this naked, moonlight swim with a girl.

"Well, there's the Arboretum," he heard himself say. "This time of night, we'd probably have the place to ourselves. . . ."

"God, that sounds fantastic!" Jenna replied. Then she kissed him on the neck. "Let's do it, let's do it. . . ." Laughing, she pulled away, then leaned out her window and let out a howl.

Jenna had two Jack Daniel's miniatures in her purse. She guzzled down one on their way to the Arboretum, and the other Ray helped her finish off once they'd parked the car.

Ray's stomach was in nervous knots as they walked down the dark, winding dirt path toward the lake. At the same time, he was incredibly turned on. Neither one of them had said anything yet about swimsuits—or the lack thereof.

He wondered if she'd keep on her bra and panties to go swimming. Maybe once they reached the lake, if he quickly undressed down to nothing, she'd follow his lead.

They came to a field, where Ray could see the lake ahead, its silvery ripples glimmering in the moonlight. A huge tree loomed at the edge of the shore—some of the branches dipping down into the water. Ray remembered there was a rope hanging from a high limb. He and his dorm buddies had swung from it and jumped into the water several times. The 520 bridge nearby had an arterial route that had never been completed. The abandoned, blocked-off piece of road veered off the bridge and abruptly ended over this secluded section of the lake.

"Oh, good!" she declared. "No one else is around! It's just us. . . ."

Ray didn't hear any laughter, chatter, or water splashing. She was right. They were alone here. It was what he wanted, but also a little scary. He'd heard stories about drug deals, muggings, and all sorts of creepy goings-on at the Arboretum late at night. The rural oasis in the middle of the city seemed the perfect place for some senseless, grisly murder.

The last time here at night with his three pals, Ray hadn't been worried. But this was a totally different scenario, because he was here alone with a beautiful girl—and he had to protect her.

As they ventured toward the lake, Jenna seemed oblivious to the potential hazards. Weaving a bit as she walked, she half-sang and half-hummed a Eurythmics tune: "Sweet dreams are made of this. Who am I to disagree?" She started to run ahead of him. Ray watched her pull her T-shirt over her head, and then she shook out her long brown hair. Her skin almost looked blue in the moonlight. His mouth open, he gaped at her as she reached back and unhooked her bra.

"No one else is around," she said again. "This is perfect, Ray . . . perfect . . ."

Ray started to undress, too. Jenna was already naked—and at the water's edge. Tossing aside her clothes, she let out a scream and plunged into the lake. Ray got only a brief glimpse of her beautiful, ripe ass before the water came up to her waist. Then she was completely submerged.

Ray shucked down his jeans and undershorts. He hurried into the cold water to catch up with her, but she hadn't resurfaced yet. The soft bottom of the lake felt slimy between his toes as he made his way toward deeper water. He kept glancing around for her, wondering where she'd swum off to. For a few moments, he panicked—until, finally, she bobbed up, and grabbed the rope that hung from a branch of the huge tree.

Ray felt at once relieved and awestruck by the sight of her. She took his breath away. She was a vision with her long, wet hair slicked back, and her flawless, creamy skin. Her breasts were small, and her nipples—hard from the cold water—looked like gumdrops.

Jenna smiled at him. "If you can catch me," she called playfully, "you can have me as your love slave! I'll do anything for you!"

Ray broke into a grin. "Then prepare to be caught, wench!" he announced, trying to sound like a swashbuckling pirate. He started toward her, keeping his head above water so he wouldn't miss one moment of her in the moonlight.

Jenna scowled at him. "Did you just call me a *bitch*?"

"No, I said, *wench . . . wench!*" he explained, a little out of breath. "I was like—joking, y'know? I'd never seriously. . . ."

Jenna let out a squeal, then splashed him in the face.

Momentarily blinded, Ray heard her swimming away and singing again, "Everybody's looking for something. Some of them want to use you . . ." Blinking, he turned and saw her backstroking farther into the deep end, toward the unfinished arterial road off the 520 bridge. He glanced back at the shore to make sure their clothes were still there. He saw them, still in a pile by the big tree.

But Ray saw something else on the shore, too—something or someone.

The pinpoint of light in the darkness was far away, maybe in the meadow or perhaps in the parking lot. He couldn't tell if it was someone with a flashlight—or a single headlight. Whatever it was, the thing seemed to be coming toward them and getting brighter. Then suddenly it disappeared.

Ray stared off into the darkness for another few moments. But he didn't see the strange, solitary light again.

All at once, everything was quiet. He couldn't hear Jenna singing or splashing in the water anymore. Ray swiveled around and gaped at the end of the aborted roadway jutting over the lake. Jenna was hoisting herself up to one of the support beams. "What are you doing?" he called. "Jenna, are you nuts?"

He swam toward her as fast as he could. But he wasn't the best swimmer. He lost all sense of direction when his head was underwater. After several frenzied strokes, Ray paused to catch his breath and see where he was going. He'd veered away from the bridge. But he spotted Jenna climbing over the guardrail to the unfinished section of road.

She paused at the abrupt edge, about ten or twelve feet over the water. Headlights from passing cars on the bridge briefly illuminated her lean, nude silhouette. She looked so defiant, uninhibited, and utterly gorgeous as she stood there. Ray was mesmerized—until she slowly raised her hands over her head. He could see she was preparing to dive, and a panic swept through him.

His dad's best friend in high school was paralyzed after diving into a quarry and hitting a boulder. Ray imagined blocks of concrete under the water by that unfinished road. "Don't dive in there, Jenna!" he called, swimming toward her. He got water in his mouth and nose, and he began to cough. "You—you could get hurt! It's too dangerous. . . ."

"I don't care," she replied, a tremor in her voice. It sounded like she was crying. "It doesn't matter. . . ."

Helplessly, he watched her push off from the edge. She executed a flawless dive, plunging into the lake's placid surface with only a small splash. Ray anxiously waited for her to emerge again, but there was no sign of her for several, long, unendurable moments.

He imagined having to carry her limp nude body all the way to the car, and then speeding to the UW Hospital.

"Jenna?" he called out, glancing around. He didn't see her near the shore. But he noticed the little point of light again—closer than before, yet still too far away for him to figure out what it could be.

Right now, he was more concerned about Jenna. He knew she was drunk; but her mood swings were absolutely nuts. Just five minutes ago she'd been so excited, laughing and singing and flirting with him. Then up on the edge of that unfinished road, he could have sworn she was sobbing. Was she trying to commit suicide again?

For all he knew, she'd just succeeded. It had been at least

a minute since Jenna had plunged into the inky water—and she still hadn't resurfaced.

"Jenna?" he yelled, frazzled. "Goddamn it, Jenna . . ."

He turned at the sound of splashing water and saw her clutching on to the rope again. This time, there was nothing sexy about it. She was crying and gasping for air.

"Are you okay?" Ray asked, swimming toward her.

She didn't answer him. She started to pull herself up the rope.

"Jenna, what the hell is going on?" he called. "Why are you acting like this?"

She didn't even glance at him. A determined expression on her face, Jenna continued to shimmy up the rope. He was amazed at her strength and agility. He knew guys back in high school gym class—even a few of the jocks—who had trouble with the rope climb. Yet Jenna pulled herself up, passing the lower branches. He heard her sobbing the whole time.

"What are you doing?" Ray called, heading toward the shore now. "For God's sake, Jenna, you're going too high!"

She disappeared amid the top branches of the tree. But he could still hear her crying.

Naked and shivering, Ray staggered onto the muddy bank. He spotted her again, standing on one of the high branches. Jenna was shivering, too. She still held on to the rope and braced herself against another limb. She hoisted up the thick, braided cord, and then took the slack and wrapped it around her neck.

"Oh, Jesus, no," Ray murmured, horrified. He raced to the tree and began climbing it. The branches and rough bark scratched his bare feet and scraped against his naked torso. But he pressed on, grabbing one limb and then another, struggling to reach her before she jumped. "NO!" he yelled with what little breath he had.

She gazed down at him. The rope was twisted around her neck.

"Please, Jenna," he gasped, climbing to a higher branch. "Even if you're kidding, cut it out. You're giving me a heart attack here. I don't want—I don't want anything bad happening to you. Why are you doing this anyway?"

Numbly, she stared back at him. "Why not?" she muttered. "Who would care?"

"I would, I'd care!" he answered, pulling himself up to the same branch as her. She backed away—farther out on the limb. He didn't want to scare her off, so he stayed close to the base of the tree. "Listen, if you're doing this for some kind of attention, you don't need to. You've always had my attention, Jenna. If—if I see you in a room, you're all I see. I gotta tell you, I—I'm crazy about you." He clung to the tree branch and let out a frightened laugh. "And I'd be really pissed if I lost you this early in the game. . . ."

Jenna cracked an uncertain little smile. "You like me?" she asked quietly.

He nodded. "A lot—even when you're acting weird, like now. In fact, it makes me like you even more. How screwed up is that?"

She wiped the tears from her eyes and managed to laugh. "Pretty screwed up . . ."

"We make a terrific pair," he said. Despite the fact that she stood precariously on that limb with a rope wound around her neck, Ray couldn't help looking at Jenna's beautiful breasts, her long limbs, and that triangle of dark pubic hair.

He noticed she was looking him up and down, as well. She started to unwrap the thick cord from around her neck.

Then she suddenly lost her footing.

Ray heard a branch snap. Jenna let out a shriek. Her arms flailing, she teetered to one side. The rope was still partially looped around her neck as she started to fall.

Paralyzed, Ray watched her careen down toward the lake. Twigs cracked and broke as her body hit them on the way down. For a few moments, everything was a blur. Ray didn't recall scrambling out on the limb and then diving into the lake to rescue her. He just remembered plunging into the water, then bobbing up to the surface and gasping for air.

Jenna was only a few feet away, amid a whirlpool of leaves and twigs. She held her forehead and laughed while treading water. Somehow, the last loop of the rope had uncoiled during her fall. He noticed some blood on her elbow—and fresh scratch marks on her arms. But her neck and face were unmarred.

"My God, are you okay?" he asked, wiping the water and snot from his nose.

Nodding, she drifted toward him. "I can't believe you dove in after me," she murmured. "Do you know how high that was? You risked your life for me. . . ."

She put her arm around him, then kissed him.

Ray was too numb to feel aroused. Exhausted, they clung to each other and made their way to the shore. He kept checking her arms for cuts and scratch marks. Jenna said she'd be okay. As they both emerged from the water, they paused to catch their breath. They gazed at each other.

Her eyes seemed to focus on his torso. She gently touched his hip. "You nicked yourself, poor baby," she whispered.

Ray glanced down at a scrape mark along his right rib cage.

"Should I kiss it and make it better?" she whispered.

Before he could answer, she bowed down. He felt her warm breath against his cold, wet skin as she planted kisses along his rib cage. Ray shuddered gratefully. He was about to close his eyes.

But he noticed that solitary light again—coming closer.

"Wait, no . . . wait, Jenna, no," he whispered, pulling her up. "Someone's coming. . . ."

She looked out toward the meadow—toward the beam of light. "What is that?"

Ray urgently pulled her toward the base of the tree, where they'd left their clothes. "Let's get dressed, c'mon. . . ." He reached for his undershorts.

"What is that?" she repeated. Then she called out, "Who's there? Is somebody there?"

Ray put on his boxers, then grabbed her bra and shook it at her. "Y'know, Jenna," he whispered, "it might be a good idea to put some clothes on."

With a perturbed look, she took the bra and slipped it on.

Ray swiped up her panties and handed them to her. He glanced toward that eerie, single spot of light again. Now he could see a person behind it. Someone with a flashlight was coming toward them. Ray quickly stepped into his jeans and threw on his shirt. To his utter frustration, Jenna was taking her sweet time getting dressed. She stood there in just her bra and panties, squinting at that lone figure with a flashlight.

Ray tried to get a good look at the man, but the flashlight was blinding him. He heard the man's feet shuffling as the light got closer and brighter. Ray shielded his eyes. "Who's there? Can I—can I help you?"

The light shined on Jenna. She sneered at the man behind it. "What the hell do you want?"

Now Ray could see the lean, tall man in a police uniform. He was about thirty-five, with black hair and a thin, weather-lined face. His police cap was tucked under his arm. "Seattle Police," he announced. "Are there any more of you out here? Or is it just you two kids?"

Ray swallowed hard. "It's just us. . . ."

"Is that your red Volkswagen in the lot?" he asked.

Ray nodded. "Yes, that's my car. I'm sorry. Were we making too much noise?"

"It's not a case of too much noise," the cop said, directing the light at him again. "This park closes at ten p.m. So it's a case of trespassing—and indecent exposure."

"Oh, for Christ's sake," Jenna hissed, defiantly standing there in her bra and panties. "Don't you have anything better to do? It's not like we—"

Ray swiveled around. "Shut the hell up!" he said under his breath. "You want to get us arrested? Let me handle this. . . ." He turned around and shrugged at the cop. "I'm sorry, it was my idea that we come here. If we've broken any laws, it's my fault. I wasn't thinking. . . ."

The cop switched off the flashlight. "I'll let you folks finish dressing," he said coolly, "and then I'd like to have a word with you."

"Yes, sir," Ray answered.

The tall policeman wandered back a few paces. He took a pack of gum from his shirt pocket and unwrapped a stick.

Ray grabbed his socks and shoes. "Get dressed, and don't say a word," he whispered to Jenna. "I know I'm sucking up. But why antagonize him? I don't want to spend the night in jail or have an arrest record with indecent exposure listed on it. That would kiss off my plans to become a teacher. Please, just let me talk to him. Maybe he'll let us go with a warning if I apologize and grovel enough."

Jenna stared at him for a moment; then she nodded. "You handle it."

Ray apologized profusely while the cop escorted them back to the parking lot. Lagging behind them, Jenna didn't utter a syllable. The policeman let them go with a warning and a few cautionary tales about the different muggings, rapes, and murders that had occurred at the Arboretum after dark.

An hour later, over pancakes at the Dog House—one of Seattle's most popular late-hour roadhouse-style diners—Ray and Jenna discussed whether or not any of the cop's horror stories were really true. Ray felt so elated to have survived the night's adventures with just a few scratches. All his terror and all of Jenna's craziness—he'd never felt more alive. And the pancakes he wolfed down were the best he'd ever had—even though they'd been served up by a haggard, geriatric waitress, and the place was a dive. Despite the dim lighting, he could detect a grimy layer of grease and smoke covering everything—from the blown-up sepia photos of old Seattle on the walls to the silver tops of the salt and pepper shakers on their table.

Beneath that table, Jenna had slipped off one shoe, and her foot kept touching his. Her toes wiggled under the cuff of his jeans and worked their way up his shin. "You saved my life tonight," she said, while nibbling on a piece of bacon. "You rescued me from myself, Ray. I don't know why I do stuff like that, I really don't."

He didn't dare ask her if she'd truly intended to kill herself earlier. He didn't want to spoil the moment. He smiled at her. "You know, the Chinese say that once you save someone's life, you're henceforth responsible for them."

"*Henceforth*, huh?" she asked, sipping her glass of milk through a straw. "Well, I kind of like that." Beneath the table, she scrunched her toes, playfully tugging at the hair on his shin. "Looks like you're stuck with me, *henceforth*."

"I kind of like that, too," Ray said.

He'd been infatuated with her up until then, but that was the night Ray told himself she was *the one*—even if she was slightly screwed up. Who wasn't screwed up in one way or another? She made him feel important.

They were married two years later, the summer after their graduation. It wasn't always smooth sailing. Her demons emerged from time to time, but she never attempted suicide again.

Then, five months ago, that thing happened at the high school, and it all went to hell. He watched Jenna, his family, his career—everything—unravel. He'd rescued her once, but couldn't help her this time. Nor could he save his daughter, who had packed up and disappeared amid all the fighting and the misery.

Ray didn't see any way out—until just recently.

He remembered what Jenna had told him that night about her suicide attempts: *"I guess it seemed like the only way I could take control of things, and—I don't know—get out. . . ."*

Ray wasn't sure how long he'd been sitting inside the idling station wagon in the Arboretum parking lot. But the rain had stopped tapping on the car roof. He heard the wipers squeaking and the motor purring. He switched off the wipers. Beads of rain surrounded a clean, twin-fan pattern on the windshield. He had a clear view of Lake Washington Boulevard. There wasn't any traffic at all.

The dashboard clock read 1:04 A.M. Everything was supposed to have happened four minutes ago.

The motor died.

Ray stared at the red warning light on the gas gauge. He didn't try to restart the engine. Instead, he took out his wallet and looked for his AAA card. In his rearview mirror, he spotted a car coming up the road. A black BMW slowed to a crawl by the parking lot entrance.

Ray started shaking. He could hardly breathe—until the BMW picked up speed and continued down Lake Washington Boulevard. Then it disappeared around a curve in the road.

He finally found the card. With a trembling hand, he punched in the numbers on his iPhone. The AAA operator answered, and Ray told her that he'd run out of gas. "I managed to roll into a parking lot by the Arboretum—off Lake Washington Boulevard," he said nervously. His heart was racing. "I'll need some assistance. Do you know how long it will be before you can get a tow out here—or someone with a container of gas?"

Forty-five minutes, the operator said.

"I'll be here, waiting," Ray said. "Thanks a lot."

After he clicked off, Ray shoved the phone in his jacket pocket. He was too anxious to just sit there at the wheel and wait. So he left the keys in the ignition, opened the door, and stepped out of the car. For a moment, he thought he might be sick, but he took a few deep breaths.

From where he stood, Ray could see that old pathway between some bushes at the edge of the lot—the trail Jenna and he had ventured down so long ago. He couldn't believe it was twenty years. Where the hell had the time gone? He'd brought his young son, Todd, to this park a few months back, and discovered they'd chopped down that tree with the rope. And the Dog House, where Jenna and he had eaten those delicious pancakes, had closed back in 1994.

Out of the corner of his eye, Ray noticed a pinpoint of light in a field south of the parking lot. A chill raced through him as he watched the light get closer—and brighter. He knew this time, it wasn't a cop.

Ray started shaking again.

At a brisk, businesslike clip, the man approached the edge of the parking lot. He switched off his flashlight. Ray could see him now—about six feet tall and swarthy. He wore a hooded clear rain slicker over dark clothes. Surgical gloves covered his hands. He paused for only a moment at the lot's edge before he started toward Ray with a determined look on his face.

Ray backed up toward the car. "Hey, listen," he said, barely able to get the words out. "I—I don't know what you're planning exactly, but please . . ."

Unresponsive, the man kept coming toward him. He reached for something in the pocket of his slicker.

Shaking his head, Ray backed into his car. "Just—just stop for a second. Please, wait—"

The man pulled out a short piece of metal pipe and slammed it down on Ray's head.

Ray let out a feeble, garbled cry. He fell against the side of the station wagon and then crumpled to the wet pavement. Dazed, he lay there while the man frisked him. Ray tried to push him away, but he couldn't lift his hands.

The stranger took Ray's wallet and iPhone and then pocketed them. He grabbed Ray by the wrists and started pulling him across the lot toward the opening in the bushes. Ray was dragged down the same pathway he'd ventured with Jenna on that warm night twenty years before. He remembered Jenna's beautiful smile when she said, *"No one else is around. . . ."*

Ray tried to struggle as the man hauled him into the shadowy brush, but he couldn't move. When he tried to talk, no words came out—just muted moans. It was as if he were having a nightmare, and couldn't wake himself up. He couldn't even scream.

His vision was blurred, but he could still see the man, hovering over him with a gun in his hand.

"No . . . no . . . no . . ." Ray managed to whisper.

"Shut the fuck up," the man grumbled. He pointed the gun down at Ray.

No one else was around.

No one else heard the three gunshots.

CHAPTER ONE

"Erin . . . sweetie, eat your waffle," Jeff Dennehy told his six-year-old daughter.

There were four curved-hardback chairs around the circular, pine table with a lazy Susan in the middle of it. On top of the lazy Susan was a hand-painted vase with a bouquet of pipe-cleaner-and-tissue daisies. The creator of that slightly tacky centerpiece was seated beside Jeff. The cute, solemn-faced blond girl gazed over her shoulder at the TV and a commercial for toilet paper—something with cartoon bears. They'd been watching the *Today* show on the small TV at the end of the kitchen counter.

"C'mon, Erin," Jeff said over his coffee cup. "Molly made the waffles from scratch, and you haven't even put a dent in them."

With a sigh, Erin turned toward her plate, curled her lip at it, and pressed down on the waffle with the underside of her fork. "It's mushy," she murmured. "I want waffles from a toaster."

Dressed in a T-shirt, sweatpants, and slippers, Molly had her strawberry-blond hair swept back in a ponytail. She leaned against the counter and sipped her coffee. She thought maybe if her stepdaughter hadn't drowned the waffle in a quart of maple syrup, it wouldn't be so *mushy*. But Molly bit her lip, set down her coffee cup, and retreated to the refrigerator. She opened the freezer in search of some Eggos, anything to put an end to the father–daughter stand-off. She didn't need the aggravation this morning.

"You know, peanut," Jeff was saying patiently. "Fresh waffles are better than ones from the toaster. Good waffles aren't supposed to have the consistency of old drywall."

Of course, Jeff wouldn't touch a waffle—fresh, toasted, or otherwise—if his life depended on it. He was having his usual bran flakes to help maintain his lean, muscular build. Molly's husband was a bit vain—and had good reason to be. Dressed for work in his black Hugo Boss suit, crisp white shirt, and a striped tie, he looked very handsome. He was forty-four, with a light olive complexion, brown eyes, and black hair that was just starting to cede to gray.

"C'mon, just a few bites," he coaxed his daughter. "Molly cooked this breakfast, special for you and Chris. You don't want to hurt her feelings, do you?"

Molly couldn't find any Eggos in the freezer, so she fetched a box of Corn Pops from the kitchen cabinet.

She and Jeff had been married for ten months. Whenever Erin and her seventeen-year-old brother, Chris, returned from a weekend with their mother, Molly felt extra compelled to show them what a great stepmother she was. So she'd cooked bacon and homemade waffles for their breakfast this Monday morning.

Molly had her theories, but still didn't know exactly why Angela Dennehy had moved out of her own house, surrendered custody of her kids, and settled for visitation rights. One thing for certain, Angela didn't want her kids warming up to their dad's new and younger wife.

Molly was thirty-two and still adjusting to stepmotherhood. Obviously, her breakfast strategy wasn't scoring points with Jeff's younger child. Molly poured some Corn Pops and milk into a bowl, took away Erin's plate, and set the cereal in front of her. She patted Erin's shoulder. "Eat up, honey. You don't want to miss your bus."

Jeff gave his daughter a frown, which she ignored while eating her Corn Pops. On TV, Matt Lauer announced that *Today* would be right back after a local news break.

Molly set Erin's plate in the sink, and then unplugged the waffle iron. With a fork, she carefully pried a fresh waffle from the hot grid. "Chris!" she called. "Chris! Your breakfast is ready!"

Her stepson hadn't yet emerged from his bedroom. This elaborate breakfast—at least, elaborate for a weekday—was mostly for him. One of the first breakfasts she'd cooked in Jeff's house had been waffles, and Chris had proclaimed they were "awesome." Maybe he was just being polite, or perhaps Jeff had told him to say that. Nevertheless, Molly always unearthed the waffle iron when she wanted to get in her stepson's good graces.

"Chris, breakfast!" Molly set the plate in front of his empty chair. "I made waffles. . . ."

"Okay, in a minute!" he shouted from upstairs.

On TV, Molly glanced at the pretty, thirtysomething Asian anchorwoman with a pageboy hairstyle. *"Seattle's Arboretum became the site of a grisly murder early this morning,"* she announced.

Molly reached for the coffeepot and refilled Jeff's cup.

"Thanks, babe," he said, wiping his mouth with his napkin. "C'mon, Chris, your breakfast is getting cold!" he yelled. "Molly's gone to a lot of trouble this morning!"

She didn't want him browbeating the kids on her account. That was no way to win them over. "It's no biggie," Molly murmured, moving to the counter, and topping off her own cup of coffee.

On the television, they showed an ambulance and several police cars encircling a small parking lot. Yellow police tape was wrapped around some trees at the edge of the lot. It fluttered in the breeze. Paramedics loaded a blanket-covered corpse into the back of the ambulance. *"The victim, according to early reports, was robbed and then shot execution-style after his car broke down along Lake Washington Boulevard,"* the anchorwoman explained with a somber voiceover. *"He has been identified as forty-two-year-old, Raymond Corson, a former guidance counselor at James Monroe High School . . ."*

"Oh, God, no," Molly murmured, stunned. For a moment, she couldn't breathe.

She forgot she was holding the quarter-full coffeepot. It slipped out of her hand and crashed against the tiled floor. Glass shattered, and hot coffee splashed the front of her sweatpants. But it didn't burn her. Molly glanced down at the mess for only a moment. Then she went right back to staring at the TV—and that covered-up thing they were shoving into the back of an ambulance.

Ray Corson had been Chris's guidance counselor at the high school—until he'd been forced to leave last December. Chris still blamed himself for that. He blamed her, too.

She was barely aware of Jeff asking if she was all right or of Erin fussing about the glass and coffee on the floor. All Molly really heard was the anchorwoman on TV: *"Ray Corson left behind a wife and two children. . . ."*

"God, no," Molly whispered again, shaking her head.

". . . Corson telephoned Triple-A, reporting car trouble shortly after one o'clock Monday morning," the handsome blond-haired TV news correspondent said into his microphone. He was in his mid-thirties and wore a Windbreaker. He stood in front of a parked police car; its red strobe swirled in the early morning light.

On the TV in Chris's bedroom, another local station covered the same news story Molly had viewed down in the kitchen just two minutes before. She recognized the crime scene, a small parking lot by the Arboretum.

Molly stood in his doorway. With the curtains still closed, Chris's bedroom was dark. Swimming trophies, graphic novels, and waggle-headed *Family Guy* figurines occupied his bookcase. On his walls were movie posters for *Old School* and *Inglourious Basterds*. One wall panel was corkboard—on which he'd tacked college pennants, pictures of him with his swim team buddies, and about a dozen family photos. Of course, while his mother was in several of the snapshots, Molly wasn't in any. She often had to remind herself this was *his* bedroom, and he was free to decorate it any way he wanted. Still, would it kill him to put up one lousy little photo of her? It didn't even have to be one of her alone, either. She'd be happy if he tacked up a photo of her and Jeff, or her with Erin, or even one with her in the background, for pity's sake. *Throw me a bone here, Chris,* she wanted to tell him. Then again, she wasn't in his bedroom much—except briefly, to put his folded laundry on the end of his bed every few days. Molly told herself that he was a nice kid and certainly polite enough to her.

The TV glowed in one corner of the room, where Chris had a beanbag chair close enough to the set to ensure he'd go blind by age fifty. But he wasn't sitting in that chair right now. He stood barefoot by his unmade bed, his eyes riveted to the TV screen. He was tall and lean, with unruly brown hair and a sweet, handsome face. His rumpled, half-buttoned blue striped shirt wasn't tucked into his jeans. He didn't seem to notice Molly in his doorway.

On TV, they showed a station wagon—with the driver's door open. Two cops lingered nearby, discussing something. *"According to Brad Reece, the Triple-A responder, he pulled into the parking lot here off Lake Washington Boulevard at the Arboretum at 1:45,"* the reporter was saying. *"He found this empty station wagon. Reece tried to call Ray Corson's cell phone, but didn't get an answer. Then he noticed something down this trail. . . ."* The camera tracked along a crooked pathway, through some foliage until it reached a strip of yellow police tape stretched across the bushes. In bold black letters, the tape carried a printed warning: CRIME SCENE—DO NOT PASS BEYOND THIS POINT. The image froze on that police barrier—and the darkness that lay beyond it. *"Reece discovered the victim a few feet past this point. Ray Corson had been shot. I'm told the police found his wallet in a field just north of this spot. The cash and credit cards were missing. Investigators are still searching for the cell phone Corson used to call Triple-A."* The solemn-faced reporter came back on the screen again. *"Reporting from Seattle's Arboretum, I'm John Flick, KOMO News."*

At that moment, Chris seemed to realize someone else was there. He turned and gazed at her.

"Are you okay, Chris?" she asked, still hesitating in his doorway.

"I'm fine," he said, his voice raspy. He started making his bed.

"Listen, if you don't feel like going to school today, I can call and tell them you're sick," Molly offered.

"It's okay, I'm fine," he murmured, straightening the bed sheets. He looked at her again and blinked. "What happened to you?"

She glanced down at the coffee stains on the front of her gray sweatpants. "I dropped the coffeepot. Your dad's still cleaning up the mess. There might still be some glass on the floor. So—ah, put your shoes on before you come down to the kitchen, okay?"

He just nodded, then pulled the quilted spread over his bed. He stopped for a moment to wipe his eyes again.

"I made waffles," she said, suddenly feeling stupid for mentioning it.

"Thanks, Molly, but I'm not really hungry," he murmured.

She wanted to hug him, and assure him that what happened to Mr. Corson last night had nothing to do with him—and it had nothing to do with the messy business at school five months ago. But the front of her was soaked with cold coffee, and besides, Chris wasn't big on doling out hugs—at least, not with her. So Molly just tentatively stood in his doorway with her arms folded.

He finished making the bed, then sank down on the end of it, his back to her. "I'll be down in a minute," he said, his voice strained. "Could you—could you close the door?"

Molly nodded, even though he couldn't see her. Stepping back, she shut the door and listened for a moment. She thought he might be crying. But she only heard the TV, and the weatherman, predicting dark skies and rain for the day ahead.

In a stupor, Chris wandered downstairs to the kitchen.

Molly was still up in the master bedroom, changing her clothes. Erin sat at the breakfast table, finishing a bowl of cereal and staring at the TV. Chris's dad was cleaning up the broken glass and spilt coffee. He had his suit jacket off, sleeves rolled up, and tie tucked inside his shirt to keep it from getting soiled. One faint streak of brown liquid remained on the tiled floor. *You missed a spot*, Chris wanted to say, as his dad straightened up and set a soaked paper towel on the counter.

He wiped his hands and gave Chris a hug. "Molly said you were watching the news about Ray Corson," he whispered. Obviously, he didn't want Erin to hear. "How are you holding up? Are you doing okay?"

"I'm fine, thanks, Dad," he muttered, starting to back away.

But his father held on to him and looked him in the eye. "You know I wasn't a big fan of his, but still, I'm—I'm sorry this happened. Do you want to talk about it?"

Chris shook his head. "Not really."

I don't want to talk to anybody, he felt like saying. *I just want to be left alone.* He still couldn't believe his former guidance counselor and friend was dead. If it weren't for Mr. Corson, he never would have made it through last year. The only person he wanted to talk to right now was Mr. Corson, and he couldn't.

His dad hugged him again. He always smelled like the Old Spice cologne Chris gave him every Father's Day. "Thanks, Dad, I'm okay," he murmured. He grabbed his books and his jacket.

He heard the car horn honking—four times. That was Courtney's signal. His ride to school was here. Molly called to him from upstairs to take a couple of her Special K breakfast bars "to keep body and soul together" until lunch—whatever the hell that meant. She had some weird expressions—like that one, and *beats having a sharp stick in the eye*, and *six of one, half a dozen of the other,* and a bunch more. Maybe they were Midwestern expressions or something. He wasn't sure.

His dad had married Molly less than a year ago, and it had seemed way too rushed for Chris. He'd still been adjusting to his mother moving out and his parents divorcing, and then *wham,* his dad got remarried. Suddenly, this pretty artist was taking his mother's place. Nice as Molly was to him, Chris still couldn't get used to her constant presence in the house.

He yelled upstairs to her that he wasn't hungry; then he hurried out the front door.

"Did you hear about Corson?"

It was Courtney calling to him from the open window of her red Neon.

Chris was halfway up the driveway, but he could see the iPhone in her grasp. Courtney Hahn was always texting or Twittering. That damn iPhone was practically glued to her hand. It didn't matter to her that it was against the law in Washington state to operate a handheld phone while driving. Courtney considered herself the exception. Her and her iPhone—it was one of several things about her that drove him crazy for the two months they dated last year. Still, she was blond, pretty, and popular—so for a while, he'd convinced himself that he was damn lucky to be her boyfriend. Well, maybe not *that* lucky. Except for feeling her breasts on a few occasions, and three intense make-out sessions during which he'd come in his jeans, they'd never gotten very far in the sex department. They'd had a pretty amicable breakup, probably because they hadn't been all that crazy about each other in the first place. But Courtney was a good kisser— and a good sport. As part of her campaign that they remain friends, she still gave him a lift to school in the mornings.

"Did you hear the news about Corson?" she repeated, glancing up from her iPhone keypad for a moment. "Somebody shot him. . . ."

Chris nodded glumly, and then he opened the passenger door and scooted into the front seat.

"If you ask me, it just proves Corson was a major perv," Courtney's *best friend forever*, Madison Garvey, remarked from the backseat. "The guy probably went to the Arboretum last night to have sex in the bushes or something. Ha! He went there to get blown, and got *blown away* instead."

Chris buckled his seat belt and sighed. "Gosh, Madison, think maybe you could wait until lunch—or at least third period—before you start making bad jokes about our guidance counselor getting murdered last night? I don't think his body's cold yet."

"Yeah, Maddie, shut up," Courtney said. With a tiny smirk, she glanced in the rearview mirror at her friend.

"Oh, kindly remove the sticks from your butts and get over yourselves," Madison muttered, eyes on her cell phone. Like Courtney, Madison was blond, but almost albino-pale with a slightly goofy-looking face. She had her feet up on the back of Chris's seat. She wore her bright orange Converse All Star high-tops today. She'd made that brand of gym shoe her trademark, sporting it in several different colors and patterns. Madison didn't wear any other kind of shoes in public. She'd even worn Converse All Star high-tops—silver—to the prom last year.

Madison lived with her divorced mother in the three-bedroom house next door to Chris. Courtney's family was across the street and two houses down. Along with two more families, they all lived on the same North Seattle cul-de-sac, which had been part of an ambitious development that started two years ago—and never got finished. A dozen beautiful, distinctive, modern houses were supposed to go up, but only five were completed. Construction halted when the recession hit. So several lots on the cul-de-sac were bare—or occupied by half-finished skeletons of houses. There still weren't any sidewalks yet, and not quite enough streetlights. At night, it was always dark and slightly sinister, because the cul-de-sac lay in the shadow of a forest. The street was named Willow Tree Court, which Chris thought was pretty lame, since they never got around to planting the willow trees on the barren divider strip down the middle of the curved, dead-end roadway.

Chris glanced at the NO OUTLET sign as Courtney came to a stop at the end of the block. It amazed him that she managed to navigate the road with only one hand on the steering wheel and her eyes on her iPhone eighty percent of the time. Whenever he rode in the car with her, Chris figured they'd end up dead poster kids for the dangers of driving while texting. Then people at school would be making the bad jokes about them—rather than about Mr. Corson.

"Tiffany thinks one of Ian's wacko parents shot Corson," Courtney announced, glancing up from her phone for a few seconds while she turned left at the intersection.

"Shauna agrees with me," Madison said, consulting her phone from the backseat.

"She thinks Corson was meeting another guy there at the park for some kinky sex thing. I mean, really, his car just happens to break down at a park at night—with a ton of bushes. Major perv alert! Corson was just asking for it."

"C'mon, shut up," Courtney said, slowing down to a stop at a traffic light. "You're talking about Chris's *hero*."

"Oh, yeah, that's right. Chris used to think Corson peed perfume."

Both girls laughed. But Chris remained silent. He kept his head turned away and stared out the window—at a dead gray cat on the side of the road.

CHAPTER TWO

"Honey, I talked with him," Jeff sighed. He was wheeling the tall recycle bin toward the end of the driveway. Molly walked alongside him with a Hefty bag full of cans. She'd put Erin on the school bus five minutes before, and now Jeff was about to leave for work.

"Obviously, Chris is shaken up," Jeff went on, talking over the bin's squeaky wheels. "But he'll be okay. We just need to downplay this thing. If he sees you making a big deal out of it, he'll start thinking it's a big deal—"

Molly stopped in her tracks and set down the Hefty bag. The cans rattled. "Jeff, honey, it *is* a big deal. The man was murdered."

"What I'm saying is, if you—if *we* make a big to-do about this and fuss over him, Chris will end up rehashing the entire episode from five months ago—and he'll be blaming himself all over again."

"He blamed me, too," Molly murmured.

"You did the right thing," Jeff said, setting the receptacle by the end of their driveway. He grabbed the Hefty bag from her and leaned it against the bin. "Personally, I'm not shedding any tears over the guy's demise. I'm not as forgiving as my son is." He rubbed his hands together to brush off some residue from the bin handle. "Anyway, for Chris, let's just downplay this whole thing, okay?"

Nodding, Molly glanced down at a crack in the driveway. "Don't forget to swing by the optical place today," she murmured. "You wanted to get your glasses tightened for your trip."

Jeff put his arm around her, and they headed back toward the garage. The automatic garage door was locked in the open position. Earlier, he'd tossed his briefcase into the front seat of his silver Lexus. "You know, I'm not so sure I should go off to Denver tomorrow, not when I think about that family in Renton last week."

Molly shuddered. "God, don't remind me." She'd read all about the Renton killings online and in the *Seattle Times*.

"Jesus, the whole family." He sighed. "It's enough to make you sick. The twin girls were Erin's age." He gave Molly's shoulder a squeeze. "I don't feel good leaving you and the kids alone for two nights—not while this maniac is on the loose."

Molly shrugged. "You can't go changing your work schedule because of some nutcase. It could be a while before the police catch him." She tried to smile. "Besides, we'll be okay, because I'm going to that Neighborhood Watch potluck today. I'll know just what to do in case a serial killer comes knocking on our front door. . . ."

The lunch would be across the street at the Hahns' house. A police detective had been invited to speak to the residents of the cul-de-sac. That included Jeff's ex-wife's two best friends, Lynette Hahn and Kay Garvey.

Angela would be attending, too. She was still chummy-chummy with her Willow Tree Court pals, even though she lived on another cul-de-sac—in Bellevue with her new boyfriend and his thirteen-year-old daughter. The new relationship didn't keep Angela from meddling in Jeff's life. Apparently, it wasn't enough that she talked to her kids every day and asked them to convey messages to their dad. At least once a week, she was back in her old stomping grounds to visit Lynette or Kay. She even tried to make friends with Molly early on. But Molly quickly figured out this was just another way for Angela to have some kind of control over Jeff—albeit indirectly. It seemed pretty damn manipulative. So Molly did her best to avoid Jeff's ex—and stayed distantly polite to her.

She wasn't looking forward to this Neighborhood Watch potluck with Angela and her cronies. She'd almost just as soon take her chances with a serial killer.

"I thought that lunch wasn't until tomorrow," Jeff said, opening the car door. "And aren't those neighborhood watch things held on weekends and evenings so it doesn't interfere with people's work schedules?"

"Not this one. Lynette pulled some strings. It's in four hours, and I still have to make chocolate chip cookies for it. Do you want me to pass along any messages to the former Mrs. Dennehy?"

"Just that I'm blissfully happy," he said, kissing her. Then he climbed into the car and buckled his seat belt. "Good luck with that crowd."

Molly gave him a wry smile. "We who are about to die salute you."

Shutting his door, he blew her a kiss, and then started up the car. He backed out of the garage. Molly waved at her husband.

The garage door started to descend. As the Lexus drove off, Molly caught a glimpse of a strange car parked in front of Dr. and Mrs. Nguyen's house. She hadn't noticed the metallic blue minivan earlier when she'd walked back from Erin's bus stop. Then again, she hadn't really been paying attention.

She ducked inside—through the garage entrance, then past the closed door to the basement, through the kitchen area, the dining room, and finally the living room in the front of the house. At the big picture window, she pushed aside the sheer curtain and glanced out at that minivan again. It was too far away for her to tell if someone was in the front seat.

This would probably be one of the first items the cop would address at the Neighborhood Watch potluck in a few hours: *Look out for unfamiliar cars parked on your cul-de-sac.* The Nguyens lived in Denver eight months out of the year, and sometimes, they had friends using the place. Molly had to remind herself that it wasn't so unusual to see a strange car parked in front of their house.

Stepping away from the window, she wondered if—before last week—the mother of those twin girls had been on the lookout for strange cars in their cul-de-sac in Renton.

She remembered the front-page headlines in the *Seattle Times* last Tuesday. She remembered, because she'd looked up the article again online just last night. She'd become a bit fixated on the murders.

RENTON FAMILY SLAIN

4 dead in Another Cul-de-Sac Killing

PARENTS AND TWIN DAUGHTERS STABBING VICTIMS

A photo of the murdered family ran under the headline. It showed the dark-haired, husky father and his pretty, somewhat mousy, blond wife. Grinning proudly, they posed behind their blond daughters in one of those family portraits from Sears or JCPenney. The twins looked darling. They were laughing in the picture. One of them was missing a front tooth.

SENSELESS MURDER, read the caption. *Renton residents, Lyle Winters, 33, and wife, Terri Anne, 31, in a photo taken last October with their 6-year-old twin daughters, Claudia and Colette. The family was brutally slain in their Loretta Court home late Sunday night. This is the fourth in a series of bizarre cul-de-sac killings in the Seattle area since February.*

The news article had been broken up with different subheadlines in boldface print: **Neighbors Heard Nothing, No Screams—Every Light Was On** and **Bodies in Closets, A Killer's Calling Card.**

Each time this Cul-de-sac Killer struck, he left nearly all of the lights on inside the house—and his victims shut inside closets.

Lyle Winters, his throat slashed, was found in the closet off their guest room. His wife, strangled and stabbed repeatedly, was discovered in the master bedroom closet, curled up amid some shoes and a pile of blouses that had fallen off their hangers. Both children were stabbed and left—one on top of the other—in their bedroom closet.

Like nearly everyone who lived on a cul-de-sac in the Seattle area, Molly was constantly on her guard now. That was why she walked Erin to the bus stop every morning and waited there with her. It was why she kept a lookout for strange cars on the block. They never used to turn on their house alarm at night, but they did now.

The newspapers didn't mention if any of the Cul-de-sac Killer's victims had home security systems.

Molly had read so much about the murders that she'd almost become an expert. She didn't know why she'd become so preoccupied with the cul-de-sac killings—except perhaps to make sure it didn't happen to her new family.

The first to die had been an elderly woman, Irene Haskel, who lived alone in a split-level house on a dead-end street in Ballard. A neighbor had noticed nearly all of Irene's lights were on for three nights in a row. She stopped by to discover Irene's front door ajar—and a foul odor permeating the seemingly empty house. Irene's neighbor followed the pungent smell to a bedroom closet in the upper level. The *Seattle Times* reported that Irene had thirty-eight stab wounds.

The killer struck again a week later, stabbing three coeds who lived in a townhouse on a dead end near Seattle Pacific University. A fourth roommate, who had spent that night at a friend's apartment, returned the following afternoon to find all the lights on inside the townhouse. She also found all her roommates' bodies, stashed in closets on the second floor.

A month passed, and it happened again—this time, a married couple in their fifties, who lived at the end of a cul-de-sac in the Queen Anne neighborhood. Coming home from college for a weekend visit, their son discovered the blood—and then their bodies, stuffed in two upstairs closets.

And now this family of four was slaughtered just last week.

Nervously rubbing her arms, Molly returned to the kitchen. Going through the cabinets and the refrigerator, she started to pull out all the ingredients for Toll House cookies. She didn't want to think about the cul-de-sac murders now, not while she was the only one home. She felt uncomfortable enough in Angela's house.

The place still seemed to belong to Jeff's ex-wife. Hell, half the spices in the kitchen cupboard had been bought by Angela. The glasses she drank from, the plates the family used—they were all Angela's.

Molly started mixing up the white and brown sugar, eggs, and butter in a bowl. She kept glancing over at the sliding glass doors in the big family room off the kitchen area. The backyard was rather small—with just enough room for a gas grill, a patio, and a small strip of grass. The forest started only fifteen or twenty feet behind the house. Some evenings, raccoons came right up to the other side of the sliding glass door. When Molly was alone in the house at night, she occasionally got scared and imagined something else emerging from that dark forest to watch her through the glass, something on two legs instead of four.

She thought about closing the drapes, but they were so damn ugly—maroon with gold fleur-de-lis on a heavy, velvet-like material. *Hello, Angela, what were you thinking?*

Given her druthers, Molly would have redecorated the entire first floor. She didn't share Angela's fondness for hunter green, maroon, and gold—and the charmless, dark, Mediterranean furniture that made the big family room look like the lobby of a small, cheesy Best Western. She also thought the tall grandfather clock that didn't work was kind of ugly. But Molly told herself that Jeff's kids were going through enough changes in their lives. They probably didn't want to see their mother's house transformed into something else entirely. Nevertheless, every other week, Molly would make a subtle alteration to Angela's drab, almost impersonal design scheme. One week, she added jazzy throw pillows to the hunter-green sofa. Another week—and about time—she got rid of a tall, ugly standing vase with a dried flower arrangement in it.

Molly figured three dozen cookies were enough for Angela and her pals. They'd probably turn up their noses at dessert anyway. It was a competitively thin crowd.

She left the cookies out to cool and started washing the dishes. The phone rang. She grabbed the kitchen cordless on the third ring. "Yes, hello?"

"It's above the heart now," whispered the woman on the other end. At least that was what it sounded like she said.

"Pardon me?" Molly said. She pulled the phone away from her ear for a moment so she could glance at the caller ID screen on the receiver. CALLER UNKNOWN, it said.

"Pardon me?" Molly repeated into the phone. "Hello?"

There was a click on the other end of the line.

Frowning, Molly hung up. She moved over to the glass doors and peered out at the backyard once more. The sky had grown dark, and the woods looked gray and a bit sinister. Trees and shrubs swayed in the wind. She wondered if the cul-de-sacs where the killer had struck were in wooded areas.

"Would you cut it out already, Molly?" she muttered to herself. She checked the lock on the sliding door.

She really wished Jeff hadn't mentioned the cul-de-sac murders earlier. Of course, before Jeff brought up the serial killings, she'd been unnerved by the news of Ray Corson's death—another senseless murder.

Molly heard the washing-machine buzzer go off downstairs in the basement. She'd put her coffee-spattered sweatpants and some other clothes in the quick cycle a half hour ago. With a sigh, she plodded to the basement door. Opening it, she switched on the stairwell light. It sputtered and went out.

"Oh, terrific," she muttered. "I really need this now."

She could see the overhead in the rec room still worked. The staircase was a bit dark, but Molly held on to the banister and quickly made her way down there. The rec room was the kids' domain. In one corner sat a rowing machine belonging to Jeff, but in the ten months they'd been married, Molly had yet to see him use it. She guessed Jeff and Angela bought the maroon sectional sofa and black end tables at Ikea. The fat, clunky big-screen TV was from before the day of HD and plasma. Chris must have been in charge of the art on the walls—which included a Mariners poster, a lighted Hamm's Beer clock, movie posters of *Zoolander* and *Avatar*, and four pictures of dogs playing poker. The Ping-Pong table had become a catchall for everything from Erin's Barbie Dream House to a science-project volcano Chris had built with papier-mâché, paint, and some chemicals.

There was also a small walk-in closet—with shelves full of board games, sports equipment, and toys. The door was open a crack. Molly paused in front of it. She imagined Jeff lying dead on the floor in there, his throat slit—just like Lyle Winters. The thought made her skin crawl. She tried to push it out of her mind.

Nervously rubbing her gooseflesh-covered arms, Molly retreated to the laundry and utility room. With its bare floor, exposed pipes overhead, and shadowy nooks around the furnace and water heater, the big room was kind of creepy. It had become cluttered with unwanted furniture and knickknacks from Jeff's years with Angela. There were also some collapsed folding chairs leaning against a square support beam, and boxes of Christmas decorations.

Molly emptied out the washer and tossed the damp clothes in the dryer. While she threw in a strip of Bounce, her mind started to wander toward that morbid direction again.

Why does he put the bodies in closets? Why does he leave practically all the lights on inside the houses of his victims? The police must have come up with some theories. Maybe she'd ask the cop at the potluck.

While setting the timer for the dryer, Molly thought she heard a creaking sound above her. *Quit it,* she told herself. *It's the house settling, stupid—or maybe something outside. You're all alone here.* From everything she'd read, the Cul-de-sac Killer usually struck at night. And right now, it was ten o'clock in the morning. *Quit it,* she told herself again.

Molly closed the dryer door and pushed the start button. The dryer drum began rolling and roaring. But the sound she heard past the racket was unmistakable.

Upstairs someplace, a door slammed shut.

"Shit," Molly whispered, a hand over her heart. She quickly reached over and switched off the dryer. The rumbling noise stopped, and the hot air gave out one last wheeze. Molly stood perfectly still, and listened. She didn't hear anything upstairs.

Glancing over at Jeff's worktable, she made a beeline for it and snatched the crowbar from a hook on the wall. She took a deep breath and crept back into the rec room. Then she made her way up the darkened stairs to the first floor. She cautiously looked around. Everything seemed just the way she'd left it five minutes ago.

"Hello? Is anyone home?" Molly called, a nervous tremor in her voice. She wondered if maybe Chris had decided not to go to school today after all—and he'd come back. "Chris? Is that you?"

No one answered.

Molly checked the locks on the front door, the garage door entrance, and even the sliding glass doors—which she'd just checked minutes before. All of them were locked. But that didn't make her feel any better.

Tightening her grip on the crowbar, she headed up to the second floor. At the top of the stairs, she saw Erin's bedroom door was closed. Erin never shut her door—not even while she was sleeping in there.

Molly tiptoed down the hallway and slowly opened Erin's door. She felt a cool breeze against her hands and face. The window was open. The lacy white curtain billowed. *The wind slammed the door shut, it's that simple,* she told herself. Still, she checked Erin's closet before she went to the window and shut it with one hand. She wasn't ready to let go of the crowbar, not just yet.

Molly looked in the guest room and Chris's bedroom— the closets, too. She poked her head in the kids' bathroom, and then scurried down the hallway to the master bedroom. It was empty—as was the big walk-in closet and master bath. Molly even peeked behind the closed shower curtain. Nothing.

Jeff had let her redecorate their quarters. But even with the bedroom's new Mission-style furniture, a recent paint job (sea-foam green), new carpeting, and photos of her and Jeff prominently displayed—it still seemed like Angela's domain. Angela had been with Jeff in that bedroom first.

Molly still held on to the crowbar, but it was down at her side. She paused at the doorway to the third floor. Maybe she was being silly, but it was worth checking up there—just to put her mind at rest. She climbed up the stairs.

The third floor was the only place in the house Molly felt was totally hers. With her own savings, she took Angela's unfinished attic and transformed it into an art studio. She'd even had a bathroom installed up there. There was also a very comfortable chaise longue on which life-study models could pose—and Molly could nap.

She glanced inside the bathroom: nothing. Her one closet was so narrow and crammed with easel frames, canvas, and paint supplies, if someone could hide in there, he'd need to be half her size and a contortionist. She was alone up here.

With a sigh, she looked at the painting-in-progress on her easel in front of the dormer window. It showed a shapely, gorgeous, tawny-haired woman in a torn bodice—which still needed some detail painted in. Standing proudly, she looked skyward as a shirtless hunk knelt behind her with his brawny arms wrapped around her trim waist. In the background, a full moon illuminated a castle by the sea. This would be the cover to *Desiree's Destiny*, the latest in a series of romance novels. Molly had already gotten the advance money for it: $1,750, minus her agent's commission. She would get the same amount once she delivered the finished painting. She'd created all seven of the *Desiree* covers, so far. Both Desiree's resemblance to Angelina Jolie and the always-shirtless Lord Somerton's similarity to Jude Law were no mistake.

It wasn't exactly what Molly had intended to do after six years in art school, but book covers, magazine illustrations, and ads had become her bread and butter. Occasionally, she sold one of her more serious works. She was proud of those paintings, mostly still-life studies or moody portraits that seemed to tell a story. Her *Woman Playing Solitaire* (at a dinette table with a melancholy look on her face and a ciga-rette in one hand), went for $2,600 at the Lyman-Eyer Gallery in Provincetown. But sales like that were few and far between.

Before marrying Jeff, she'd barely eked out a living as an artist, so Molly had taken on an assortment of part-time and temp jobs: everything from office worker to waitress to hotel desk clerk. She'd figured she was paying her dues. Molly felt a bit guilty for not needing to work those kinds of jobs anymore. She had quite a nice setup here. She wondered if Angela and her friends said as much behind her back.

She was glad for this space on the third floor, where Angela had no claim. The studio was Molly's escape, a haven for old family knickknacks she couldn't part with, photo albums, and her collection of elephants.

When she was a kid, she'd heard elephants brought good luck, so Molly started collecting elephant figurines—in marble, jade, porcelain, mahogany, plastic, you name it. She'd given most of them to Goodwill two years ago, but kept about forty figurines—all of them now neatly arranged on a bookcase along one wall of her studio. No photos of her family were displayed. It just didn't seem right. Her dad and her brother were dead, and she and her mother weren't on the best of terms.

Considering how her brother had died, Molly wondered if those elephants were really so lucky. A few of the elephants on that bookshelf had originally belonged to him. He'd collected them, too.

Nearly every time Molly looked through her family albums, she ended up crying. So it seemed pretty masochistic to frame those pictures and put them on display. Jeff and his children were her family now.

Though she sometimes felt like a houseguest they merely tolerated, Molly still really cared for Jeff's kids. It was why she waited at the bus stop with Erin this morning. And it was why she worried about Chris getting through his school day when Ray Corson had just been murdered last night. It was why she tried to be cordial—albeit distantly cordial—to Jeff's ex. After all, she was their mother.

At the same time, she dreaded this Neighborhood Watch potluck with Angela and all her pals. Molly glanced at her wristwatch. It was less than an hour from now.

Downstairs, the phone rang, and it startled her. Molly hurried down to the second floor and rushed into her bedroom. She snatched up the cordless from the nightstand. "Yes, hello?" she answered, a bit out of breath. She set the crowbar down on the bed.

"Molly?" the woman whispered. It was the same voice from before. What she murmured next still sounded like gibberish: *"It's above the heart now. . . ."*

"I can't understand what you're saying," Molly cut in. "Could you talk louder, please? Who is this?"

"I said . . ." She still spoke in a whisper, but the words were very clear this time. *"It's about to start now."*

"I don't understand. What's about to start? Who—"

Molly heard a click on the other end of the line—and then nothing.

CHAPTER THREE

It was stupid of her to think he might be grieving, too.

Chris Dennehy seemed to go about his morning as if it were a normal day. Walking through the corridors between classes, he didn't appear disturbed or troubled—only slightly aloof toward all his fellow students, who couldn't stop staring at him. He didn't make eye contact with anyone.

He certainly hadn't seemed to notice her.

She felt invisible in the crowded second-floor hallway of James Monroe High School. Now and then, someone bumped into her and kept walking as if she weren't even there.

She was just like the others, watching Chris, waiting for him to snap or start crying—or show some kind of emotion, for God's sake. His former guidance counselor had just been murdered last night. They'd been very close at one time, and everyone knew it.

"Are you—like—totally freaked out, man?" she'd over-heard a tall, lanky basketball player ask him in the stairwell an hour before. She'd strained to hear Chris's answer. But there were too many other students stomping up and down the stairs, and too much noise. Chris had shrugged, muttered something to his classmate, and then he'd continued up the steps. He'd seemed pretty nonchalant about it.

Now he walked down the corridor by himself, close to the lockers on the wall. Even though his brown hair was a mess, and his blue-striped shirt needed ironing, he still looked handsome. He was on his way from Ms. Kinsella's trigonometry class to third-period study hall.

She knew his class schedule. She knew he occasionally rode his bike to school—though most of the time, he carpooled with those bitches from his cul-de-sac, Courtney Hahn and Madison Garvey. He had swim practice from 3:30 until 5:30, and usually caught a ride home from a teammate or took a bus.

Not counting three empty lots and the skeletal frames of two unfinished homes, the Dennehys' was the second house down from the start of Willow Tree Court. She knew every inch of that cul-de-sac. From the forest that bordered the backyards, she'd spied on the Dennehys and their neighbors. They never bothered to lower their blinds or shut the drapes on that side. She had a direct look into their day-to-day private lives. She'd thought it might make her more compassionate toward them, but it didn't change how she felt—not at all.

She didn't care much that some of them would die soon.

But Chris Dennehy was different—at least, she used to think he was. That was why she'd come to his high school to follow him around today. She wanted to see if he would shed any tears for Ray Corson.

She trailed about twenty feet behind him in the hallway as he shuffled toward the study hall just around the corner.

"Hey, Dennehy!" another student called to him.

She stopped—and so did Chris, up ahead of her.

A handsome, blond-haired jock swaggered toward him. He wore a varsity jacket and carried a backpack. She could see—as he approached—he was a bit shorter than Chris. "Dennehy," he said, slapping him on the shoulder. "Wow,

you must be so glad someone killed that slimy fuck. . . ."
Then with a cocky grin, he said something else—under his
breath.

Chris glared at him. Suddenly, he grabbed the blond-
haired jock by the front of his shirt and slammed him into
the row of lockers. There was a loud clatter, and a girl nearby
screamed. Still holding onto the guy's shirt collar, Chris had
his fist under the jock's chin. He kept him pinned against the
lockers for another moment. Everyone around them froze—
and it was suddenly quiet.

She heard Chris growl at the young man: "Get the hell
away from me." Then he let go of the other guy, and turned
away.

"What's your fucking problem?" the jock yelled. He was
shaking. "Jesus, you're crazy! Crazy fuck!"

Chris kept walking.

Her heart racing, she pushed her way through the crowd
to catch up with him. She wanted to see his face.

"Can't you take a joke?" the jock was saying. "What's
wrong with you, man?"

As he started to turn the corner, Chris looked back and
scowled at the other guy.

She stopped in her tracks. Chris looked so angry and agi-
tated. But he had tears in his eyes, too.

He turned and disappeared around the corner.

She'd figured he would cry. That was what she'd wanted
to see today.

She stood there, invisible to the others, and wondered
about him. She still wasn't quite sure if—once the killing
started—Chris Dennehy would die like the others.

He certainly would suffer. That much she knew.

"I really wish you'd let me in, Chris," Mr. Munson said in
his customary mellow tenor, which made him sound slightly
stoned. "I'm sensing some hostility from you, and that's

okay. You own those feelings, Chris. They're valid. But I'm your friend, and I'm here to help you. . . ."

Mr. Munson leaned back in his chair and scratched his gray-orange goatee. He was about forty with thinning, red hair, a pasty complexion, and a stud earring. He wore an ugly paisley tie and a denim shirt. Some sort of weird stone charm hung on a chain around his neck.

Chris squirmed in the hard-back chair facing Munson's desk. The little office had a wide window in one wall, looking out to a corridor full of lockers. Munson kept a bunch of self-help books and pamphlets on the shelves behind his desk. There was also a really cheesy poster of a guy dressed as a clown, flying a kite by a lake at sunset. It said: *To Thine Own Self Be True*

Mr. Munson had pulled Chris out of third-period study hall for this impromptu touchy-feely, new-age, psycho-babble session. Chris could barely tolerate the guy, but he kept telling himself that Munson meant well.

Munson was Mr. Corson's replacement. This was Mr. Corson's old office. Chris remembered the cool Edward Hopper *Nighthawks* print—of those lonely-looking people at a café at night—that had been where the stupid-ass clown poster was now. He remembered pouring his heart out to Mr. Corson in this office and feeling better for it. He couldn't open up in the same way to Munson.

"I'm fine, Mr. Munson, really," Chris said, slouching in the chair a little. He tried to keep from tapping his foot, but the restless, nervous tic was almost involuntary now. "I'm— I'm sad Mr. Corson is dead, of course. And it's a real shock. I feel really bad for Mr. Corson's family, too." He shrugged, and glanced down at the tiled floor. "I don't know what else to tell you."

"How are the other kids at school treating you today?"

Chris kept looking at the floor. "Fine," he lied. "Just fine . . ."

He realized what this session was all about. Somehow,

word must have gotten to Munson that he'd shoved Scott Kinkaid against the lockers.

All morning long, Chris had felt people staring at him. In the corridors and classrooms, he heard people whispering about what had happened last December with Mr. Corson and him—and another classmate, Ian Scholl. If they weren't whispering about it, they were Twittering and texting about it. They rehashed old jokes that had circulated around school after the incident in December. And they told new ones, making fun of Mr. Corson's brutal murder last night. Madison Garvey's wiseass comments in the car this morning had been just a sneak preview of the snickering remarks Chris overheard in the school hallways.

Several of his classmates—even kids he barely knew—approached him this morning with comments and questions about Mr. Corson's death:

"Isn't it weird what happened to Corson? God, what a trip. . . ."

"Have any TV news people talked with you yet? After all, you're the reason he got fired. . . ."

Then there was Scott Kinkaid: *"Wow, you must be so glad someone killed that slimy fuck. . . ."* He added, under his breath: *"After he tried to get into your pants, you must figure the faggot had it coming. . . ."*

That was when Chris lost it. Before he knew it, he grabbed Scott by the front of his shirt and threw him against the lockers. It was all he could do to keep from punching his face in.

And that was why he'd ended up here in Munson's office. He was certain of it.

"I don't know if you heard," Chris muttered, unable to look Munson in the eye. "I kinda shoved Scott Kinkaid, because he said something creepy about Mr. Corson. But it was nothing."

"Do you want to talk about it?" Munson asked.

"Not really," Chris answered.

"Is there someone else you can talk with?" He leaned forward in his chair. "Have you discussed with anyone how you feel about Mr. Corson's death?"

"My dad and I talked this morning," Chris said. "It's cool."

"And your mom?"

"They don't live together anymore," he replied. "My dad remarried and my mother lives in Bellevue now."

"Oh, um, well, I see. . . ." Munson nervously cleared his throat and started searching through some papers in a file folder on his desk. Obviously, the guy hadn't done his homework. "Give me a minute here," he said.

Chris glanced over his shoulder. He caught a glimpse of a girl on the other side of the window to Munson's office—or it could have been a teacher, he wasn't sure. She'd ducked away so quickly he didn't even get a look at her face, just her shoulder-length brown hair and her black coat. She must have run down the corridor.

A stocky young man with thick glasses and brownish-blond hair stopped at the window. He was Chris's best friend, Elvis Harnett. They'd known each other since sixth grade. A stack of books under one arm, Elvis peered into the office. He looked concerned. "Are you okay?" he mouthed to Chris.

Chris glanced warily at Munson, still searching through his paperwork. He turned toward his friend and nodded furtively.

Elvis half smiled, but then he suddenly looked away and retreated down the corridor.

Chris swiveled around in his chair. Munson was staring at him. Eyes narrowed, he scratched his goatee again. "You had several sessions here with Mr. Corson, didn't you?"

Chris nodded.

"Did Mr. Corson take any notes during these sessions?"

Chris nodded again. "Yeah, he—he used to scribble stuff down."

Munson glanced at the papers in front of him. "That's

odd, there aren't any notes here. These records are from your freshman year. There's nothing from the last two years." Shaking his head, Munson got to his feet and grabbed the file. "I need to go figure this out. Be right back. Stay put, okay? While you're waiting, here . . ." He reached for one of the books on his shelf and handed it to Chris. "Take a look at this. I think you'll find it very useful."

Chris glanced at the book's cover. It had bright purple lettering against an orange background. At the very top was the banner: *"A breakthrough in getting yourself on the road to happiness and self-fulfillment!"—Dr. Tim, National Syndicated Radio Personality*

HELP *YOURSELF!*

A Cathartic Cookbook of Easy Recipes for Overcoming What's Holding You Back & Finding a Better You

By Dr. Sonya Swinton
Bestselling Author of You First!

"She's got a fantastic chapter in there about dealing with anger and grief," Munson said, on his way out the door.

"Fantastic," Chris muttered, once he was alone in the office. He glanced up from the book in his hand to the empty chair that used to be Mr. Corson's.

"Psssst, hey, Chris . . ."

He turned to see Elvis poking his head in the doorway. "Is Mellow Man Munson guiding you on a personal-growth journey? Or are you in here because you kicked the crap out of Scott Kinkaid?"

Chris rolled his eyes. "All I did was push him against some lockers."

"Well, depending on whose Twitter you're reading," Elvis said, hovering at the office threshold, "you either had a slight altercation with Scott or you beat him bloody and put him into a coma. Personally, I'd hoped the coma story was true. I've always hated that douche bag—ever since eighth grade, when he called me Goodyear Blimp in front of our entire homeroom class. Remember that?"

Chris nodded. "Vividly."

"Hey, listen, I'm really sorry about Corson," Elvis whispered, suddenly somber. They hadn't had a chance to talk this morning. "How are you holding up?"

Chris nodded again. "I'm okay."

"You're not going to talk about this, are you?" Elvis whispered. "Even though it's eating away at you inside."

"Probably not," Chris murmured. "Listen, you should scram before Munson comes back. I'll call you later."

Elvis sighed. "You better." Then he headed down the corridor.

Chris turned and faced the empty desk.

Besides Mr. Corson, Elvis was just about the only person who could get him to open up and talk about things that truly upset him. And even then, it took Elvis a lot of prodding.

"You're so tight-lipped about everything," Elvis had observed a while back. "You care too much about what people think. Always putting on your best face, no matter what—I think you get that shit from your mom."

Elvis's own mother was a lost cause. With her drug and alcohol problems, her terrible taste in men, and her penchant for dressing like a slut, Mrs. Harnett would have been a terrific guest on *The Jerry Springer Show*. Chris rarely went over to the Harnetts' place.

While he'd dated Courtney Hahn, his image-conscious girlfriend had wanted very little to do with Elvis. "I'm sorry, but how can you let yourself even be seen with him?" she'd asked at one point toward the end, when they were breaking up. "I mean, he's a nice guy and all, but he's poor white trash. You'd think he'd try to lose a little weight or dress in something besides *farmer clothes*. And when's he going to get those stupid glasses fixed?"

One of Mrs. Harnett's loser boyfriends had slapped Elvis for mouthing off to him, and he'd broken the hinge on his glasses. For the next three months, Elvis had silver electric tape bunched around the corner of his progressives.

Elvis couldn't help that he didn't have money for new glasses or new clothes. He couldn't help that he was overweight from being raised on junk food. He never even ate a vegetable until he had dinner at Chris's house. Elvis slept over at least once a week. Chris felt the overnights gave his friend a taste of what a fairly functional, *normal* family was like.

Just two weeks before his parents sat down with him for *the talk*, Chris had watched them at a block party at the Hahns' house. They looked so happy, and it made him feel lucky—not only compared to Elvis's situation, but also compared to his neighbors, Courtney and Madison. Madison's parents had split up three years before; and as for Courtney, she admitted that her father could barely tolerate her mother. Chris could tell, too. Mrs. Hahn would act all lovey-dovey around him, and Mr. Hahn would hardly crack a smile. He'd get a sort of constipated, slightly annoyed look whenever she started to hang on him.

But at that party, Chris watched his parents sitting together on the floor by the Hahns' fireplace. His mom looked especially pretty that night. Snuggled next to his dad, she whispered in his ear. His father chuckled and kissed her on the cheek.

Two weeks later, on a Friday last March, his mother called him at school on his cell, saying he shouldn't make plans for the evening. She and his dad needed to talk with him about something. Chris wondered if maybe his mother had discovered the two adult DVDs he'd hidden in his desk drawer: *Slutty Betty* and *Hot Meter Maids 2: Violation!* He'd stashed them beneath a collection of old birthday cards, some of which were sent from his now-deceased grand-mother. Had he no shame? His parents probably thought he was a major pervert.

But that wasn't it at all.

He came home from school that Friday at 4:30 to find his dad sitting at the kitchen table with a scotch and soda. He wore his blue suit. His dad never came home from work before six—unless someone got sick or had an accident. Chris's mom was pouring herself a glass of wine at the counter. It was kind of early for them to be drinking. The house was quiet, no TV blaring in the family room, no sign of his sister.

Hanging his coat in the pantry closet, Chris gave them a wary look and asked where Erin was. His dad hugged him, and said they thought it best Erin spend the night at Aunt Trish's.

Chris didn't understand. "Are you guys mad at me about something?"

His dad shook his head.

"We wanted to discuss this with you first—and then we'll talk to Erin," his mom explained. She sat down at the break-fast table.

Chris suddenly thought of something he hadn't considered until just that moment: cancer. Panic swept through him. "Is somebody sick?" he murmured. "Is that what this is about?"

With a sigh, his dad shook his head again. "Nobody's sick, Chris," he said. "Sit down, son."

Numbly he obeyed him, taking his usual spot at the kitchen table. "What's going on?"

His dad sank down in his chair and reached for his scotch and soda. The ice clinking in his glass seemed loud against the silence. He took a gulp. "It's this," he said, clearing his throat. "Your mom and I have decided to live apart for a while. . . ."

Chris let out a stunned little laugh. "You're joking."

He looked at his mother, whose eyes met his for the first time since he'd walked through the door. She didn't appear sad or apologetic or angry. It was as if all her feelings had shut down. She quickly looked away—and gazed down at her glass of wine. She took a sip.

Chris realized this was no joke.

He couldn't remember anything else they'd said—just that his mother was moving out. All the while, he kept looking at his dad's hands, one around his highball glass and the other clenched in a fist on the kitchen table. His mother kept fiddling with the saltshaker—picking at the little grains of salt stuck in the pour holes. She and his dad wouldn't look at each other.

When Chris finally asked if he could go upstairs and they let him go, he saw the clock on his nightstand read 4:58. He'd been sitting at that kitchen table with them for only twenty-five minutes, but it had seemed like hours.

He kept thinking of the way they'd seemed so affectionate at the Hahns' party two weeks before, and he realized it had been a lie. Chris hated admitting that to himself. And he didn't want to admit it to his friends—especially Elvis. So he didn't talk about it at all.

He felt bad Elvis had to find out about his parents' separation from someone in school. Apparently, Mrs. Hahn had told Courtney, who broadcast it on her Facebook page. Chris had kept hoping—right up until the day his mother moved out of the house—that his folks would work things out.

Her new home was a two-bedroom apartment in a tall, eighties-era condominium on Capitol Hill. She showed them the indoor pool off the lobby—and off her balcony, a sweeping view of downtown Seattle, Elliott Bay, and the Olympic Mountains. She kept going on about how they were walking distance from Volunteer Park and all these great restaurants, movie theaters, and shops. So when he and Erin visited, they'd never be bored.

Chris couldn't figure out why his mother had moved out of the house and given his dad custody. It didn't make sense. It wasn't practical. His dad was hardly ever home.

It wasn't as if he liked his mother more than he liked his dad. In fact, he felt a stronger connection to his father—even though his dad was away so often. Chris remembered when he was a kid, and his dad used to give him the white cardboard eleven-by-eight sheets the cleaners put inside his folded dress shirts. It was heavier than regular paper, and Chris used the cardboard inserts for elaborate drawings of *Lord of the Rings* scenes. But mostly he used them for the posters he created to welcome his dad home from business trips. Chris would post one sign on a tree at the end of their block: WE MISSED YOU, DAD! He'd tape another welcome home sign on the lamppost at the start of their driveway, and another on the front door. It was always special when his dad came home. Chris would get a T-shirt or snow globe from an airport in another city, and he'd bask in his dad's presence for the next few days—until another business trip took him away.

His dad might not have been home much; but when he was around, he spent a lot of time with Chris—and attended his swim meets (something his mom never did). All of his friends' mothers had crushes on his dad. So when people told him that he was starting to look like his father, Chris took that as a big compliment.

He wondered what they'd do now whenever his father went away on business. Hire a live-in housekeeper? Go stay with Aunt Trish in Tacoma? Chris didn't like it there. Aunt Trish had a house that smelled like rotten fruit and a cat who hated him. Plus she was vegan, and there was never anything decent to eat in her place.

It didn't make any sense that his mother was the one moving out. Was she sick of looking after him and Erin? Was that why she'd decided to leave?

"Your father and I have already told you—several times— this separation has nothing to do with you and Erin," his mother pointed out. "And neither does my moving out of the house."

She was behind the wheel of her SUV. Chris, in the passenger seat, couldn't see her eyes behind her designer sunglasses. Wind through the open window blew her close-cropped hair into disarray. She'd recently highlighted it with some silvery-brown rinse, a new look for her new life.

It was his and Erin's first weekend visiting her in her new condo. He and his mom were driving on Interstate 5 back from North Seattle, where they'd just dropped off Erin at ballet class.

"You had to know, Mom," he said, squinting at her. "You had to know that Erin and I would really miss you. It just screws up everything with you moving away. I mean, if Dad was the one who got a new place, I don't think it would have made that big a difference, because he's away so much anyway. Y'know?"

"I had to know that you and Erin would really miss me," she paraphrased him in a cool, ironic tone. She looked stone-faced as she stared at the road ahead. "The way you used to miss your father when he was away? Do you think it was easy for me, raising the two of you practically on my own? Yet every time your father came home, you kids treated him like visiting royalty. You were always so happy to see him. Always the hero's welcome . . ."

"I thought you felt the same way whenever he came home," Chris murmured numbly.

"See how much of a hero he is to you and Erin when he's the one who stays put and does all those thankless household chores," she growled.

Chris swallowed hard. "Then it's true, you're sick of us."

"No, goddamn it, I'm sick of him!" she cried. She twisted the wheel to one side. The driver behind them blasted his horn. Chris braced a hand against the dashboard as his mother pulled over onto the shoulder of the road. She slammed on the brakes and the tires screeched beneath them. "I'm sick of you and Erin thinking he's so goddamn wonderful when he's never really been there for you—or for me."

Stunned, Chris stared at her.

One hand gripping the wheel, she swiveled toward him. "He fucked around. Did you know that? Did you know your father—your hero—can't keep his dick in his pants?"

Chris just shook his head. He'd never heard his mother use such language, and he couldn't believe what she was saying. He still braced himself against the dashboard, though the Saturn was idling on the shoulder of the road. Other cars whooshed by.

"Every time he goes out of town, it's just another opportunity for him to screw whomever he wants. Five years ago, he came back from Boston and gave me a dose of chlamydia—at least I think it was Boston where he must have caught it. I can't be sure. For a while, he even had regular, steady girlfriends in some of those cities. Of course, he couldn't stay faithful to them any more than he could stay faithful to me. One, her name was Cassandra, she lived down in Portland, and she was crazy. I'm talking certifiable. She was calling the house day and night, threatening me, for God's sake. She even left a decapitated squirrel by our front door, the insane bitch. Your father can sure pick them. That was last year. . . ."

Chris vaguely remembered for a while the previous May, when his mom had instructed him not to answer the phone and not to let Erin pick it up. She'd said some crackpot had been calling. He couldn't comprehend that the *crackpot* had been a woman his father was screwing. He just kept shaking his head at his mother. He couldn't say anything. He felt sick to his stomach.

"Now you know," she said, her voice cracking. From behind her dark glasses, tears started down her cheeks. She leaned back in the driver's seat, took off the glasses, and sobbed. "This is no way for a mother to be talking to her son," she muttered, plucking a Kleenex from her purse. She wiped her eyes and nose. "But I couldn't stand to have you go on worshiping him, when—when he's been a terrible husband and at best, a part-time father."

A few cars sped by, and Chris cleared his throat. "How long have you known he was—messing around?" he asked timidly.

"It's been going on since you were about five, maybe even before that. I'm not really sure. He hasn't exactly been honest with me." His mother blew her nose, and then turned to him. Her red-rimmed eyes wrestled with his. "You said earlier that my moving away screwed everything up—and that if your father was the one getting a new place, it wouldn't make such a big difference. Well, sweetie, you're right. His life wouldn't change much at all. It would be very easy for him. He'd get a bachelor pad and probably have a live-in girlfriend within six weeks. Well, I'll be damned if I let that happen. It's why I moved out, honey. Maybe if he actually had to be a full-time father for a while and keep house for you and Erin—well, perhaps then he'd grow up. He might even begin to appreciate me a little more, though I doubt it."

"I think he appreciates you already, Mom," Chris whispered. "I really do. He's going to want you to come back, I know it."

His mother took a deep breath, readjusted her seat belt, and put her sunglasses back on. "I'll tell you what's going to happen. Your father will cancel his business trips for a while, but he'll hire a housekeeper to do the cooking and cleaning. After about a month, he'll need to go out of town, and he'll get the housekeeper to stay with you and Erin. And pretty soon, he'll start traveling on a regular basis again. . . ."

She glanced over her shoulder and pulled back onto the highway. The SUV began to pick up speed. The sound of the wind through the windows and the motor humming almost drowned her out. But Chris could still hear her. "And then one day," she muttered, "he'll come home from one of those trips with a woman he's very serious about—some woman who's younger and prettier than me. . . ."

It was scary how accurate his mother's prediction was. His dad did indeed stay home for a few weeks. They went through two housekeepers: one who stole and one who was lazy as hell. Then he found Hildy, an honest, hardworking Russian woman who didn't speak English very well and smelled like an open can of vegetable soup. Hildy stayed with him and Erin when his dad started traveling again.

What his mother hadn't predicted was how miserable Chris would be. He was utterly disappointed in his dad—to the point of contempt. His grades started sliding, and he didn't care. His timing at swim practices and meets was atrocious. He hated disappointing his swim coach, Mr. Chertok, because he was such a nice guy. Mr. Chertok tried to get him to talk about what was bothering him. But Chris was so ashamed. He couldn't talk to Mr. Chertok, or any of his teachers, or Elvis.

He never uttered a word to his dad about what he knew. At this point, he didn't want much to do with him.

He wasn't too happy with his mother, either. In order to get even with his dad, she was willing to screw up his and Erin's lives. Neither she nor his dad were around to hear Erin crying in her room at night. Hildy, who slept on an air mattress in a curtained-off corner of the basement rec room, didn't hear her, either. So Chris always came in and sat in a white wicker rocking chair that was usually reserved for a big stuffed giraffe she called Bill. Chris would keep her company until she nodded off.

"At least Erin has you to lean on," Elvis pointed out to him, while they wandered around Northgate Mall one Saturday night. "But who do you have? Why don't you ever tell me what's really going on with you? Something's bugging you big-time, and it's more than just your parents' splitting up. . . ." He grabbed hold of Chris's arm. "Are you even listening to me?" he asked, raising his voice. "I'm worried about you, man. I mean it, you're acting really weird."

Frowning, Chris glanced over at the entrance to a clothing store. "A little louder. One or two people in The Gap didn't hear you." He started walking again—toward the food court.

Elvis caught up with him. "Listen, if you don't want to unload on me, then you should talk to a shrink or maybe Mr. Corson at school."

Chris squinted at him. "Corson? Are you nuts? Only losers, psychos, and problem cases go to him. No thanks."

Elvis cleared his throat. "Maybe you forgot that I had a few sessions with Corson a while back."

Chris remembered, and immediately felt bad. After meeting with Elvis, Corson had tried to get Mrs. Harnett to join AA, but it didn't take. Nevertheless, Elvis liked him a lot—as did most of the kids at school. Corson's claim to fame was that two years back, he'd decided to quit smoking, and gotten over a hundred students to pledge they'd quit, too. The final number of students who actually stopped smoking was seventy-something, but it was still a big deal.

Chris gave his friend a limp, apologetic smile. "If I buy you a Cinnabon, would you forget that last remark—and drop this whole conversation?"

Elvis frowned at him. "That's really disgusting. Do you think just because I'm slightly overweight, that I'd trade in my dignity and my deep concern for your psychological well-being—all for a Cinnabon?"

Chris nodded. "Absolutely."

"Make it a Caramel Pecanbon, and we have a deal."

As they headed for Cinnabon, Chris thought about Mr. Corson. He couldn't go to him for help. It was like admitting to himself—and everyone else—that he was indeed very screwed up.

Instead, Chris exercised every day—to the point of exhaustion. After swim practice, he ran laps around the track or lifted weights. It was a good excuse to avoid going home for a while, maybe even miss dinner, especially when his dad was in town. He'd come in late, make himself a sandwich, and then hole up in his room with the TV and his homework.

This routine went on for about three weeks, but it didn't make him any happier. The only sliver of happiness he knew was a weird, warped satisfaction whenever he made it obvious to his dad that he politely loathed him.

His mother had been right about another thing. Sure enough, his dad brought some woman home from one of his trips. And she was indeed younger and prettier than Chris's mother. She worked at the Hilton in Washington, D.C., where his dad attended a pharmaceutical convention. But she was *really an artist*, so his dad said—whatever the hell that meant. The way the two of them talked, they'd known each other only a few weeks. But Chris wondered if his father had been screwing her long before the separation. Was this Molly person the reason his parents had split up?

He was thinking about that as he ran the track at dusk on a chilly Tuesday in early May. It was the second of three laps he intended to make around the football field. But his lungs already burned, and he felt depleted. Cold sweat soaked his jersey. He hadn't gotten much sleep the night before. He'd spent most of it in Erin's room, comforting her from nightmares. She'd woken up screaming—*twice,* for God's sake.

He started to run faster and faster as he thought about his poor little sister, who was always so frightened at night now. He thought about the last time he'd stayed at his mother's, when she'd been so concerned about how skinny he'd become—and the dark circles under his eyes. But within moments, she was grilling him about his father's new girlfriend, Molly. His mother was far more concerned about that situation than she was about his health. She was pathetic. So was his father, already *smitten* (at least that's the word he used) with this young woman—just two months after separating from his wife. What an asshole.

Chris poured on the speed until it felt as if his heart was

about to burst. He staggered off the track and collapsed onto the cold, damp grass. He started crying.

He didn't know how long he sat curled up on the ground, shivering and sobbing. But he noticed someone else on the track, rounding the turn and making his way toward him. Chris quickly tugged the bottom of his jersey up to his face and wiped away the tears and sweat. He tried to catch his breath. He recognized the other runner now, in gray sweats. Tall and lean with wavy, dark hair, it was Mr. Corson. *Just keep moving, pal,* Chris thought. *Get the hell away from me. I don't feel like talking to anybody.*

Slowing down, Corson smiled and waved at him. Glaring back, Chris just nodded.

Corson must have gotten the hint, because he trotted past him and started to pick up speed again. Chris let out a sigh. He didn't mean to be rude. He just wanted to be left alone.

"Goddamn it!" he heard Corson cry out. "Son of a bitch!"

Chris saw him hobble off the track and stumble to the ground. Corson grabbed his right leg below the knee and rubbed it furiously. "Damn it!" he howled. He was wincing in pain.

"Are you okay?" Chris called. His throat was a bit scratchy from crying.

"I think I pulled a muscle or something," Corson replied, still grimacing. He rocked back and forth while he massaged his calf. "This seriously hurts. . . ."

Chris got to his feet. "Maybe it's just a leg cramp," he said, approaching him. "I get those when I don't have enough sleep or I'm stressed. It's best to walk it off." He stood over the guidance counselor and held out his hand. "Let me help you."

Corson frowned at him. "Are you a sadist? Walk it off? I'm practically crippled here." He continued to rub his calf, then gazed up at Chris again and nodded. "Okay, okay, I'll try walking on it."

Chris helped him to his feet and led him back to the track.

"Ouch . . . ah . . . damn it . . ." Corson grumbled. With an arm around Chris's shoulder, he hobbled along. He kept sucking air through his gritted teeth. But his faltering walk seemed to improve. "I think you're right," he admitted at last. "Must be a leg cramp. I've just never had one this severe. Then again, I've been stressed a lot lately. My daughter's driving me crazy. How old are you—sixteen, seventeen?"

"Sixteen," Chris replied. Corson was still leaning on him and limping a bit.

"That's how old Tracy is," he said. "So—do you hate your parents, too? Does everything they say and do seem stupid or shallow or phony to you?"

"Kinda," Chris admitted.

Corson pulled away slightly, but still kept a hand on his shoulder. "Well, then maybe it's normal for the age. Or have you always felt this way about your folks?"

"Not always," Chris heard himself say. "Just lately."

"Why the sudden change? That's what I'd like to know. Tracy used to be such a loving child, and now she acts like she can't stand me. All she and her mother do is fight." He broke away and rubbed his calf again. "So—what happened with you? Did you just suddenly decide on your sixteenth birthday that your parents were losers? Is that how it works?"

"No. At least that's not how it worked with me," Chris mumbled, glancing down at the ground. "My parents are getting a divorce. And they're both being pretty selfish, so I'm pissed at them. In fact, lately, I'm pissed all the time—at everyone."

Corson stared at him. "That sucks." He seemed to work up a smile, and then held out his hand. "I'm Ray Corson, the guidance counselor."

Chris suddenly felt his guard go up, and he wasn't sure why. Still, he shook Corson's hand. "I know who you are. I'm Chris Dennehy."

"Well, Chris, if you ever want to talk, just let me know and I'll block off an hour for you. It'll get you out of study hall."

Chris shrugged. "I don't see how talking about it is going to help. They're still getting a divorce. And no disrespect, but you can't even figure out how to connect with your own daughter. So how are you going to help me?"

Corson let out a stunned laugh. "You're a real wiseass, aren't you? But I like that. Listen, it's always easier to help other people with their problems than to solve your own issues. That's why I was asking how you got along with your folks. I recognize that I need help dealing with my daughter." He bent down and massaged his calf again. "So—Chris, when you recognize that you need help dealing with your parents, come see me in my office. Or you can usually find me here between five and six on weekdays. I could use a running partner—if for nothing else, in case I ever get another leg cramp."

He straightened up, and still limping slightly, started toward the school. "Take care!" he called over his shoulder.

Two days later, Chris came and saw him in his office.

Between the scheduled appointments and the impromptu running sessions together, Mr. Corson helped him to understand his parents better and forgive them for not being perfect. Mr. Corson also urged him to give Molly a chance, and Chris realized his soon-to-be stepmother was actually kind of nice. From what he could tell, she had nothing to do with his parents' breakup. And she was a good artist. In fact, Molly even had him pose as the hero for the cover of a young adult novel that could end up being the start of a series.

Though he liked Molly, he still felt a loyalty to his mother, who clearly disdained her. Mr. Corson helped him deal with those conflicts. Chris took drivers' education at school during the summer, and he met up with Corson at the track once or twice a week. The guidance counselor had become his friend, and Chris depended on him. He didn't mean for Mr. Corson to take the place of his father, but that was what sort of happened.

And just as his father ultimately disappointed him, so would Mr. Corson.

In the end, Chris would wish he'd never walked into this office, where he now sat waiting for Munson to return.

Slouched in the chair, he nervously tapped the cover of the self-help book and sneered at the *To Thine Own Self Be True* clown poster on the wall. He heard someone coming and quickly straightened up in the chair.

"That's the damnedest thing," Munson muttered, stepping back into the office with a file folder. He sat down at his desk again. "There are no records of your visits here with Mr. Corson."

Chris just stared at him and shrugged.

"Corson made evaluations and progress reports of every student who consulted him—even the onetime visits," Munson explained. "Your evaluation—along with your progress reports and all the notes he took during your sessions—they're missing."

Chris shook his head. He remembered all the deep, private conversations he'd had with Mr. Corson in this room, all the things he could admit to his trusted counselor and no one else. Corson was taking notes during all those sessions. "What happened to them?" he asked numbly. "You sure Mr. Corson didn't just take them with him when he left?"

"No, I checked the files from last semester, and his critiques and progress reports are there for the other students," Munson said.

"Well, who would want to steal Mr. Corson's notes on our sessions? Those conversations were private." Chris felt a pang of dread in his gut—as if realizing he'd lost his wallet. Only this was far more valuable—and personal. "Maybe we should call Mr. Corson, and ask—"

Chris remembered and stopped himself. He swallowed hard. He hated the look of pity in Mr. Munson's eyes. "I just don't understand why anyone would take something like that," he murmured. "Who would do that? What would they want with it?"

Munson continued to study him in a pained and wondering way. He sighed and shook his head. "That's what I'd like to know, too, Chris," he replied.

CHAPTER FOUR

"Last night, a stranger to everyone here was cruising up and down this cul-de-sac," the handsome cop announced. "This man was trying to determine which one of your homes would be the easiest to break into."

Everyone in the room fell silent. They stopped passing around the tray of cookies. The policeman had them hanging on his next words.

Molly guessed he was about thirty-five. He had short, chestnut-colored hair and pale green eyes. Tall and athletically lean, he looked sexy in his black suit and a blue shirt with the collar open. He was probably a big hit with all the bored, lonely housewives at Neighborhood Watch meetings like this one.

Hands in his pockets, he stood in front of the Hahns' fireplace, above which hung a large studio portrait of the Hahn family: Jeremy and Lynette and their kids, Courtney, seventeen, Carson, eight, and Dakota, five. They were in front of a forest backdrop. Jeremy and Carson had matching blazers, and the girls were decked out in their yacht-club-dinner best. It was odd to see their frozen smiles in the portrait while the police officer made such a disturbing announcement.

"This stranger checked out every house on the block," the

cop continued. "He made observations of who was home and who wasn't, how well-lit your backyards were, and whether or not you had home security systems. . . ."

The residents of Willow Tree Court were gathered in the Hahns' family room for the down-to-business portion of the Neighborhood Watch potluck. Molly sat next to Henry Cadwell, a stocky forty-five-year-old work-at-home architect, who lived on the other side of a vacant lot next door to her and Jeff. Henry and his partner, a chiropractor named Frank, had an adopted daughter in Erin's class, Su-Li. *Hank and Frank*, Chris called them. They were moving soon, and Molly didn't want to think about it. Henry was her only real friend on the block. Among this clique, she and Henry were the outsiders. Perhaps that was why they sat in folding chairs while everyone else was ensconced on the sofa or in a cushioned easy chair.

Occupying the chair was Mrs. Kim Nguyen, the quiet, middle-aged, not-altogether-friendly neighbor at the end of the cul-de-sac—on the other side of Hank and Frank. At least, she wasn't too friendly with Molly. Then again, they'd only met a few times. Molly had asked her earlier—at the buffet table—if she and Dr. Nguyen had had a visitor this morning, someone driving a blue minivan. "I guess I'm already starting to neighborhood-watch," Molly had explained, trying to make light of it.

Mrs. Nguyen had frowned. "My friend picking us up at airport," she'd explained in her fractured English. "She driving blue van."

Molly had been relieved to hear that. Yet Mrs. Nguyen had seemed annoyed by the question. Molly had asked how long she and Dr. Nguyen would be in town.

"Three days," Mrs. Nguyen had replied curtly. Then she'd moved over to the other end of the buffet table, where Angela had stood.

A few minutes later, Molly had seen Mrs. Nguyen and Angela laughing about something.

Angela had the middle spot on the couch, with her gal pals, Lynette Hahn and Kay Garvey, on either side of her. Her mink-colored hair was perfectly styled, but she'd laid the makeup on a bit thick. Plus she was slightly over-dressed—in black pants and a black V-neck sweater with a shimmering silver striped weave. Her girlfriends, Lynette and Kay, had raved about how gorgeous she looked, and they wanted to hear all about the man in her life—the one with the beautiful house on a cul-de-sac in Bellevue. Angela had brought a quiche to the party—along with a bit of attitude.

"Hi, Molly," she'd said to her coolly. "You look so pretty—but then, you always do. I love your blouse." Molly had been in the middle of thanking her and was about to re-turn the phony compliment when Angela had excused herself to instruct Lynette on how to heat up the quiche. That was the extent of their conversation so far, after ninety minutes.

While grazing around the buffet table earlier, Angela, Lynette, and Kay had whispered about Ray Corson's murder. "I knew something like that would eventually happen," Lynette had concluded. "You have to wonder what he was doing in that park so late at night. He went there looking for trouble, and he found it."

Molly had steered clear of the conversation.

The Toll House cookies she'd baked that morning were on a plate in a hard-to-reach spot on the buffet table. Though Lynette knew she was bringing chocolate chip cookies, she'd baked a batch herself. "I thought you might forget or bring store-bought," Lynette had cheerfully explained. "And be-sides, I have to admit, I make the best chocolate chip cook-ies in the universe."

Molly hated Lynette. She had this phony perkiness to her—like a sitcom mom moonlighting in a commercial for deodorant. She was just a little too self-satisfied cute. She had a slim, tennis-taut figure, and frosted brunette hair with bangs. She seemed to think of herself as *Supermom!* But her daughter Courtney was shallow and selfish, and the two younger kids were utter brats. On several occasions, Molly had spotted Carson and Dakota and their friends throwing dirt balls at passing cars from an abandoned lot at the start of the cul-de-sac. She'd tried to tell Lynette about it, but Supermom was in total denial: *"I'm sure you're mistaken, Molly."* Her kids could do no wrong. For a while, Lynette had talked about suing a local restaurant, where the owner had had the unmitigated gall to ask if her children could please use their quiet voices so as not to disturb the other patrons.

Madison's mom was rather plain, with blond hair and a pale complexion. She was friendly enough when Lynette and Angela weren't around. But Molly was dead certain Kay talked behind her back to the other two. They seemed to regard her as this flaky, vapid successor to Angela—and only a temporary one at that.

And it hurt.

"Why do you care what those bitches think of you?" Henry had asked her at one point.

Molly couldn't quite explain why. Maybe it was because she was living in their friend's house, or because their daughters were in Chris's class. Once Henry moved away, she wouldn't have any friends on the block. He was her only friend in Seattle.

"Your cookies are infinitely better than Squeaky's," Henry had whispered in her ear—after sampling one of Lynette's from the tray being passed around the family room. Unbeknownst to Lynette, he called her Squeaky—after Lynette "Squeaky" Fromme, the one-time Manson follower who tried to assassinate Gerald Ford.

The detective had missed the potluck brunch portion of the proceedings earlier. Lynette had gotten up to present him to the group. She'd given a long, sickeningly cute introduction, which included a story about how her dear, sweet Dakota had once mistaken a guard at the zoo for a policeman (*"Is he going to arrest the elephant, Mommy?"*). Then she'd finally called on their guest speaker, Detective Chet Blazevich.

Molly could tell her neighbors were still wondering about this stranger who had been cruising around their cul-de-sac last night, studying the lay of the land.

"Didn't any one of you notice a dark green Toyota Camry going up and down your block around eight o'clock?" Detective Blazevich asked, with a hint of a smile.

Angela and her friends glanced at each other and shrugged.

Molly cleared her throat, and half raised her hand. "Do *you* drive a dark green Toyota Camry, Detective?"

He smiled and nodded. "Very good, Ms.—?"

Molly tried to ignore Angela out of the corner of her eye. She hesitated. "Dennehy."

"Ms. Dennehy is correct," Blazevich announced. "I scoped out your cul-de-sac last night, and found some things that might make you vulnerable to a break-in—just the kind of stuff a burglar would look for. . . ."

Molly glanced over at Angela and her pals on the sofa. Lynette shot her a look, and then whispered something in Angela's ear.

Molly turned away—just as Henry leaned in close to her. "Hell, if I knew this hunk was driving around our block, looking to break in to somebody's home, I'd have left the front door open."

Molly patted his knee and then turned her attention to Chet Blazevich. She felt a bit sorry for him. As he explained about their need for more streetlights and recommended spotlights for their back and side yards, the trio on the couch were still whispering to one another. Mrs. Nguyen pulled out some knitting and went to work on an ugly pink and maroon scarf—or maybe it was a sweater, Molly couldn't tell for sure. Blazevich had to talk loudly over the *clink, clink, clink* of her knitting needles. Then Henry's cell phone rang, and he went to talk on it in the kitchen. For a while, Molly felt like the only one paying any attention to the poor cop.

He was talking about how if they noticed any kind of maintenance truck on the block—a plumber, electrician, or a carpet cleaning service—it was best to check with neighbors to make certain the service truck was legitimate. That was when Kay Garvey raised her hand. "Excuse me. Do you know anything about this murder last night at the Arboretum?"

Gaping at her, Blazevich looked stumped for a moment.

"This Ray Corson person who was killed," Kay explained. "He was the guidance counselor at our kids' high school. So naturally, we're concerned."

Blazevich shoved his hands in his pockets. "I understand, but—um, I can't tell you any more than what's been on the news. It's not my case."

"Is it really true he just happened to run out of gas by that park?" Lynette pressed. "Or is that something the media is saying to protect his family or his reputation or whatever?"

Blazevich shrugged. "I'm sorry. As I said, it's not my case."

"You were talking about service trucks on the block," Molly spoke up. "Is that something burglars do when they're casing a house or a neighborhood?"

He smiled at her. "Yes, thank you, Ms. Dennehy."

"And is that something this Cul-de-sac Killer might do when he's figuring out where to strike next?"

Blazevich's smile faded and he nodded somberly. "Yes, we believe these killings are well planned. He knows ahead of time exactly where, when, and how he's going to gain entry into a house. And we think he has a pretty good idea of how many people are in that house. . . ."

Mrs. Nguyen ceased knitting, and Angela's group suddenly stopped whispering to each other. Henry quietly returned to the folding chair beside Molly.

"So—be cautious, be concerned," the policeman said. "Just the few extra seconds it takes to watch for strangers driving or walking around your cul-de-sac may be enough to prevent a crime."

Molly was thinking of all the strangers who house-sat for the Nguyens. It would be tough to keep track of who was supposed to be there and who wasn't. "Is there anything else we should be on the lookout for?" she asked. "Any warning signs specific to these—killings?"

Folding his arms, the cop hesitated before answering. "This hasn't been made known to the general public, for reasons I'll explain later. But if you notice your no-outlet or dead-end sign at the start of the cul-de-sac is missing, report it to the police immediately. With each murder, the sign at the beginning of the street was gone. We believe the killer takes the signs—possibly ahead of time—and keeps them as souvenirs or trophies of his crimes. We're doing our best to warn people who live on cul-de-sacs like this one. Unfortunately, some teenagers have heard about it, and we've had a rise in incidents with kids stealing the dead-end signs as a prank. So—if you do see a sign is missing, don't panic, but definitely report it to the police right away."

The policeman glanced around the room. "Now, even if you're taking all the proper precautions," he said, "you still might be a bit nervous in the house after dark—especially if your spouse is away, or if one of your children has seen the news stories about these murders, and they're scared. One thing you don't want to do is turn on all the lights in the house. Since this has become part of the killer's ritual, you don't want to alarm the neighbors. Instead, call a neighbor if you're scared or you suspect trouble. Count on each other for help. You might even agree on a code word to use if you have reason to believe an intruder is in the house, listening in. . . ."

Molly found herself clinging to Henry's arm. Once he

and Frank moved away, she wondered who she'd call if she
got scared.

After Detective Blazevich finished his presentation, he
passed around some Neighborhood Watch leaflets and had
everyone sign an official attendance form. It was all so they
could post a NEIGHBORHOOD WATCH placard by the NO OUTLET
sign at the start of Willow Tree Court—as if that would keep
away a serial killer.

Henry had to hurry off to an appointment. Molly retreated to the kitchen for the Tupperware container in which
she'd brought her Toll House cookies. Only a couple had
been eaten, and she didn't want Squeaky throwing the rest
away, which she most certainly would do—out of spite. Jeff,
Chris, and Erin would be happy to eat them.

She was at the buffet table, transferring the cookies from
Lynette's plate to the plastic container, when Detective
Blazevich came up to her side. Standing this close to him
now, Molly felt a certain electricity from him that she hadn't
experienced with anyone since first meeting Jeff a year ago.
She could tell he was attracted to her—and it was flattering,
embarrassing, and titillating.

"I'd like to thank you, Ms. Dennehy," he whispered.

"Molly," she said, with a cordial smile.

"For a while there, Molly, you seemed to be the only one
listening to me. . . ."

She stole a glance at Angela in the kitchen, watching their
every move. From the family room, Kay and Lynette were
staring at them, too.

"Well, it seems you certainly have their attention now,"
Molly said under her breath.

"Something tells me you're the new neighbor on the
block," he said, helping himself to one of her Toll House
cookies. "You don't seem to be part of the clique here."

Molly nodded. "You're a very good detective."

"Damn, these are great," he said, munching on the cookie. "Better than the other batch. Why weren't they passing *these* around?"

"Because *I* baked them," she replied quietly. "Our hostess made the other batch. It's a long story, Detective." Grabbing a napkin from the table, she wrapped a few cookies in it and handed it to him. "Here, take some home with you."

"Well, thanks." His fingers grazed hers as he took the napkin.

Molly glanced at Angela in the kitchen and Angela's gal pals in the Hahns' family room. They were still staring.

Blazevich reached into his pocket and pulled out a business card. "Listen—Molly, I appreciated your thoughtful questions earlier." He handed her the card. "If you have any more questions or concerns, please don't hesitate to call. My cell phone number is on there, too."

Molly took the card. She saw the others were still watching and took a tiny step back from the cop.

"Well, I should head out," he said. "Thanks again for the cookies."

"Good-bye, Detective."

Molly watched him return to the family room, where he also gave Lynette his card. He thanked everyone for their hospitality and said they should call if they had any questions.

Blazevich wasn't quite yet out Lynette's front door when Angela sidled up beside Molly at the buffet table. She took one of Molly's cookies, broke off a corner, and nibbled at it. "He was very good looking," she said. "And he was flirting with you."

"Well, if that's true, I'm flattered," Molly replied, not looking at her. She kept busy putting the cookies in the Tupperware. "But he was wasting his time."

"He gave you his business card," Angela went on. "The rest of us have to share one. Of course, you're the youngest

and prettiest woman here. Why shouldn't he pay more attention to you? So—how's Jeff doing?"

Molly nodded a few more times than necessary. "He's
fine. Everyone's fine, Angela. Erin's looking forward to seeing you at her ballet recital on Saturday."

"I was thinking it must be scary with this killer on the
loose, and Jeff going out of town all the time," Angela remarked. "I know all of his traveling drove me crazy after a
while—along with the fact that he couldn't keep it inside his
zipper. . . ."

Molly stared at her and blinked.

"I'm sorry, but if I were you, Molly, I'd have flirted more
with that detective. Jeff doesn't have any self-restraint. Why
should you?" The way Angela spoke, she almost came off as
a concerned friend who had had too many glasses of
chardonnay—rather than the bitch she was.

Shaking her head, Molly snapped shut the lid to the plastic container. "I don't need your advice, Angela," she said
evenly. "That problem doesn't exist in my marriage."

Angela gave her a smug smile. "You keep telling yourself
that, honey." Then she turned and joined her friends in the
Hahns' family room.

Molly didn't waste much time getting out of there. After a
few brief good-byes, she was out the door and walking down
the cul-de-sac with her Tupperware container and what was
left of her dignity. The sky was an ominous gray, and the
wind started to kick up. It would be raining soon, she could
tell.

She kept thinking that she shouldn't have let Angela have
the last word. She should have said, *"The only problem Jeff
and I have is you, Angela. Get over him, and get out of our
lives."*

But she couldn't have said anything like that to Angela's
face—not without feeling like a total ass afterward. In truth,
Angela had every reason to be bitter. It was true. Jeff had
been unfaithful on several occasions during the last few

loveless years of their marriage. Jeff had told Molly all about it when they'd first started seeing each other.

At the time, Molly had been working part-time under a real bitch who was the events coordinator at the Capital Hilton in Washington, D.C. Jeff had been there for the New Drugs in Development Conference with the American Pharmacology Association. Molly was working the registration desk when Jeff walked up, introduced himself, and asked for his badge. She was immediately drawn to him. Not only was he drop-dead handsome, but he had such a warm, friendly, confident manner. She'd grown so tired of dodging passes from businessmen at these conferences, most of them with their wedding rings in their pockets.

Her time in D.C. had been like an exile. She'd gone there to forget—and feel somewhat anonymous. She didn't know a soul in Washington, D.C. But after a while, the loneliness was too much. All she'd had were a few illustration assignments, a job she tolerated, and a boss she loathed. On more than one occasion, out of sheer desperation, she'd succumb to the charms of some lonely businessman. She didn't ask too many questions or expect anything more than one or two nights of company.

But Jeff was different. The conference went on for three days, and on day two, he asked if she had time the following afternoon to go with him to the National Gallery. How could she refuse? On top of everything else, he appreciated art.

At the gallery, right in front of a Jackson Pollock painting, Jeff told her that he and his wife had separated only six weeks before. Molly didn't want to date someone who was on the rebound. Reluctantly, she told him so, and Jeff seemed to understand. Then he showed her pictures of his kids on his cell phone, and he seemed so genuine, so proud of them. She couldn't help falling for him, despite her resolve.

Jeff said he'd be back in D.C. for another pharmaceutical

conference in three weeks. Could he take her out to dinner while he was in town again?

She said yes. Six weeks later, she flew into Seattle to meet Chris and Erin.

Two months after that, they were married. If it seemed rushed, that was probably her fault as much as Jeff's. She was in love with him and eager to start a new life. She'd been so miserable in Washington, D.C., and the dark, gloomy paintings she'd produced during this period reflected that.

Then into her life stepped this handsome, sweet guy with two kids who was going to change everything around for her.

Yes, he'd had affairs and one-night stands while married to Angela. But Molly had to give him a second chance. She knew what it was like, not being let off the hook. Before her exile to D.C., she'd spent her last weeks in Chicago seeking forgiveness—and not finding it.

She still remembered standing at that woman's front stoop on West Gunnison Street. She'd come there to tell her how sorry she was. "I don't mean to bother you," she'd told the middle-aged woman. "My name is—"

"I know who you are," the woman had hissed, glaring at her. She'd had tears in her eyes and started trembling. She suddenly spit in Molly's face. "Don't come crawling around here, hoping I'll accept any apologies from you, because I won't! It's not going to change a damn thing. Now, get the hell out of here—or I swear to God, I'll kill you."

Sometimes, Molly could still feel the woman's spittle running down her cheek and hear her harsh words. She'd moved to D.C. to forget, but it hadn't worked. She'd thought her chances might be better in Seattle.

She and Jeff were both starting over. She told him about Chicago. And Jeff kept her secret. There was no reason his kids needed to know about it, not for a while at least.

As she headed home, the wind seemed to whip right through her. Molly felt a few drops of rain. She wished she'd worn a coat for the half-block jaunt down to Lynette Hahn's house.

She couldn't get that conversation with Angela out of her head. Molly told herself the Jeff she knew was different from the Jeff who had been married to Angela

Shielding her head with the Tupperware container, she trotted up the walkway, unlocked the front door, and stepped inside the warm foyer. She set the container on the hallway table and headed up to the master bedroom. In Jeff's closet, Molly started checking the pockets of his suits and his khakis. She was looking for matchbooks or cocktail napkins with phone numbers scribbled on them. But all she found were three wrapped Halls cough drops, a stick of Juicy Fruit, several wads of Kleenex, and about $1.30 in change.

She still felt uncertain and retreated downstairs—to Jeff's study off the front hallway. The small room had a built-in, U-shaped mahogany desk—along with matching cabinets. A large-screen computer sat in the middle of the desk—in front of a picture window. Photos of her and the kids decorated the walls and desktop.

Molly opened the desk drawers and glanced at old bills and bank statements. She opened his appointment book and browsed through it. Nothing even remotely suspicious.

With a sigh, she plopped down in his chair and switched on the computer. She glanced at his e-mails—the ones he sent and received. Almost all of them were business-related, with a few correspondences to friends she knew. Four were from Angela, all within the last few days. They were curt inquiries about some book or CD that she'd accidentally left behind. Jeff was just as curt with his responses:

I'll make sure Chris brings the Moody Blues CD to you next time he visits. —J.

Molly had no idea Angela was still bugging him about little things like that. His poor ex-wife just couldn't let go—

and that was why she'd tried to put these doubts about Jeff's fidelity in her head. Molly felt stupid, listening to her.

She shut off the computer.

Carrying the Tupperware full of cookies into the kitchen, she set it on the counter, and then pulled Detective Blaze-vich's card from her jeans pocket. She fixed it to the front of the refrigerator with a magnet.

She had to work on her painting. But before heading up-stairs to her studio on the third floor, Molly wandered back into Jeff's study. She gazed out the window—toward the start of the cul-de-sac. She could see the NO OUTLET sign was still there.

She just needed to make sure.

Incoming Call
206-555-0416
Angela Dwyer

Chris frowned at the little screen on his cell phone. He still wasn't used to his mother going by her maiden name.

The phone was on vibrate, but it had still startled him. Chris had been slouched over a long desk in the school li-brary, his arms folded on the tabletop, resting his head on them. He was a little out of it, but hadn't really fallen asleep. He couldn't stop thinking about Mr. Corson.

During swimming season, he was excused from gym, his last class of the day. So he often came here to kill time, get a head start on his homework, or nap before swim practice. He liked the arched windows and the quiet. Plus he had a little crush on the head librarian, Merrill Chertok. The pretty brunette was his swim coach's wife. She got him hooked on books about time travel. When things hadn't been so great at home, he'd sometimes stay at the library until it closed at five. Unlike the assistant librarian, who had a burr up her butt, Ms. Chertok let him nap there. He'd wake up and see her behind the desk, and somehow he'd feel all right for a while.

At the moment, Ms. Chertok was at her desk, shaking her head at him. She pointed to the door.

Chris got her drift: no talking on cell phones in the library. Nodding, he quickly got to his feet and stepped out to the empty hallway with his cell. He clicked it on. "Hi, Mom," he said, leaning against the wall. "What's going on?"

"I've been thinking about you all day—ever since I heard about Mr. Corson," she said. "How are you doing, sweetie?"

Chris rubbed his eyes. "I'm okay." He really didn't want to talk to her about Mr. Corson's death. His mom had played as pivotal a role as anyone in banishing Mr. Corson from the school.

"Listen," she said, "if you're confused or feeling bad, I want you to know that I'm here for you, Chris. You can talk to me. Or you can talk to your father. He's a smart man, a very compassionate man."

He couldn't believe she was actually praising his father to him. It was touching that in order to make sure he had someone to talk to, his mom put aside her personal grievances with his dad.

"Thanks, Mom," he said into the phone. "Dad and I talked this morning, and I'm okay." He wanted to change the subject. "How are you? What's going on?"

"Well, I was in the neighborhood today," she said. "Lynette Hahn had one of those Neighborhood Watch meetings at her place, and this attractive, young policeman told us all about the Cul-de-sac Killer. Very scary stuff! Oh, and afterwards, he flirted shamelessly with Molly. Of course, she's so pretty. Still, I didn't see her do anything to discourage him. Sometimes, I really wonder about her. You get along with her, honey. Has she said anything to you about her family or her past? I mean, I'm absolutely clueless as to who she is or what she did before she met your father. And I'm supposed to entrust you and Erin in her care? It's crazy."

Chris wondered why—after all these months—his mother was suddenly dying to find out more about Molly. "Well, I don't know what to tell you, Mom," he said. "She doesn't talk much about her background or her family. . . ."

He remembered helping Molly move her stuff up to the third floor after she'd converted it into an art studio. A photo of a good-looking guy in his twenties had fluttered out of an open shoebox full of snapshots and postcards. Chris has asked who it was, and Molly had stared at it for a moment. Her eyes had filled with tears. "That's my brother, Charlie," she'd said at last. "He's dead."

"How'd he die?" Chris had asked.

"He—ah, he killed himself," she'd admitted, her voice a little strained.

Not wanting to upset her any more, Chris had decided to stop asking questions about her dead brother.

He never asked Molly about her mother, either. But apparently, she was a widow who lived in St. Petersburg, Florida. Every once in a while, Chris could hear Molly talking on the phone to her—usually behind the closed door of the master bedroom or in her art studio on the third floor. The conversations didn't last long, and Molly never sounded too happy. "Yes, Mother, I'll get a check to you this week," she'd say in a dull monotone.

Chris didn't want to tell his mother any of this. It seemed wrong somehow. Besides, he needed to get off the phone and go to swim practice.

"Listen, Mom, I gotta wrap it up here, okay?" he said into the phone.

"Well, I'll see you weekend after next—if not sooner," she said. "I love you. And call me if you start to feel sad or blue. Promise?"

"I promise," he said. "Bye, Mom." Chris clicked off the cell phone.

He ducked back into the library to grab his jacket and

books. After a quick wave to Ms. Chertok, he headed out again.

The pool was in a different wing on the other side of the school. Chris kept his head down and eyes to the floor all the way there. It had become his posture of the day. He just didn't want to talk to anybody.

As he stepped inside the locker room, he was hit with a familiar combo-waft of chlorine-chemical smell and B.O. Most of his teammates had already gone to the pool area, but a few still lingered at their lockers. He could hear them in the next row, belt buckles clinking against the tiled floor, locker doors banging.

"Hey, did you hear this one?" one of the guys was saying. It sounded like Dean Fischer, who was kind of a wiseass jerk. "What was Ray Corson's favorite song?"

There was a silence. While Chris worked the combination of his locker, he imagined the other guy shaking his head.

"'Don't Let Your Son Go Down on Me'!" Fischer said, cackling. "Get it? That old song by Elton John . . ."

Chris started to unbutton his shirt. He'd first heard that joke when Mr. Corson was forced to leave the school.

"Don't you get it, moron?" Fischer was saying. A locker door slammed. "Corson and Ian Scholl, remember back in December? And at the same time, Corson was trying to get into Chris Dennehy's pants, too. Dennehy's the one who walked in on them. . . ."

In his blue Speedo, George Camper, the captain of the team and a nice guy, strode past Chris. George shot him a concerned look before he disappeared past the row of lockers. "Hey, Fischer," George said. "Do me a favor and shut the hell up."

"'Don't Let Your Son Go Down on Me'? Get it?" Fischer was saying to his buddy. "Are you brain-dead or something? Don't you remember? Chris Dennehy and Ian Scholl—"

"Shut up already!" Chris heard George growl. Then there was whispering.

Chris buttoned his shirt back up. He quickly collected his jacket and backpack of books. He just couldn't stick around there. He closed his locker, spun the combination dial, and then ducked out of the locker room.

It was raining out, so Chris stood under the bus shelter while waiting for the number 331. Only a few other students were at the stop. They looked like freshmen. Chris didn't have to wait long before the bus showed up. He took a seat near the back. Staring out the rain-beaded window, he thought about Ian Scholl.

Ian was thin and pale with jet-black hair. There was something weird about his looks—he seemed *pretty* instead of handsome. Courtney claimed he must have sculpted his eyebrows to get them to look the way they did. Yet he didn't have a metrosexual thing going on. He always dressed very neat and conservatively in what Courtney called Mormon clothes. Ian was a mess of contradictions. He was obviously gay, and just as obviously uncomfortable with it. His effeminate manner—paired with a rabid homophobia—alienated everyone and made him a prime target for teasing.

Chris didn't talk to him much. They were in the same English lit class, but that was about it. Mostly, he just saw Ian in the hallways, carrying his books like a girl—until some guy inevitably knocked those books out of his grasp or tripped him. On one of those occasions, Chris had felt bad for Ian, and he'd picked up one of Ian's books for him. "Are you okay?" he'd asked.

Ian had snatched the book out of his hand. "I don't need any help from some dumb jock," he'd hissed.

Chris had let out a surprised laugh. "Well, screw you, then." He'd turned and walked away.

So later, when Mr. Corson had asked him to be nice to Ian, Chris resisted. They'd been jogging around the track to-

gether. Chris told him about the episode with the schoolbooks in the hallway. "The guy's a jerk," Chris said, between
gasps for air. "I already tried to be friendly with him, and he
got all pissy on me. And you want me to be his pal? No
thanks!"

Mr. Corson slowed to a stop, and then caught his breath.
His Bruce Springsteen and the E Street Band Concert Tour
T-shirt was soaked and clinging to him. Jogging in place at
his side, Chris had only a few beads of sweat on his forehead.

"You weren't offering Ian friendship," Mr. Corson said.
"You were offering him your pity. He was mad and humili-
ated. So he snapped at you. Give him a second chance. I'm
not asking you to be best friends with him. Just be nice, and
maybe persuade some of your pals to stop tormenting him."

Chris suddenly stopped running in place. "I've never tor-
mented him," he pointed out. "And the guys who pick on
him aren't my friends, so I doubt they'll listen to me when I
tell them to lay off. I don't have that much clout around
here." He shook his head. "Really, I'm sorry, but I can't help
you out, Mr. C."

"Fine, I understand," Mr. Corson muttered.

"We've still got two more laps," Chris said. He started
running in place once more. "You aren't pooping out on me,
are you?"

Mr. Corson nodded. "Yeah, I am," he sighed. "You go
ahead and finish up without me, Chris. I'm beat." He turned
and lumbered toward the school's athletic wing.

Chris remembered watching him walk away. He'd almost
called to him. But instead, he'd just let him go.

Chris heard the bus driver announce his stop. He let out a
sigh and started to reach for the signal cord above his head.
But then he hesitated. He didn't want to go home just yet. He
couldn't pretend for Molly that everything was okay. He just
didn't have it in him right now. Slowly, his hand went down
and he watched the bus speed past his stop.

He realized there was someplace else he had to go.

The bus made three more stops, and Chris was the only passenger left. He wasn't too familiar with this part of the route, but he knew they must be getting close to his destination. He'd only been there once before.

Getting to his feet, he made his way toward the front of the bus. The driver was a cinnamon-skinned, thirtysomething woman with short-cropped, shiny, dark auburn hair. Chris caught her looking at him in the mirror.

"Excuse me," he said, grabbing an overhead strap to keep his balance. "Does this bus go to the—the Evergreen Wasabi Cemetery?"

"Ha!" She grinned up at him in the mirror. "You mean, Evergreen *Washelli,* honey! Wasabi is Japanese horseradish. Ha!" She gazed at his reflection; and obviously she saw he wasn't smiling. She shifted in her seat a bit, cleared her throat, and nodded. "Evergreen Washelli Memorial Park is coming up in two more stops. Why don't you sit down, honey? I'll tell you when we get there."

Chris plopped down on the handicapped seat behind her. He figured the bus driver must have thought he was related to someone buried in the cemetery, and maybe that was why she got serious all of the sudden. "Thanks a lot," he said.

Chris thanked her again a few minutes later as the doors whooshed open and he stepped off the bus. He was about a half block from the open gates of the Memorial Park entrance. By the time Chris started down the private drive of the park, his hair was wet and matted down with rain. His jacket had become soaked. The cold dampness seeped through to his shoulders, and he shuddered. He passed the administration building, which resembled a modern-looking chapel. He'd gone in there on his last visit for help finding the grave.

But he was pretty sure he still remembered where the marker was. Taking a curve in the road, he started up a gentle slope and kept a lookout for a tall statue of St. Joseph. That had been how he'd found his way when he'd been here back in January. The trees were bare then, and the grass had some brown patches. But everything was in bloom now, and the lawn was a lush, misty green—punctuated by squares of gray, rose, and white marble. There were only a few other people in the park, and they'd had the good sense to bring umbrellas. No one was close enough to see him muttering to himself: "I'm sure this is the way. I know St. Joseph is around here someplace. . . ."

He finally spotted the statue behind a huge evergreen. Just beyond that was a section of the cemetery with no upright markers. The grave he wanted to find was near one of the two Japanese maples on the far side of the section.

As Chris trudged on the grass, he felt water seeping into his Nikes, soaking his socks. The rain seemed to be getting worse. His hands were wet and cold. He rarely strapped on his backpack, but he resorted to that now—so he could shove both hands in his jacket pockets. Shivering, he imagined catching pneumonia, maybe even dying.

Well, he deserved to die.

Perhaps they would bury him here among these flat markers, where people could walk over the gravestones, as well as the graves—and not give a damn. He realized that without any standing tombstones, it might be tough to find the right grave—a lot tougher than he thought.

Chris reached the Japanese maples—with rain dripping from their red spidery leaves. He started looking for the marker. *Near the end of the row*, he reminded himself. He couldn't remember the color. He walked up and down the end row of markers with his head down, looking at the ground. It was his posture of the day, because he didn't want to talk with anyone.

The only people he wanted to talk to were dead.

And they hadn't buried Mr. Corson yet.

After a few minutes, the names started to blend together, and Chris retraced his steps. "You're here someplace," he whispered, running a hand through his wet hair. "I know you're here. . . ."

Then at last, he saw it—a gray marker, a bit newer than the others. Chris stopped in his tracks and stared down at it. His throat started to tighten.

IAN HAMPTON SCHOLL
1994 – 2010
Beloved Son – Rest with the Angels

As he gazed down at the marker, warm tears mingled with the cold rain on his face. "I'm sorry," Chris said. He shook his head over and over. "God, I'm so sorry. . . ."

CHAPTER FIVE

"Why are you doing this to us?" she heard her friend, Leslie, cry out.

Marianne Bowles sat up in bed for a moment. She was thirty-two and single, with blond hair, blue eyes, and a lovely figure—though Marianne felt she stood to lose about ten pounds. She was in from Boston on business with Microsoft, and decided to spend the weekend with her old college roommate, Leslie and her husband, Kurt.

At the moment, it sounded like the two of them might be having a fight. In a weird way, it was kind of a relief to know Leslie and Kurt Fontaine weren't so damn perfect after all. Marianne envied her old college pal. Leslie was still a knockout. She and Kurt seemed terribly happy. They lived in a gorgeous little English cottage–style house at the end of a cul-de-sac in the Madrona neighborhood. It had a sweet English garden with a stone pathway to the garage, which Kurt had converted into an office for Leslie and her thriving website-design business. It made ideal guest quarters—with its full bath, mini-fridge, microwave, and comfortable sofa bed, on which Marianne now slept. At least she'd been sleeping—until the voices from the house woke her up.

They'd dined out at Cactus in Madison Park and had a

few too many margaritas. But it had been a wonderful time, with lots of laughs and old college stories. Marianne had staggered down the stone pathway to her guest quarters at around 11:30, and she'd been asleep by midnight.

She squinted at the clock on the end table: 1:55 A.M. She couldn't believe Leslie and Kurt were still awake—and arguing, no less. Maybe they'd hit that wall some people hit after a certain amount of happy drinking—and then they become angry-drunk.

"Oh, God, no!" Kurt yelled. "Wait, wait!"

Marianne slumped back down in the bed and put her hands over her ears. She didn't want to hear their private discussion, which sounded almost violent. She could still detect some muffled yelling from Kurt. So Marianne rolled over on her side and pressed the extra pillow to the side of her head. That seemed to block it out.

She must have drifted off, because then she heard a tapping noise and glanced at the clock again: 3:17 A.M. It took her a moment to realize someone was knocking on her door. She'd locked it earlier. There was just enough light in the room for her to see the knob turning back and forth a bit.

Pulling back the bedcovers, Marianne was about to climb out of bed. She hesitated—she wasn't sure why. She already had a bit of a hangover, and didn't want to have to listen to Leslie's version of what they'd been arguing about. Marianne was just too tired.

There were a few more taps on the door.

She figured if Leslie wanted to talk that badly, she'd go fetch the key and let herself in. Marianne fell back into bed. After a few moments, she saw a shadow in the window—moving back toward the house.

Her eyelids grew heavy and she felt herself drifting off to sleep again. Marianne's last thought was about the light coming through the window. Strange, how bright it seemed outside. It was as if every light was on inside the charming English cottage–style home.

* * *

"Chris? Erin?" Molly called from the bottom of the stairs. They were both in their respective bedrooms. Erin had a ballet recital at 2 P.M. Chris was getting together with Elvis this afternoon. Molly had emerged from the shower an hour ago and was still in her bathrobe. She'd promised to drive Erin to her recital and attend the show.

That had been two weeks ago—before she'd found out Angela would be there, too.

Perhaps that was why Molly had been on edge most of the morning. It was Saturday, and the ballet show was in an hour.

"Did either of you take the MapQuest directions from the basket on the kitchen counter?" she called upstairs to them.

No response.

"Erin? Chris?" she yelled.

"I didn't take'm!" Chris yelled back, his voice muffled by the closed door.

"Me neither, and please, I'm trying to get dressed!" Erin screamed, very much the prima donna ballerina.

Molly checked her purse for the directions. The night before last, she'd printed the MapQuest directions and set the printout by the phone on the kitchen counter. Now it wasn't there. All she could remember was the recital hall was someplace where God lost his shoes in Mountlake Terrace.

The printout wasn't in her purse, either.

She didn't even want to go to this stupid thing. Why the hell couldn't Angela drive Erin? Wouldn't a mother want to spend that time with her daughter? What an incredible jerk. Molly really didn't want to see her today. Angela was probably ready to dole out some more *Don't Trust Jeff* advice, too.

It had been a little over a week since Molly had spoken with Angela at the Neighborhood Watch potluck. They'd learned about Ray Corson's murder that same morning.

The police still hadn't found his killer yet. Molly heard they'd interviewed Ian Scholl's parents. They'd even spoken with Jeff at his office that day. They didn't dare let on that he was a suspect, or even a person of interest. But he must have been—for a brief while anyway.

From what Molly had read, the police figured Corson's death was the result of a random robbery that had gotten out of hand. The Arboretum was close enough to the University District, where there had been a rash of armed robberies lately.

Chris had told his dad he wanted to attend Mr. Corson's wake this weekend. He wanted to pay his respects, and maybe even apologize to Mrs. Corson for that whole mess back in December. But Jeff insisted it was a private service, and Chris wouldn't be welcome there. Besides he didn't need to apologize to anybody for anything.

In the end, Chris had ceded to his father's ruling and sulked about it for the better part of an evening.

Jeff had spent the last four nights in Denver. He was coming back in time for dinner tonight—if his flight wasn't delayed.

Molly had endured the last few nerve-wracking nights without him. The Cul-de-sac Killer had struck again last weekend, slaying a Madrona couple. An old college friend visiting from Boston had been asleep in a guesthouse behind the residence. She hadn't heard about the Cul-de-sac Killer, so she hadn't been alarmed when she noticed nearly every light on inside her friends' house when she awoke Sunday morning. She found her friend's husband in a coat closet on the first floor. His hands were tied behind him, and he'd been stabbed repeatedly. The wife was in the master bedroom closet with her throat slit. The woman from Boston told police that she'd heard them in the middle of the night—and thought they were arguing. And later, someone had tapped on her door, but she hadn't answered it.

Of course, Molly read every article she could about the murders—and then she wasn't able to sleep at night.

Last night had been the worst. Chris had gone out for a

movie and pizza with Elvis. Molly had let him take her car. But when Chris still hadn't come home by midnight, she grew more and more anxious—not only about her stepson but also for Erin and herself. After tucking Erin in bed, she'd been reluctant to go up to her studio and work. If someone broke in, she might not hear anything until it was too late. She imagined coming down from her studio to discover Erin's empty bed—and her body in the closet.

So Molly sat in the family room with the TV on. She kept expecting to see someone through the glass doors, lurking at the edge of the forest in the back. Finally, she closed Angela's ugly drapes, blocking the view entirely. She almost telephoned Henry down the block, but stuck it out until 12:25, when Chris finally came home.

Just having a semi-adult in the house made her feel safer—which was also kind of silly, because three of the killer's victims were adult males. Still, Molly was able to relax a bit with Chris there.

He'd asked to use her car again this afternoon to hang out with Elvis, but she had to drive Erin to her ballet recital.

Molly still couldn't find the damn MapQuest directions. She decided to go into Jeff's computer, check the sites she'd last visited, pull up the page, and print it again—a solution she should have thought of ten minutes ago.

On her way to Jeff's study, she ran into Chris coming down the stairs. His hair was carefully combed, and he wore a pair of pressed khakis, a crisp-looking blue shirt, and black loafers, shined and buffed. He carried a lightweight, dark jacket.

"Well, you look nice," Molly commented. "I thought you were getting together with Elvis. You look more like you're going out on a hot date."

He frowned at her a bit. "No, we're just hanging out, that's all," he muttered. At the front door, Chris threw on his jacket. "We—um, we might go to the art museum. I just didn't want to look like a bum."

"Can I drop you at Elvis's? It's on the way, and there's still time before Erin's *Swan Lake* stint."

"It's okay. I'm taking the bus downtown and meeting him."

"Well, try to be back in time for dinner," Molly said, patting his shoulder. "Your dad's coming home, and I'm fixing lasagna. Tell Elvis he's invited, too."

Chris just nodded distractedly. "I'll call and let you know. Bye." Then he headed out the front door.

Molly glanced at her wristwatch. She still had to get dressed. "Erin, honey!" she called upstairs. "Just to let you know, we're leaving in about twenty minutes!" Then she murmured to herself. "If I can ever track down how to get to this damn place . . ."

She headed into Jeff's study, sat down at his computer, and got online. She clicked on the browsing history arrow. She was about to scroll down to MapQuest.com Search Results when she noticed two sites listed near the top: King County Metro Online Trip Planner and Bonney-Watson Funeral Home, Seattle.

Molly shook her head. "Oh, that sneaky son of a . . ."

She stood up and peered out the window. She could see Chris at the end of the cul-de-sac, near the NO OUTLET sign. Molly felt a little sad pang in her stomach as she watched him. His head down as he walked, Chris pulled a tie from his jacket pocket and started to fix it around his neck.

The bus was late.

Chris stood at the stop, by the pole with the route table listed on a small placard. It was a chilly, overcast afternoon, but he wore his sunglasses anyway. He hiked up the collar of his jacket, and then felt his tie knot again. He figured it was crooked, but he could always straighten it out when he got to the funeral home.

He wondered if he'd read the bus schedule wrong when

he'd checked it online. From his jacket pocket, he pulled out the piece of scrap paper on which he'd written the bus numbers and pickup times. On the back of the scrap paper was a MapQuest printout to someplace in Mountlake Terrace. He turned it over and glanced at his notes. He had to make three transfers, and it would be a ninety-minute trip each way.

He wondered if attending this wake was such a good idea. He didn't want to upset Mr. Corson's family, and chances were good he'd upset them—big-time. But he had to make amends and apologize to *someone.*

He remembered trying to get ahold of Mr. Corson after he left school in December. But his guidance counselor, who had always been there for him, changed his cell phone number and e-mail address. Chris used to run the high school track alone late afternoons, hoping against hope that Mr. C would surprise him and show up. He knew it was a crazy notion.

Mr. Corson once mentioned he sometimes ran on the Burke-Gilman Trail along north Lake Union in Seattle. So for three nights in mid-February, Chris took two buses to the University Bridge and then strolled along the trail in search of Mr. Corson. He didn't spot him until the fourth trip.

It was unseasonably warm, and the setting sun marked the sky with streaks of red, orange, and plum. The colors glistened off the lightly rippling water of Lake Union. The trail had a steady stream of people running, walking, and riding their bikes. Chris was momentarily distracted by a pretty blonde in a clingy black jogging suit, and he almost missed Mr. Corson—jogging a few feet behind her.

"Chris?" he said, slowing to a stop.

Chris gaped at him. He looked so different. He had a heavy five o'clock shadow, and his hair was longer. He appeared tired—and older, somehow. He wore a Huskies sweatshirt and black knee-length workout shorts.

"Um, hi, Mr. C," Chris murmured.

Mr. Corson wiped the sweat from his brow. "What are you doing here?"

"Trying to find you," Chris admitted. "I—I feel awful about everything that happened."

Mr. Corson nodded. "So do I, Chris." Frowning, he glanced over at the sunset and then sighed. "The big difference is you're still in school and you still have a future—and me, well, I doubt I'll be able to get a job in any school again. That's a done deal."

Chris shook his head. "I'm so sorry, Mr. C," he said meekly.

Mr. Corson nodded toward a nearby park bench that faced the water. "C'mon, I need to sit down and take a break anyway. I'm so out of shape lately, it's not even funny."

He lumbered toward the bench, and Chris walked alongside him. Mr. Corson brought his hand up toward Chris's shoulder, but then he hesitated. Chris noticed him pull away slightly. They sat down—with a gap between them, big enough for another person.

"I don't really blame you for anything, Chris," Mr. Corson said, staring out at the water. "It's just that Courtney Hahn and her pals made all those accusations about me on Facebook and Rate-a-teacher-dot-com. So many parents—especially the Willow Tree Court group—they got all stirred up, and it was over absolutely nothing."

He leaned forward and ran a hand through his brown hair. "You know, there's a big difference between folks who look out for the welfare of their kids, and the ones that spoil them rotten and let them get away with anything, simply because they're *their* kids." He let out a defeated laugh and shook his head. "Do you have any idea how difficult it is for teachers nowadays? We have to put up with kids texting and Twittering during class and then rating us online. We have these self-righteous parents calling us up and screaming at us about why *their* kid didn't get a better grade or more time playing in a varsity game or more pages in the yearbook. Shit, I should be glad they fired me. I guess I'll survive this. But your neighbors on Willow Tree Court and the ones like them, they'll have to pay. They've raised a bunch of coddled, selfish brats who have an overblown sense of entitlement and absolutely no accountability. It's going to bite them on the ass eventually. It reminds me of this saying my wife has: '*Time wounds all heels.*'"

Dumbfounded, Chris just stared at him. He wasn't quite sure what Mr. Corson meant. He'd never seen him this upset and angry before. Did Mr. Corson consider him a *selfish, coddled brat*?

It turned darker—and colder—in a matter of minutes. Chris shivered and rubbed his arms to fight off the chill. "Is there anything I can do—anybody I can talk to—that will help you get your job back?"

"No, it's too late for that," Mr. Corson sighed. "The damage has been done. When I think of poor Ian Scholl . . ." He rubbed his eyes. "No, Chris, you can't fix it. All the gossip and lies have taken their toll. My marriage is pretty much a shambles now—along with my finances. Plus my daughter, Tracy, this has really hurt her, and she's been acting out in all sorts of—disturbing ways. I'm really worried about her. Fortunately, Todd is too young to understand what's happening. I think maybe we'll sell our home here and move to the East Coast, try to start over. . . ."

Biting his lip, Chris tried to think of something he could say to make Mr. Corson feel better—the way Mr. Corson had always seemed to know exactly what to say to him. The only thing that came to mind was one of Molly's expressions: *This too shall pass.* But he was worried he might sound like a smart-ass. And besides, it hardly seemed true in this case.

"You didn't come here to listen to how shitty my life has become," Mr. Corson said. "You came here because you feel bad and don't want me blaming you. Well, I don't blame you, Chris."

"But you got such a raw deal, Mr. C, and I feel like—"

"You saw something that confused and disturbed you, so you went to your stepmother about it, and things just got out of hand. It wasn't your fault, Chris." He gave him a sad smile. "Even if I was mad at you for a while, I couldn't stay angry at you. It sounds corny, but you've been like a son to me—and I'll always think of you that way."

Chris could see the tears in his eyes. Mr. Corson cleared his throat and then suddenly stood up. "Listen, I should go. Obviously, your mom and dad don't know you're here meeting with me. If it ever got back to them—well, there'd be hell to pay for both of us."

Chris quickly got to his feet. "Can I get your new e-mail address or—or—or phone number? I don't want this to be—"

"No," Mr. Corson said, cutting him off. "That's a bad idea. Your parents wouldn't want you communicating with me, Chris." As he spoke, he kept glancing down at the ground—and not at him. "I don't want it, either. I don't think we should see each other again. . . ."

"Oh, c'mon, Mr. C, you can't mean that."

But Chris saw the tired, defeated look on Mr. Corson's face—and he knew his beloved guidance counselor meant every word.

Chris's heart sank. He went to hug him.

"Don't," Mr. Corson muttered, backing away. "That's what got me into trouble in the first place. You should know better than anybody." He took a deep breath, then grabbed Chris's hand and shook it. "Good-bye, Chris. Good luck."

"Bye," Chris murmured. Dazed, he watched him turn and start toward the trail. "Mr. C!" he called, his voice cracking. "Mr. C, if it weren't for you, I never would have made it through the last year! Mr. Corson?"

A few people on the track stared at him. But Mr. Corson

didn't even turn around. He started running down the trail, and never looked back.

That was the last time Chris saw him.

And now he was going to his wake.

At least, he hoped to go—if the bus ever showed up. With a lump in his throat, Chris glanced at his wristwatch: 1:35. The bus was fifteen minutes late. He felt so lonely and lost. He hated going to this wake alone—and facing all those people who might hate him. He should have asked Elvis to come with him.

He took off his sunglasses and anxiously peered down the street. No sign of the bus. But he recognized Molly's dark green Saturn coming up the street. It was close enough that she probably saw him. And from what he could tell, she was alone in the car.

His mouth open, he watched her pull over to the stop. With a hum, the front passenger window descended. Chris leaned toward the car and suddenly remembered he was wearing a tie. His hand came up to cover it, but too late. "Um, what's going on?" he asked.

"I could ask you the same thing," Molly said with a wry smile. "I like your tie."

Mortified, he took his hand away. He noticed she was wearing a dark, formal coat and a black dress. Her blond hair was all done up.

"Where's Erin?" he asked, still hovering close to the car.

"I called Marlys Bourm to see if Erin could get a ride with Allyse. They just picked her up five minutes ago. She's a little disappointed I'm not going to the recital, but she'll survive. Besides, your mother will be there."

"So—where are you going?"

"To a wake—with you," Molly said. "C'mon, get in."

Chris stared at her and blinked. "How did you—"

"I'll tell you on the way," she said, cutting him off. "Get in—before we cause a traffic jam."

Chris quickly opened the passenger door and climbed inside.

"If you're so determined to go to this wake, despite everything your father told you and all his warnings," Molly said, glancing in the side mirror, "well, honey, you shouldn't have to face that crowd all by yourself."

Chris felt the lump in his throat return. He was so grateful for the company, for the ride, and for her uncanny intuition. He almost went to hug her. But he held back and strapped himself in with the seat belt.

"Thanks, Molly," was all he said.

"Okay, here's what I think we should do," Molly whispered to Chris as they stepped into Bonney-Watson Funeral Home's elegant lobby. It resembled the foyer of a rich, old estate. Vases of flowers and Kleenex boxes were strategically placed on mahogany tables between cushioned chairs and love seats. "Once you see Mrs. Corson," Molly continued, "we'll wait until she's alone or down to just one person talking to her—and then we'll make our approach. Say what you need to say, and then let's beat a hasty retreat."

Chris looked nervous. "Um, Molly, I—I don't know what Mrs. Corson looks like. I've never met her."

She was thrown for a loop for a moment, but then she nodded and straightened his tie. "Well, okay, we'll just figure it out. You look nice."

By a double doorway at their right, a small placard on the wall had CORSON spelled out in white plastic letters on a ribbed black velvet background. Molly and Chris stepped into the crowded room and made their way toward the closed bronze casket at the far end. Molly guessed there were about a hundred people attending the wake. She stopped and asked a skinny, twentysomething woman if she could point out Mrs. Corson for them.

The woman nodded in the direction of the casket. "Mrs. Corson's over there in the black dress." she said. Then she moved on.

"Well, that narrows it down to about twelve women in the general vicinity," Molly muttered to Chris. "C'mon, let's see if we can weed her out."

Hesitating, he glanced around the room. "I'm not so sure about this now."

"Well, personally, I agree with your dad," Molly whispered. "It's a bad idea, Chris. You have no idea how she's going to react. My guess is we won't be welcomed with open arms. So just say the word and we're out of here. If you're so determined to apologize to her, you can always do it in a sympathy card."

Biting his lip, he stood there for a few moments. He shifted his weight on one foot and then the other.

Molly remembered over a year ago, going to that woman's front door on Gunnison Street in Chicago and trying to apologize to her—only to end up with a face full of spittle for her efforts.

"I vote we leave," Molly said.

But Chris shook his head. "No, I need to do this." He started toward the casket.

Molly followed him. She spotted a pale, dowdy, brown-haired woman in an unflattering wrap-around black dress. Two people were talking to her—and one of them was holding her hand in a consoling way. Beside her stood a bored-looking teenage girl with heavy Goth eye makeup and stringy black hair. She had on a black skirt and a ratty, black sweater with sleeves that came down to her fingers.

"Do you think that might be her?" Molly whispered.

"I—I guess," Chris replied under his breath. "It sounds mean, but I always thought Mr. Corson's wife would be really pretty. They have a daughter around my age—and she's supposed to be kind of weird. So maybe . . ."

The two people moved away from the woman, and Molly meekly approached her. "Mrs. Corson?"

The woman stared at her. "I'm *Ms.* Corson. I'm Ray's sister, Sherry." She held out her hand.

Molly shook it. "Hello, Sherry. I'm so sorry for your loss. My name's Molly Dennehy."

"This is my daughter, Serena. . . ." Ray Corson's sister started to gesture toward the teenage girl. But she hesitated. "Did you say *Dennehy*?"

"Yes," Chris piped up. "I'm Chris. Mr. Corson was my guidance counselor at James Monroe. I was hoping I could talk with Mrs. Corson. . . ."

"*Dennehy*," the woman repeated, scowling at them. "I know that name. I've heard about you from Jenna."

"I'd like to talk with her—and—and—and explain some things," Chris said in a shaky voice.

Molly put a hand on his shoulder. She could feel him trembling.

Ray Corson's sister slowly shook her head. "You have a lot of nerve showing up here."

Molly cleared her throat. "If we could just talk to your sister-in-law . . ."

"Jenna is in Yakima with her sister," Sherry whispered. "She's in no condition to see anyone. . . ."

"Well, she went there before Uncle Ray was killed even," the girl piped up. "She was ready to leave him—"

"Serena, please," her mother growled.

"Well, she was!" the girl said, rolling her eyes. "And still, Uncle Ray left everything to her. Anyway, Aunt Jenna's not even in Yakima right now—"

"That's enough, young lady," her mother hissed. "Why don't you see if Grandma Berry needs a glass of water or something?"

The girl rolled her eyes again. "Excuse me for living," she muttered, wandering off.

"Do you happen to have her address in Yakima?" Molly asked. "Someplace we can send a card or flowers?"

"Haven't you done enough damage?" she asked. "For God's sake, leave her alone. She's been through hell, thanks to you people."

"Is—is their daughter okay?" Chris asked suddenly. "The last time I talked with him, Mr. Corson said he was worried about her, because she was having a lot of problems."

"Tracy ran away two months ago," Sherry said. "She hasn't been seen or heard from since. Now, if you don't have any more questions, would you please leave? I have nothing more to say to you."

"I'm sorry," Chris murmured. "I really am."

"My condolences," Molly said to the woman. She gave Chris's shoulder a squeeze. "C'mon, honey."

She steered him toward the exit. She noticed Serena, the Goth girl, talking with an old woman. She gave Chris a crooked smile, but he seemed oblivious. Molly waited until they reached the lobby before she patted him on the back. "Are you okay?" she whispered. "I know that was rough. But you have to remember, people say things they don't really mean when they're grieving."

He jerked away from her. "Would you leave me alone?" he grumbled.

Perplexed, Molly backed off. "Fine. . . ."

"I'm going to take the bus home, okay?"

"Why? Chris, honey, that doesn't make sense. Are you upset at me about something?"

Chris hurried for the door and ducked outside. Molly went after him. He paused by the entry—under an awning that was flapping in the wind. He put on his sunglasses.

"Chris, what's wrong?" Molly asked him. "Are you angry with me?"

"You're the one who insisted we go to the principal about Mr. Corson." He shook his head. "I never should have told you what I saw. None of it would have happened if I'd just kept my mouth shut."

"You're blaming me?" Molly asked. "For this?" She motioned toward the glass double doors to the funeral parlor. "Chris, Mr. Corson isn't dead because of us. What happened back in December—"

"Leave me alone!" he yelled, cutting her off. "God!"

A passerby on the sidewalk stared at them. Chris glanced down at the pavement. "I'm taking the bus back," he said quietly.

Molly sighed. "Suit yourself. But can I say something?"

"What?" he muttered.

"Why is it, Chris, every time I start to feel we're really connecting, you pull the rug out from under me? And once again, I'm just this stranger you resent, living in your mother's house."

"*Pull the rug out from under me,*" he repeated. "Is that another one of your expressions? Because I don't understand it."

"Yes, you do," she replied. "You know exactly what I'm talking about. You did it to me again just now."

She turned and started down the sidewalk. "Be home in time for supper," she called over her shoulder. "Your father's expecting you."

Molly knew she'd worry about him until then.

CHAPTER SIX

Outside the north entrance to Seattle Central Community College, she blended in with a few other students who had stepped outside for a smoke. But she didn't talk to them. She was too focused on what was happening across the street in front of Bonney-Watson Funeral Home.

Chris Dennehy was wearing a tie and some nice khaki pants. In all the times she'd followed him, she hadn't seen him this dressed up before. She'd had a feeling he would be here today.

Chris hadn't noticed her at all, and neither had anyone else.

He seemed to be having a heated discussion with his stepmother. *"Leave me alone! God!"* His voice boomed over the traffic noise.

His stepmother said something to him and then walked away. Chris stood there on the sidewalk, rubbing his forehead. He'd certainly gotten his wish. His stepmother had left him alone—and maybe even a bit stranded.

She smiled.

It was just how she would get to him—when he was all alone.

* * *

Chris paced back and forth under the funeral parlor's awning. He didn't know why he'd gotten so mad at Molly. Mostly he was disappointed. After coming all this way, he hadn't even had a chance to see Mrs. Corson.

There had been only Mr. Corson's sister making him feel horrible.

Despite everything she'd said, he still wanted to talk with Jenna Corson. Part of him wanted to apologize and explain his side of things to her. But mostly, he needed to connect with someone else who grieved for Mr. Corson. Maybe he could even help her somehow. After all, wouldn't she want to know how important her husband had been to him?

Chris took off his sunglasses and stepped back inside the funeral home. At the doorway of the viewing room, he scanned the crowd for Mr. Corson's niece, Serena. At the same time, he kept an eye out for her mother. He dreaded another run-in with her.

For a few moments, he found himself just staring at the bronze casket at the far end of the room. It was hard to fathom Mr. Corson lying inside it. Chris imagined the three bullet wounds in him, now plugged up by some mortician.

He went back to looking over the crowd and finally spotted the Goth girl with an elderly man. She nodded at something the old man said, but still had a bored look in her heavily madeup eyes.

Threading through the crowd, Chris made his way to her. She glanced at him and let out a little laugh. Then she looked at the elderly man again. "Really nice talking with you," she said loudly.

Turning toward Chris, she rolled her eyes. "Shit, there are so many old people here, and all of them are close talkers—with bad breath. And I'm stuck here until seven, too. Please, kill me now." She sighed, then looked him up and down. "So you're the one who caused all the fuss. Well, I heard you were cute. That's certainly true."

Chris shrugged. "Thanks, I guess. Where did you hear—"

"I have a friend at James Monroe, and she has a blog," Serena explained before he finished asking the question. "I see you didn't let my mother, the Wicked Bitch of the West, scare you away. What happened to the woman you were with? She's not your mother, is she? She looked too young."

"She's my *step*mother," Chris explained. "She's on her way home." He spied Mr. Corson's sister across the room and pulled Serena into a corner. He hoped a potted palm by the wall blocked the woman's view of them. "You said something about your aunt getting ready to leave your uncle before he was killed," he whispered.

She nodded. "More than 'getting ready.' She actually moved out, took my bratty three-year-old cousin, Todd, and went to her sister's in Yakima. Uncle Ray had to drive to Yakima to visit Todd. But he didn't complain. In fact, he renewed his life insurance and kept Aunt Jenna on as the beneficiary. My mom's still pissed off about that."

"But you said your aunt was back again. . . ."

"That's right. While she was in Yakima, she had movers take her stuff from the house to this apartment she rented in Kent. I guess she wanted to be closer to Seattle in case my crazy cousin, Tracy, ever decides to come home. Aunt Jenna's there now, only my mother wants everyone to think she's still in Yakima, crying her eyes out or something like that. Todd's in Yakima with her sister, but my aunt's at her new apartment in Kent. She just didn't want to come to Uncle Ray's wake."

"Why not?" Chris asked, frowning.

Serena shrugged. "Beats me. And Aunt Jenna's paying for this thing. You'd think she'd want to put in an appearance. I heard my mother on the phone with her last night, begging her to come, saying 'How do you think it'll look if you don't show up?' and shit like that. If you ask me, Aunt Jenna just didn't want to be a hypocrite." She squinted at Chris. "Why are you so anxious to see my Aunt Jenna?"

"I want to tell her that I'm sorry," Chris admitted. "Maybe explain things to her, set the record straight."

"You mean, about you and Uncle Ray?"

He nodded.

"I heard he was trying to fuck you," she said.

"You heard wrong," Chris replied soberly. "Was that on your friend's blog, too?"

"Yeah," she said, half smiling.

"Terrific," he grumbled. He glanced over toward where her mother had been earlier, and she was no longer there. Chris looked around, but didn't see her. A panic swept through him. He didn't want another chewing-out from her. He turned toward Serena again. "Listen, do you know where in Kent your aunt is staying? Do you have the address?"

She shrugged. "Well, not on me. It's one of those new apartment complexes near Southcenter Mall."

Chris suddenly spotted Mr. Corson's sister emerging from a group of mourners nearby. She started toward him and Serena.

"Oh, shit," he murmured. "Listen, I got to go, thanks a lot—"

Ms. Corson was pointing at him. *"You . . ."*

Just then, a smartly dressed older woman with silver hair grabbed her arm. "Sherry? Sherry, dear, I'm so sorry about Ray. I remember when the two of you were just kids, and you had those skateboards. . . ."

Ms. Corson stopped and talked to the older woman. Her smile looked forced.

"Thanks again," Chris whispered to Serena. He almost knocked over the potted palm as he hurried out of the room. He saw a sign on the wall between a tall grandfather clock and the edge of a corridor: RESTROOMS, OFFICES.

Chris retreated down the hallway and into the men's room. It smelled like cinnamon-scented urinal cakes. Ducking into a stall, he caught his breath and waited for a few minutes. He figured Serena's mother wouldn't come after him in there.

He stood by the toilet with hands in his jacket pockets. He wondered why Mr. Corson's wife hadn't come to his funeral. Did Mrs. Corson believe the lies broadcast on the blogs?

More than ever, he needed to see her and explain that her dead husband had never done anything inappropriate—at least, not with him. He owed Mr. Corson that much. He wished he could get her address somehow.

He took his hands out of his pockets, and his sunglasses fell out. They landed beside the toilet. He was about to pick them up off the floor, but he heard the bathroom door squeak open, then footsteps. Chris froze. The person seemed to stop just outside the stall. He tried to peek through the gap where the door was hinged, but he couldn't see anybody.

"Chris?" he heard someone whisper. It was a girl's voice.

"Serena?" he said, ready to open the door. But when she didn't answer right away, he hesitated. "Serena?" he asked again.

"Chris, it's about to start," she whispered. The voice didn't belong to Serena, he could tell.

"Who's there?" He fumbled with the door lock, trying to undo it. "What are you talking about?"

"The killing is about to start."

"What?" he murmured. A chill raced through him.

There was no response, just footsteps on the tile floor again, and the restroom door yawning.

Chris twisted the lock another way and finally pulled open the stall door. He raced out to the corridor. It was empty. How could she have moved that fast? He knocked on the women's room door. There was no response, so he peeked inside at the small lounge area with a settee, chairs, and a dressing table—with two boxes of Kleenex on it.

He ventured through the next doorway. He heard a steady drip from one of the sink faucets. The washroom looked empty, but two of the three stall doors were closed. Chris crouched down and peered at the openings between the floor and the bottom of the doors. He didn't see anybody's feet. He straightened up.

"What are you doing in here?"

Chris swiveled around and saw a middle-aged woman with stiff-looking platinum-blond hair gaping at him from the doorway.

"Um, sorry," he managed to say. "I was looking for my sister."

She just stared at him, a hand on her pearl necklace.

"You didn't—you didn't happen to see a girl run up the hallway a minute ago, did you?" he asked. "Maybe she was in the lobby?"

Frowning, the blond lady shook her head. "If you don't mind, young man, I'd like to use the facilities."

"Sure, sorry, excuse me," Chris muttered, brushing past her, and then out the doorway.

He glanced down the corridor again, thinking maybe Serena had ducked into an empty office. That must have been her in the bathroom, playing a joke on him. She knew his name. Who else could it have been? She'd done a good job disguising her voice. But why would she say that? *The killing is about to start.* Leave it to a Goth girl to think that was funny.

Chris noticed a long window along the wall farther down the hallway. The wooden venetian blinds on the other side of the glass were slanted open wide enough for him to look into an office. A pale, balding, thirtyish man with black-rimmed glasses sat in front of a computer screen on one of the two sleek mahogany desks. The small office was nicely appointed with hunter-green walls, bookcases full of what looked like catalogs, and a window overlooking Cal Anderson Park. In his black suit, black tie, and dark blue shirt ensemble, the man at the desk seemed to take his job in the funeral parlor very seriously.

Chris knocked on the door, and then opened it. "Excuse me, hi," he said.

The man glanced up at him, thinly disguising his annoyance. "Can I help you?"

"Yes, did you see a girl run down the hallway here a few minutes ago?" Chris asked.

"No, I'm sorry," he said. He slid a printed sheet of paper inside an eight-by-ten envelope so the address appeared through a little window. It looked like a bill.

Chris stared at it. He remembered something Serena had said: *"Aunt Jenna's paying for this thing. You'd think she'd want to put in an appearance."*

The man gazed at him over the rims of his glasses. "Is there anything else?"

"Yes, sir," Chris said. "My mother sent me in here to get the address for Jenna Corson. She's Ray Corson's widow. It's a new address in Kent, and my mother wants to send Mrs. Corson some flowers."

With a pinched smile, the man reached for a business card from a little silver tray on his desk. "Your mother can send the flowers care of us, and we'll see that Mrs. Corson gets them."

"Well, that's just the thing," Chris said, taking the card with *Bonney-Watson Funeral Home* and the man's name on it. "See, the last time she did that here, Mr. Decker, her friend never got the flowers, and my mom was really ticked off. So she sent me in here for the address. *Corson.* It's a new address—in Kent."

Frowning a bit, the man turned to his computer keyboard and started typing. Then he copied down the address on a memo pad.

"And the phone number, too," Chris thought to say. "The florist is gonna want it."

The man sighed and scribbled down the address.

Five minutes later, Chris was near the side of the Bonney-Watson building to get some distance from all the traffic noise on the cross street, Broadway. He was dialing the number for Jenna Corson on his cell phone. He wasn't sure what he'd say if he got her machine, or if he'd even leave a message. He started to count the ringtones.

Someone picked up on the third ring. "Hello?" It was a woman's voice.

"Hello, is Mrs. Jenna Corson there, please?"

"Speaking."

Chris covered his free ear as a floral delivery truck pulled into the driveway beside the funeral parlor. "Mrs. Corson, this is . . ." He hesitated and glanced at the truck. "This is Emerald City Flowers calling. We have a delivery for you. Are you going to be home for the next hour?"

There was a pause on the other end of the line, and Chris held his breath.

"Yes, I'll be home," she said finally.

"We have you at 22013 Forty-second Avenue in Kent, Unit 2-F, is that correct?"

"Yes."

"We'll be there within the hour, Mrs. Corson, thank you," he said.

"Thanks," she said. Then he heard a click on the other end.

Chris switched off the cell phone. He had a strange feeling of dread in the pit of his stomach. It had been stupid of him to pretend he was someone else on the phone; but he'd figured she would hang up if she knew it was him. Now she'd be even angrier once she found he'd lied to her.

He heard a door slam and saw a young, heavyset woman

with red hair unloading a blooming plant from the back of the truck. "Excuse me?" he called to her. "Is that for Corson?"

She hesitated, and then glanced at the card on the plant. "Yeah," she said.

"I'll take it, thanks," he said, holding out his hand.

She gave him a crooked grin. "Wait a sec. Who are you?"

Chris straightened his tie. Then he pulled out the business card with *Bonney-Watson Funeral Home* and the man's name on it. He flashed it at the woman. "We were expecting you an hour ago."

"Oh, well, sorry." The redhead handed him the mum plant.

"It's okay," Chris said. "Mrs. Corson will be glad to get it."

Minutes later, Chris sat in the back of a Yellow Cab, balancing the blooming plant in his lap. He was on his way to Kent. The card on the little plastic holder read: *To Jenna— Thinking of you, with love, Dennis & Debbie Gotlieb.*

Chris felt inside his jacket pocket for his sunglasses, but they weren't there. Then he remembered—they were on the bathroom floor in the funeral parlor. An eighty-five-dollar pair of Ray-Bans, right down the toilet—or in this case, right beside the toilet. He checked his other pocket just to make sure. No, he had his cell phone in there, and nothing else.

His cell phone.

"Shit!" he whispered. He realized—after thinking he'd been so damn clever with the funeral parlor guy and the florist—he'd done something really bonehead stupid. He'd called Mrs. Corson on *his cell phone*, pretending to be someone else. She almost certainly had caller ID. She might have forgotten to check it when she'd picked up the phone. But chances were she would check it before he showed up at her door. Maybe she already knew it had been him calling.

He felt that knot in his stomach again and wished he'd

just been honest with her. He expected his cell phone to ring any minute—with Mrs. Corson on the other end, ready to chew him out. And he would deserve it.

"Stupid," Chris muttered to himself. He adjusted the mum plant in his lap and pressed a hand to his stomach.

He felt the knot tightening.

CHAPTER SEVEN

Molly was driving on the interstate, halfway home. "Tuesday Afternoon" played on the car radio, and a cool breeze whipped through the half-open window.

She thought again about calling him, but told herself that Chris was a big boy. He had bus fare and a route schedule. He could get home on his own. He was a responsible kid.

As she watched the road ahead, Molly remembered six months ago and how they'd tried to do the responsible thing. But then it all spiraled out of control.

Before that, back in October, she still hadn't known Chris well enough to read his various moods. She'd been married to Jeff for only three months. She'd figured most teenagers were sullen and withdrawn all the time. Chris was still getting used to this strange woman in the house, moving in on his mother's turf. His behavior seemed normal considering the circumstances. But Jeff was deeply concerned about him.

"Since Angela moved out, he's been getting worse and worse," Jeff observed. "Every time he comes back from a weekend with her, all he does is snarl at me. I'm sure Angela's bad-mouthing us to him every chance she gets. And poor Chris is her captive audience."

Molly tried to reach out to Chris. Having him pose as the teen hero for the cover of the young adult novel, *Conquer the Night,* helped thaw him out a little. And in early November, when he asked her to come with him to Zales to pick out a bracelet for Courtney, Molly felt she'd finally won him over. She told him in the jewelry store how flattered she was that he'd solicited her opinion.

He shrugged. "Well, Mr. Corson thought I should ask you—since you're a woman and you know this kind of stuff."

She and Jeff had been hearing more and more about his guidance counselor, Mr. Corson. At first, Jeff had been grateful Chris was even talking to them—about anything. But after a while, Molly could tell he felt a bit threatened. Ray Corson seemed to have become Chris's new father figure. "I'm not sure I like Chris going on these late-afternoon runs with this guy—just the two of them," Jeff told her one night. "It's just weird."

But Molly considered Mr. Corson a godsend. Until the guidance counselor came along, Molly hadn't realized Chris could be so sweet and friendly. She guessed he might have been that way before his parents' separation; and if so, they had Ray Corson to thank for bringing back the old Chris.

But he started to backslide in late November. His mother had suddenly fallen in love with Larry Keegan, a Bellevue divorced dad. She didn't waste much time moving in with him. So Chris had a potential stepdad and teenage stepsister, and obviously, he wasn't crazy about either one of them. Making matters worse, he and Courtney had broken up.

It seemed to come to a head one night the week after Thanksgiving, when Jeff was out of town. Molly had been holding dinner for Chris, who still hadn't come home from school. He hadn't answered his cell phone, either. She finally fed Erin at eight-fifteen. Chris crept in at a quarter to nine, while she and Erin were washing the dishes. Erin wanted him to guess what she drew in art class. Molly asked where he'd been and why he hadn't called.

"Could you both just leave me alone?" he muttered, retreating upstairs to his room.

After tucking Erin in bed, Molly went to his door and gently knocked. "Chris, can I come in?"

"I don't feel like company, okay?" he replied from the other side of the door.

"Well, I didn't feel like worrying about you for the last four hours, but I did," she replied. "You owe me an explanation. I'm coming in." She opened the door and found him on top of the bed with his hands clasped behind his head, staring up at the ceiling.

"I know you're having a tough time lately," she said, standing in the doorway with her arms folded. "What happened today? Why didn't you call? You were very curt with Erin when you came in. That's not like you. Her feelings were hurt."

"I'm sorry," he said, rolling over on his side. His back was to her.

"Did something happen with Courtney?"

"No. It's got nothing to do with her," he murmured.

"But something happened," she said.

His voice was strained when he finally answered. "I—I can't talk to you about it, Molly."

She sat on the edge of his desk. "Well, if this is as serious as it sounds, maybe you should talk to your dad."

"He's too busy," Chris grunted.

"He's never too busy for you, Chris. You know that. You should call him."

"It's almost midnight in D.C. He's probably asleep. It is D.C. where he's at this week, right?"

Molly didn't respond right away. He sounded so bitter. "Well, it's not too late to call your mother."

"She can't be bothered right now. She's in love."

"What about Mr. Corson? Do you have his number? You trust him."

"Not anymore," he muttered.

"Why? Did something happen with Mr. Corson?" Molly remembered what Jeff had said a while back: *I'm not sure I like Chris going on these late afternoon runs with this guy—just the two of them. It's just weird.*

She walked around the bed so she was facing him. "Chris, did something happen with Mr. Corson?"

He rubbed his eyes. "Damn it, you'd think I'd learn. People always let you down. What a disappointment—first, my mom and dad, and then Courtney, and now, Mr. C. . . ."

Molly sat on the edge of his bed. "Chris, what did Mr. Corson do to you?"

With a sigh, Chris half sat up. He pushed his pillow up against the headboard and leaned back on it. "He didn't do anything to me. It's just . . . I needed to talk with him. I've missed him on the track the last couple of days—and I've had a lot of stuff on my mind."

Molly nodded. "I know you have."

He picked at a loose thread on his bedspread. "I'm not sure whether or not I told you about Ian Scholl."

"Isn't he the boy everyone picks on?" Molly asked. "He snapped at you when you tried to help him pick up his books. . . ."

Chris nodded. "Mr. Corson asked me to be nice to him—and be his pal. I wasn't so gung ho about the idea. I mean, I tried to be nice to him before, and look how he reacted." Chris shifted on the bed, and the springs squeaked. "Anyway, I went looking for Mr. Corson this afternoon. It was kind of late, and he wasn't at the track. He sometimes takes a shower in the varsity locker room after his run. So I went looking for him in there. At first, I thought the place was empty. But then I heard this strange, moaning sound a few

locker rows down from where I was. I went to check it out
and . . ." Frowning, he took a deep breath. "Well, Mr. Corson
was standing there hugging Ian Scholl. No one else was in
the place. Mr. Corson had his shirt off, and it wasn't buddy-
buddy hugging, y'know? I mean, it looked like he was kissing the top of Ian's head. . . ."

"Go on," Molly said somberly.

He shrugged. "Ian suddenly saw me, and he just freaked.
He practically knocked me down running out of there. I
couldn't believe it. I just stared at Mr. Corson, and I think he
started to say something. But I didn't stick around. I bolted.
I heard Mr. Corson call to me, but I just kept running. A few
minutes later, he phoned my cell twice, but I didn't pick up.
I finally switched it off." Chris shook his head. "It really disgusted me, and I'm not sure why. I don't think I'm homophobic or anything like that. I just—"

"What if you found him with a female student, doing the
exact same thing? How would you have felt?"

He sighed. "Just as disgusted, I guess. I didn't think of
Mr. Corson as the type of guy who would make a move on a
student—any student."

Molly patted his leg. "You're not homophobic, Chris.
You're just very disappointed in Mr. Corson. So am I—if
that hug is what you say it was. Are you sure it was sexual? I
mean, don't guys sometimes hug in the locker room after a
game?"

"Not when one of them is half naked, and no one else is
around—and there's no game," he muttered. "It looked
pretty sexual. So now, I'm wondering why he wanted me to
be friends with that creepy Ian, and why he's been so nice to
me. I think back to all the times we were alone, and—shit."
Chris shook his head. "How come I feel so pissed off and
disgusted about this? I mean, why should I care if they want
to get it on?"

"Because you looked up to Mr. Corson, you trusted him,"

Molly said. "And then you found him doing this—this wildly inappropriate thing. Ian's a student—and a minor. It's not just inappropriate, it's against the law. What Mr. Corson was doing was wrong."

Chris turned away and rubbed his eyes.

"You said he tried to call you?" Molly asked quietly. "Did he leave a message?"

Chris frowned. "No, I checked. I was hoping he could explain. . . ."

Biting her lip, Molly realized she was out of her element here. This was a matter Jeff needed to handle. The new stepmom had no business trying to resolve it.

So she heated up leftovers from that night's ham-and-mac dinner for him. Though Chris had claimed he wasn't hungry, he wolfed it down—alone in his room. Molly retreated downstairs to the kitchen and phoned Jeff at the Hilton in Washington, D.C. Jeff had been sleeping. He sounded groggy at first, but after Molly explained why she was calling, he became wide awake—and angry.

"I knew that guy was bad news!" he declared. "What have I been telling you? There's something basically wrong with a teacher spending so much time alone after school with a student. Damn it, I should have nipped this in the bud months ago. Jesus, it's a good thing I'm not there right now. I'd kick the crap out of that SOB."

"Well, then I'm glad you're not here," she said. "Jeff, we can't be one hundred percent positive about what Chris saw. We should at least listen to what Mr. Corson has to say, maybe get him together with Chris—"

"What? Are you nuts? He's not getting near Chris again. Listen, listen—put Chris on, honey. I need to talk with him, make sure he's okay. . . ."

She let Chris talk to his father in private for a few minutes. When Molly got back on the line, Jeff explained that Chris had agreed to tell his story to the school principal in the morning. Could she set up the appointment? Could she go with him to see the principal?

They met with the principal during lunch hour the next day. Molly's heart ached for Chris, who sat across from her in Principal Carney's office. His foot shook nervously, and he kept glancing down at the ugly gray carpeted floor—unable to look anyone in the eye. Molly's chair was hard and uncomfortable, and she figured his was, too. They were probably that way on purpose for students being disciplined in there.

Carney was a large, fiftysomething black woman who looked like she didn't smile much. Behind her desk was a blown-up photo of the Seattle skyline and several framed certificates. She listened solemnly as Chris recounted what he'd seen in the varsity locker room the previous evening.

When he was finished, the principal cleared her throat, reached for her phone, and pressed three numbers. "Shannon, have Ray Corson come to my office. . . . Yes, right away . . ."

Chris seemed to go pale. He shot Molly a panicked look.

She reached over and put her hand on his arm. "Chris and I aren't comfortable with this," she said to the principal. "I thought we'd be talking with just you, Principal Carney. We weren't expecting a face-to-face with Mr. Corson."

The principal gave her a dubious sidelong glance. "Well, if Mr. Corson has an explanation, you want to hear it from him, don't you?"

Molly just sighed and said nothing. She noticed Chris's foot started to shake so bad it looked like a spasm.

Principal Carney began typing on her computer keyboard. Molly wasn't sure if she was writing up a summary of what Chris had just told her or if she was answering e-mails. The principal didn't explain. No one said anything. Molly listened to the *click-click-click* of those fingernails on the keyboard for about five excruciating minutes.

At last, she spotted Ray Corson through the window in the office door. At least, she was pretty sure he was Ray Corson. He reminded her a bit of Jeff, only not quite as handsome—and a few years younger. Still, he was pleasant looking. He wore a blue striped shirt, jeans, and a loosened tie. He knocked on the office door and then opened it.

Chris slinked down in his chair.

When Corson saw him, a sad half smile came to his face. "Hi, Chris," he said. Then he approached Molly with his hand out for her to shake. "Mrs. Dennehy?"

She hesitated. All she could think about was Jeff, going ballistic because she actually shook the guy's hand. "Molly," she said finally. She didn't want to be mistaken for Angela. She went ahead and shook his hand.

"Have a seat." Principal Carney nodded at a single chair against the wall. He sat down in it. The principal folded her hands on her desktop. "Mr. Corson, Chris happened to see you in the locker room last night with a student, and he was concerned that something inappropriate might have happened there. Maybe you can clarify for us exactly what was going on."

Ray Corson frowned. "I was counseling a student on a personal matter."

"Would you care to elaborate?" the principal asked.

"I don't see why I should. It's nobody else's business." He glanced at Chris. "I'm disappointed you didn't come to me about this, Chris."

Squirming, Chris rubbed his forehead. "I'm sorry—"

"Excuse me," Molly interrupted, gaping at Corson. "But *you're* disappointed? Chris walked in on you and a student—in the locker room, *embracing*. You had your shirt off, and no one else was around. What was he supposed to think?"

"Ray?" the principal said. "I'll ask you again. Would you care to elaborate?"

In that isolated chair, he might as well have been sitting on the witness stand. He stared at Chris. "I was running laps around the track when Ian Scholl came to see me about some problems he's having at home and at school—as you often do, Chris. We spoke for about twenty minutes. He agreed to make an appointment to see me in my office this week. We shook hands good-bye. Then I went to take a shower. . . ." He turned toward the principal. "I sometimes shower in the varsity locker room when it's not in use."

"Go on," she said.

He looked at Molly, and she involuntarily shrank back a bit. "I started to undress," he said. "After I took off my shirt, I realized Ian had followed me into the locker room. He still had some issues he wanted to discuss—very personal, very emotional issues. Maybe you think I should have put my shirt back on, Mrs. Dennehy, but it never crossed my mind. I was listening to this young man, who was hurting. Do you understand?"

Molly almost nodded, but she held back.

"Anyway, Ian started to cry—and I hugged him. That's when Chris saw us. I know how it must have looked, but I also know Chris. . . ." Corson had a wounded look on his face as he turned to him. "I figured you trusted me, and wouldn't jump to any wrong conclusions about what you saw. I figured you'd talk to me about it if you had any questions or concerns. I guess I figured wrong."

Chris let out an unsteady sigh. "Why did Ian run away like that?"

Mr. Corson shrugged. "I honestly don't know. Why did *you* run away, Chris?"

Chris opened his mouth but didn't say anything.

Frowning, Principal Carney tapped the end of a pen against her desk. "Mr. Corson, considering the time and place—and how you were dressed—I don't think hugging this student was an appropriate action."

He straightened in the chair. "Considering the fact that Ian was crying and in anguish, I think hugging him was very appropriate." He turned to Molly and then Chris. "Anyway, that's what happened. Do you believe me, Chris?"

"Yeah—I guess, of course," he murmured with his head down. Molly barely heard him,

"Then that's all that matters," Corson replied, standing. "As far as I'm concerned, we're done here." He headed toward the door.

"Wait a minute, Ray," Principal Carney said.

"Please, let him go," Chris interjected woefully. "Can we—can we—just drop this?"

Glaring at the principal, Corson paused by the door. "May I go now, Hannah?"

"Yes." She nodded. "But this isn't completely over yet."

Mr. Corson turned and walked out of the office.

As far as Molly was concerned, it was over—mostly because she could tell Chris regretted it had come to this. Still, the principal seemed to have a valid point. Mr. Corson might have inadvertently crossed a line when embracing that boy in the locker room after hours. And didn't Chris say it looked as if Mr. Corson was kissing the top of Ian Scholl's head?

Molly didn't want to analyze it any more. That was Principal Carney's job. If Chris wanted to drop it, that was fine with Molly. She could tell he was already wishing he'd never confided in her about what he saw.

But Jeff wasn't quite ready to let it go—though Chris begged him to forget the whole mess. Jeff mentioned to Angela what had happened, and she went nuts. She acted as if Chris had been sexually abused. Molly suspected Angela was trying to show everyone what crappy parents Jeff and his new wife were—allowing her son to consort with a potential pedophile.

Her gal pals, Lynette Hahn and Kay Garvey, got involved, too. Lynette and Kay asked their daughters if they'd heard anything about Mr. Corson making advances on any of the male students. Had Chris said whether or not Corson had ever come on to him?

Courtney Hahn had four hundred thirty-one friends on her Facebook page—all over the United States, and even overseas in London, Sydney, and Paris. On Saturday night, thirty-six hours after Chris and Molly had met with Principal Carney and Mr. Corson, Courtney broke the news to her Facebook friends:

> **One reason I broke up w/Chris Dennehy was cuz he spent so much time w/Ray Corson & I wasn't interested in a 3-way! Thursday night, Chris walked in on Corson with his shirt off molesting Ian Scholl (ick!) in the boys' locker room after hours. I wouldn't be surprised if he tried to do the same w/Chris. Pervert alert! Chris's parents are pissed. I think Corson will be forced to leave the school.**

By Sunday night, Courtney, Madison, and all their friends were texting, Twittering, and discussing on Facebook what they thought had really happened between Ray Corson and Ian Scholl—and Chris. That sad, private little moment in the varsity locker room was analyzed, joked about, and condemned by teenagers all over the country.

The word spread fast to many of their parents, too.

By eleven o'clock the following Monday morning, Principal Carney had asked Mr. Corson for his resignation, and he left the school.

That had been almost six months ago, and Chris still hadn't quite forgiven himself—or her. Molly thought about what he'd said outside the funeral home: *"I never should have told you what I saw. None of it would have happened if I'd just kept my mouth shut."*

Molly hadn't noticed Principal Carney or any of Chris's

peers or their parents at the wake. Then again, why would they attend Mr. Corson's memorial service? They'd all turned their backs on him months before.

Watching the highway ahead, Molly took her exit toward home. She glanced at her cell phone on the passenger seat. She'd taken it out of her purse just in case Chris called. As she turned into the cul-de-sac, Molly noticed the NO OUTLET sign was still standing. She'd been checking it quite often lately.

That little precautionary habit reminded her of when she was a teenager, babysitting at night in someone else's house. When she got scared, she'd pick up the phone receiver every once in a while, then listen for a dial tone to make sure no one had cut the wires. The weird part about it was hearing a dial tone didn't really make her feel safe. It merely reminded her how vulnerable she was.

She passed the NO OUTLET sign and headed toward home. Molly knew she would check it again before the night was over.

"Hello, is this Mrs. Corson?" Chris said into the intercom. Holding the mum plant, he stood by the gated entrance of a new apartment complex—four uniform beige buildings, each housing about twenty apartments. It was one of those charmless places that looked as if it had gone up in a hurry. He imagined residents coming home drunk probably had a tough time figuring out which building and apartment were theirs. It was in a cul-de-sac, between two more apartment complexes just like it.

The taxicab idled in the driveway in front of the closed electric gate. Chris had paid the man and asked him to wait until he got inside the complex.

He heard a voice though the intercom static: "Yes?"

"Um, floral delivery for you, Mrs. Corson," Chris said, keeping up his lie.

"C'mon in," she said. "Second building, second floor, unit 2-F."

The lock to the tall gate made an obnoxious buzzing sound. Chris pushed at the handle and then waved at the cab.

At the second building, he found an alcove and stairway marked UNITS E–H. He went up the stairs to Unit 2-F, and saw her name handwritten and taped above the doorbell: *J. Corson.* He adjusted the mum plant, took a deep breath, and rang her bell. The door must have been pretty cheap and thin, because he could hear her coming.

The lock clicked and the door swung open. The woman in 2-F stared at him. She looked skinny in her oversized long-sleeved henley T-shirt and sweatpants. She had shoulder-length, frizzy brown hair, a fair complexion, and a birthmark on her cheek. Chris thought she looked a bit older than Mr. Corson. "Are you Mrs. Corson?" he asked.

Nodding, she held out her hands. "I'll take that, thanks."

Chris carefully handed the plant to her. She didn't look as if she'd been crying or anything. He lingered in the doorway. He could see a stack of unpacked boxes in the front hall.

She looked like she was about to shut the door in his face, but then hesitated. "Am I supposed to sign for it or something?"

He shook his head. "Um, no, I . . ."

"Were you expecting a tip?" she asked, adjusting the plant in her grasp. She seemed a bit impatient.

"Mrs. Corson, I'm Chris Dennehy," he said finally. "I—I'm very sorry about Mr. Corson. He was a really good man."

She stared back at him and blinked.

"I apologize about coming to see you this way—under false pre—pretenses." He struggled to get the words out, he was so nervous. "You—you know who I am, don't you?"

She nodded.

He wished she'd say something. "It's mostly my fault that Mr. Corson had to leave school back in December. It was all just a misunderstanding. Mr. Corson never did anything wrong. You should know that. I'm not sure if he ever mentioned it to you, but I tracked him down a few months ago, and told him how sorry I was. But I—I never got a chance to apologize to you, Mrs. Corson."

"Is that it? Are you finished?" she asked.

"I guess," he said. "Only I hope you don't think any-thing—inappropriate ever happened with Mr. Corson and me. He was always—very kind to me. He helped me get through a lot of stuff. . . ."

She just kept staring at him over the top of the mum plant in her hands.

"I thought you should know," he went on, a tremor in his voice. "I mean, you didn't come to his wake, so in case you're mad at him or anything, I wanted to tell you he never did anything wrong. He was a nice guy. I miss him."

"Are you done now?" she asked. Her eyes were dry.

Chris swallowed hard. "Yes, I'm sorry, Mrs. Corson."

She set the plant on the floor, and wiped her hands on the front of her sweat pants. "Listen . . . Chris," she said in a very quiet voice. "Because of you, my husband lost his job. More than that, our lives were destroyed. All of your snivel-ing apologies aren't going to change that. So—leave me alone with my grief. I'm moving to the East Coast soon. But while I'm still here, I don't want to see you ever again. You make me sick. Is that clear? Do you understand?"

She didn't wait for him to answer. She shut the door in his face.

Stunned, Chris stood there for a moment. Through the thin door, he listened to her walking away. He felt as if someone had just sucker punched him in the stomach. He didn't know what he'd expected. He only knew what he'd wished for. He'd hoped to feel some connection with her, because they were both so close to Mr. Corson.

But there was nothing—just the feeling he'd intruded on an angry stranger.

She was right. All his stupid apologies weren't going to change anything.

Wiping his eyes, he retreated down the staircase and headed toward the exit. He slowed down as he approached the high gate. Something was dangling from one of the gate's crossbars—at chest level.

Chris stepped closer, and a chill raced through him. He recognized the eighty-five-dollar pair of Ray-Bans.

CHAPTER EIGHT

"I didn't want to be alone in the house tonight," Kay Garvey admitted, over her third glass of cabernet. "I'll admit it, these cul-de-sac killings have made me a nervous wreck."

Molly sat on the other side of the sofa from her. Between them was an open Pagliacci Pizza box—with three pieces remaining. In front of them, the big flat-screen TV had the frozen images of Paul Newman and Eva Marie Saint. Kay had gabbed throughout the first forty-five minutes of *Exodus* until Molly finally put the movie on pause.

She'd planned to work on a new painting and then treat herself to pizza and a movie to keep her mind off being alone that Saturday night. Jeff had a seminar in Denver, and Chris and Erin were at their mother's boyfriend's house in Bellevue for the weekend.

Molly felt even more isolated and anxious, because she'd said good-bye to Hank and Frank that morning. Her only true friends on the cul-de-sac had moved away. Hank had been her designated Neighborhood Watch "Call Me If You Get Scared" buddy. They'd shaken hands on it two weeks before, during the potluck at Lynette Hahn's place.

Now, Hank and Frank were gone. Their house at the end of the cul-de-sac stood empty and dark.

Kay had phoned her this afternoon, "just to chat," mentioning several times that she was all by herself, because Madison had gone to her dad's and stepmother's place for the weekend. Of Angela and her two gal pals, Kay was the easiest to tolerate. At least, she came across as friendly enough. Molly figured a surface friendship was better than nothing. She just wouldn't share anything personal with Kay.

That had been her resolve when she'd halfheartedly invited Kay over for dinner. "I'm by myself tonight, too," she'd admitted. "I rented *Exodus,* and was about to order a pizza. You're welcome to join me, Kay."

"Paul Newman's in that, isn't he?" Kay had replied. "Well, I'm all over that! I'll bring some red wine. We can have a regular slumber party."

With a little red wine in her, Kay had started talking during the movie about the brief period when Angela's and Lynette's kids had dated. Apparently, when the class heartthrob had dumped her, Courtney set her sights on Chris. He wasn't as popular as her ex, but Chris was handsome and well-liked. It seemed like a pretty good match. But all the while she and Chris were dating, Courtney shamelessly flirted with their guidance counselor.

"Madison told me that Courtney used to come on to Ray Corson like gangbusters," Kay had said while slouched in the corner of the sofa, finishing her second glass of wine. "She thought it would be really cool to hook up with a teacher, especially one who was so popular. But old Ray wouldn't give Courtney a tumble. He kept their counseling sessions strictly professional. I used to think he had morals, but—well, obviously, he preferred teenage boys to teenage girls. I think that's why Courtney really let him have it with her Facebook postings. Hell hath no fury like a teen queen scorned. . . ."

At that point, Molly had put the movie on pause. "I noticed Madison had a few choice comments about Mr. Corson on her Facebook page, too," she'd pointed out.

Kay had just laughed. "Oh, that daughter of mine certainly has a wicked sense of humor!"

"Well, personally, I thought Ray Corson may have gotten a raw deal," Molly had said, frowning.

That was when Kay had poured a third glass of wine and changed the subject to the Cul-de-sac Killer. She was pretty inebriated. "When's the last time he killed somebody?" Kay asked.

Molly knew—exactly two weeks ago, when he'd murdered that Madrona couple. But she didn't want to admit she was keeping track. She felt silly enough checking the NO OUTLET sign at the end of the cul-de-sac earlier tonight. She just shrugged.

"He's probably overdue to strike again, isn't he?" Kay said.

"Let's hope the police catch him before that happens," Molly replied. She got to her feet and took the pizza box. "Last call before this goes into the fridge."

Kay shook her head. She turned quiet for a few moments while Molly put the pizza in the refrigerator. "You're going to think I'm crazy," Kay said, glancing down into her wineglass. "But I have a feeling someone's been in the house while Madison and I aren't there."

Her hands on her hips, Molly stepped into the family room again. "What do you mean?"

Kay gave a pitiful shrug. "I'm not sure. It's just a feeling I get. I know for a fact someone has been through our garbage. I've double-checked. I can see stuff has been rearranged in the bins."

"Are you sure it's not just raccoons?"

Kay frowned. "Raccoons don't put the trash bin lids back in place."

"Well, when I was living in an apartment building in

Chicago, we used to have these Dumpster divers." Molly sat down on the sofa again. "They look for credit card or bank statements or anything with a Social Security number on it for identity theft—stuff like that. Maybe that's what's happening."

"Lately, I've been getting these really strange phone calls, too," Kay murmured. "This woman with a scratchy voice has been calling me and saying these weird things—and then hanging up."

Molly squinted at her. "What kind of weird things?"

"The last two times, she asked me, *'Kay, do you think you're a good mother?'* Just like that, she said it. I don't know who she is or how the hell she knows my name. I think it might be Ted's wife—or a friend of hers. From what I hear, Madison's new stepmother doesn't think much of my parenting skills. Well, screw her and the horse she rode in on."

Molly didn't say anything. She was thinking it was a very valid question. Kay wanted everyone to like her—including her own daughter. As a result, she was a pretty ineffectual mother. She spoiled Madison rotten and let her do whatever she wanted.

"Anyway, thanks for having me over tonight," Kay said. "I'd just as soon not be home in case that creepy bitch calls again." She drained the rest of her wineglass and sighed. "So—this apartment you had in Chicago, were you living there alone or did you have a roommate?"

Molly hesitated. "I—ah—I was living alone."

"No boyfriend?"

Molly shook her head.

"With your face and figure?" Kay pressed. "I can't believe it. What were you doing there, your art thing?"

"Part-time," Molly said, nodding. "And part-time temp work wherever I could find it."

"Aren't you from Chicago originally? Do you still have family there?"

"Not anymore," Molly said. She picked up the remote and switched off the TV. "You know, speaking of my painting, I really need to work on this new piece. I hate to be a party pooper, but it's getting late. . . ."

Kay just stared at her, looking a bit confused. "What about the movie?"

"Oh, it's an epic. It has another three hours to go. I think I'll finish it up tomorrow." Molly stood up. She took the empty wineglass from her. "Anyway, I'm really glad you could come over, Kay."

She stayed seated. "Will you be okay by yourself in this big house? Because, listen, I could crash in Erin's room tonight—"

"Oh, that's sweet of you, but I'll be fine," Molly said.

With a defeated little shrug, Kay got to her feet.

"You'll be okay, won't you?" Molly asked, walking her to the door. She knew Kay was a bit scared to go back to her empty house. She wondered how Madison being there could make much of a difference in how secure she felt. Maybe Kay was just lonely. It would have been neighborly of her to invite Kay to spend the night, but Molly just didn't want her there. She didn't want to answer any more questions about Chicago.

"You'll be okay?" Molly asked again.

"Oh, sure, I—I'm hunky-dory," Kay said.

Molly opened the front door for her, and Kay gave her a hug. It seemed sincere, too—unlike the phony hugs she'd seen Kay share with her pals, Angela and Lynette. "Thanks, Molly," she said. "Let's do this again, okay?"

She nodded. "Of course, that would be nice."

Kay teetered a bit as she stepped down the front stoop and continued along the walk.

Her arms folded, Molly stood in the doorway, looking after her. The night air gave her a chill. "Kay, listen," she said. "Call me if you get scared or anything, all right?"

Stopping near the end of the driveway, Kay turned. A streetlight was behind her, and she was just a silhouette. But Molly saw her nod.

"We'll be Neighborhood Watch buddies," Molly said.

"I'd like that," Kay replied. Then she moved on.

Molly watched her from the front stoop. She could tell Kay was drunk. She weaved a bit as she walked up the darkened cul-de-sac.

For weeks, someone else had been carefully watching Kay Garvey. And Kay had no idea. She was clueless—as were her neighbors on Willow Tree Court. None of them knew how vulnerable they'd become after a month of constant observation.

The intruder on their cul-de-sac had already figured out that Kay Garvey kept an extra key under the flowerpot by the screen-porch door in the back. That was just one of many things this uninvited visitor to Willow Tree Court knew about its residents.

Kay drank a lot, too. Her daughter, Madison, had once confided in Mr. Corson about the woes of having an alcoholic mother. Ray Corson had taken extensive notes on his sessions with Madison, who had repeatedly gotten into trouble and been sent to him for guidance:

> When she has an "audience" of any kind, Madison too often lapses into a Catskills comedy routine—full of bile about her classmates & teachers. She's very insecure, probably due to her borderline gawky looks. Madison must know, at some level, that if it weren't for her close friendship with Courtney Hahn & her affectation of wearing Converse All Stars 24/7, no one might notice her at all. There must be some truth to Madison's claim that her mom has a drinking problem & tries too hard to be her best friend. . . .

Madison loathes her stepmother (often the brunt of
her comic quips). I believe this "bitch on wheels"
isn't at all cruel, but rather stuck with the thankless
task of correcting years of unchecked bad behavior.
More time with the stepmother might help Madison
become a better person, but that would mean she
would have to move away from her indulging mom &
attend a different school. Her whole social identity is
wrapped up in being Courtney's best friend. Without
that, I believe Madison would see her popularity
plummet & she'd be utterly miserable. . . .

At this very moment, Kay Garvey had no idea someone
planned to make her daughter, Madison, a better person—
and for a while utterly miserable.

Kay started up her driveway and glanced back at Molly,
still standing on the front stoop of the Dennehy house. It was
sweet of her to make sure she got home safe.

Kay kind of felt guilty for all the nasty things she'd said
about Molly to Lynette and Angela. She really never had
anything against Molly, but had to go along with the others.
Until last year, when Angela and Jeff split up, Kay's two best
friends had treated her like a second-class citizen, because
she was a divorcee. Both Angela and Lynette had considered
themselves happily married—as deluded as that notion
might have been. *Poor, pathetic Kay*, seemed to have been
their attitude. But since Angela and Jeff's marriage had gone
kaput, the second-class citizen on Willow Tree Court was
Jeff's new wife. Anything Kay could say to tear down Molly
to her two friends raised her stock with them.

"You should see how she fawns over Erin," she'd told
Lynette two weeks ago. "I have a view of the bus stop on the
corner. Honestly, she acts like Erin's her own child. I want to
tell her, 'Hello, you know, her real mother is still around!'

Angela would be livid if she saw how Molly smothers that little girl. It's creepy."

Now, Kay felt bad for saying that—and for all the other embellished bits of gossip she spread about Molly Dennehy.

At the front stoop, she paused by some bushes that blocked her view of the Dennehy house. She heard Molly step back inside and close the door.

With the sound of that lock clicking, Kay suddenly felt all alone.

She'd left a few lights on inside the house—as she always did when she stepped out. Pulling her keys from her purse, she put the key in the lock but realized the door was open. "What the hell?" she murmured.

She was almost positive she'd locked it when leaving for the Dennehys'. But that had been a few hours and three glasses of wine ago. She wondered if Madison had come home from her overnight. Kay warily stepped inside. "Madison?" she called. "Maddie, honey, are you here?"

No answer.

For a moment, she stood in the front hallway, listening. The lights were on in the living room and kitchen. She didn't see any movement in either room, nothing out of place, either. "You're fine," Kay told herself. She closed the front door and double-locked it.

Heading into the kitchen, she went right for the liquor cabinet and poured a glass of wine. "A dose of courage," she murmured, taking a hearty gulp. She always hated it on these rare occasions when Madison spent the night at a friend's house. Usually, it was Courtney spending the night here. The Garveys' house got to be known as Party Central. Kay actually liked having a lot of teenagers around. She didn't mind the noise.

It was being alone in a deathly quiet house that she hated.

She switched on the TV in the family room—just for company. Some movie with Sarah Jessica Parker came on.

Kay wasn't sure what it was; she'd check it later. Right now, she just needed the noise.

Her wineglass was already down to the last few sips. How did that happen so fast? Kay retreated toward the kitchen for a refill. Weaving slightly, she bumped against the edge of the kitchen's entryway. She knew she was drunk, but that didn't stop her from emptying the bottle. There was only a little bit left anyway.

On the TV, Sarah Jessica Parker stopped talking for a moment. Kay heard something upstairs. It sounded like water running in one of the bathrooms. She told herself it was just the toilet tank refilling. She must not have flushed it right earlier. That had to be it. Still, she couldn't relax until she went upstairs and checked it out.

Setting down her wineglass, Kay grabbed the empty cabernet bottle by the neck and brandished it like a weapon. A few drops spilled out and slithered down her arm. She quickly licked it off, then headed up the stairs.

She'd left the light on in the second-floor hallway. In the bathroom at the top of the stairs, the toilet wasn't making any noise. It seemed to be coming from the master bathroom. It sounded more like a faucet running than a toilet tank.

Moving down the hallway to her bedroom, Kay tightened her grip on the empty wine bottle. She stepped into the bedroom. She'd left the bedside lamp on, but it was still dim in there.

She didn't see the man standing in the shadowy corner until it was too late.

"Oh, my God," Kay gasped. Staggering back, she knocked over the nightstand lamp. A brief flash of light blinded her as the shade flew off. Kay dropped the bottle. The lamp hit the carpeted floor, but the bulb didn't break. The wine bottle rolled next to it, also unbroken.

"Take it easy," the man whispered. He wore a black jogging suit with a hood—and surgical gloves. He had a gun pointed at her. "I'm not going to hurt you. You're a little unsteady there. Have you been drinking?"

Terrified, Kay quickly shook her head. She backed into the edge of the bedroom doorway.

She couldn't really tell what he looked like. The light on the floor cast strange shadows all over the room—and on his face. He stepped toward her. "You look pretty drunk to me, Kay," he said. "Were you guzzling that wine? Were you a naughty girl? Did you drink the whole bottle, honey?"

Tears stung her eyes as she stared at him. "Yes, I—I've had several glasses of wine," Kay admitted. "In fact, I probably wouldn't even be able to describe you to the police later, if they asked. I'm so—I'm really so drunk."

It wasn't true anymore. She'd been tipsy a few minutes ago, but he'd scared that right out of her. She couldn't move. Her back was still pressed against the edge of the doorway. "Listen, you—you can help yourself to anything," she said, her voice cracking. "There's a silver service in the dining room downstairs. It's worth a lot. And—and—and my daughter has a new laptop computer in her bedroom. I have some cash and credit cards in my purse. Take whatever you want, really . . . please. . . ." She started sobbing.

"This works out perfectly," he said—almost to himself. He pointed the gun at her. "Take off your shoes and unbutton your blouse."

Kay shook her head. "Please . . ." she repeated.

"I just want you to be comfortable," he said, with a tiny smirk. "C'mon, Kay . . ."

Her hands trembling, Kay struggled with the buttons of her lavender blouse until it was open. She had a camisole beneath it. Bracing herself against the doorway, she pried off her shoes. All the while, she kept glancing over at the bedroom closet and wondered if they'd find her body in there.

"I'm not going to hurt you, Kay," he cooed. "But I do

need you to sit there on the floor, right by the nightstand. Okay? There's a good girl. . . ."

Tears streaming down her face, she was obedient. She fell to her knees and then sat down on the floor. He stood over her and began to stroke her hair. "There now, Kay, there now. . . ."

All at once, he grabbed her by the hair and slammed her head against the corner of the nightstand. Stunned, Kay flopped down on the floor. Blood from the gash on her temple began to soak the plush, pale yellow carpet. She started blacking out.

"I'm supposed to make it look like an accident," she heard him murmur as he stood over her.

It was the last thing Kay Garvey ever heard.

Minutes later, her killer took out a small pair of scissors and carefully cut off a corner from the shirttail of her lavender blouse.

It was such a small cutting, no one would notice.

CHAPTER NINE

"So—in all this time that she's been married to your dad, Molly hasn't once talked about her family?" his mother asked.

"Not really," Chris replied, ensconced in front of her boyfriend Larry's computer.

His mother didn't see him roll his eyes. She was arranging the sheets on the foldout sofa bed in Larry's study, which served as Chris's bedroom whenever his mother had him and Erin for the weekend.

He tolerated Larry Keegan, a stocky, balding older guy who seemed to think they were really connecting because they could talk about sports. Chris hadn't told his mother, but Larry's habit of always calling him *dude* drove him nuts. Larry obviously suffered under the delusion that this made him a very cutting-edge guy. He had a thirteen-year-old daughter, Taylor, who was kind of a pill both times Chris had met her. She was with her mother this weekend, thank God.

Since his mom had moved in with Larry, these alternate weekend visits had become more and more of a drag. Chris didn't know anyone in Bellevue, so all he could do was bus it to Bellevue Square Mall or hole up in Larry's study and play computer games. The study was in the basement and had its own bathroom, so at least Chris had his privacy. Larry had gone mallard crazy decorating the place. There were pictures of ducks on the wall, and duck-decoy lamps, and even a duck pattern on the sofa his mother was preparing for him so he could bed down for the night.

It was just past eleven. Erin was already asleep up in Taylor's room, and Larry had nodded off in his La-Z-Boy recliner in front of one of those *CSI* shows.

Chris's mom was tucking the bottom of the sheet under the mattress. "The father's dead, the mother's in Florida, and her brother killed himself, is that right?" she asked.

"Yeah," Chris said, staring at the computer monitor. He was playing Cube Runner, and really didn't feel like answering questions about Molly. Lately, it seemed every time he saw his mom, she wanted a full report on Molly's every activity. Did his dad seem happy with her? Did Molly get any calls from her family or old friends?

It had been a week since he'd gone against his dad's orders and attended Mr. Corson's wake. Molly had been nice enough to drive him to the funeral parlor, and he'd been pretty creepy toward her. As far as Chris knew, she hadn't said anything to his dad about it. After Molly had covered for him, it just didn't seem right to spy on her for his mom. Besides, he really didn't have much to report.

"And you've never met her mother—or even talked to her on the phone?" his mom pressed.

"No, I haven't," Chris mumbled, his eyes on the computer screen.

"Don't you find that odd? I mean, after all . . ."

He did think it was pretty strange. The lady was his step-grandmother, and she hadn't even spoken with him yet. It was like she didn't exist.

"Do you know *how* her brother killed himself?" his mom asked. She was slipping a flower-patterned case over the pillow. "Did Molly say anything to you about it?"

"Nope," Chris said.

"What was his name again?"

"Charlie, I think."

"Do you know if he killed himself in Chicago or in Washington, D.C.?"

He leaned back in the cushioned swivel chair. "I really don't know, Mom."

Frowning, she tossed the pillow on the foldout bed. "You probably wouldn't tell me even if you did know. You're starting to like her, I can tell."

"She's okay, I guess," he replied. Chris consciously kept his eyes on the monitor. "It's just kind of weird that you keep asking me about her, Mom—practically every time I'm here. Molly never asks about you at all."

His mother clicked her tongue against her teeth. "Well, excuse me if I want to know about this woman who's looking after my children part of the time. She had a brother who committed suicide and a mother who never calls or visits. Who's to say some kind of mental illness doesn't run in her family? I'm just concerned, that's all. I can't help thinking about that crazy stalker your father was—*seeing*, that Cassandra character. He's not exactly discriminating. . . ."

"I think Molly's pretty normal, Mom," Chris said quietly. He switched off his computer game, and then faked a yawn. He turned the swivel chair to face her. "Boy, I'm beat. I think I'll hit the sheets. Thanks for making up the bed."

She stared at him. He could tell she was hurt he didn't want to talk anymore. She seemed to work up a smile, and then kissed his forehead. "You know, I love these weekends with you and Erin. Larry really enjoys having you, too. Anything special you'd like to do tomorrow?"

He shrugged. "I can't think of anything."

She mussed his hair. "Well, sleep on it. G'night, Chris."

Twenty minutes later, as he tossed and turned on Larry's lumpy sofa bed, Chris thought about how it drove him nuts whenever his mom started criticizing his dad. Didn't she realize that kind of talk only made them *both* seem awful? It had been one reason he'd come to depend so much on Mr. Corson last year.

Attending his wake a week ago had been pointless and painful. First, Mr. C's sister had chewed him out, then his widow had told him what a creepy little shit he was. He had to remind himself that Mr. Corson had forgiven him—and so had the niece, Serena. Chris was still baffled over his encounter with her. He was convinced Serena had been the one who had snuck into the funeral parlor men's room and said whatever she'd said to screw around with his head. She must have picked up his sunglasses and followed him to her aunt's apartment complex. Chris couldn't think of anyone else who might have done that.

He'd had a pretty miserable week. It was hard to kick back and have anything resembling a good time when he knew certain people hated him. And he still wasn't over Mr. Corson's murder. But finals kept him busy—as did rehearsals for *Aquanautics*, the show the boys' and girls' swim teams put on twice a year to raise money for charity. This time it was for leukemia. There were races, diving competitions, and the girls put on a synchronized swimming routine. Chris was surprised they'd decided to have it again—especially after what had happened at the last show.

He remembered four months ago, throwing himself into rehearsals for the January *Aquanautics*. He still hadn't had a chance to talk with Mr. Corson, who had left school about three weeks before. Ian Scholl had lasted only a few days once Mr. Corson had gone. It was all over school and the Internet about the two of them in the boys' locker room. Even people who assumed Mr. C was merely consoling the kid had figured it was because Ian had finally admitted to his counselor—and himself—that he was gay. He'd spent so much time trying not to be identified as homosexual, and now everyone knew—including his crazy, Bible-thumping parents.

When Ian had failed to show up to school the first Thursday in January, rumors flew about what had happened to him. Elvis heard that Ian's parents had pulled him out of school and stuck him in some clinic in Encino that was supposed to cure his homosexuality. "They may as well try teaching him to breathe underwater," Elvis commented. "Even if Ian figured out how to pull off something like that, it would still be a constant struggle."

By the time Chris was practicing for *Aquanautics* in mid-January, people had stopped talking about Mr. Corson and Ian. Chris still felt miserable for his part in what had happened. But he couldn't do a damn thing about it.

So he focused on mastering a reverse one-and-a-half-tuck-position dive for the show—even though he was a swimmer, not a diver. He really punished himself, trying to get the routine right. He went home every night with a headache from all those repeated botched dives from the high board. Coach Chertok kept telling him to lighten up and do a simpler routine. This was for a charity show, not some competition. But Chris was obsessed with getting this particular dive just perfect in time for the show.

All the while, he wondered if Mr. Corson would be in the audience for *Aquanautics*. It was a popular event at the school, and Mr. Corson had originally suggested the charity they ended up choosing: Big Brothers Big Sisters of Puget Sound. So it wasn't totally implausible that he'd attend. Chris imagined himself perched on the high dive, spotting Mr. Corson in the crowded stands. He would salute him, and announce to everyone there, "I dedicate this dive to my guidance counselor, Mr. Corson," and then he'd perform a flawless gainer-one-half.

But the day before the show, Chris still hadn't mastered the dive. He'd only been able to pull it off a few times in about sixty attempts. Coach Chertok said his form was poor most of the time. Either his arms weren't extended high enough at takeoff, or his feet were apart when he hit the water. Chris didn't have a lot of confidence he could get it right for the show.

He had this weird notion that if Mr. Corson came to *Aquanautics*, he'd be able to tackle the dive—for him. Chris furtively looked for him in the crowded stands as he filed out of the locker room with the boys' team. Meanwhile the girls marched out from their locker room on the other side of the pool. Both teams dove into the water in perfect synchronization. All the while, the theme to *Hawaii Five-O* played over the tinny-sounding intercom. Between his swimming routines, Chris scanned the bleachers again, hoping to see Mr. Corson, but he didn't spot him. Then came the diving portion of the program, and they turned off the music. Coach Chertok provided color commentary, whispering into a mike a little something about each diver—and how amazing they'd been in this meet and that meet. Chris tried to tune him out as he climbed up the ladder to the high board. He had to focus on his dive. Yet he couldn't help looking around from his lofty vantage point, still hoping to spot Mr. Corson in the audience. Again, there was no sign of him.

". . . not only that, but Chris is one of the nicest guys you ever could meet," Coach Chertok finished up.

Chris was really touched by that comment, but he told himself to think about the dive. He paused at the top of the ladder. *Push off with your arms high over your head, and then tuck tight—like a little ball.* He slowly, deliberately started toward the end of the diving board, ready to raise his hands over his head.

That was when he heard the screams.

Chris stopped dead. The board wobbled beneath him. He gaped down toward the source of the noise and saw someone in the bleachers, pushing his way past people in a row of seats. He barreled toward the aisle. A few women cried out, and there was a rumbling. People ducked and recoiled from him, anything to get out of his way. One mother in the next row up tried to shield her two young children as he passed in front of her.

Precariously standing on the end of the high dive, Chris gazed down at the person causing all the commotion and panic. He recognized Ian Scholl and saw the gun in his hand. It was hard to miss. Ian waved it at everyone around him.

More people started screaming as Ian charged down the aisle steps toward the pool area. In their dark blue one-piece swimsuits and matching bathing caps, the girls' team had lined up along a dividing wall from the bleachers, right beside those steps. Suddenly the girls scattered in many different directions. The pool area was like an echo chamber, and their horrified shrieks were deafening.

Some of them were too scared to move. They stood there with their backs pressed against the wall. Ian grabbed one of them by the arm. It was Margaret Riddle, a petite, pale girl with freckles. She struggled to pull away from him, but he jabbed the gun barrel against the side of her neck. Margaret let out a scream.

"Shut up!" Ian yelled. "Everyone, shut up!" He hoisted his gun in the air for a second and fired. The shot reverberated through the pool area.

There were more shrieks. "Goddamn it, shut up!" he cried. "All of you!" He held Margaret in front of him—almost like a human shield. He pressed the gun under her chin. She shook and wept uncontrollably.

Everyone turned quiet. The crying from people in the stands became muted. It was as if they were suddenly too scared to make a sound. Margaret's bare feet squeaked against the tiles as he hauled her closer toward the other side of the pool, where Chris stood paralyzed on the high dive.

Ian looked up at him. Slowly, he took the gun away from Margaret's chin.

Chris started to tremble. The diving board teetered beneath him. He suddenly felt cold and naked in his blue

Speedo—so vulnerable. He clutched his arms in front of his chest. Horrorstruck, he watched Ian point the gun up at him. All at once, he couldn't breathe.

Chris thought for certain he was a dead man.

"I'M NOT QUEER!" Ian yelled.

His mouth open, Chris shook his head at him. He wanted to say, *It doesn't matter.* But he couldn't get any words out. He took a step back on the board.

Ian glanced around at the people in the bleachers, randomly waving the gun at them. "Do you hear me?" he shouted over the muffled crying. "I'm not a queer! I'm sick of people saying that! You're all liars!"

Helpless, Chris gazed down at him. Ian turned, and his back was to him for a moment.

Out of the corner of his eye, Chris saw Coach Chertok through the window of his office. He was on the telephone in there. Chris began to notice a few people in the stands furtively whispering into their cell phones. He wondered if all the calls to the police would do any good. Would the cops make it there before Ian started shooting?

"Nothing happened with me and Mr. Corson!" Ian shouted. "You're all liars! What did I ever do to any of you?" He seemed to clutch Margaret even tighter, and his face was pressed up against hers. He stuck the gun under her chin again.

Squirming, she let out a shriek. "God, somebody help me!"

"Ian, stop it!" Chris managed to say. "Please, you don't want to do this. . . ."

Ian swiveled around and gazed up at him again. All at once, he shoved Margaret away. She screamed again as she hit the tiled floor. He aimed the gun at her.

"No, Ian, don't!" Chris yelled.

Ian stared up at him. Tilting his head back, he opened his mouth, then stuck the gun barrel in it.

The shot rang out, and Chris recoiled, almost falling off the board. He managed to grab on to the railing.

Stunned, he watched Ian's body flop down on the tiles. The gun dropped out of his hand, and his head hit the edge of the pool.

Everyone was screaming. Chris could hear Coach Chertok yelling over all the noise that the police were on the way, and everybody should stay calm. Mrs. Chertok hurried from the stands and helped the traumatized Margaret to her feet.

Doubled over, Chris clutched the diving-board rail and gazed down at Ian Scholl's lifeless body.

Sometimes, when Chris lay in bed in the dark, he could still see Ian—with his eyes open and his face turned sideways against the pool's edge. Chris remembered the puddle of blood under his head, some of it running into the pool, billowing in the blue water.

He suddenly bolted up in Larry's sofa bed and tossed back the covers. He started to reach for the duck decoy lamp on the end table, but changed his mind.

He could hear someone walking around upstairs. He wasn't sure if it was his mother or Larry. Either way, he didn't want anyone to know he was awake.

So he sat there in the dark.

He didn't want anyone to come down and see he was crying.

CHAPTER TEN

The teddy bear on the rumpled bed was splattered with blood.

Molly didn't want too much blood—just enough for people to notice when they saw the book on the store shelves. She stood at her easel in her studio on the third floor, painting the cover to the latest Sally Shortridge mystery, *The Teddy Bear Killer*. After saying good night to Kay, she'd changed into an old pair of jeans and a paint-stained sweatshirt. Linda Ronstadt's *Greatest Hits* spun on her old CD player.

Past Linda's rendition of "You're No Good," Molly thought she heard a noise downstairs.

Putting down her paintbrush, she moved over to the CD and pressed the PAUSE button. Molly listened for a moment, but didn't hear anything. She told herself it was probably just the house settling.

One of the great things about having a studio on the third floor that she became oblivious to everything happening two levels down. The kids could have the TV on, and she couldn't hear it. She was shut off from the rest of the house.

That was also a bad thing sometimes—especially when no one else was home. Since the cul-de-sac killings had started, Molly wasn't completely comfortable up in her studio during these nights alone.

She almost wished she hadn't sent Kay home. Having another person in the house would have made her feel better—even if that person was drunk and a bit too inquisitive.

Molly glanced at her wristwatch. It was just past ten o'clock. She'd been up here less than an hour, and this was the third time she'd put her CD player on pause because of a noise downstairs. She hadn't made much progress with *The Teddy Bear Killer* cover. It would just have to wait until morning—when she'd be a little less nervous up here.

Putting away her paint and brushes, she switched off Linda Ronstadt and went downstairs to Jeff's and her bedroom. She pulled her paint-splattered jersey over her head and changed into a long-sleeved tee. Molly glanced out the window at Kay's house next door. She'd figured Kay would have passed out by now. But several lights were still on inside the house—including one in Kay's bedroom. There was a glass door and a little balcony off the master bedroom, and through the sheer curtain, Molly noticed a shadow moving around.

Somehow, it made her feel better. In case she got too scared, someone was awake just next door. She wasn't so alone after all.

Molly decided to check her e-mail on the computer in Jeff's study. She switched on the radio, and "American Pie" came on while she accessed the Internet. It looked like two junk e-mails, something from her agent, and a message with the subject head "A Blast from the Past" from Dcutland@windycityart.com.

"Oh, wow," she murmured, staring at the computer monitor. She opened the e-mail.

Dear Molly,

It's been too long, at least 2 years. The last address I have for you is in Alexandria, VA. Are you still there? If not, you should contact the gallery & update us. We still have 3 of your paintings for sale in our online catalog. Once in a while, I see your work on some book cover, and it's always fantastic. But you're way too good for them!

Anyway, there's a reason for this e-mail (besides the fact that I often think of you). Yesterday this guy came by the gallery, asking about your paintings, but pretty soon he started grilling me on your background & your family. I don't know who he was, but I told him if he wasn't interested in buying your art, he could get lost. Anyway, I just thought you should know that someone has been snooping around, asking questions about you. I'm not sure if he knows about Charlie or what, but I have a feeling that's what he was getting at with all his questions.

I hope I was right to contact you about this. I don't want to cause you any unnecessary worry or heartache.

Feel free to give me a call. I'd love to catch up & find out how you're doing.

Take Care,
Doug

At the bottom of the e-mail, he'd included Windy City Art Gallery's phone number, as well as his cell phone number—the same old one. Molly could see he'd sent the e-mail at 4:52 that afternoon, Chicago time. She glanced at her watch again. It was after midnight in Chicago, but it was also a Saturday, and Doug liked to stay up late. At least, he'd been a night owl back when they'd dated.

She didn't think she could wait until morning to call him. She had to know more about this man who was snooping into her past.

Getting to her feet, Molly headed into the kitchen, where her purse hung on the back of a chair at the breakfast table. She dug out her cell phone. It just didn't seem right calling an old boyfriend on the house line—and in Jeff's study, no less.

She sat down at the table and punched in Doug's number. She didn't have to look at it again. She still remembered. She wondered if he still lived in that third-floor apartment on North Kenmore. Doug had curly, light brown hair and Clark Kent glasses that made him look slightly bookish—and very sexy. He was an assistant manager at the gallery that had commissioned six of her pieces years back. They'd dated for almost a month—until he met Charlie. Then things got fouled up.

Charlie had a way of fouling things up.

Molly was counting the ringtones. Doug answered on the third one. "Molly?"

"Hi, Doug," she replied. "I hope I didn't wake you."

"Of course not," he said. "It's great to hear your voice again, Molly. I guess you got my e-mail. I hope it didn't freak you out or anything."

"Well, it did—kind of," she admitted. "You said this man came into the gallery and asked all sorts of questions about me?"

"Yeah. He was about fifty years old with black hair that looked like a bad dye job, and he talked out of one side of his mouth all the time. Does that sound like anybody you know?"

"No, it doesn't," Molly murmured.

"He didn't seem like an art aficionado," Doug continued. "He didn't give me his name. He wanted to see your paintings, and asked if I knew you, stuff like that. I showed him the three pieces of yours we still have for sale. But I could tell he wasn't really interested in the paintings. He started asking about your family—if you'd been married, and didn't you have a brother who died? That's when I told him to take a hike."

The phone to her ear, Molly was frowning. "How did he figure you knew me?"

"My guess is he went on the Internet, looked up Molly Wright, and found your paintings on our website. He didn't seem like a stalker. There was something kind of snaky about him, but it was more *professionally* snaky, if you know what I mean. I think he may have been a private detective or something along those lines. Anyway, I didn't tell him anything about your family—or your brother. Like I say, when his questions started to veer in that direction, I figured something was fishy, and I gave him the heave-ho. I hope I did the right thing to tell you about this—I wasn't sure."

"No, I'm glad you did, thanks," Molly said. She rubbed her forehead. If this guy asking questions about her was indeed a private detective, it didn't take much guesswork to figure out who had hired him. This had *Angela* written all over it. Jeff's ex and her buddies were always trying to stick their noses into her background and personal life. Hell, Kay was just grilling her about Chicago earlier tonight.

"So—are you still living in Alexandria?" Doug asked.

She suddenly realized that they hadn't said anything for a few moments. "Oh, no, I—I'm married now. I moved to Seattle."

"So who's the lucky guy? Another artist?"

"No, Jeff's an executive for Kendall Pharmaceuticals."

"Pharmaceuticals? Well, then I guess you guys must be doing okay."

"We're doing all right," Molly said.

"Are you?" he asked, a sudden serious change in his tone. "I think about you a lot, Molly, and everything you've been

through. I've always wished I was more—*there* for you
when things got so horrible. Anyway, I hope you are okay.
You deserve to be happy."

"Thanks, Doug," she murmured, staring down at the
kitchen table.

They talked for another ten minutes. Doug had been seeing a concert cellist named Kate for the last year. She was
the one. And if Molly had any new paintings, he wanted her
to send him some slides. And should that guy come into the
gallery again asking questions, Doug would find out who the
hell he was—and who had sent him.

Molly already had a pretty good idea who might have
hired the man. She just told Doug to keep in touch.

After she clicked off the phone, she remained seated at
the breakfast table. *So what if Angela and her gal pals find
out about Charlie?*

They were bound to learn about him eventually. Jeff already knew. Molly had planned to tell Chris about her
brother sometime soon. Still, it was just so damn creepy that
Angela had gone to the trouble of hiring someone to go to
Chicago and pry into her family past.

Molly imagined some snaky, fiftysomething guy talking
out of the side of his mouth as he asked her old family doctor about Charlie's condition.

Her brother had been bipolar, which seemed like a blanket label for all kinds of emotional problems. Seventeen
months younger than her, he was a very handsome, charming little boy with black hair, beautiful blue eyes, and long
lashes. Maybe that had been why everybody cut him so
much slack. He'd do something wicked, then start crying
and apologizing, and people just caved. He was a bit of a
manipulator that way.

But by fifth grade, Charlie started getting into trouble at
their grade school, and it just wasn't so forgivable anymore.
That was when her parents had him diagnosed. They talked

about putting him into a special school. He begged Molly to intercede so they wouldn't send him away. Early on, she'd felt responsible for him. She was always trying to neutralize things when her crazy, erratic kid brother acted up. Sometimes, he'd go nuts and hit her—or he'd mess up her room, or destroy some drawing she was working on. And then, he'd be so sorry.

Molly always forgave him—eventually. He started collecting elephant figurines—like her. By the time he was thirteen, he had a hundred elephants to Molly's thirty. Whenever he did something really awful, he'd give her one of his elephants, and tell her it was his favorite—a total lie, of course. She knew Charlie's favorite: a detailed, six-inch gray marble elephant with its trunk up. But she also knew giving up *any* of his prized elephants practically killed him. So she always sucked it up, thanked him, and assured him that all was forgiven.

By the time Charlie hit puberty, he became more and more unpredictable. The guys he'd befriended were trouble-making morons. Molly couldn't have any girlfriends over, because he was always hitting on them—or hitting them, anything to get their attention.

One Friday night while their parents were out at a party, Molly heated up a Lou Malnati's pizza for the two of them. She was sixteen at the time and had gotten away with renting *The Big Easy* from the video store. Charlie was so excited, because of the video's R rating. He anticipated ninety minutes of nonstop sex and violence ahead. He was hyper to the point at which he started to go out of control. Molly kept telling him to calm down. They were waiting for the pizza in the oven when he picked up the pizza cutter and started shaking it at her.

"Cut it out!" she yelled, backing against the kitchen counter.

"Cut out what, your heart?" Laughing, he moved closer

to her, waving the cutter in front of her face. "I'm the Pizza Killer, and I'm gonna slice you up!"

But Molly wasn't laughing. She threw the oven mitt at him. "Stop it! I'm serious, Charlie! I mean it, back off. You're getting too close with that thing. . . ."

He wasn't listening. He brandished the pizza cutter, slashing an X in the air—just inches away from her nose.

"Damn it, Charlie!" she screamed, putting up her hand. "I said, back off!"

Suddenly, she felt the cutter slice into her arm—inches below her elbow. For a few seconds, Molly thought he'd merely grazed her. She saw a pink line along her pale skin— a long scratch.

Charlie was still laughing. He raised the pizza cutter as if ready to strike again.

Then the two-inch line below her elbow turned red. Blood seeped out and started dripping down her arm.

"Oh, shit!" Charlie said, dropping the pizza cutter.

Grabbing a dish towel, Molly hurried over to the sink and stuck her arm under the cold water. She frantically wrapped the dish towel around the wound. "Damn it, Charlie, what did I tell you?" she cried. "Why do you have to be this way? Oh, God, I think I'm going to need stitches. . . ."

She glanced over her shoulder at him. He sat at the breakfast table, sobbing.

Molly kept her arm up over her head, and with a second dish towel, she had Charlie make a tourniquet and wrap it tight above her elbow. She had to coach him through the whole process. Taking her mom's Chevy Celebrity, Molly drove to Highland Park Hospital. She'd gotten her driver's license only two months before. While she steered with one hand, she kept her right arm raised. Charlie sat in the passenger seat, silent. By the time they reached the hospital's emergency room, her makeshift bandage was drenched with blood.

Three hours and fifteen stitches later, Molly was back home, sitting at the breakfast table with a bag of Birds Eye frozen peas on her bandaged arm. And she was lying to her parents about what had happened. A burnt, dried-up Lou Malnati's pizza sat on the rack inside her mother's oven. Charlie had retreated to his room, claiming he didn't feel well.

Molly wasn't sure if her mom and dad really believed that she'd accidentally cut herself while fooling around with the pizza-slicer.

She tried to convince herself that Charlie's condition had nothing to do with what had happened. Two years ago, her friend Cathy Brennan had had her nose broken when her brother had accidentally hit her with the rim of a tennis racket. Screwy mishaps like that happened in families all the time. But Cathy's brother had owned up to it, and he'd been three years younger than Charlie at the time. Cathy didn't have to cover up for him.

Molly knew Charlie would never take responsibility for cutting her. She was just as certain that her parents would agree to put him on some kind of medication soon, and maybe even send him to a boarding school for kids with special needs. Her dad had been talking about that for a while. Molly almost wished for it. She hated herself for thinking that way.

She remembered going up to her bedroom that night, holding the bag of frozen peas against her sore arm. On her pillow, Charlie had left his prized gray marble elephant, the one with its trunk up. Molly plopped down on the bed. Clutching the elephant figurine, she allowed herself to cry for the first time that evening.

That had been almost twenty years ago.

She still had the scar. Sitting at the kitchen table, Molly rolled up her sleeve and studied the long, pink line below her elbow. The wound looked just like it had that night—for those fleeting seconds before the bleeding started.

Molly glanced at her sad reflection in the darkened window.

Suddenly, something darted across the backyard. Molly only glimpsed the shadow of a person—or a thing—streaking by. It seemed to come from Kay's house.

"Oh, Jesus," she gasped. She stood up so quickly, her chair almost tipped over. She hurried to the light switch in the family room and turned on the outside spotlight—illuminating the small backyard and the first few rows of trees to the forest beyond it. A hand over her heart, she peeked out the sliding glass doors. Nothing.

She ran to the other window and looked next door at Kay's place. There were still some lights on within the house—including one up in the bedroom. Not *all* the lights were on, thank God.

Molly couldn't get over the feeling that someone was just outside the house, looking in at her. Earlier tonight, she'd told Kay they were now Neighborhood Watch buddies. Even though it was late, she figured Kay couldn't be sleeping with all those lights on.

Molly grabbed her cell phone and dialed Kay's number. It rang twice, and then she heard a click. "Kay?" she said anxiously.

"Hi, you've reached the Garveys!" announced a recording of Kay's voice. *"But you're out of luck, because we can't come to the phone right now. Leave a message after the beep, and we'll get back to you. Better luck next time!"* A few bars from "Maybe Next Time" from *Cabaret* played over the recording until the beep finally sounded.

"Kay?" Molly said into the phone. "Kay, this is Molly next door. Can you pick up? I know it's late, but—well, could you please pick up? I see your lights are still on. . . ." She wondered if maybe Kay was in the bathroom. "Listen, call me back once you get this message, okay? I'm kind of concerned about something. Thanks."

Clicking off the phone, Molly went to the window again and peered out at Kay's house.

She couldn't detect any movement over there. She retreated into Jeff's study and looked out his window—down toward the start of the cul-de-sac. The NO OUTLET sign was still standing.

But she still felt on edge. Wringing her hands, Molly checked to make sure the front, garage, and sliding glass doors were all double-locked.

She really missed Henry right now. If he was still down at the end of the block, she would have called him, and he'd have been over within two minutes. They'd be cracking jokes right now and having a glass of wine.

She decided if Kay called back, she'd invite her over to spend the night. Kay could ask as many questions about her family as she wanted. Molly didn't care at this point. She just didn't want to be alone. She kept looking at the phone, hoping it would ring.

Finally, she returned to Jeff's study and picked up the cordless on his desk. "Sorry, Jeff," she murmured, dialing his cell number. He was supposed to be in Denver, and it was past midnight there. She would probably wake him. It rang four times before he answered, sounding groggy. "Hey, honey, what's up?" he whispered. "You okay?"

"I'm so sorry I woke you," she said with a nervous sigh. "I'm just a little paranoid tonight. I thought I saw something outside the kitchen window just a few minutes ago. It was probably nothing, but I tried calling Kay, and there's no answer. I know she's home. Her lights are on. She might be passed out or something. She was over here earlier tonight, and belted back a lot of wine, but still . . ."

Molly realized she was babbling. She peered out the window at Kay's house again.

"Well, Kay does like her cabernet," Jeff said. "You're right, she's probably passed out. I mean, the woman has a problem. You sure you didn't just see a raccoon or something?"

Molly moved into the family room. Through the sliding glass doors, she stared out at the spotlit, empty backyard. "Whoever or whatever it was—it's gone now." She sighed. "I'm sorry, honey. I feel awful for waking you up."

"Well, if you really think you saw someone outside, don't hesitate to call the police. I mean it, babe. Don't take any chances."

"No, I'm sure it was nothing," Molly said. She didn't want to call 911 about a little scare she'd had. She could get a reputation for sounding false alarms. The cops probably had enough residents on cul-de-sacs doing that to them lately.

"I guess I'm just feeling on edge," she admitted. "I got a strange e-mail from an old almost-boyfriend tonight. He works at an art gallery in Chicago. He said someone was in there, asking all sorts of personal questions about me, my family—and Charlie. He said the guy seemed like some kind of sleazy private detective. I'm sorry, but I can't help thinking of Angela. I mean, she's always trying to pry into my past. I wouldn't be surprised if she hired this—this *creep* to go to my old hometown and ask questions about me."

Jeff sighed. "Listen, sweetie, I'll talk to Angela, and get to the bottom of this. If she's resorted to this kind of crap— well, I'll put a stop to it. That's ridiculous. I'm so sorry. No wonder you're feeling jumpy. Anyway, Molly, I'm going to take care of it. Okay?"

"Okay," she said. "Thank you, honey." The cordless phone to her ear, she was still looking out at the backyard.

"I'll be home in just about twelve hours," Jeff said, soothingly. "Why don't you pour a glass of wine and look for something good on TV, take your mind off things?"

"Well, I'm about a third of the way through *Exodus*. I think I'll go back to it and watch until I get sleepy. I'm feeling better already. I think I just needed to hear your voice. . . ."

After she said good-bye to Jeff, Molly hung up the phone. Just about twelve hours until he was home.

Molly told herself she could be all right by herself till then.

Sitting in a cushioned chair by the window, Jeff clicked off his cell phone. The room in the Jantzen Beach Red Lion was dim, and from the window he had a view of the Columbia River and the Portland Bridge. He was in his undershorts.

He strolled into the bathroom, took a pee, and washed his hands. Stepping out of his shorts, he slipped back under the covers.

"Was that your wife?" the woman lying beside him in bed asked.

Jeff nodded, and then nuzzled up next to her, kissing her shoulder. "Yeah, she just had a slight case of the jitters. . . ."

Their legs were still tangled together under the sheets, and he kissed her shoulder. "I love the way you welcome me home when no one else is around," Jeff whispered.

Smiling, Molly lazily ran her fingers through his dark hair. The curtains in their bedroom were closed, but she could hear rain tapping against the windows. She felt so satiated—and safe.

Last night, she'd had another glass of wine and watched the rest of *Exodus*, which went on until nearly three in the morning. Then under a cozy throw from Restoration Hardware, she'd read four chapters of the latest Susan Wiggs. It was starting to get light out when she finally fell asleep on the sofa.

Kay had never called back. But Molly wasn't too worried about it. The NO OUTLET sign had still been standing at the end of the block when she'd checked shortly after waking up at ten o'clock. And then Jeff had come home a little after one, and suddenly nothing else had mattered.

"I'll wait until tomorrow to call Angela," he said, caressing her arm. "I just want you to know I haven't forgotten. I'll phone from the office, and find out if she has anything to do with this guy in Chicago. I'd do it today, but I don't want the kids around, getting wind of this. They shouldn't know their mother can be pretty awful sometimes. Anyway, rest assured, I'll get to the bottom of it."

Molly leaned over and kissed him on the forehead—and then on his lips. "And they say chivalry is dead," she whispered.

He gave her a wry smile. "You know, another thing I haven't forgotten about is this old boyfriend e-mailing you. . . ."

Molly started to laugh. But then she heard a car coming up the cul-de-sac, and it sounded like it stopped right in front of their house.

"Oh, God, is she bringing the kids back *now*?" Molly muttered, jumping out of bed. "She's at least two hours early." Swiping her discarded jersey top from the floor, Molly held it in front of her as she ran naked to the window. She pushed back the curtain, and peered outside.

An SUV had stopped next door in front of Kay Garvey's driveway. Madison climbed out of the car, and hurried toward the front door. She was wearing hot-pink Converse All Star high-tops today. She shielded her head from the rain.

With a sigh of relief, Molly turned away from the window and tossed aside the jersey. "False alarm," she said. She jumped back under the covers and nestled next to Jeff's warm, naked body. She heard Kay's front door slam, and the SUV driving away.

Jeff kissed the side of her neck, and she shuddered gratefully. "So—why was your old boyfriend e-mailing you?" he asked. "Should I be worried?"

"He just wanted to tell me about that guy coming around the gallery," Molly said.

"So what's this old boyfriend's name?" Jeff asked, gliding a hand down her stomach. "And how long were you two an item?"

Molly giggled. "You're jealous, I like that. His name is Doug, and we dated for only a month. But we were pretty crazy about each other for a while." She nudged Jeff. "As much as I relish torturing you, I have to be honest. He's now seeing a concert cellist named Kate, and it's *serious*. So you have nothing to worry about, sweetie."

"That's a relief." He kissed her cheek. "I was thinking I might have to hire my own private detective to keep tabs on you."

Molly worked up a smile. It was a little too soon to joke about private detectives. But she decided not to say anything. She just stroked his hair.

Next door, she heard muffled screams. It sounded like Madison was laughing—way too loud—about something. Molly resented the noise. It intruded on this rare quiet moment with her husband.

Jeff sat up halfway, reclining on one elbow. He shot a look over his shoulder toward their window. "Well, that's annoying as hell. Jesus, listen to her. . . ."

Molly realized it wasn't laughter coming from next door. Those were screams. A chill raced through her.

Tossing back the covers, she climbed out of bed and grabbed her jersey off the floor. She quickly put it on, then went to the window and pulled back the curtain. She peeked out the rain-beaded window.

The door off Kay Garvey's bedroom flung open, and Madison staggered out to the balcony. Her screams were much louder now. "Oh my God!" she shrieked. "Someone help me! She's dead! My mom's dead! Dear God . . ."

Stunned, Molly stared out the window at her. Automatically, she glanced toward the start of the block—at the NO OUTLET sign still standing there. She looked over at Madison again, screaming and crying hysterically on her mother's balcony, the rain drenching her.

"No," Molly whispered, clutching her stomach. "No, it can't be. . . ."

The dollhouse sat on a worktable in the private little room. It was a perfect replica of Kay Garvey's house, right down to the small balcony off the master bedroom where Kay was murdered. Constructing the miniature house was the result of two weeks of intense work.

The man who killed Kay Garvey wasn't much of a photographer. Still, out of the hundred photos he'd taken, he'd managed to snap twenty good shots after breaking in two weeks ago when Kay and Madison weren't home. Between the photos and the intruder's description, the dollhouse-builder had a pretty accurate idea of the layout. No time was wasted working on the first-floor rooms. That section of the dollhouse was closed off, boarded up.

The murder was planned for upstairs, and that was where all the detail work was done in the miniature house. Kay's bedroom, along with its furnishings, was almost an exact match—down to the yellow carpet and the peach-colored curtains and bedspread.

And in that little bedroom was a hard rubber, flesh-colored doll about the size of an index finger. It was a woman—with hair quite close to Kay's pale straw color. The blond doll was lying on the floor of that miniature bedroom—beside a nightstand.

Wrapped around the small figurine was a tiny piece of lavender silk, cut from Kay's blouse.

She was just the first.

CHAPTER ELEVEN

Six months later

The three seniors primping in front of the lavatory mir-
rors weren't the most popular girls at Roosevelt High
School, but it wasn't from lack of trying. They were in-
tensely concerned about their appearances and getting noticed. But they were also just a bit too full of themselves and
catty for anyone to really like them. Still, as long as they
stayed within their little clique, they didn't have to worry.

At least that was the snap judgment of the woman who
entered the girls' room and briefly interrupted their conversation. The three girls stopped gossiping and fussing with
their hair to stare at her in the mirror. They probably thought
she was a teacher. One of them whispered to the other two.

"I don't care," remarked the tallest one, a tawny redhead.
"It's between classes. We have every right to be in here."

The woman stepped into a stall and closed the door. But
she didn't sit down on the toilet. She just stood there, listening to two of them argue about whether or not a popular teen
heartthrob was gay. The third one seemed to be having a different conversation—with someone else. The woman figured she must have called another friend on her cell phone.

She flushed the toilet and emerged from the stall to wash her hands at the sink. She was right. One of the girls was on her cell phone, and another had just pulled out her Black-Berry. That left the tall redhead with no one to talk to, but she was busy applying lip gloss to her mouth.

The woman made eye contact with her in the mirror. "You don't happen to know Madison Garvey, do you?" she asked.

The girl glared at her and shook her head.

Not looking up from her keypad, the one with the Black-Berry piped up: "Oh, God, Madison Garvey? Isn't she the weird-looking freak with the Converse high-tops?"

"Shit, I know who you're talking about now," the redhead said, rolling her eyes. She went back to her lip gloss application. "She wears those dorky Converse shoes all the time. I guess when you look like an albino you have to do something. She thinks she's really funny, too. As if. . . ."

"I hear she used to be a big deal at James Monroe High," the BlackBerry girl said, eyes still riveted to her apparatus. "But she moved here, because her mother died. Now she's living with her father and her stepmother. I guess her old lady got really drunk one night and killed herself—"

"Suicide?" the redhead asked, looking at her friend's reflection in the mirror.

"No, she passed out and hit her head on the toilet or a table or something. Like I say, she was a drunk. She bled to death."

"If I had a dipshit daughter like that, I'd drink, too."

The one with the BlackBerry laughed.

"You guys!" the girl on her cell phone said. "We're going to be late for Lawson's class. Remember last time?"

"Oh, shit!" the redhead said, throwing the lip gloss tube into her purse. She started giggling, and so did her friends. The three of them hurried out of the bathroom, their laughter echoing off the tiled walls.

The woman stood there for a moment. The tall redhead

had merely glanced at her, and the other two hadn't even bothered to look up from their gadgets. Kids with cell phones and BlackBerries had a way of not noticing things around them.

Obviously, they hadn't seen under the far stall door, the feet of another girl—and she was wearing a pair of green Converse All Star high-tops.

The woman heard her muffled sobbing.

She knew who was on the other side of that stall door—a slightly gawky-looking girl whose stepmother didn't let her get away with anything.

Madison Garvey's onetime counselor, Mr. Corson, would have been happy to know—as miserable as she felt right now—Kay's daughter was on her way to becoming a better person.

"Stop . . . just a sec . . . stop it," she whispered, pushing him away. "Did you hear that?"

"Hear what?" Rob Sessions asked. The handsome, blond-haired eighteen-year-old stopped nibbling on her ear for a minute. He was practically on top of Sarah Manning. Tangled up in one corner of the couch in the Sessions' family room, they had an old *Seinfeld* rerun on the big-screen, plasma TV.

This was Rob's third date with the pretty brunette, whose breasts—he thought—could have been bigger. Then Sarah would have been a real knockout. Still, that Thursday night, three days before Halloween, he was discovering that Sarah was a good kisser. Damn good.

"Didn't you hear the noise outside?" Sarah said, squirming out from beneath him. She grabbed the remote control and turned down the volume on the TV. "It was like somebody walking on gravel. Didn't you hear it?"

Rob shook his head. But there was a small strip of gravel

along the north side of the house—below the family-room windows. Rob squinted at the darkened windows and saw nothing. He listened for a few moments. "I don't hear anything. Maybe it was the TV." He leaned over and kissed her. "Now, where were we?"

He started to fondle her breasts over her blouse, and Sarah didn't protest or push his hands away. This was a very good sign. Rob was beginning to wish he'd sent his best friend, Luke, home—instead of out to score some beer and pot. Rob realized he had a pretty good chance of getting laid tonight. And Luke would be back any minute now, damn it.

He figured once his pal returned with the brew and the bong-feed, he'd allow him a few hits, and then give him his walking papers. Luke was a good buddy. He'd understand. Opportunities like Sarah didn't come along every day.

Rob's parents had left two days ago for Phoenix to visit his older sister, Cathy, and her husband, Mike. That left Rob alone in the house for a week, and he intended to make the most of it.

Last night, Luke and two other friends had come over. They'd all eaten McDonald's and drank Thunderbird while watching porn on the big TV. Tomorrow night, Rob was thinking of having a bunch of friends over. In fact, word was out all over Federal Way High School: *Party at Rob Sessions' house on Laurel Lane.*

Maybe that explained why the DEAD END sign at the start of the cul-de-sac had gone missing this morning. Somebody was playing a joke. Just two weeks ago, Rachel Porter, one of the most popular girls in their class, claimed someone had stolen the NO OUTLET sign at the end of Larkdale Court, where she lived. It turned out Jim Hall and some of his buddies from the football team had swiped the sign as a gag.

Sarah had noticed the missing sign when Rob had turned down Laurel Lane in his dad's BMW on their way here tonight. She'd freaked out a little. But Rob had assured her

that someone was just probably playing a gag. Besides, together, he and Luke could take on this Cul-de-sac Killer nut
job.

Obviously, Sarah wasn't totally reassured, and every little
noise outside threw her into a panic. Rob didn't mind her
being a little scared and vulnerable, except when it put a
crimp in the make-out proceedings.

"Everything's fine," he whispered between soft kisses on
her neck. He'd read somewhere once that it was a woman's
erogenous zone. "Just chill out and relax. . . ." He started to
unbutton her blouse.

That was when he heard the noise, too—gravel crunching
underfoot. Someone was just on the other side of the windows. "Shit," Rob said, pulling away from her. "Did you hear
that?"

"Yes." She sat up. "See? I'm not crazy."

Rob gazed over toward the darkened windows. Again, he
didn't see anything. But he heard the footsteps retreating.
Someone was creeping around out there.

Sarah squeezed his hand. "What is that?"

Biting his lip, he reached over and turned off the lamp on
the end table so he could get a better look outside. Sarah
wouldn't let go of his hand as he climbed off the sofa. He
moved toward the windows—with her hovering behind him.
He saw their reflection in the dark glass, and they both
looked so scared. Rob studied the bushes alongside the
house. They swayed a little with the breeze. "Nobody's out
there," he told her—and himself, too. His mouth was suddenly dry. He reached up and made sure both windows were
locked.

Rob wondered if Luke or one of his buddies from last
night was trying to punk him or something. "I bet you anything it's a gag," he mumbled. "Luke's screwing around with
us."

"What do you mean?" She followed him as he headed
back for the coffee table, where he'd left his cell phone.

"Check this out," he said. His hand was a bit shaky as he speed-dialed Luke. If his pal was right outside, Rob would hear the phone go off. Luke's ringer was the first few bars of Beethoven's Fifth. Rob crept toward the window again, waiting to hear that ominous tune on the other side of the glass.

But it was dead quiet.

"What are you doing?" Sarah asked. "Are you calling the police?"

Luke's voice mail clicked on: *"Yo, it's Luke. You know what to do. Talk to you later!"*

Rob waited for the beep. "What's going on?" he asked. "Where are you? Why am I talking to your stupid machine? Call me back, okay?" He clicked off.

Frowning, he turned to Sarah. "That's weird, Luke's not picking up."

She was shaking her head. "I don't like this. You should call the police. . . ."

"Are you nuts?" he asked. "Just because Luke isn't answering his cell phone?"

"Because the dead end sign at the end of your cul-de-sac is missing!" she said, edgily. "And because we heard someone outside. Those are both pretty damn good reasons for calling the cops." She glanced toward the windows, and nervously rubbed her arms. "I just want to go home—only not now. What's going on out there? I swear to God, Rob, if this is some sort of setup to scare me, I'm going to be so pissed off at you."

Rob headed toward the front of the house to make sure the door was locked. She trailed behind him, her hand clutching his belt along the back of his jeans.

"If it's a setup, Sarah, I'm not in on it," he admitted. He prayed to God it was a joke. But obviously Luke wasn't in on the gag, either.

At the front door, he discovered he hadn't locked up after Luke. "Oh, shit," Rob muttered. He quickly turned the lock and deadbolt.

He heard footsteps—just on the other side of the door. Someone was coming up to the front porch of the house. Sarah heard it, too. She gasped and grabbed his arm. Rob automatically backed away from the door for a moment.

The doorbell rang.

Rob swallowed hard. He stepped toward the door again, and checked the peephole. Someone had their hand over it.

The bell rang again—and again.

"Luke, is that you?" he called in a shaky voice. "Stop screwing around, man. Sarah's scared. . . ."

She was squeezing his arm, almost cutting off the circulation.

Rob gazed into the peephole again. It was still blocked. "Goddamn it," he muttered.

But then he saw his friend take his hand away from the security viewer. Luke was standing so close to the other side of the door that his face filled the viewer. He smiled this weird—almost maniacal—grin.

"Oh, thank God, it's Luke," Rob said. He unlocked the door and flung it open.

Then he saw the man standing beside his friend. He saw the tears streaming down Luke's face—and the desperation behind that fake smile. The man held a gun inches away from Luke's head.

Sarah gasped.

The man shoved Luke, and he staggered inside, dropping a grocery bag full of beers. With a clamor, the cans rolled across the front hallway's Oriental rug and hardwood floor. Luke grabbed hold of the newel post at the bottom of the stairs to keep from falling.

Rob and Sarah backed away. Rob hoped against hope this was some kind of sick joke—that Luke had hired this icy-eyed stranger and given him a fake gun. But Rob knew his friend wouldn't drop a six-pack of beer and let it spill for the sake of a gag. And Luke's tears weren't an act. In the five years they had been friends, he'd never seen Luke cry.

The man quickly stepped inside and shut the door behind him. "I don't want to hurt anybody," he announced in a calm, quiet voice. He glanced toward Luke. "Get over there with your friends."

Nodding, Luke obeyed him—until he and Rob were almost shoulder to shoulder. "Please, man," Luke said. "Just—just don't shoot, okay?"

The stranger aimed the gun at Rob.

His heart seemed to stop beating. He stood there, paralyzed. Sarah clung to him. He could feel her shaking.

"Just do what I tell you," the man said. "And I promise, I'll be out of here in twenty-five minutes. You'll have a great story to tell your friends at school tomorrow. Now, I need you upstairs." A tiny smile tugged at the right corner of his mouth. "We're going to get those nice designer sheets out of your mama's linen closet and start tearing them into strips. I want to see how good you are at tying each other up. . . ."

Terrified, Rob backed toward the stairs, taking Sarah with him. With her face pressed against his shoulder, she sobbed quietly. "C'mon, man, you're scaring her," Rob pleaded. "We'll—we'll cooperate. Just take whatever you want, okay?"

The stranger nodded. "I intend to." He nodded at the light-switch plate on the wall by the foot of the stairs. "Is that for the lights down here or outside?" he asked.

"Both," Rob said.

"Listen, please, you've got the gun," Luke said, his hands half raised. "You don't have to tie us up. . . ."

"I'm not going to tie you up," the man said—in a gentle, almost condescending tone that some people used on kids. He still had that flicker of a smile on his face. "Weren't you listening? *You're going to tie each other up.* Now, switch off those lights. I don't want anybody to see me at work down here."

He's only going to steal stuff, Rob told himself. *Just do what he says.*

Obedient, he reached over and turned off the lights.

The front part of the house was suddenly dark.

"Okay, let's go upstairs," the stranger said, with his face now in the shadows. His voice was so calm—almost reassuring. "Don't be scared. I promise you, I won't hurt anyone. . . ."

Within two hours, nearly every light in the Sessions house would be on.

CHAPTER TWELVE

It seemed like the start of a crisp, overcast autumn day as Natalie What's-Her-Name trotted up the cul-de-sac, back from her morning run. Natalie wore black bicycle shorts and a clingy blue top. Molly guessed the thin, thirtysomething ash-blonde might have been a lot prettier at one time, but she had a hard-edged look to her now. For the last six weeks, Natalie had been house-sitting for Dr. and Mrs. Nguyen. She had guys going in and out of the place at all sorts of hours. Jeff had a theory that Natalie was turning tricks in the Nguyens' house. But according to Lynette, she was a secretary in an ad agency downtown. Whatever, it was unsettling to have strangers cruising up and down the cul-de-sac—especially after midnight, especially when a serial killer was still on the loose.

Molly had tried to introduce herself to Natalie a while back. She'd been standing just where she was now—at the end of the driveway. And she'd been retrieving the morning-delivered *Seattle Times* then, too. She'd spotted Natalie, power-walking up the cul-de-sac—with a baseball hat, a Windbreaker, and the bike pants that showed off her bony ass. Two fingers to the side of her neck, Natalie had been consulting her wristwatch.

Molly picked up the newspaper, and waved at her. "Hi, I'm Molly!" she called as Natalie approached her. "I've been meaning to welcome you to the block—"

Her lip curled, Natalie glared at her. It was such an annoyed look that Molly fell silent. Natalie pulled her cell phone from her Windbreaker pocket and started muttering into it. Then she continued up the cul-de-sac to the Nguyens' house.

To this day, Molly still didn't know if the sneer was directed at her—or at whoever had phoned Natalie at that moment. Molly tried not to take it too personally. Just the same, she never made another effort to introduce herself to Natalie. They nodded to each other on occasion, but that was about it.

Molly didn't even get that now. She waved at Natalie, who glanced away and ran past her—toward the Nguyens' house.

"Yeah, good morning to you, too, Nat," Molly muttered—almost to herself. Rolled-up newspaper in hand, she paused near the start of the driveway. "You're a real sweetheart. . . ."

Molly wasn't too crazy about her other new neighbor, either. A forty-year-old widow named Jill Emory had moved into Hank and Frank's house. She had a little boy and worked at the Art Institute of Seattle. Plump, with tawny, auburn hair, she'd seemed down to earth. Molly had hoped to connect with a fellow art lover. But Jill was in Human Resources and pretty much a cold fish—at least, toward her. However, she'd instantly bonded with Lynette—and Angela, who still made her presence felt on Willow Tree Court.

Molly really missed Henry. She still felt so isolated and friendless. Jeff seemed to go out of town on business even more frequently. And whenever she started to feel close to Chris or Erin, they'd spend another weekend with Angela and come back treating her like a housekeeper they barely tolerated.

Glancing next door at Kay Garvey's house, Molly noticed the fallen leaves scattered across the front lawn, some blowing over onto their driveway. The real estate sign was still standing. It had gone up with the SOLD placard already on it. There had been an offer on the house before it had even gone on the market during the summer. A divorcee with no children had bought the place, but she'd yet to show her face on Willow Tree Court. Her name was Rachel Cross. Molly knew, because she'd already gotten a few pieces of her mail by mistake last week—some junk mail, but also what looked like a personal letter from someone in Portland.

For now, the house next door stood empty.

Molly had blamed herself for letting Kay go home so intoxicated that night six months ago. Of course, Lynette Hahn and Angela just had to get in a few jabs about that. At Kay's funeral, Molly had overheard Lynette telling the mother of one of Madison's classmates: "Everyone knew Kay had a drinking problem. At parties, I always used to get some coffee in her before sending her home. Poor Kay, she needed a real friend looking after her that night. . . ."

Apparently, Kay had at least one more glass of wine at home before tripping and hitting her head against the nightstand in her bedroom. Madison found an empty wine bottle beside her mother's body on the bedroom floor. Her mother had passed out and bled to death.

On her Facebook page, Courtney Hahn had provided all the details about her BFF's mother's death, and said, *"We all have to be real supportive of Madison right now."* Courtney texted several friends from Mrs. Garvey's wake, and she loaned her cell phone to a friend and had her snap a picture of her comforting Madison at the cemetery. She featured the photo on her Facebook page, too.

Molly attended the funeral and thought Courtney's behavior was obnoxious. Lynette's other two children, Carson and Dakota, were extremely bratty, too. One of them got a case of the giggles in the cemetery. Lynette didn't seem to notice.

Jeff kept telling Molly that she was in no way responsible for Kay drinking too much that night. "You were supposed to walk her home and tuck her into bed?" he'd asked, incredulous. "It's not like you let her *drive* home drunk—and I've seen Angela and Lynette do just that several times, because they didn't want to leave a party early. Don't listen to those bitches. . . ."

Jeff had talked to Angela about that mystery man in Chicago, the one asking all those questions. Angela insisted she knew nothing about it. Molly didn't believe her for a second. She e-mailed Doug at the art gallery, and apparently the nosy guy had never come back. She was pretty certain Jeff's little talk with his ex had inspired her to call off her private detective.

Molly felt very lucky to be married to such a sweet, considerate guy. Last night Jeff, Erin, and she carved pumpkins together. Even Chris had gotten into the act at the last minute, helping Erin with her jack-o-lantern.

She turned and looked at the carved pumpkins by their front door, a reminder of how good she had it. Molly just wished she had some close girlfriends who could tell her what it was like in the first trimester.

Jeff didn't know yet. The home pregnancy test had come up positive on Wednesday, and she'd made the doctor's appointment for the coming week. She'd tell Jeff once she got confirmation from her doctor.

So far, the morning sickness wasn't too bad at all, just a few mild bouts of nausea. She hadn't even thrown up yet.

Still, she felt sick to her stomach when she thought about having to see "those bitches" in just a few hours. They were having another Neighborhood Watch potluck at the Hahns', a Saturday session. Jeff would be missing it, the lucky stiff. Chris had a swim meet this afternoon, and that took precedence. But Angela would be attending again. The same cop as last time, Chet Blazevich, was making a return engagement as their guest speaker. Molly kind of looked forward to talking with him again.

Of course, the handsome cop wasn't coming there to socialize—or flirt with her. It was all about neighborhood safety.

As far as Molly knew, the last cul-de-sac killing had been over two months ago. In her current condition, she felt even more vulnerable. She couldn't help thinking about Sharon Tate, the victim of a ritualistic murder while in the last stages of pregnancy. Molly remembered reading that Sharon's baby had been a boy. She tried to blot out the thought, but with this maniac out there, the same thing could happen to her and her unborn child.

Was it too much to hope—after two months with no murders—that perhaps this killer had moved on or died? This was the longest he'd gone without killing someone. Molly had actually stopped checking the NO OUTLET sign at the beginning of their block every day. She'd stopped obsessing about it.

Now she had something else to obsess about, something good—a baby on the way.

With a contented sigh, Molly headed toward the house. She started to unroll the newspaper and suddenly stopped dead. As she stared at the headline, a wave of nausea swept through her:

3 TEENS SLAIN IN ANOTHER
CUL-DE-SAC KILLING

An hour before the Neighborhood Watch potluck, Molly was alone in the house. Jeff was dropping Erin at Debi Donahue's birthday party on the way to Chris's swim meet.

Sitting on the tiled floor of the master bathroom, Molly

listened to the toilet flush. The last time she'd thrown up had
been two years before—as a result of some questionable
shrimp she'd eaten at the Bounty Buffet in Alexandria. She'd
almost forgotten how horrible it felt after vomiting: the
burning in her throat, the bilious taste in her mouth, the
shakiness, and the awful sensation that she just might hurl
again.

Her mother used to give her Saltines and 7UP when she
was sick to her stomach. Did that help for morning sickness,
too? She missed her mother so much right now. She still felt
nauseous, but rode it out.

She hadn't had this problem until two hours ago. Seeing
that newspaper headline triggered something. Before stepping inside the house, she'd paused at the front stoop and
scanned the story on the front page. The murdered teens
were Chris's age, two boys and a girl. The girl's parents, Mr.
and Mrs. Wallace Manning of Federal Way, had become
concerned when their daughter, Sarah, hadn't returned home
from a friend's house by midnight—and on a school night,
too. Sarah hadn't answered her cell. Mr. Manning had finally
called one of her friends, and learned Sarah was at the house
of a new boyfriend, Rob Sessions, whose parents were out of
town. Mr. Manning got the Sessions' address from his
daughter's friend and drove to the house on Laurel Lane. He
noticed all the lights were on.

When no one answered the door, Mr. Manning phoned
the police. Officers found the front door unlocked. The bodies of the two boys were discovered, bound and gagged, in
the master bedroom closet. They'd been stabbed repeatedly.
Sarah Manning's body was in a guest room closet. Her hands
tied behind her, she'd been strangled and stabbed.

The *Seattle Times* reported that the DEAD END sign at the
start of Laurel Lane was missing.

When Molly had come inside with the paper, Jeff had noticed right away that she looked sickly. "You okay, babe?"

he'd asked, staring at her. He'd stood at the kitchen counter, pouring coffee into the WORLD'S GREATEST DAD mug Erin had given him last year. "Jesus, you're white as a ghost. . . ."

Her hands shaking, she'd shown him the newspaper. Molly had felt sick for the rest of the morning, but managed to keep from throwing up until just now. She'd vomited three times in a row.

Unsteadily, she got to her feet. She gargled with mouthwash and splashed her face. In the mirror above the sink, Molly could see she was starting to get some of her color back. She took a few deep breaths, and then sprayed the place with Glade. It didn't quite eliminate the vomit odor. Instead, it merely smelled like someone had puked in a pine forest.

Five minutes later, while picking out what to wear for the potluck, Molly couldn't believe it, but she was actually hungry.

The doorbell rang, startling her.

Molly glanced out the bedroom window and recognized Angela's SUV in the driveway. "What the hell?" she muttered.

Zipping her jeans back up, she threw on the periwinkle top she'd planned to wear and hurried down the stairs. Molly unlocked the front door and opened it. "Hi, Angela," she murmured, puzzled.

Jeff's ex stood on the front stoop with a tray of hummus, raw vegetables, and pita bread. Her silver-brown hair was slicked back in a small ponytail. She wore big gold earrings and a silky bronze-colored V-neck top over black jeans. She'd laid the makeup on a bit thick.

"The potluck is at Lynette's," Molly said, her hand on the doorknob.

"I know," Angela replied sheepishly. "Can I come in?"

Molly opened the door wider. "I'm just getting ready. It's in forty-five minutes, isn't it?"

Angela didn't seem to hear her. She stood in the front hallway, gazing around. She took a deep breath. "It's exactly the same. I thought it would be different."

Suddenly, it dawned on Molly that Angela hadn't been inside the house for well over eighteen months. She noticed the tears in Angela's eyes. "Here, let me take that for you," she said, relieving her of the hors d'oeuvre tray. She carried it into the kitchen and set it on the counter.

Following her, Angela pulled a handkerchief from her purse and blew her nose. Molly watched her assessing the kitchen and family room. Two months ago, Molly had gotten rid of Angela's ugly maroon drapes with the fleur-de-lis design and replaced them with some heather-green curtains from Pottery Barn.

"I see a few changes," Angela announced, "but nothing really drastic. If I were you, moving into another woman's house, I'd have gutted the place and started all over again."

"The kids were going through enough transitions," Molly explained. "So—Jeff and I decided to take it slow with the redecorating. I didn't throw anything out. I put it down in the basement. If you want your old curtains—"

"God, no," she said, with a wave of dismissal. "I don't care. Give them to Goodwill." She wandered over to the breakfast table and stood behind Molly's chair.

Molly realized it used to be Angela's chair. She hadn't thought about it until now.

Angela put her hand on the top of the chair's backrest and sighed. "I took everything I wanted out of here when I left. Anything you decide to replace, you can throw out. Except one thing—the white wicker rocking chair in Erin's room—it used to be my mom's. She rocked me in it when I was a baby, and I rocked Chris and Erin in it when they were babies. I want Erin to have it."

Molly nodded. "I know, Jeff told me. Erin's room is just the same as when you left."

"Would it—would it be okay if I went up there?" Angela asked.

Molly gazed at her. "Is this why you've dropped in in—because you want to see the house again?"

Angela nodded. "I knew Erin had a birthday party, and Chris had a swim meet—which Jeff wouldn't miss for the world. I didn't want to come back here while anyone else was home. I didn't know how I'd react. . . ." Her voice started to quiver. "I lived here for two years, and some of that time was very happy. I've missed this place. . . ."

Molly didn't say anything. She wasn't quite sure she believed Jeff's ex had dropped in for solely sentimental reasons. Up until now, she'd been so manipulative and catty. She watched Angela dab her eyes with the handkerchief again.

"Sure, you can take a look at Erin's room," Molly said finally. She started up the stairs. "For a change, it doesn't look like a cyclone hit it." While Angela followed her up the stairs, Molly wondered if she'd ask to see the master bedroom, too. She didn't want Angela in there. It was just too weird.

Letting Angela step inside Erin's room first, Molly stood in the doorway. Angela reached down and rearranged two stuffed animals—a giraffe and a pig—on Erin's pillow. She moved to the empty rocker and tipped the arm, so it rocked back and forth for a few moments. The squeaking sound filled the silence between them.

"I hear you turned the attic into an art studio," she said, at last. "Would you mind if I took a peek?"

Molly worked up a smile. "Sure, why not?" She led the way up the third-floor stairs to her studio.

"Oh, this is wonderful," Angela said, glancing around. "You put in a skylight. I didn't realize how gorgeous the light is up here. What a great use of this space . . ."

Molly watched Angela wander over to the bookcase. "I don't see any pictures of your family around."

"I have them in photo albums," Molly said.

"I know your father passed away. But your mother's still alive, isn't that right?"

Molly stared at her. "That's right," she said steadily. "Are you going to ask about my brother now?"

"What do you mean?" Angela let out a skittish little laugh. "Molly, if I've made you uncomfortable, I—"

"Aren't you going to ask about my brother? Or did you already find out enough about him from your—detective or whoever he was?"

"Jeff said something to me about that a few months ago," Angela replied with a hand on her hip. "And I'll tell you what I told him. I have no idea what you're talking about. I didn't hire anyone to snoop into your family background, Molly. I'm not getting that much alimony. I really can't afford to waste my money on something so silly."

Molly's eyes wrestled with hers. She could tell Angela was lying.

"Oh, what's the use? You don't believe me." Angela brushed past her on the way to the stairs. "When you first married Jeff, I tried to reach out to you and be your friend, but you were cold and distant. . . ." She stomped down the steps.

"Why in the world would I want to be friends with my husband's ex-wife?" Molly shot back. She trailed after her down the stairs. "My God, practically every time I see you, Angela, you tell me what a lying cheating sack of shit Jeff was to you. Well, I'm sorry, but I really don't need to hear that!" Molly paused at the top of the second floor landing. "And I don't think your son needs to hear it, either. . . ."

From the bottom of the stairs, Angela glared up at her. She opened her mouth to say something but quickly shook her head. She flounced toward the kitchen.

Molly hurried down the stairs and found Angela by the kitchen counter, the hors d'oeuvre tray in her trembling hands.

Angela stared down at it. The bowl full of hummus was moving slightly. Tears ran down her cheeks.

"Goddamn him!" she screamed, throwing down the tray. It hit the tiled floor with a clatter. The bowl of hummus smashed, and the thick brown goo splattered against the lower cabinet. Pieces of pita bread and vegetables scattered across the floor. "God, I'm so stupid!" she cried, bracing a hand on the countertop. She shook her head. "I thought if I gave him custody of the kids, he wouldn't be able to raise them without me. I thought he'd beg for me to come back, and he'd finally grow up. Instead, Jeff just moved on. And the worst thing is—a part of me knew he would. On a certain level, I knew he'd find someone younger and prettier to replace me—and look after *my* children. Now I don't have anything. I gave up my kids, hoping somehow . . ." Angela trailed off. She dug out her handkerchief again and blew her nose.

With uncertainty, Molly moved toward the kitchen, but she stopped at the breakfast table, giving Angela a wide berth.

"God, how could I be so stupid?" Angela asked with a pathetic little laugh. "I can't believe I'm telling you this—you of all people." She wiped her eyes, and then shook the wadded-up handkerchief at Molly. "You know, I carry these around all the time now. I keep having these—these crying jags. They just sneak up on me sometimes. God, I think I'm losing my mind." She shook her head. "I shouldn't even be talking to you about this."

Molly took a deep breath. "You're right, Angela, you shouldn't," she said, very carefully. "You ought to confide in a therapist or maybe a good friend—like Lynette."

"Lynette? Are you kidding?" With a sigh, Angela bent down and turned over the serving tray. She started to collect the scattered pieces of pita bread and cut vegetables, and then tossed them on the tray. "Lynette would only say,

'That's too bad, I'm so sorry,' and then she'd tell me about how Jeremy chases her around the bedroom. And that's such a crock of shit. Have you seen the two of them together? I mean, please, anyone who has half a brain and one good eye could see Jeremy can't stand her. Talk about stupid—and self-delusional. I don't need any marital advice from my friend Lynette. No, thank you very much."

Angela missed some stray pieces of broccoli and baby carrots on the floor. She also left the broken bowl and spilt hummus. But she set the tray on the kitchen counter. "You're right, Molly. I shouldn't be telling you any of this. I've said too much already. I should go." She wiped her hands on a dish towel that hung from the oven door handle. "I'm sorry I left you with this mess," she said in a shaky voice. "Please, make my excuses to the girls at the potluck. I don't think I could face them right now. I just don't have it in me."

She touched Molly's shoulder as she hurried past her and headed for the front hall.

Bewildered, Molly didn't walk her to the door. Before she could even react, she heard the door open and slam shut.

From a second-floor window, she watched Angela Dennehy storm out of the house. She spied her through a pair of binoculars, but still couldn't quite tell whether or not the ex-Mrs. Dennehy was crying. She certainly looked upset as she hurried toward her SUV in the driveway.

Fifteen minutes ago, when Angela had first arrived at her former home, she'd brought in a tray of something that might have been hors d'oeuvres. But she didn't have it with her now. She jumped into her car, backed out of the driveway, turned around, and headed out of the cul-de-sac.

Funny, she'd thought for sure Angela would be attending the Neighborhood Watch potluck at Lynette Hahn's house.

She wondered what this visit between the two Mrs. Dennehys had been about—and what exactly had gone on in there. Whatever had happened, it was upsetting enough for Angela that she must have changed her mind about the potluck.

It was scheduled for 12:30—fifteen minutes from now.

She knew, because she'd been invited.

Something else she knew: Soon, there would only be one Mrs. Dennehy.

She'd already started building the dollhouse.

CHAPTER THIRTEEN

The hors d'oeuvre tray of neatly arranged pita bread and raw vegetables sat on Lynette's dining room table. Molly had been in such a hurry to make the potluck on time, she'd left some spilt hummus and a few stray baby carrots and broccoli crowns on her kitchen floor. She'd quickly dusted off the bread, and rinsed the vegetables, then dried them in the salad spinner. She'd had a container of low-fat dill dip in her fridge from one of her cravings a few days ago; and she'd substituted that for Angela's hummus.

A tiny smile on her face, she now watched Lynette help herself to bread and dip for the umpteenth time. "I'll have to get this dill dip recipe from Angela," she said to Jill, who stood at the table with her. "It's fantastic!"

In a bowl beside Angela's serving tray, the pasta salad Molly had made went untouched.

"Oh, I shouldn't do this again, but I'm going to!" Lynette was saying, reaching for a raw vegetable now. "Jeremy likes me skinny! In fact, he can't keep his hands off me. He's insatiable!" She let out a little laugh. "Ha, maybe I should eat up! Maybe he'll leave me alone if I gained a few pounds. At least, I'd get a little rest. Honestly, that man of mine . . ."

Lynette's "insatiable" husband was supposed to have attended the Neighborhood Watch potluck, but something had come up at his office at the last minute. Apparently, Natalie had been invited, but Miss Congeniality pulled a no-show. Lynette had told the Realtor for Kay's house about the potluck, and Molly had wondered if this Rachel Cross person who had bought the place would attend, but no dice.

With Angela suddenly backing out, that brought the Neighborhood Watch attendance down to three: Lynette, Jill, and Molly. Lynette forced her daughter, Courtney, to attend, just for another body in the room, when Chet Blazevich showed up.

Molly felt sorry for the handsome cop, making a special trip to talk to three women—and one teenager who was text-messaging throughout his whole presentation. Jill asked him if the police had any new leads from Thursday night's triple murder in Federal Way. He admitted they hadn't made too much progress. After that, no one seemed interested in his Neighborhood Watch safety tips—Molly included.

She tried to pay attention but kept replaying in her head what had happened with Angela less than an hour before. She'd always suspected Jeff's ex wasn't really over him. A part of her felt sorry for Angela, but she still didn't trust her. Before Angela had had her little meltdown, when they'd been talking in the art studio, she'd looked Molly in the eye and claimed she hadn't hired anyone to investigate her family background: *"I have no idea what you're talking about."*

The hell she didn't. Molly knew she'd been lying.

She wondered just how much information Angela's sleazy investigator had uncovered. He'd probably figured out by now that her brother, Charlie, was the person the news stories from Chicago referred to as Roland Charles Wright. No had ever called him that; he'd always been Charlie ever since he was a baby—just as she'd always been Molly, though Mary Louise was the name on her birth certificate.

The only person who called her Mary Louise was her mother when she was mad about something: "Mary Louise, this room is a pigsty!"

Now, that was all her mother ever called her. "I'm fine, Mary Louise, you don't need to send me any money, thank you," she'd tell her during those painful, brief conversations over the phone once a month.

Of course, Charlie was why their relationship had deteriorated.

A few weeks after Charlie had cut her with the pizza slicer, Molly's parents stuck him in a special boarding school called New Horizons. He still came home on weekends. When not hanging out with Molly, he'd get into trouble with his creepy friends. It really put a crimp in Molly's social life, but she felt responsible for him. It was why she didn't go away to college.

She day-hopped at Northwestern University for four years, and it was with mixed feelings she went off to the Art Students League of New York. Like it or not, for so many years her main purpose in life had been looking after her needy, troubled kid brother. Suddenly, she was looking after herself, and it felt strange.

Charlie used to write her long, rambling, sometimes incredibly sentimental letters, asking when she'd come home. Occasionally, he even sent her one of his elephants. She felt so guilty—as if she'd deserted him.

Still, Charlie seemed to do all right at New Horizons. He finally got his high school diploma—or at least its equivalency—but stayed on at the school, working as a janitor for his room and board.

Molly planned to stay on in New York after graduation, but then her dad died. The way Charlie dealt with the loss was to get drunk, break several windows in the school, and punch a sixty-two-year-old security guard in the face. New Horizons fired him and sent him packing.

Molly's mother announced she was too frail to look after

Charlie. She wanted to put him in a state-run halfway-house facility. Molly got an unscheduled, unofficial tour of the place. It was a run-down old boardinghouse, full of ex-cons on probation and mentally ill tenants, packed in three to a room. She noticed a pile of feces—which she suspected were human—in the second-floor hallway. Charlie cried and cried, begging her not to let their mother put him in there.

So Molly stayed in Chicago. She sold the occasional painting, got temp work wherever she could find it, and rented a two-bedroom apartment on Clark Street for Charlie and herself.

For a while, it was actually kind of comfortable. After all, Charlie knew her better than anyone else. He was a good cook and handy to have around for chores. In fact, the building manager paid him thirty dollars a week to vacuum the common areas and change burnt-out lightbulbs. People in the building liked him—despite his quirky personality. But sometimes Molly felt like one half of the building's token weirdo residents: the artist and her handyman brother—with their collection of elephant figurines in the living room. Did she still want this arrangement when she was thirty?

Charlie got a job bagging groceries at the Jewel. He was on medication, which made him pretty manageable. But sometimes Molly felt like she had a kid living with her, a kid who occasionally brought home some skanky woman he'd pick up in a bar. It was easy for Charlie to score with an undiscerning female who didn't realize he was a little off. He was a handsome guy, despite the fact that he gave himself some pretty terrible haircuts at times.

Often Molly just wanted a break from him. But there was no one to spell her, because their mother had moved to a retirement village in Vero Beach, Florida. She had friends down there.

At least one of them had friends. Molly couldn't really keep any, not after she brought them home. Each one of her female friends became the object of Charlie's affection. He

deluded himself into thinking they were hot for him. Molly
tried, but couldn't stop him from pestering these women—to
the point of stalking them.

Molly didn't have much of a love life with Charlie around,
either. He was boyfriend-repellent—maybe because he'd
taken to wearing this ratty, secondhand Hells Angels jacket
wherever he went. It was embarrassing. Molly waitressed
part-time at T.G.I. Friday's, the lunch and early dinner shift.
She got asked out frequently. But Charlie tried to be best
friends with every guy she dated, and he scared them off.
Doug Cutland from Windy City Art Gallery valiantly tried to
make a go at it. He even took Charlie to two Bears games.
But he just didn't have the patience to put up with a girlfriend who came with a needy, oddball twenty-six-year-old
kid brother.

Poor Charlie seemed almost as devastated as she was
when Doug had pulled away. On some level, Charlie must
have known he was the reason things didn't work out there.
He started drinking more as a way of self-medicating. He
even showed up drunk and surly to the Jewel, insisting on
wearing his Hells Angels jacket in the store, because his
checkout stand was by the automatic doors, and it was cold
out. Rather than fire him, the ever-patient manager at the
Jewel cut back Charlie's hours.

To keep him busy on his new days off, Molly enrolled
him in a creative writing class at Central Evanston Township
Community College. His instructor was an author Molly had
never heard of, Nick Sorenson, who published one novel,
The Eskimo Pie Breakfast. Molly found his e-mail address in
the college catalog's course description. She wrote to him
about Charlie:

> . . . He's on medication for bipolar disorder, and may
> seem a little odd, but he's very sweet. He's really
> looking forward to your class & is hard at work on a
> short story. If Charlie should disrupt the class or act

inappropriately in any way, please don't hesitate
to contact me by phone or e-mail. Thank you very
much & I'll have to buy THE ESKIMO PIE BREAKFAST!

Sincerely,
Molly Wright

Nick Sorenson's e-mail reply came the next day:

Dear Molly,

Thanks very much for your heads-up about your
brother. My favorite niece has special needs, like
Charlie. So I'm pretty familiar with the struggles &
challenges. I'm looking forward to having Charlie in my
creative writing class.

Good luck tracking down a copy of *The Eskimo Pie
Breakfast*. It's out of print. I think there are some
cheap, used copies on Amazon.com. Literally, dozens of
people have read it!

Sincerely,
Nick Sorenson

Molly looked up Nick Sorenson, Author on Google.com,
and came across a good review of his book, and a photo of
him. The three-quarter-profile author portrait showed a trim,
thirtysomething man with dark, wavy hair and a relaxed
smile. His tie was loosened, and he stood in front of Buck-
ingham Fountain. She knew it was silly, but she didn't have a
crush on anyone, and he seemed like a good candidate—
even if it was just a fantasy crush. It would be a nice change
of pace if she *found* a boyfriend because of Charlie instead
of losing one because of him.

Molly ordered a used copy of *The Eskimo Pie Breakfast*
on Amazon.com.

She took it as a good sign when Nick Sorenson sent her a

friendly, unsolicited e-mail after Charlie had had his first class with him:

> **Dear Molly,**
>
> I know you were concerned about how your brother would get along in my creative writing class. Today, he read his short story, which was rather violent, but entertaining. He seemed to have some difficulty taking criticism of his work during the critique session. But I was impressed by the way Charlie praised a story by one young woman when it didn't go over well with the others. It was very chivalrous of him. I think he'll do all right in the class.
>
> **Sincerely,**
> **Nick Sorenson**
>
> **PS: Charlie proudly mentioned to me that you're an artist & have sold your paintings in a few local galleries. I never miss a First Thursday art walk. Keep me posted on any upcoming exhibits of your work, Molly. I like to support local writers & artists!**

She couldn't help thinking that perhaps Nick was a bit interested in her, too. She asked Charlie about the piece he wrote. He bragged that everyone loved his story, but he didn't want to show it to her yet, because it was part of a novel he planned on publishing. "It'll probably be a bestseller," he said.

When she asked about Mr. Sorenson, all Charlie said was, "He's pretty cool."

Charlie says you're "pretty cool," she wrote in her e-mail to Nick that night. Molly mentioned she'd shown a few paintings in participating First Thursday art walk galleries, and she'd ordered *The Eskimo Pie Breakfast* on Amazon.

I could only find a used copy, which means you won't
get a dime out of it. So I hope you'll let me treat you to
coffee sometime. I like supporting local writers &
artists, too!

Molly thought she was being pretty damn clever with the
oh-so-casual way she'd asked him out. But two days went by
without a response. In the meantime, Charlie had had his
second class with Nick Sorenson. The reply finally came on
that third day:

Dear Molly,

Thanks so much for buying my book. It doesn't matter
if it's used. I just like the idea that my work is still out
there being read.

J. Simmons Gallery & Stafford-Lombard Gallery are 2
of my favorites. Your work must be quite extraordinary
if it's displayed in those galleries.

Would it be possible to get together for lunch or coffee
on Monday? The cafeteria here at the school isn't bad,
and as you must know, Charlie seems to like it. Are you
available around lunchtime on Monday?

Sincerely,
Nick

Molly wondered what he meant about Charlie liking the
cafeteria. She casually asked her brother where he had lunch
on the days he had writing class. "The school cafeteria, of
course," he said, looking at her as if it was the dumbest question he'd ever heard. "They've got excellent food."
Molly found someone to fill in for her at T.G.I. Friday's
and e-mailed Nick that she could meet him in the school
cafeteria at one. She wondered if this would be purely social

or if Nick wanted to talk about Charlie. Maybe he expected Charlie there, too. It wasn't quite clear. *No, it's a date or at least a semi-date*, she told herself. Charlie worked at the Jewel on Mondays. Even if it was just a cafeteria in a community college, she was considering this a date.

Molly received her copy of *The Eskimo Pie Breakfast* from UPS late Monday morning. She brought it along when she caught the El to Evanston. The overcast skies looked ominous, as if it might snow at any minute. While waiting for a cab at the Evanston station, Molly decided to call Charlie at the Jewel, just to double-check that he wasn't part of this lunch with Nick.

"You want to talk to Charlie Wright?" asked the woman who picked up the phone at the store.

"Yes, this is his sister," Molly said into her cell. She covered her other ear as the El started up with a roar.

"Charlie quit," the woman told her. "He hasn't been here in—like—two weeks. In fact, we have his last paycheck here. Do you want us to mail it to him?"

Baffled, Molly asked to talk to Charlie's boss. He got on the line and confirmed that Charlie had given his notice: "He just waltzed in here late two Fridays ago and said he was finished," the man told her. "He said he's going to publish a book—or something like that."

Molly wondered what the hell Charlie was thinking. Where had he been every workday for the last two weeks?

No cabs were stopping, and while she stood there stranded, it started to snow. By the time a taxi pulled over, and she ducked into the backseat, Molly was frazzled. She remembered what Nick had said in his e-mail: *The cafeteria here at the school isn't bad, and as you must know, Charlie seems to like it.* She figured her brother must have been hanging out at the community college's cafeteria all this time, maybe writing his stories or chatting up the other students and the cafeteria workers. He had a way of starting conversations with total strangers wherever he went. About

one time in twelve he'd hit the jackpot and find someone
who actually didn't mind talking with him.

She was furious at Charlie for quitting his job and not
telling her. Plus the people at the Jewel had been so good to
him. Not many places would hire someone like Charlie.
What was she going to do with him now?

About six blocks from the college, the snow became
thicker, and Molly realized that this date with Nick would almost certainly include her now-unemployed brother. That
was one more reason to be furious at Charlie.

And now that she thought about it, she was pretty mad at
her mother, too. Why did she have to look after Charlie
while her mother played shuffleboard with friends down in
Vero Beach? Wasn't she allowed to have a life? She remembered how her mother had planned to stick Charlie in that
horrible halfway house. *"Well, it's either that or you'll have
to be responsible for him, dear,"* she remembered her mother
saying. *"I simply can't do it anymore."*

Molly glanced at her wristwatch: ten after one. She was
already late for this stupid lunch meeting.

Two blocks from the college, the taxi's windshield wipers
had fanned a clearing on the snow-covered glass. Molly noticed something that looked like an accident on the road
ahead, right in front of the community college. Ambulances
and about a dozen police cars—their red strobes swirling—
had arrived on the scene. At least a hundred people stood
huddled in the snow just outside the school.

"This is Chicago," the taxi driver muttered. "You'd think
some of these idiots on the road would learn how to drive in
the snow. Looks like a pile-up ahead. We'll get caught in this
gridlock if we keep going."

"It's okay," Molly said, reaching for her purse. "I can get
out and walk from here." She paid the man, thanked him,
and climbed out of the taxi. With Nick's book tucked inside
her coat, Molly treaded through the snow toward the school.
The sidewalk was already starting to get slippery. She didn't

see a car wreck ahead—just the emergency vehicles, and all the bystanders. What were they gaping at?

As she got closer to the school, Molly passed several people who weren't wearing jackets. They huddled together on the sidewalk and the snow-covered grass. Molly spotted a policeman escorting a young woman to an ambulance, and she was crying hysterically. She wasn't wearing a jacket, either. There was blood on her white blouse.

"What's going on?" Molly asked a thin, young Asian man who stood shivering in his shirt and jeans. He clutched some schoolbooks to his chest.

"They evacuated the school," he said. "There was a shooting in the cafeteria."

"What?" Molly murmured. Nick Sorenson was waiting for her there—probably with Charlie. She could just see her brother trying to be a hero in a situation like this and getting himself shot. "Do you know if anyone's hurt?" Molly asked him, panic-stricken. "I think my brother's in the cafeteria. Do you know what happened?"

"I was there!" gasped a short young woman with stringy blond hair. Tears streaming down her face, she stood beside Molly. She was in a short-sleeved blouse, and she frantically rubbed her bare arms. "I saw it all," she cried. "This guy walked in the cafeteria and just started shooting people! I don't know who he was—some creepy guy in a Hells Angels jacket. He pulled out a gun and just started shooting. . . ."

Molly shook her head. She told herself she hadn't heard it right. She glanced around at the police cars and ambulances. In the distance, someone gave instructions over a static-laced police radio. TV-news vans were just arriving on the scene. Molly gazed at the crying, shivering, scared people. She could hear their sobbing. Her brother couldn't have been responsible for all this.

"How many people did he kill?" Molly heard someone ask.

"At least seven are down, maybe more," answered an older man standing nearby.

Molly turned toward him. "Do you know what happened to the man doing the shooting? Do the police have him?"

Frowning, the older man shook his head. "A security guard shot the son of a bitch. He's dead, thank God."

The man turned away.

Molly numbly stared at his back as he threaded through the crowd. Then she glanced up at the snow. She felt the cold, wet flakes on her face.

Nick Sorenson's book slipped from under her coat and landed in a puddle on the ground. Molly's legs buckled.

She had no memory of collapsing and hitting her forehead on the sidewalk. She barely remembered them sewing up the gash at the hospital. Four stitches—the doctor did an exceptional job. Within a few months, the scar disappeared completely.

It was the only thing that ever really healed from that day.

Rubbing her forehead, Molly shifted in the cushioned chair in Lynette Hahn's living room. She glanced up at Lieutenant Chet Blazevich, standing by Lynette's fireplace, giving his talk. His pale green eyes seemed to stare right through her, and Molly realized she hadn't heard a word he'd said. Blinking, she straightened in the chair.

She felt clammy and light-headed, and hoped to God her morning sickness wasn't coming back. She didn't want anyone here putting two and two together and guessing she was pregnant. She would have hated for Lynette, Angela, and company to know about the baby before Jeff.

She took a few deep breaths and tried to focus on what the handsome cop was saying. But all the while she wondered how much Angela's investigator had uncovered about Roland Charles Wright, who shot seven people in a cafeteria at Central Evanston Township Community College—before a security guard put a bullet in his throat. Of the seven people shot on that winter day, two died, one of them his teacher, Nick Sorenson. The other was a twenty-year-old student from the Philippines named Tina Gargullo, who worked part-time in the cafeteria. According to some news reports, Roland Charles Wright had been pestering her for a date, but Tina had refused his advances. He'd also alienated some of his classmates in the creative writing class in which he was enrolled. Five other people were wounded in the shooting spree: a cashier in the cafeteria and four students. All of them were treated and released within a day or two—except for one. Janette Wilder, a divorced thirty-two-year-old mother of two, had been taking a Spanish class at the community college. She was shot twice in her right leg, and then confined to a wheelchair for the next three months. Even after she endured extensive physical therapy sessions, the doctors said Janette would probably walk with a limp for the rest of her life.

Molly sent letters of apology to every one of the wounded—and to Tina Gargullo's parents in the Philippines. After some research, she found the address of Nick Sorenson's widowed mother—on Gunnison Street in Chicago—so she could visit her in person. Mrs. Sorenson was the woman who spit in Molly's face.

Molly had wanted to tell her that she'd read Nick's book, a coming-of-age story that was sweet and funny and sad. She wanted to impress upon Mrs. Sorenson how sorry she was. But it was a futile gesture. She didn't blame Nick's mother for hating her.

But Molly had expected some support from her own mother, who refused to come to Chicago for Charlie's meager, furtive funeral. "I'm so disappointed in you," she'd told Molly over the phone. "How could you let this happen? He was your responsibility. How did he get his hands on a gun? For God's sake, you should have been watching him more closely. . . ."

Her mother claimed that if Molly had let her put Charlie in the state-run halfway house, they could have avoided this tragedy.

After that conversation, Molly didn't talk to her mother for four months.

But she talked to several doctors and psychologists, who assured her there was no way she could have anticipated what Charlie was about to do. They tried to counsel her in grief and guilt, but nothing they said really helped.

Her mother broke the silence when she phoned Molly, needing money. They were polite to each other and kept it brief. From then on, Molly phoned her once a month to ask if she needed funds. Molly always sent the check inside an artsy greeting card, scribbling *Hope you're well—Molly* on the inside.

Sixteen months ago, Molly had written inside the card bearing the check: *Met a very nice man a while back & was married last week. Please note the new home phone number and address. Hope you're well—Molly.*

Part of her felt horrible for being so impersonal about it. Yet another part of her got a strange satisfaction letting her mother know she wasn't part of this milestone in her life. Mostly, she was fishing, hoping her mom would care enough to phone and ask about her new son-in-law. But her mother didn't phone. When Molly called her a month later to inquire if she needed more money, she had to ask, "Did you get the last check—and my note?"

"Yes, thank you, Mary Louise," she replied coolly. "Congratulations."

Tears filled Molly's eyes, and the hand holding the cell phone began to shake. "His name is Jeff Dennehy, and he was married before—and divorced. He has two children—Chris, he just turned seventeen, and Erin, she's six. They're really nice kids. And Jeff's wonderful." She paused, and then sighed. "Not that you give a damn. Am I right?"

There was silence on the other end of the line.

"I'll call you next month, Mother," Molly murmured. Then she clicked off the phone.

Her mom hadn't always been like that. She used to have a wicked sense of humor. She'd start telling stories at dinner, and soon the whole family would be laughing hysterically— to the point at which whatever Charlie was drinking started coming out of his nose. She was a good artist, too. Molly remembered her designing their family Christmas cards every year. And it was her mother who taught her how to paint and draw. She'd made it so fun.

After her dad had died, when her mother was moving to Florida, Molly had helped clean out her parents' old house. She'd found dozens of homemade cards her dad had saved that her mother had drawn. They were cute, clever, and very endearing. *I'm Crazy About You!* she'd written on one of them, under a cartoon of a woman with birds and stars swirling around her head—while she admired a muscle man on the beach. The cartoon characters even had a passing resemblance to Molly's parents in their younger days.

Her mom's sense of humor and fun seemed to have died along with her dad. Whatever was left must have died with Charlie.

That was something Angela's hired snoop couldn't know about her family.

Molly tried to pay attention as Chet Blazevich talked about what they should do to better protect their homes against intruders. But she was still fighting the nausea and light-headedness. She felt even sicker as she imagined Angela sharing the detective's findings with her gal pal, Lynette, and the new girl on the block, Jill.

"Excuse me," she whispered, unsteadily getting to her feet.

Chet Blavevich stopped talking for a moment. But Molly didn't look up at him—or anyone for that matter. Eyes downcast, she retreated toward Lynette's powder room, through a hallway off the kitchen. Her legs were wobbly, and once Molly closed the bathroom door, she dropped down to the tiled floor and sat by the toilet. She took a few deep breaths and managed to hold back. She didn't want to throw up in Lynette's fancy powder room with its gold fixtures, pedestal sink, and shell-shaped mini-soaps. She rode it out, splashed some cold water on her face, and then sucked on a peppermint Altoid from her purse. She started to feel halfway human again.

By the time she emerged from the bathroom, the detective had finished his talk. Lynette and Jill had migrated to the kitchen, Courtney had disappeared completely, and Chet Blazevich was standing by the buffet table.

"Are you feeling all right?" Lynette asked, with a raised eyebrow.

"Just a headache," Molly lied. "I hope you don't mind if I cut out early."

Lynette frowned a bit. "Of course, if you're not feeling well."

Molly brushed past her and worked up a smile for Chet Blazevich in the dining room. She signed his Neighborhood Watch attendance form. "I'm sorry I missed the end of your talk," she said.

"It's okay, you didn't miss much." He smiled at her. "I was hoping you'd baked cookies again. Those were really good last time." He turned toward the spread of food on the table. "Which dish is yours? Is it the pasta salad?"

"How did you guess?" Molly asked.

"It's the one thing on the table that appears untouched. I remember the last time, they didn't eat your chocolate chip cookies, either."

"Good memory," Molly told him.

"So—still not part of the clique?" he said in a quiet voice. She just shrugged and shook her head.

"Well, it's their loss."

Molly smiled. "Can I interest you in taking home some delicious pasta salad?"

He nodded. "You certainly can."

In the kitchen, she retrieved the Tupperware container in which she'd brought over the pasta salad. Lynette smirked at her. "Well, Molly, I see you weren't so headachy that you couldn't stop and chat up our good-looking, green-eyed guest," she said under her breath.

"I'm just being polite," Molly replied. She held up the empty Tupperware container. "I'm giving him the pasta salad to take home, since neither one of you touched it. And by the way, Lynette, that recipe for Angela's 'fantastic' dill dip? It's Nalley low-fat dill dip, which you can buy at any old Safeway. Angela had a meltdown and dropped the hors d'oeuvres tray on my kitchen floor. I'll be cleaning up spilt hummus when I get home. I rinsed off the vegetables that had been on the floor and, as for the bread—I blew on it, Lynette."

"What?" Lynette said, scowling at her. "Are you crazy?"

"That's disgusting," Jill muttered, a hand on her hip.

"If you want details about Angela's meltdown, you'll just have to ask Angela," Molly said. "I'm sure she'll tell you. And she'll probably tell you all about my family, too—if she hasn't already, Lynette."

"What are you talking about?" Lynette shot back. "Have you lost your mind?"

"Just my patience—with you, with all of you," Molly grumbled. She marched into the dining room, where Chet Blazevich gaped at her.

"What's she talking about?" she heard Lynette saying.

Molly handed him the Tupperware bowl and lid. "Here you go," she said briskly. "Take as much as you want and keep the container. Thank you for the talk." She touched his shoulder. "I think you're very nice," she whispered, and then she headed for Lynette's front door.

She hurried down the block toward the house. Fallen

leaves drifted across the road, and Molly kept her arms folded to fight off the chilly breeze. She couldn't believe the crazy things she'd just said to Lynette and Jill. What the hell was wrong with her? *Raging hormones,* she told herself, *just part of the pregnancy package.*

That handsome cop probably figured she was crazy.

Heading up the walkway, Molly pulled her keys out of her purse. She was still a bit shaky, and wasn't looking forward to cleaning up Angela's mess on the kitchen floor. She was almost at the front stoop when she stopped dead.

Someone had bashed in the faces of their pumpkins.

"Oh, shit," she murmured. "Who would do this?"

She thought about Angela, but as nasty as she could be at times, Jeff's ex wouldn't have done that to her own child's jack-o-lantern. Erin would be devastated.

Molly wondered if Lynette's brats might have been the responsible parties. After all, they got their kicks throwing dirt balls at passing cars from the vacant lot at the edge of the cul-de-sac. Smashing pumpkins seemed like a perfect outlet for the little shits. But Lynette's brother had taken them to a Seahawks game today—along with Jill's son.

Bending down, Molly ran her fingers over the bashed-in face of Erin's smiling jack-o-lantern. It was beyond repair. With a sigh, she straightened up and started to unlock the door. But then she balked.

The door was already unlocked.

Molly could have sworn she'd locked the door after leaving the house two hours before. She hesitated and then stepped into the front hall. The house was quiet. She glanced around to make sure nothing was different, and no one was lurking. She headed into the kitchen. As she moved around the island of kitchen cabinets, she looked down at the floor, where Angela had dropped the tray earlier.

The floor was clean—no globs of hummus or shards of glass from the broken dipping bowl, no stray broccoli crowns or baby carrots.

Molly frowned. All she could think was that perhaps Angela had snuck in and cleaned everything up. Maybe Angela still had an old key.

But Angela wouldn't have smashed those pumpkins.

So it must have been someone else.

She turned toward the sink and saw something that didn't seem like Angela's work at all.

On the clean granite counter, three baby carrots were carefully arranged in the shape of a smile—below two broccoli crowns that might have been eyes.

The raw vegetables had been scattered over her kitchen floor earlier.

Now they formed a jack-o-lantern's grin.

CHAPTER FOURTEEN

She glanced over the top of her *Vanity Fair* magazine as the elevator door opened. Ensconced in the cushioned love seat across from the front desk, she'd been waiting forty-five minutes. The W Hotel's lobby was all black and gray, with sleek steel and glass. She blended in well in her black power suit and tan trench coat.

She was there for Jeremy Hahn's last-minute "business meeting" that Saturday—the day before Halloween. Jeremy's meeting must have ended a few minutes ago. The person with whom he'd been doing business was just now stepping off the elevator.

The thin, nubile blonde in the Catholic schoolgirl's uniform was a prostitute named Tara. She was sixteen, but trying hard to look even younger. Lynette's husband met Tara once or twice a week in the same room at the W Hotel in downtown Seattle for an extended lunch hour.

"Why always the same room?" she'd asked Tara a while back.

"Cuz in that room, he's got like four or five porn magazines stashed under the mattress—in the middle, where the maid can't see 'em when she changes the sheets," Tara had explained. "He likes to take 'em out, look at 'em, and warm up before I get there. Usually, by the time I come knocking, he's so horny and coked out, he practically attacks me."

It hadn't made sense why Jeremy planted his porn in the hotel room—rather than just bring it with him. But Tara had enlightened her: "If he was caught with that shit *on his person*, they'd lock him up and throw away the fucking key. Jeremy likes 'em young—illegal young, if you get what I'm saying. I mean, shit, I'll be too old for the son of a bitch in a year. Anyway, if anybody finds the porn in that room, Mr. Hahn can always say it's not his. Ha! He's a lot less nervous about toting around all the coke he puts away."

Tara wasn't adverse to a bit of cocaine herself. That was how the woman in the tan trench coat got her cooperation. She started out by giving Tara eight hundred dollars and two grams of quality cocaine for some information on Jeremy Hahn—and the promise to keep her informed about when these sessions at the W were scheduled. That had been three weeks—and four "business meetings"—ago. Tara could be pretty reliable if the payoff was another gram or two of coke—something the dealer called an eight ball, whatever that was. She just knew it cost over two hundred dollars a pop.

The woman in the lobby thought it was rather amusing that she now consorted with killers, drug dealers, and prostitutes. Just a year ago, she'd been happily married with two children, and she made a little money on the side custom-building dollhouses for people in the neighborhood and their kids.

She stood up as Tara walked through the lobby. She wondered if Jeremy liked Tara to stay dressed in the white blouse, Black Watch plaid skirt, kneesocks, and saddle shoes while they did the deed. But as she seriously thought about it, she really didn't want to know.

She followed Tara into the ladies' room. Another woman was in there, putting on some lipstick in front of the mirror. Tara ducked into one of the stalls.

The woman in the trench coat waited until the other woman left. Then she dug the little Baggie out of her purse and slid it under the stall door. She watched it get snatched up. "Anything new to report?" she asked.

"Well, I guess he scheduled me today because he knew his wife would be busy with some block-party meeting or something," Tara replied. "He wants to see me again on Thursday at one."

"That's it?" the woman asked.

There was a silence on the other side of the stall door, and then she heard Tara snorting. According to Tara's earlier descriptions of her sessions with Jeremy Hahn, the two of them did quite a lot of coke up in that room. She couldn't believe the girl wanted yet another hit of the stuff. She listened to her snorting again—and then, a long sigh.

"He bought us a bottle of champagne from room service," Tara finally said. "It cost like two hundred and fifty bucks. I saw the bill, and asked how he could afford it. He said he was charging his company. Isn't that funny? I wouldn't be surprised if he puts *me* on the company expense account, too. Some of these executive pricks think they can get away with just about anything. . . ."

In her head, the woman listed the possible charges against Jeremy Hahn: *Statutory rape, supplying drugs and liquor to a minor, solicitation, possession of drugs and illegal pornography, and now corporate theft.*

"Y'know, I was thinking," Tara said, "I don't really understand how you're friends with his wife, and why you're keeping tabs on him. I mean, I remember you saying they had an open marriage, but still . . ." There was a click, and the stall door opened. Tara was face-to-face with the woman. Her head cocked to one side, Tara stared at her inquisitively.

For a moment, she looked eleven years old. "Anyway, I just don't get it. . . ."

The woman in the trench coat smiled. "His wife just wants to make sure he doesn't get himself into too much trouble," she explained. "And besides, dear, you don't have to 'get it.' Just call me whenever he schedules you for a session. See you on Thursday."

She gently pinched the girl on the cheek, and then headed out of the women's room.

The three murdered teenagers from Federal Way—that was all everyone talked, Twittered, and texted about at school that Monday after Halloween. As he walked down the crowded hallway toward his locker, Chris overheard people chattering. Apparently, a lot of kids from James Monroe High knew Rob Sessions, Sarah Manning, and Luke Brosco.

During first period, they'd announced over the intercom that any students who wanted to attend a group counseling session led by Mr. Munson in the auditorium during sixth period had to sign up by lunchtime in order to be excused from class. Touchy-feely Munson was slated to talk about grief, loss, fear—and how to cope.

Chris didn't sign up. He didn't know any of the kids who were murdered.

Courtney started texting and Twittering about it late Friday night, when people first found out about the latest cul-de-sac killings:

I'm pretty sure I met the 3 kids who were murdered. I went to a lot of parties w/that crowd from Federal Way last year. It's a scary time 4 us people who live on cul-de-sacs!

Just a few minutes ago, as the school day ended, Courtney was really milking the situation with her latest and extremely lengthy Facebook status update:

> When I think of my friends Rob, Sarah & Luke, I just
> want to cry. Munson's meeting was no help at all, a
> waste of time. Some of us living on cul-de-sacs are
> really scared. My dad mentioned over the weekend that
> he's thinking of moving us to a hotel until this killer is
> caught. But we're sticking it out at home. If we moved
> or changed our lives around, then the CDS Killer would
> win.

It was funny about Courtney. She didn't seem to realize
what a major phony she was. Chris remembered all her postings on Facebook and all the texts she'd sent when her "best
friend forever" Madison was burying her mother. But once
Madison moved in with her dad and her much-loathed stepmother, Courtney saw a lot less of her. And Madison's dad
didn't live all that far away, either. By the time Madison
started senior year at Roosevelt High School in another part
of town, Courtney already had a new "best friend forever,"
Cindy McBride, whom Chris couldn't stand.

Of course, why should he have been surprised? Courtney
had gotten over him pretty fast, too.

Yet he still had a thing for Courtney, maybe because she
was so beautiful—and insecure. She'd admitted to him once
that by the time she'd turned thirteen her dad seemed to lose
all interest in her. "He used to make me feel so special,"
she'd said. "I was his little girl. Now that I'm older, I feel
like I'm turning into my mother, and he hates her."

Chris couldn't fathom what that was like. As screwed up
as his parents were, at least he felt loved.

He walked around a couple who were making out by his
locker and then he stopped dead. The combination lock was

gone. Chris glanced at the number again: *216*. It was his locker, all right. "What the hell?" he murmured. He squinted at some fresh dents and silver scratches near the handle, where the combination lock had been. Someone had knocked it off.

Chris carefully opened the locker door, not sure what to expect. Everything appeared just as he'd left it before last period. His school jacket hung from the hook. His backpack was stashed at the bottom of the locker, and on the upper shelf were his books.

He glanced around the corridor to see if anyone was watching him. Maybe the culprit was still around. The couple making out by his locker had moved on, and the crowd of students had thinned out. But there were still some stragglers by their lockers.

Chris pulled his backpack out and rifled through it. Nothing seemed to be missing. He wondered if maybe the cops had gotten a bad tip, and they'd broken off his lock to search his locker for drugs or something like that. But wouldn't they have told him?

"This sucks," he muttered. Now he'd have to clear out his locker if he didn't want anything stolen tonight. He stuffed the books in his backpack. Then, as he put on his jacket, Chris felt something in the inside breast pocket.

With two fingers, he fished out a folded-up piece of spiral notebook paper. He unfolded it. In an almost childlike handwriting, someone had written a brief, cryptic message:

Ask your stepmother about Tina Gargullo and Nick Sorenson.

Baffled, Chris stared at the note in his hand. He slowly shook his head.

Then something else caught his eye. It was along the red, ribbed cuff of his school jacket.

Someone had cut out a perfect, small square of the material.

Most of the Google results for *Nick Sorenson* were articles about a Cleveland Browns defense back, Nick Sorensen. It wasn't even the same spelling. There was another Nick Sorenson from Des Moines, Iowa, on Facebook. He had 231 friends, and neither Molly nor this Tina Gargullo person was listed.

With a sigh, Chris glanced up from the computer screen. Only a few other students were still in the school library at this hour, most of them using the computers. There was a row of monitors and keyboards on a long table by the big windows. Outside, it had started to get dark already—a typical autumn afternoon.

He wondered who had written that weird note about Molly. The only person he could think of was Courtney. She never had anything nice to say about his stepmother, but she was always pretty open about it. Why would she break into his locker to pass along this bizarre message? And why cut off part of the cuff to his jacket? Already one small thread had unraveled along the freshly cut edges.

He tried searching for Tina Gargullo on Google. But a message popped up along the top of the results. Google asked: Did you mean Tina Gargiulo?

He tried that for two pages, but it seemed like a dead end. Pretty soon, Chris was aimlessly staring out the window at the red, brown, and golden treetops. He was thinking of the other mysterious notes he'd gotten—over the summer, when he'd been a lifeguard at the Lake Forest Park Community Pool.

He'd pedaled his bike three miles to the pool every day. One Tuesday, during a hot, dry spell in late July it was particularly crazy—with some loud, unruly kids and their equally obnoxious mothers, who objected to his tone when he reprimanded their darling little brats over his bullhorn. He was glad for the end of the day, near twilight. The pool was closed, and he washed down the lounge chairs and the deck area with a hose. He looked forward to hanging out with Elvis that night and maybe going to a late movie. After locking up, Chris headed for his bike—the only one still at the bicycle rack outside the chain-link fence behind the pool house.

He stopped abruptly when he saw something white on one side of his handlebars. As he got closer to his bike, he noticed it was a piece of paper, rolled up and fixed on there with a rubber band. He unrolled the paper, and read what was scrawled across it:

Meet me here behind the pool house at 9:00.
It's inportant.

Chris looked up from the note and glanced around the empty parking lot. He figured this was some kind of prank. Someone was screwing around with him, some idiot who didn't even know how to spell *important*.

"I don't have time for this shit," he muttered to himself. He had no desire to wait around there until nine. He shoved the note inside one of the pockets of his cargo shorts, and forgot about it—until the following night.

At quitting time, he found another note wrapped around his bike's handlebar—in the same spot as before, by the left-hand grip.

Why didn't you meet me? I'll be waiting for you here tomorrow night at 9:00. It's very, very important we talk. I know you are a nice, thoughtful person, and you will be here.

The next day, as Chris sat on his lifeguard perch—slathered with sunscreen, wearing his pith helmet, sunglasses, and red trunks—he looked down at the crowd around the pool. He wondered who was jerking him around with these weird notes. Why didn't they just tell him who they were? Was it one of a gaggle of girls who hung out at the pool every day? Did one of them have a crush on him? Maybe he was about to get punked, and they were all in on the joke. Or was it that overly tanned older-woman regular who always looked at him kind of weird behind her designer sunglasses? A bunch of guys his own age hung out at the pool, and he'd had to discipline a few of them from time to time when they acted like jerks. Maybe they were setting him up, so they could beat the crap out of him or something. Finally, there was a guy about twenty or so, who may have been gay—and he was always friendly. Was he the one leaving him these notes?

During his lunch break, Chris went out and checked his bike for another note on the handlebars. But there was nothing. So he ducked into the pool house office and wrote his own note, then secured it with a rubber band to his handlebars. It said:

Who are you?

For the rest of the afternoon, Chris kept checking the crowd to see if anyone was watching him. Near closing, he saw a burgundy-haired girl around his age, hanging outside the chain-link fence—near the pool house. She had that Goth look, and wore a black T-shirt, black jeans, and black wristbands. She was so pale—almost sickly looking. And he imagined she had to be sweltering as she stood in the sun in those black clothes. She put a hand up to the other side of the fence, her fingers hanging on the crisscrossed chain links.

She stared right at him—to the point that Chris became uncomfortable.

He finally had to look away. A few moments later, when he glanced back toward the pool house again, she was gone.

She reminded him of Mr. Corson's niece—whatever her name was. It had been months before. Sabrina? No, *Serena*. He'd been convinced she was the one whispering to him in the men's room at the funeral parlor during Mr. Corson's wake. Who else but Serena would have left his lost sunglasses—the pair of Ray-Bans he now wore—on that gate outside Mrs. Corson's apartment complex? It would have been just like her to plant those strange notes for him.

But it wasn't Mr. Corson's niece in the community pool's parking lot. This girl was taller, and so skinny she looked emaciated.

At closing time, Chris checked his bike, and the note he'd left on the handlebars was gone. Nothing was there in its place. After a bit of deliberation, he jumped on his bike and pedaled home. He thought about driving back to the pool at a quarter to nine, but decided to get together with Elvis instead.

For the next few days, he kept an eye out for that Goth-looking girl. And he always expected to find another note on his bicycle handlebars at quitting time every night.

Pretty soon, Chris forgot about the girl in black. He didn't see her again until late August—on another hot afternoon. He just happened to glance over toward the pool house from his lifeguard's perch, and there she stood on the other side of the fence. She was glaring at him. It looked like she was wearing the exact same clothes she'd worn last time. And she looked sick, or drugged out, or both. She seemed to hang on to the fence to keep from collapsing.

Chris grabbed his bullhorn: "Office?" he said, holding his hand up. That was the sign that he needed someone to relieve him. One of his coworkers, Karen Linde, a pretty, college-age blonde with a boyfriend, hurried out of the office. "What's going on?" she asked.

He climbed down from his post to meet her. "I just need to check on something for a few minutes," he said distractedly. "Thanks, Karen. Be right back."

He hurried toward the gate by the pool house. The Goth girl started to back up. She weaved a bit, like she was drunk or about to faint. Chris glanced over his shoulder at Karen, taking his place on the lifeguard's perch. When he looked forward again, the girl was gone. It was as if she'd just vanished. Chris didn't have any shoes on, but he ventured out to the parking lot with its hot asphalt and pebbles. He scoped the area for any sign of the girl, but didn't see her.

Before heading back inside the fenced area, Chris checked his bike. There wasn't anything on the handlebars.

For the rest of the day, he kept his eyes peeled for the Goth girl. But she never returned. Then at quitting time, he went out to his bike. There wasn't a note on the handlebars.

But someone had slashed both his tires.

Chris never set eyes on the sickly looking Goth girl again. But he thought about her now. It was happening again. Another strange, anonymous note; and someone had broken into his locker to leave it for him: *Ask your stepmother about Tina Gargullo and Nick Sorenson.*

Chris couldn't help thinking this was yet another little mystery that would go unsolved. He wondered what would end up slashed this time.

Hunched in front of the computer monitor, he noticed most of the other students had left. Outside the streetlights were on. He glanced over his shoulder at Mrs. Chertok, who gave him a patient half smile and pointed to her wristwatch. Chris checked his own watch: 5:23. The library was closing in seven minutes.

His fingers started working on the keyboard again. Under the Google subject head, he typed in all three names—Molly

Wright, Nick Sorenson, Tina Gargullo—and then pressed
ENTER.

The first item that came up didn't show Molly's name,
and yet Chris somehow knew this was what he was supposed
to find:

3 Dead, 5 Wounded in Campus Shooting Spree
The gunman, Roland Charles **Wright**, 26, was shot by a security
guard . . . a teacher, **Nick Sorenson**, 32, and a cafeteria worker,
Tina Gargullo, 20, both died on the scene. **Wright** fired three
rounds into **Sorenson** . . .
www.thechicagotribune/news/1302007.html

All he could think about was Molly's younger brother,
Charlie, who was supposed to have committed suicide.

"What?" Molly murmured into her cell phone.

She sat on the edge of the chaise longue in her attic art
studio. The door at the bottom of the stairs was closed. Two
levels down, on the first floor, Erin was parked in front of the
TV in the family room and Chris was on the computer in
Jeff's study. Jeff had asked Molly to take her cell where the
kids couldn't hear her. So she'd come up here.

She'd been on edge most of the day. Jeff had kept asking
if she wanted him to cancel his trip to Washington, D.C. But
she'd insisted he go, and so he'd gone—at 11:35 this morning. She'd tried to act brave about being alone with the kids
so soon after the latest cul-de-sac murders. It wouldn't be for
long. Jeff would be back the day after tomorrow—the same
day she'd be seeing her doctor.

Chris had come home late and immediately barricaded
himself in Jeff's study. He'd emerged for dinner: sloppy joes,
green beans, and fries in front of a *Simpsons* rerun in the
family room. Molly kept weekday dinners without Jeff casual.
During a commercial, Chris announced he was spending to-

morrow night at Larry's place. His mother would be there alone, because Larry was helping chaperone an overnight field trip to Olympia with his daughter's class.

"I think my mom could use the company," Chris said, gazing at the TV—and not her. "She shouldn't have to be alone in that house. You'll be okay with Erin, won't you?"

"Of course," Molly said. "If it's okay with your dad and mom, that's fine with me," Molly continued. "I can drop you off in Bellevue tomorrow afternoon."

"Can I stay with my mom, too?" Erin asked, almost kicking her TV table.

"That's fine," Molly said, with a pale smile.

She wasn't looking forward to tomorrow night all by herself—with an empty, dark house next door. And while Chris's reason for leaving her alone seemed rational enough—even sweet, in that he was looking out for his mother—there seemed more to it. Molly felt him pulling away. He'd hardly looked at her all night.

After dinner, Chris called his dad from the phone in the study. He had the door closed. Molly was watching TV with Erin, but she could hear him down the hall murmuring. He raised his voice a few times, but the words were indistinguishable. He was talking in there for twenty minutes, which was something of a record. He and his dad usually kept their phone conversations brief.

Finally, Molly heard the study door click open, and Chris lumbered into the family room with the cordless in his hand. Eyes downcast, he gave her the phone. "Dad wants to talk to you," he muttered. Then he retreated back to the study and closed the door.

"Erin, honey, could you turn down the TV a bit," Molly said. Then she spoke into the phone. "Hi, there . . ."

"Hi, babe, we need to talk," Jeff said. "If you can get away from the kids for a few minutes, I'll call you back on your cell. . . ."

It was raining lightly; so instead of stepping outside with

her phone, Molly had retreated up to her studio. Jeff had called after only a minute or so—and he'd told her what had been bothering Chris tonight.

"What?" Molly repeated into the cell phone. She got up from the chaise longue and clutched a hand to her stomach. "So that's why he's been in your study all night. He's been holed up in there, looking up articles about my brother. My God, no wonder he can't bring himself to look at me."

"I think his biggest concern was making sure I knew," Jeff said gently.

"So—he just assumed I'd keep something like that from you?" Molly asked. She started pacing around the studio space. "Is that the kind of person he thinks I am?"

"Honey, look at it this way. Together, we kept him in the dark about this for well over a year. You can't blame him for wanting to check with me to find out how much I know."

"Yeah, well, I'll tell you who we can blame for this—Angela!" Molly said, exasperated. "God, she's a piece of work. Is she so out to get me that she doesn't give a damn about traumatizing her own son? Just the other day, I was starting to feel sorry for her. I was starting to feel she might be halfway human. And then she turns around and smashes our pumpkins. It doesn't seem to matter that it broke poor Erin's heart. And now, she's pulling this shit with Chris. She's crazy! Breaking into his locker, leaving notes. . . ."

"I'll talk to her," Jeff said.

"She'll just deny it," Molly shot back. "The same way she denied smashing our pumpkins on Saturday, and then using her old key to get back in here and leave that—that weird smiley-face jack-o-lantern arrangement for me to find on the kitchen counter. I'm sorry, but I've had it with her. She's certifiable, she really is."

"You're right, you're right." Jeff sighed. "You shouldn't have to put up with this. I'll have it out with her tomorrow. The gloves are coming off, I promise. By the way, I told Chris that he and Erin are staying home tomorrow night. You shouldn't be alone there. Besides, I don't want them spending any time with Angela until I've talked to her. I don't think she realizes how much she's hurting her own children in her efforts to hurt us."

Molly plopped down on the chaise longue again. "No," she said resolutely into the phone. "I'll have it out with her. It's high time I handle this. You're too nice, Jeff." She took a deep breath. "I'll talk to Chris tonight and straighten things out with him. And I'll talk to Angela tomorrow. And when you come home on Wednesday night, this will all be in the past. . . ."

As she assured her husband that all their fears and troubles would soon be behind them, Molly almost believed it herself.

Almost.

There was a knock on his bedroom door.

Chris had been expecting it—and dreading it, too. He'd hoped maybe if he came up here and shut the door, she might not bother him. He really didn't want to talk to Molly right now. He just couldn't wrap his head around the fact that her brother had shot all those people in that college cafeteria. One of the articles he'd read online said that Roland Charles Wright fired nineteen shots from a handgun, which meant the son of a bitch probably had to stop and reload while people around him were screaming and dying.

And this creep was his uncle.

No wonder Molly and his dad had kept it a secret.

At his desk, Chris turned his swivel chair. "Yeah, come in," he grunted.

Molly opened the door. She had a photo album tucked under her arm. Chris had glanced through it one night when he'd been bored and alone in the house. Molly kept it on the bookcase in her art studio—along with those elephant figurines. Chris had been a lot more fascinated by the nudes in her figure-study drawing books than snapshots of Molly's childhood.

She stepped into the room and set the photo album on his bed. "So—now you know why I don't talk about my family much."

He frowned at her. "You told me that your brother committed suicide."

Molly shrugged. "Well, in a way he did. I don't think he expected to live through that—*nightmare* he inflicted on so many people. Anyway, it's easier for me to tell people he killed himself. Usually it shuts them up and keeps them from asking any more questions—at least out loud." With a sigh, she sat down at the edge of his bed. "I'm sorry I treated you like just *people*. Your dad and I should have trusted you with the truth, only—well, it's been difficult enough for you to get used to me without me dragging my family skeletons out of the closet."

Chris's eyes narrowed at her. *Family skeletons out of the closet*, there she went with another one of her weird expressions. It sounded gay-related, but he wasn't sure.

She opened the photo album and brought it to him. "That's Charlie and me when we were about eleven and twelve. . . ."

Chris glanced at the photos of two kids, bundled up in jackets, earmuffs, scarves, and boots, playing in the snow. They were building a snowman that was taller than both of them. It looked like a scene from the movie *A Christmas Story*.

"When I look at these pictures," Molly said, "I still can't believe he did what he did. But I'm sure your dad explained to you that Charlie was mentally ill. Anyway, if you have anything you'd like to ask me about my brother or my family, feel free."

"Is that why you and your mother aren't close?" Chris asked. "Because your brother shot all those people?"

Molly nodded. "Yes. And it's a shame, too, because I

really miss her. But I guess we're both having a hard time forgiving each other—and ourselves."

Chris turned the page in the photo album—to some pictures of Molly on what must have been her thirteenth birthday. At least, in the photos, there was a 1 candle and a 3 candle on the cake. She was kind of gawky looking, with braces and braids. At the dinner table with the cake and the stack of presents, it was just Molly, her brother, and one parent. In some photos, it was the mom, in other photos, the dad. The parents must have taken turns snapping the picture. It was sad. There was no one else at her birthday. And there was no one else playing in the snow with them. "Didn't you guys have any friends?" he heard himself ask.

Chris noticed the slightly pained look on her face. Then he cleared his throat. "Sorry."

"Don't apologize," she murmured. She sat back down on his bed. "Charlie didn't make friends too easily, and I felt responsible for him. It sort of became my job, my role in the family. Plus, to be honest, I was embarrassed to have people over to the house, because of him. So as freakish as it sounds, I guess the two of us were very close growing up." She glanced down at the bedspread and smoothed it out with her hand. "You'd think I would have known him a little better, and known what he was capable of, but obviously I didn't."

"After it happened, did you ever talk to any of the people he shot?"

She nodded soberly. "I wrote to all of them. A couple of them wrote back. This one woman who was severely wounded, God bless her, she said she'd already forgiven Charlie, and she was praying for me. On the opposite side of that, I visited the mother of the man who was killed, and she spit in my face. I'm not sure if I lost a son, I wouldn't do the exact same thing."

Chris said nothing. He was thinking of his visit to Mrs. Corson.

"Anyway—" She sighed. "I just couldn't stay in Chicago

after that. So—I moved to Washington, D.C, and tried to put the past behind me. Then I met your dad, and I fell in love. I guess you know the rest."

Chris closed her photo album and set it on his desk. "So who do you think broke the lock on my locker and left me that note?"

She glanced down at the carpet and shrugged uneasily. "I—I really can't say."

Chris stared at her. He'd thought she was being so honest with him, but now he could see she was holding something back. "You can't think of anybody? I mean, it's like they have it out for you or something. Could it be one of the people your brother shot—or a relative of one of them?"

"Well, it happened over three years ago, Chris. I can't imagine they'd wait this long to try to get back at me." Molly got to her feet. "Anyway, whoever's responsible, I hope the only damage they did was to the lock on your locker." She put a hand on his shoulder. "Are *we* okay, Chris?"

He hesitated, but then nodded apathetically. "Sure."

She started to bend forward—maybe to kiss him on the cheek or hug him. But he turned away in his chair and reached for the photo album. He handed it to her. "Thanks for letting me see this."

"Oh, yeah, you bet," she said awkwardly. Clutching the album to her chest, she backed toward the door. "I—I have a lock on my bike that might fit your locker at school. Remind me to get it for you tomorrow morning, okay? The combination should be easy for you to remember. It's your dad's birthday—eight-oh-eight."

"Thanks, Molly," he said, unsmiling. "Good night."

"G'night, Chris," she said. Then she stepped out to the hallway and closed his door.

Part of him felt bad for not being a little friendlier toward her. But he couldn't help it. She was covering something up, just as she'd covered up for over a year now the fact that her brother was a murderer. He could tell Molly had a pretty good idea who had broken into his locker and left that note. That same person had probably been watching him all day—maybe even longer. They were screwing around with his head, and he didn't like it.

And he didn't like Molly, because she wouldn't tell him who it might be.

CHAPTER FIFTEEN

"Are you crazy?" Angela asked, with a glass of white wine in her hand. They sat in a booth at Palomino in the City Center Building. The elegant restaurant was busy and noisy with the lunch-hour crowd. Gorgeous, opulent Chihuly glass vases were strategically placed between booths; and the wait-staff all wore black pants, white shirts, and ties beneath their aprons.

Angela had been sitting in the booth and sipping her wine when Molly had arrived promptly at one-fifteen. It reminded Molly of a line she'd heard in a gangster movie once, something about always arriving extra early when meeting with the enemy. With her navy-blue dress and pearls, Angela looked like she was going to a wedding. Molly felt under-dressed in her black slacks and a sage-colored sweater.

She wished she'd chosen another restaurant for their rendezvous, ideally a cafeteria where diners paid up front. This lunch with Angela promised to be very confrontational, and they'd both be stuck there at the table, hating each other and waiting for the bill.

Right now, Molly was waiting for her Diet Coke. They hadn't even ordered their food yet, and already things were getting a bit hostile.

"Molly, you're not making any sense," Angela said, rolling her eyes. "I mean, really, why in God's name would I break the lock off Chris's school locker and leave him some snide note about you? Talk about crazy. It's as nutty as you accusing me of smashing the pumpkins on your front stoop—and then breaking into the house. I know how much Erin loves Halloween. Why on earth would I want to ruin that for her?"

"Well, if you didn't do it, who did?" Molly pressed. "Who else has a key to the house?"

Angela leaned forward. "I don't have a key to the house anymore. I gave it to Jeff when I left. And I don't know where Chris's locker is at school. If I was sneaking around the school hallways, don't you think Chris would have noticed—or one of his friends would have seen me and told him? Why would I do something so silly? If I wanted to tell Chris something, I'd sit down with him and tell him—face-to-face."

"No, you wouldn't," Molly countered. "You wouldn't want your son to know you hired a private detective to look into my family background. So you planted that note in his jacket. You have a history of being underhanded and sneaky and . . ."

The waitress returned with her Diet Coke, and Molly fell silent. She worked up a smile, shifted in her seat, and tried to look interested in her menu.

"We still haven't decided on lunch yet," Angela told the waitress. "Give us a few minutes."

"Certainly, take your time," the waitress said.

Angela waited until the waitress walked away, and then she turned toward Molly. "You know, I'm getting pretty sick of all your accusations," she said. "And I don't appreciate the threatening phone calls on my cell, either."

"What calls?" Molly scowled at her.

"Are you on the level?"

"Yes," Molly said. "I haven't a clue what you're talking about."

Angela took a sip of wine. "Someone called me on my cell three or four times this week. It was one of those blocked numbers, and all they said was, *'You're going to pay for what you did.'* That wasn't you?"

Baffled, Molly shook her head.

"It's a woman's voice—all raspy and crawly. At first, I thought it was that crazy Cassandra, who Jeff was seeing on the sly while we were married. But then I figured, why would she call me? She'd be calling and harassing you now. So— then I figured *you* had to be the crank caller."

"Well, it's not me," Molly murmured.

"I have a tough time believing you," Angela replied. "I mean, who else would be calling me like that? You're the one accusing me of doing all these bizarre things—things that hurt my own children. It doesn't make any sense." She shook her head. "You need help, Molly. I'm serious. Insanity must run in your family."

The reference to Charlie stung. At the same time, Angela was finally admitting that she knew about him. Molly glared at Jeff's ex and told herself she wasn't going to tear up. "Nice, Angela," she said in a low voice. "Now that you found out from your private detective what my brother did, I suppose from now on you'll get your little digs in wherever you can. Have you sprung the news on Lynette and Jill yet? Is it going to turn up in one of Courtney Hahn's texts or Facebook announcements soon?"

Frowning, Angela didn't say anything for a moment. She glanced down at the tablecloth. "I'm sorry, Molly," she whispered finally. "I apologize. That was—that was a terrible thing to say. You should know, I haven't told anyone about your brother." She sipped her wine, and then shrugged. "Don't get me wrong, that's just what I intended to do when I—when I hired a private detective to dig up whatever he could on you. I'd hoped he'd find something to make you look bad, some good dirt I could share with Jeff and your neighbors. I didn't expect something so—tragic and awful. It made me ashamed that I hired someone in the first place."

Molly studied her, and as much as she felt sorry for Angela, she didn't trust her one bit.

"Believe it or not, Molly, I used to be a nice person," she said. "I think having an unfaithful husband turned me bitter. Maybe you're luckier than me. Maybe Jeff has changed his ways. I suppose some people can change." Angela leaned forward. "I'm being honest with you now. So can you return the favor? Tell me the truth about these calls on my cell. You really don't know anything about them?"

Molly shook her head.

Angela slumped back in the booth. "Damn, I was almost hoping it was you," she admitted. "Then at least I'd know who was threatening me. I'm a nervous wreck. It's no help that someone tried to break into Larry's house two weeks ago. They didn't get in—at least the police didn't think so. Nothing was missing. But they'd pried a screen off a kitchen window. Don't say anything to the kids. I don't want them worried about me—or about staying there. I thought I'd have to be alone in that house tonight. Larry was supposed to chaperone an overnight in Olympia with Taylor's class. Thank God it got canceled."

At that moment, the waitress returned to their booth.

"I'll have another one of these," Angela said, pointing to her near-empty wineglass. "And the chop salad, dressing on the side."

The waitress looked at Molly, who shook her head. "Nothing else for me, thank you." She had no intention of sticking around.

As the waitress left, Angela nervously drummed her fingertips on the tabletop. "Listen, Molly. Let's call a truce and put our heads together on this. I didn't break into Chris's locker and leave that note. And I didn't smash the pumpkins on the front stoop or let myself into the house. And you say you're not the one calling and threatening me. That means someone else is behind all this, some woman—at least it was a woman calling me. Do you think it's possible somebody is trying to pit us against each other?"

Molly frowned. "For what purpose?"

"I don't know, but it doesn't seem to matter to her if my kids get hurt, and that really scares me. We've both been married to Jeff—you in the present tense, and me in the past. I wonder if that crazy Cassandra woman is back in his life— or if maybe Jeff has found someone new, and she wants to sit back and watch us scratch each other's eyes out. I don't know."

Shaking her head, Molly grabbed her purse. "Okay, I've had enough." She fished a five out of her wallet and slapped it down on the table. "I'm sick of you implying that Jeff is screwing around on me. I don't need to hear it—and it's not true. Of course, the truth and you have always been strangers. Lying seems to come easily to you. . . ."

"Now, wait a minute—"

"Screw you, Angela." She scooted out of the booth. "Last May, you denied over and over again that you'd hired a private detective. And now, you admit you did. You're a real piece of work. Why should I believe anything you say?"

"Molly, wait!" she said loudly.

A few people at nearby tables stopped and gaped at them. Molly hesitated.

Angela glanced around for a moment, and then she cleared her throat. "I didn't hire a private detective in May," she whispered. "I was telling the truth back then." She nodded at the other side of the booth. "Please, Molly, sit down."

She didn't budge. She stood by the booth, scowling at Angela.

Jeff's ex-wife stared right back at her. "I hired my guy last month," she explained carefully. "I got the idea after Jeff accused me. But I didn't act upon it until last month. My guy got all his information off the Internet. It only took him two days. He never went to Chicago."

Bewildered, Molly sat down at the booth's edge. "But back in May, who. . ."

"That's just what I'm saying," Angela whispered. "It's someone else doing all this."

Molly shook her head. She felt a little sick.

She had the horrible feeling Angela was telling the truth.

With her tan trench coat draped over the back of her chair, the woman sat at a small table in Palomino. She hadn't touched the Cobb salad set in front of her ten minutes ago. There wasn't much chance of anyone recognizing her, but she wore a black pageboy wig just to be on the safe side. She watched the two Mrs. Dennehys talking heatedly in a booth on the other side of the crowded restaurant. She wished she could hear what they were saying.

She wondered if Angela Dennehy realized how pathetic she was. Ray Corson had figured her out immediately. Chris Dennehy's old guidance counselor had taken some notes after meeting her:

I'm guessing Angela Dennehy was very beautiful once. She still has some panache, but there's a lot of bitterness in her, and it shows on her face. Clearly, her husband's womanizing has taken a toll, and she's trying to turn Chris against him. As difficult as it was for Chris to adjust to his father's remarrying, it must have been utterly defeating for Chris's mother. The new Mrs. Dennehy is younger & prettier. Plus she seems like a good person. Chris's mother can't be happy about that. I don't know why she gave up custody of her children, but clearly, she's doing all she can to poison Chris's relationship with his dad.

*It's horrible to say this, but in many ways, Chris
would be better off without her. . . .*

She sipped her merlot, and thought, *Not just Chris, the
whole world would be better off. . . .*

She was careful not to spill wine on the small square
of cotton material she'd set by her place setting. The little
patch had a pattern of tiny blue rosebuds on it. She couldn't
resist gently running her fingertips over the fabric as she focused on Angela Dennehy across the room. She imagined
the material wrapped around a little doll with silver-brown
hair.

Had Angela noticed yet that her nightgown had a small
square cut from the hem? It had been that way for two weeks
now.

She thought about what Ray Corson had written in his
private journal, after Angela and her friends on Willow Tree
Court had waged their campaign against him:

> *Molly Dennehy handled things rather quietly & it
> might have stayed under the radar. But the former
> Mrs. Dennehy has really gone on the warpath. I
> wonder how much of her animosity toward me is
> based on genuine concern for her son. Or is it a
> means for Angela Dennehy to reestablish her
> maternal turf & show up her successor as an
> ineffectual & incompetent mother? I used to feel
> sorry for Angela Dennehy, but not anymore. . . .*

The woman carefully folded the small patch cut from Angela Dennehy's nightgown. She slipped it inside a little plastic bag and stashed it into her purse. She gazed over at the
two Mrs. Dennehys again.

She decided that Ray Corson was a better person than
her. She never felt sorry for Angela Dennehy. In fact, it gave

her great satisfaction telling Angela over the phone that she was going to pay for what she'd done.

The digital clock on her nightstand read 1:42 A.M. Molly was pretty certain both Chris and Erin were asleep. She was the only one hearing the sounds of the house settling and that one tree branch scraping against the bathroom window screen every time the wind kicked up. She pulled the sheets up around her neck and rolled over to face the bedroom door. The glow from Erin's *Cinderella* night-light spilled beyond her room, bathing the hallway in dim blue shadows.

Molly thought about how she'd given away all of Charlie's things to charity—except for a dozen of the two hundred elephant figurines he'd collected in his lifetime. Those were the only things from her past that she wanted to hold on to.

But now someone had dug everything up again. She'd thought Angela was behind it. She'd thought Jeff's ex was responsible for all the recent strange occurrences. But it was someone else.

Molly had a feeling they were just getting started.

The last thing on her mind right now was the Cul-de-sac Killer.

In a split-level home on a Bellevue cul-de-sac called Alder Court, another woman, a year older than Molly, was also lying in bed alone. Her husband was out of town on business, too. The pretty redhead named Paulette LaBlanc had two children asleep down the hall from her, Matt, six, and Brendan, three. Brendan was getting over a cold.

After putting the kids to bed, Paulette had caught up on some editing she'd been contracted to do for Boeing. Then she'd made the mistake of watching the eleven o'clock news.

They'd released one of those creepy composite sketches of a "person of interest" spotted Thursday night near Laurel Lane in Federal Way, where those three teenagers were slaughtered. The man they sought had been seen emerging from a silver Honda Civic. He was about six feet tall, approximately one hundred eighty pounds, between thirty and forty years old, and had thinning brown hair. He was wearing a tan jacket. The sketch showed a cold-eyed man with thin lips and a very high forehead. The news segment featured a brief clip of paramedics at night carrying one of the covered corpses from the house—amid swirling police lights and popping flashes.

Paulette was kicking herself for watching the news story. As she tried to sleep, she kept seeing the cold-eyed man in that police sketch again. She imagined getting out of bed and finding him in her hallway. *Stop it*, she told herself. She and the kids were safe. She'd locked up and double-checked all the windows downstairs. She even had a little canister of pepper-spray on her nightstand—within reach. Yet Paulette still felt on edge. She kept tossing and turning. She thought about taking a sleeping pill. But what if Brendan woke up coughing again—as he had last night? She'd given him two spoonfuls of children's cough syrup, and took him into the bathroom, where she let the hot water go full blast until the place was like a steam room. She'd lowered the toilet seat lid and sat there with him in her lap, telling him a story until he'd stopped coughing and fallen asleep again.

If she took a pill, and he needed her again tonight, she wouldn't be able to wake up—much less function.

She desperately needed her sleep, too. Matt would be up for school in less than five hours. Plus she still had eighty-seven pages to edit, and it was due in two days.

As she lay there in bed, Paulette tried to assure herself that the Cul-de-sac Killer couldn't possibly come to her house tonight. After all, she'd just watched that story on the news. It would be way too much of a coincidence if he broke into their home tonight. Her being scared was her insurance that it wouldn't really happen. It was like taking an umbrella outside with her to make sure it wouldn't rain.

As Paulette drifted off to sleep, she realized that kind of logic made absolutely no sense whatsoever.

"Mom? Mom, wake up!" Matt whispered.

Paulette sat up in bed and rubbed her eyes. Her son was at her bedside in his *Pirates of the Caribbean* pajamas, doing a little dance like he had to go to the bathroom. She glanced over at the clock on her nightstand: 3:21 A.M. "Honey, what's going on?" she asked, her head in a fog. "Is it Brendan?"

"There's a man in our room," he said in a scared, tiny voice.

Suddenly, Paulette was wide awake. "What?"

"I saw him sneak in, and now he's hiding in there," Matt said.

Paulette grabbed the pepper spray off her nightstand and climbed out of bed. She was wearing one of her husband's T-shirts and a pair of panties. Matt clung on to the hem of her T-shirt as she walked across the room. "It's okay, Matt," she said, trying to act brave for him. Yet her heart was racing. "You probably just had a bad dream. And sometimes they seem so real, I know. . . ."

Pausing in her doorway, Paulette reminded herself that Matt recently had monsters under the bed, clowns hiding in his closet, and a vampire outside his window. Still, she couldn't help wondering, *What if it's real this time?*

He hovered beside her, whimpering. She could feel him shaking.

"Is Brendan asleep?" she whispered.

"I don't know," Matt whined. "I couldn't see him. The man was standing between our beds."

The very notion sent a chill racing through her. Suddenly, Paulette couldn't get her breath. She started shaking now, too. She thought about telling Matt to go lock himself in her bathroom. But that might just scare him even more.

"Brendan, honey?" she called nervously. She switched on the hallway light.

There was no response. Her hands trembling, Paulette took the cap off the pepper spray. She padded down the hall with Matt trailing after her. He still clutched the bottom of her oversized T-shirt. She stepped across the threshold to her sons' room and flicked on the light switch.

She stared down at Brendan in his bed. He stirred and coughed a little, but he didn't awaken.

Paulette let out a sigh, and put the cap back on the pepper spray. She glanced around the room—with the Mariners, Seahawks, and Sonics posters on the walls and the matching *Transformers* covers on the beds. The toys and books on their bookshelves were undisturbed, and the goldfish were peacefully swimming around their bowl on Matt's desk.

"No one's in here, honey," Paulette whispered. "Now, it's late—"

"Check behind the door!" he cried.

"Hush, you'll wake Brendan," she said quietly. Obliging him, she peeked behind the door, then half closed it—so he could see no one was hiding behind it. "Okay?"

"What about under the bed?" he whispered.

With a sigh, she got down on her knees, and lifted the dust ruffle. "Candy wrappers. Have you been eating candy in bed?"

"Just on Halloween," he murmured, sheepishly.

Paulette gathered up the Reese's and Hershey's wrappers, and tossed them in the trash pail by Matt's desk. "Do you need to go to the bathroom?" she asked.

He shook his head.

"Into bed now, c'mon," she whispered. "You have school in a few hours."

Matt climbed under the covers, and she switched off the light. Paulette checked on Brendan again, feeling his forehead to make sure he wasn't running a fever. Then she came over to Matt and tucked him in.

"Could you check the closet, Mom?" he asked in a hushed voice.

Paulette hesitated for a second. Suddenly, she was scared again. She glanced across the dark bedroom at the closed closet door—with a poster of the Seahawks symbol on it. The boys had a fairly large closet. She couldn't help thinking about the Cul-de-sac Killer. He left the bodies of his victims in closets. Was that where he liked to hide, too?

She took a deep breath and moved across the room. She took the cap off the pepper spray again, then reached for the doorknob with her other hand. The hinges squeaked as she opened the door. In front of her, she could barely make out the clothes on hangers on each side of the dark closet. They were just black, bulky shapes. Her hand waved at the air as she blindly reached for the pull-string to the overhead light. At any minute, she expected someone to grab her wrist.

She found the string and pulled it. The closet light went on. Paulette glanced around. "It's all clear in here, honey. Nothing to worry about," she announced—to both her son and herself.

Paulette kissed Matt good night, and he asked if she could leave the hallway light on. "No problem," she whispered. "Now, get to sleep—and no candy in bed."

Paulette figured she wasn't going to fall asleep now. Her heart was still pounding furiously. Maybe a hit of brandy and about fifteen minutes of infomercials would calm her a bit.

She headed downstairs, and checked the front door dead bolt again. In the kitchen, she tested the back door. It was still locked. She switched on the TV in the family room, and glimpsed some before-and-after photos of a middle-aged woman whose crow's-feet, eye bags, and turkey neck had miraculously vanished.

Paulette set the pepper spray on the kitchen counter, and she poured some brandy into a jelly glass, filling it halfway. She took a belt. It burned a little, but she immediately felt better. How did she let herself get so scared?

She glanced out the kitchen window—at her neighbor's house, a two-story Colonial. The lights were on. People were still up next door in Larry's house. If she'd known that, she might not have been so nervous earlier.

Standing at the window, Paulette took another swig of brandy. She was wondering if Larry's girlfriend Angela had her two kids over tonight—the sweet little girl and that cute teenager. Was he the one who was up so late?

But it wasn't just one window with the light on.

"Oh, Jesus, all the lights are on," she whispered.

The jelly glass slipped out of her grasp and broke on the floor. But Paulette didn't look down at it.

She was staring at a tall, shadowy figure darting past the lights from Larry's front window.

He was running away from the house.

CHAPTER SIXTEEN

When the phone rang, Molly automatically looked at the digital clock on the microwave oven. She wondered who would be calling at 7:04 A.M.

In her T-shirt, sweatpants, and thick wool socks, she was at the stove, craving a verboten cup of coffee and heating up some SpaghettiOs for Erin's lunch thermos. Both Chris and Erin were up and getting dressed. In about fifteen minutes, they'd be eating their cereal at the breakfast table, and the TV in the family room would be blaring. Molly had been cherishing the quiet—until the damn phone rang.

She thought about screening the call, but figured it might be Jeff. He was due back from D.C. late tonight. Maybe he was getting an earlier flight.

Without looking at the caller ID, Molly snatched up the phone on the third ring. "Yes, hello?"

"Is this Molly?" asked the woman on the other end of the line.

"Yes. Who—"

"Molly, this is Trish, Angela's sister," she explained hurriedly. "I need to speak with Jeff."

"I'm sorry, Trish," she replied, a bit mystified. She'd heard both Chris and Erin talk about their Aunt Trish, but

Molly had never spoken to her before. "Jeff's out of town. He's in Washington, D.C. He's due back tonight. Can I give him a message?"

There was silence on the other end.

"Trish?" Molly asked.

"Angela was killed last night," she said in a shaky voice. "She was murdered—along with Larry and his daughter. The police say it's one of those cul-de-sac killings."

"What?" Molly murmured. "Good Lord, no. . . ."

She told herself it was a joke—or maybe she hadn't heard Trish right. But she listened to the quiet sobbing on the other end of the line. Her legs suddenly felt wobbly, and she put a hand on the kitchen counter to brace herself. "Trish, I—I'm so sorry. . . ."

"Listen, could you track down Jeff and let him know?" she asked. "You—you'll have some police coming by this morning. I'll try to make it over there later in the afternoon to see Chris and Erin. Tell them I love them. . . ."

"Oh, Trish, I'm so sorry," she repeated, a hand on her heart. "I just had lunch with Angela yesterday. I can't believe it."

Angela's sister was sobbing on the other end of the line. "I have to go," she said. Then she hung up.

Dazed, Molly listened to the line go dead. She finally clicked off, and then dialed Jeff's cell number. She started pacing back and forth in the kitchen. Angela's children were upstairs. How was she going to tell them their mother was dead?

Jeff wasn't picking up. It went to voice mail. Molly impatiently waited for the beep. "Hi, honey, it's me," she said, her mouth suddenly dry. "Can you call me as soon as you get this? It—it's very important, okay? Thanks. Bye."

Even though she'd worked there for nearly two years, she couldn't remember the number for the Capital Hilton in Washington, D.C. So she retreated to Jeff's study, got online, and found the number off the Hilton website. From the cordless phone in his study, she called the hotel and asked for Jeff Dennehy's room.

It took the operator a minute. "Could you spell that for me, please?"

Molly spelled it out. "He's there for a pharmaceutical convention," she said.

There was another silent lapse. "We don't show a Jeff Dennehy staying here. And we don't have anything on our schedule this week for any pharmaceutical or medical groups. Are you sure you have the right Hilton? This is the Capital Hilton on Sixteenth Street Northwest."

"Yes, that's the one I want. I—"

Molly heard a beep on the line, the call-waiting signal. "Just a second, please . . ." She glanced at the caller ID screen and saw Jeff's cell number. She put the receiver back to her ear. "Never mind, I've got him on the other line right now. Thank you."

As she clicked on the call-waiting button, she heard one of the kids coming down the stairs. "Jeff?" she whispered into the phone.

"What's going on? You sounded pretty grim on that message. Are the kids okay?"

Molly hesitated. She could hear the TV go on in the family room. "The kids are okay—for now," she said carefully. "It's Angela, honey. Trish just called. Angela's dead. She and Larry and his daughter were murdered last night. The police—they think it's a cul-de-sac killing."

She heard a sigh on the other end of the line. "Oh, my God . . ."

"I think the police are supposed to be over here pretty soon," Molly continued. "I just got off the phone with Trish about five minutes ago. I haven't said anything to the kids yet. . . ."

"Molly!" Erin yelled from the kitchen. "My SpaghettiOs are burning! And I can't reach the Cocoa Puffs!"

She turned and saw Chris treading down the front stairs

with his backpack slung over his shoulder. He wore a wrinkled blue shirt and jeans. He glanced at her. He must have seen something was wrong from the expression on her face. "Is that Dad?" he asked.

With the phone to her ear, she nodded. "Chris, could you do me a favor? Could you turn off the stove in the kitchen, and move the pan? And then could you get Erin her cereal, please? I'll be there in just a second."

He frowned at her. "Is Dad okay?"

She felt like such a coward, but she just nodded. She waited until Chris headed toward the kitchen before she got back on the line with Jeff. "Honey, are you still there?"

She heard muffled crying on the other end of the line. She swallowed hard. "Jeff, honey, what do you want me to do?"

"There are Snap, Crackle, and Pop pencil pals inside this unopened box of Rice Krispies," Chris announced as he sat down at the breakfast table with his little sister. "I'll trade you them for the remote."

Erin thought about it for a moment. He'd already poured her a bowl of Cocoa Puffs, and she was watching some inane preteen situation-comedy on ABC Family or the Disney Channel, he wasn't sure. He just knew that all the kids looked like catalog models and none of them could act worth shit.

" 'Kay," she said, at last. She set the remote on the lazy Susan and gave it a gentle spin. Then she went back to eating her Cocoa Puffs.

"Thanks," Chris said, grabbing the remote. He switched over to news for the latest sports.

He was trying to feel normal again after all the weirdness that went down the day before yesterday. He'd already replaced the combination lock on his locker. He'd had no desire to borrow Molly's bike lock. The less he had to do with

Molly right now, the better. He just couldn't get over the fact that her brother had shot those people.

He really wished he'd been able to get out of the house and away from her for an evening. Apparently Larry and Taylor had canceled their field trip, so his mom hadn't been alone last night after all.

Right now Molly was in the study on the phone with his dad, whispering and acting weird.

Chris poured himself some Rice Krispies, and then fished the little packet of pencil pals out of the box. "There you go, kitten, knock yourself out," he said, pushing the packet across the table at his little sister.

"Thanks, Chris!" she replied. She ripped the packet open with her teeth.

He was reaching for the milk to pour over his cereal when he heard the newscaster on TV. *"Breaking News this morning from a cul-de-sac in Bellevue,"* a pretty Latino reporter announced grimly. Dressed in a red coat, she stood in front of a swarm of police cars with their lights flashing. They partially blocked any view of the house in the distance. *"Three people are dead in what police sources here say has all the earmarks of another cul-de-sac killing. The identities of the three victims are being withheld for now, but I can tell you that two of the victims are adults—one male and one female. And the third victim is a teenage girl. The last time the Cul-de-sac Killer struck, three teens were slain in Federal Way. This is a quiet street in a family neighborhood—"*

Chris hit the mute button. He didn't want his little sister traumatized by this grisly news report. He was about to switch channels when he glanced across the table at Erin. She didn't seem to understand the gravity of the news story. Smiling, she scratched the top of her blond head, and then pointed at the TV screen. "Look! Isn't that Uncle Larry's house?"

Chris turned toward the TV. From the roof and the location of the trees, the house behind that pretty reporter might have indeed been Larry's. But it couldn't be. No, so many of the houses in those Bellevue subdivisions looked alike.

Yet Chris unsteadily got to his feet. He looked at the TV, and that roof of that two-story Colonial—so much like the one he'd slept under every other weekend for the last few months. He kept thinking of the reporter's description of the Cul-de-sac Killer's latest casualties: a teenage girl, and two adults—one male, one female.

Chris told himself that they would have heard from the police by now. But then, that was why the names were being withheld. The families still didn't know.

With the sound muted on the TV, he could hear Molly down the hall in the study, whispering to his dad on the phone. He couldn't make out the words, but she sounded so worried—even panicked, as if she might have just heard some disturbing news.

Chris started toward the front of the house. He saw Molly step out of his dad's study. She held the cordless phone to her ear. Biting her lip, she gazed at him with pity. "Honey," she whispered into the cordless. "I'm going to put Chris on."

He numbly stared at his stepmother. He couldn't move.

She handed him the phone. "Chris, your dad needs to talk to you."

For the next few hours, all Molly could think about was holding on until Jeff came home. It was a grueling, sad nightmare. When she and Chris had sat down with Erin to tell her that her mother was dead, the six-year-old didn't just cry, she shrieked at the top of her voice—as if she were being attacked. It seemed to take forever for Chris to calm her down. Every time Molly even touched her, Erin went into a fit—maybe it was because Molly had been the one who had actually told her that her mother had been killed. Chris rocked her to sleep in the rocking chair in her room, the same chair that had once been her mother's.

Two plainclothes police detectives arrived around nine-thirty. Molly had barely enough time to run a brush through her hair and throw on some jeans and a sweater. Chris talked with them at the breakfast table. Meanwhile Molly made them coffee and screened calls. The phone wouldn't stop ringing. One of the calls was from her doctor's office. She was being charged for missing her appointment. She didn't bother arguing with them.

Another call was from Lynette. Apparently Trish had her number, too. Lynette said she was coming over with some lunch for them in a couple of hours, and she wouldn't take no for an answer. Molly didn't argue with her, either.

Chris told the police that he hadn't seen his mother in over a week. He hadn't noticed anything unusual the last time he'd stayed at Larry's house. Once the detectives were finished with their questions, Chris retreated to his room and shut the door.

Molly was so frazzled by the time she sat down with the two cops, her thinking was muddled. She told them about her lunch with Angela the day before. She thought they'd want to know about the strange, threatening calls Angela had gotten on her cell—from that woman. But she didn't know much beyond what Angela had told her. To Molly, it seemed totally unrelated to the cul-de-sac murders. She'd read all there was to read on those killings, and at no time was it mentioned that any of the victims had been threatened beforehand.

The police asked if Angela had mentioned any other strange goings-on. Molly remembered the attempted break-in at Larry's house two weeks ago. "She said the kitchen window screen had been removed," Molly recalled. "But it didn't look like anything was missing."

The police already knew about it. Angela and Larry had reported the incident twelve days before.

The two detectives said they wanted to talk to Jeff as soon as he came home. His flight was due into SeaTac at 3:55. "Where's Mr. Dennehy flying in from?" one of the cops asked.

"Washington, D.C.," Molly replied. "He's been there since Monday."

"Where was he staying?"

"The Capital Hilton," Molly answered. But then she remembered talking to the hotel operator earlier. Molly watched the police detective writing it down, and decided not to say anything.

The cops said they'd be back to talk with Jeff.

As Molly showed them to the front door, she glanced outside. Two TV news vans were parked in front of the house. No one had rung the bell yet. But the vans had attracted a few onlookers. Three strange cars were parked on the block, and about a dozen people stood in the middle of the street, gawking at the news vans and the house. An older couple had their bikes with them. They must have been out for a ride when they spotted the TV news trucks.

Half hiding behind the door, Molly watched the reporters and cameramen rush out of their vans to interview the two policemen.

Molly noticed yet another van crawling down the cul-de-sac, but this one was a moving van.

The vehicle made an incessant beeping noise over a chorus of hissing and grinding as it backed into Kay's old driveway next door. Molly couldn't help thinking that the new neighbor had picked one hell of a lousy day to move in.

The police hadn't been gone five minutes when Lynette Hahn came by with Courtney, Carson, and Dakota in tow. She'd pulled the kids out of school so they could help Chris and Erin through this awful tragedy. Just in time for lunch, she'd also brought along enough McDonald's to feed a small army. It was actually a good call. With a Happy Meal and Lynette's bratty kids to distract her, Erin seemed to perk up a little. She and the little monsters parked themselves in front of some cartoons on the Disney Channel.

Chris remained barricaded in his room. He didn't want to see anyone—including Courtney. So she spent most of the time sitting at the breakfast table, sipping a milk shake and texting friends on her iPhone.

Molly never thought she'd be grateful for Lynette Hahn's company, but she was. Lynette helped screen the calls, and twice she chased away reporters who dared to ring the door-bell. And having not had a scrap of food all morning—when she was eating for two—Molly was glad for the cheese-burger and fries. She devoured them.

She was able to steal a moment and brought some of the food up to Chris's room. She gently knocked on his door.

"Could you go away, please?" Chris called, in a voice hoarse from crying.

"I know you don't want to see anybody," Molly said, lean-ing close to his door. "But you need to eat something. There's a double cheeseburger, large fries, and a Coke for you. I'm leaving it outside the door here."

He didn't respond.

"Chris?" she said. "I just want you to know, you were so good with Erin this morning. The way you took care of her and got her to calm down, I think your mom would have been very proud of you."

"Thank you, Molly," he said, still raspy. "Can you leave me alone now?"

"Sure, Chris," she said. Then she left the McDonald's bag and the Coke by his door.

In the upstairs hallway, she could hear Lynette down in the family room, chiding one of her children: "If you want to make yourself sick to your stomach with even more candy and more soda pop, Dakota, you just go right ahead."

Molly felt a little sick herself. Either she'd eaten that burger too fast, or the baby was stirring things up. She hurried into the master bathroom and stood over the toilet for a few minutes, hoping the nausea would pass. As she tentatively stood there, Molly began to weep. She wasn't sure why. She'd never liked Angela very much.

She remembered Angela telling her at lunch yesterday how scared she was. She'd talked about calling a truce. The person calling Angela must have been responsible for hiring the investigator in Chicago, for the smashed pumpkins, and for Chris's broken locker.

Molly hadn't told the policemen about any of those things. They just didn't seem to have anything to do with the cul-de-sac killings.

But maybe they did.

Suddenly, she felt her stomach churn, and she thought for certain she was going to throw up. But she held back and took a few deep breaths. The awful sensation passed—for now.

When she came back out to the hallway, she smiled a little. The McDonald's bag outside Chris's door wasn't there anymore. At least he was eating something.

In Erin's room, the bed covering was askew. Molly stepped in to straighten the quilt on the bed. Leaning beside Angela's rocker, she glanced out the window—at the crowd in front of the house. Now there were three TV news vans, a cop car, and about thirty people just gaping at the house.

Next door, movers were unloading furniture from the van and hauling it into Kay's old house.

Natalie, in her usual running attire, jogged down the block, passing people on her way back to the Nguyens' house. Her dark blond hair, in a ponytail, slapped back and forth between her shoulder blades. She barely slowed down to see what everyone was gawking at.

Down the block at Hank and Frank's old place, Jill's car

was parked in the driveway. In a first-floor window, Molly could see the flickering light of a big-screen TV.

Stepping away from the window, she put a hand on the back of Angela's rocking chair. Molly remembered something else the now-dead Mrs. Dennehy had said to her yesterday.

"Do you think it's possible somebody is trying to pit us against each other?"

She easily blended in with the rest of the crowd loitering in front of the Dennehys' house. Another patrol car had come up the street and parked beside the TV news vehicles. For a while, the only thing the crowd had to look at was the furniture being unloaded from the moving van parked next door. But now, Lynette Hahn was giving them a show.

Standing on the Dennehys' front stoop as if the place were hers, Lynette held her youngest child, Dakota, in her arms while the TV news cameras rolled. "Angela was a wonderful mother, a great neighbor, and my dear, dear friend," she announced with tears in her eyes. She patted Dakota on the back. "It's such a tragedy, and so senseless. Two of the nicest kids you'd ever want to meet are now without a mother. We're on a cul-de-sac here. Angela moved from one cul-de-sac to another. You never think anything like this will happen to someone you know, someone you care about and love. But it just goes to show—until this maniac is caught, none of us who live on a cul-de-sac in the Seattle area is safe. . . ."

The crowd seemed pretty mesmerized. But then, what did they know, a bunch of idiots who had nothing better to do than follow TV news vans around?

They had no idea what Lynette Hahn was really like.

Courtney Hahn's former guidance counselor at the high school had referred to Lynette as a *"royal pain in the ass."*

She used to phone Ray Corson constantly with complaints—
and at his home, too. Why wasn't her daughter given the solo
in the school concert? How could the coach let Courtney sit
on the bench for the entire first half of the volleyball game?
Why did she only get a C+ on that English literature test?

Mr. Corson wrote in his notes after a parent-teacher conference with Lynette Hahn, to which she'd brought along
Dakota:

> *For someone who considers herself Supermom, she
> does very little to keep her kids in line. Dakota was a
> terror throughout the whole session. Lynette Hahn is
> one of those parents who suffers under the delusion
> that everyone should think their children are cute. It's
> as if the rest of the world has to make concessions for
> her coddled, bratty kids. No wonder Courtney's so
> screwed up and selfish. Lynette Hahn's brand of
> motherhood is helping to turn out a generation of
> spoiled snotty kids with an exaggerated sense of
> entitlement and no accountability. . . .*

Ray Corson wrote about the only time he met Courtney's
dad. It was another parent–teacher conference:

> *I don't like Jeremy Hahn at all. The guy is very
> arrogant. He had his BlackBerry on throughout the
> entire parent-teacher session. He made one call and
> took two—neither of which were related to his
> business or his daughter. For one of those calls, he
> was talking about getting tickets to a Mariners game.
> Courtney once told me that she thought her father
> cared more about his fancy car, his clothes, and his
> high-tech toys than he did for his family. I don't think
> she was exaggerating about him, and that's very
> disturbing. It gives credence to the more sordid*

things she has told me about her father—like his
fondness for teen porn (she claims he has a collection
of adult DVDs hidden in the back of a cabinet in his
study), and the way he sometimes looks at her
girlfriends. Courtney said her mother has totally
blinded herself to it. I thought she might be making it
up to get my attention & sympathy. Now, after
meeting the SOB, I'm not so sure. . . .

She observed Lynette Hahn in front of the Dennehys'
door, holding her daughter in her arms. "I'm just stunned,"
she told the TV newspeople, her voice choked with emotion.
"I'm overwhelmed with grief. . . ."

Watching Lynette in action, she wondered how the self-
delusional Supermom would handle the press next time—
when they'd be gathering outside her door.

Molly didn't say anything.

She just slumped back in her chair and smiled at Jeff,
who sat beside her at the head of the kitchen table. She held
on to his hand.

On the countertop behind her was a large Pagliacci Pizza
box with one piece of discarded crust in it and an emptied-
out salad container. Chris and Erin had cleared their plates
away. Erin was now parked in front of the TV in the family
room. Chris was upstairs in his room with Elvis, who had
stopped by after dinner.

It almost seemed like a normal night.

Jeff looked tired. He was finishing off his second glass of
merlot. As much as she could have used a nice, big glass of
wine, Molly had insisted she was in the mood for a 7UP. "I
get the worst headache after drinking wine lately," she'd
said. And Jeff had seemed to buy the excuse.

Apparently, Jeff had managed to catch an earlier plane.

There had been some confusion when the cops had gone to meet him at the gate at SeaTac for his original 3:55 flight. But it all got straightened out, and the police detectives interviewed Jeff in the living room for ninety minutes.

While the police were still talking to Jeff, Lynette and her tribe headed home. Molly thanked her for the lunch, for talking to the TV reporters, and for being such a good neighbor. She felt beholden to Lynette—until she caught her little speech on the 5:30 news. It was tough not to take it personally when Lynette said, *"Two of the nicest kids you'd ever want to meet are now without a mother."*

The TV news vans and the crowd of onlookers had dispersed a while ago. It was quiet out there now.

Molly didn't want to talk. She just wanted to sit and hold Jeff's hand.

The doorbell rang.

Molly closed her eyes. "Oh, go away," she muttered.

Jeff sighed, and got to his feet. "I'll get it. You stay put."

But Molly followed him into the front hallway and watched him open the door.

Chet Blazevich stood on the front stoop in jeans, a rumpled shirt, a jacket, and a tie. His short brown hair was a bit messy. He had his wallet out with his police ID to show Jeff. "Mr. Dennehy? I'm Detective Blazevich, Seattle Police."

Molly could tell from his stance that Jeff was tensing up. "Oh, c'mon, give me a break," he grumbled. "It's been a lousy day, and I've already spent two hours talking to you guys."

"My sympathies, Mr. Dennehy," he said. Then he glanced over Jeff's shoulder, and shyly smiled at her. "Actually, I was hoping to talk with you, Molly. It would just be a few minutes."

"Molly?" Jeff repeated, obviously confused.

Molly stepped toward the door, and put her hand on Jeff's shoulder. "Detective Blazevich and I are veterans of two

Neighborhood Watch potlucks at Lynette Hahn's house, which makes us like war buddies. Please, come in, Detective."

Jeff and the handsome cop awkwardly shook hands. Molly led him into the living room and offered him something to drink. All the while she wondered why he wanted to talk with her.

"No, thanks, I'm fine," Chet Blazevich said. "I just had a cup of coffee at the Hahns' house." He sat down in the easy chair while Molly and Jeff settled back on the sofa in front of the picture window. She put her hand on Jeff's knee and watched the detective take a little notebook and pen from his inside jacket pocket.

"Mrs. Hahn called me," he continued. "She wanted to tell me some things she thought might be relevant to our investigation into the deaths of the first Mrs. Dennehy, her companion, and his daughter."

"Angela went back to using her maiden name, which was Dwyer," Jeff said coolly.

Chet Blazevich nodded. "Thank you. Mrs. Hahn was telling me about some phone calls that *Ms. Dwyer* had been getting." He turned to Molly. "Apparently, Angela thought you might have been the one calling her."

"Yes, I know," Molly said. "I had lunch with Angela yesterday, and we straightened that out. I didn't make those calls. But I know Angela was concerned, because the calls were sort of threatening. I discussed this already with the two policemen who were here earlier today."

"Mrs. Hahn said that Angela had hired a private detective to uncover some information on your family, your brother in particular." He glanced at his notes and winced a little. "I haven't verified this yet, but according to Mrs. Hahn, Angela said your brother was responsible for shooting several people in a college in Evanston, Illinois."

"Oh, shit," Molly muttered angrily. She rubbed her forehead. She could still see Angela sitting across from her at their booth in the restaurant, a hand on her heart, so sincere: *"You should know, I haven't told anyone about your brother."*

She didn't want to think ill of the dead, but what a goddamn liar.

"Mrs. Dennehy?" the handsome cop asked, leaning forward.

"Nothing," Molly muttered. "Yes, that's true about my brother. He was mentally ill. He shot seven people in a cafeteria at a community college in Evanston. Two of those people died. Angela led me to believe she hadn't shared that information with anyone else."

"Mrs. Hahn said you accused Angela of breaking into her son's school locker and—"

"Yes, yes, I did, I accused her of that," Molly said, nodding emphatically. "And I accused her of smashing some pumpkins on our front stoop. I'm sure Lynette told you about that, too. During our lunch together, Angela claimed she didn't do any of it. And I believed her. Though now, I'm not so sure."

Beside her, Jeff restlessly shifted on the sofa. "I don't understand the purpose of these questions."

"I'm just trying to verify what Mrs. Hahn told me," Blazevich said.

"Well, I'm verifying it," Molly said edgily. "And if Mrs. Hahn told you that Angela and I really didn't like each other, I'll verify that, too."

"What is this anyway?" Jeff asked hotly. "Is my wife a suspect or something? Do you think she's in cahoots with the Cul-de-sac Killer?"

Chet Blazevich shook his head. "No, Mr. Dennehy. I'm just trying to cover all the bases here. I didn't mean to upset you folks, especially after what you've been through today. I just have one more question, and then I'll be out of your hair."

"Go ahead," Molly said with a sigh.

He looked at Jeff. "Where were you when you got the news about your ex-wife?"

Jeff hesitated.

Molly impatiently chimed in: "He's been in Washington, D.C., since Monday. He was staying at the Capital Hilton. I already told that to the two policemen I spoke with this afternoon."

Nodding, the handsome cop quickly got to his feet. "Well, thank you, Mr. Dennehy . . . Mrs. Dennehy. Once again, I'm sorry to have intruded on you during this difficult time." He stuffed his pen and notebook inside his jacket pocket.

Molly walked him to the door. "It sounds crazy, but should I be worried? Do the police really think I had anything to do with—"

"No, not at all," he assured her. "Like I say, I'm just following up on things."

Molly nodded, and opened the door for him. "Well, I apologize if I got a little snippy. It's been a long, tough day, and I'm a bit on edge. You're just doing your job."

"You shouldn't apologize," Blazevich said with a kind smile.

"You're damn right she shouldn't apologize," Jeff said, standing behind her.

Chet Blazevich nodded at him sheepishly. Then he turned and retreated down the walkway.

The November night air was chilly, but Molly remained in the doorway with her arms folded. Behind her, Jeff put his hands on her shoulders. She reached up and took hold of his hand. "You know, his last question reminded me of something," she said. "It's weird, but this morning, when you didn't pick up on your cell right away, I phoned the Capital Hilton. The operator said you weren't registered there."

"Oh, I should have let you know, this thing was at the other Hilton," Jeff said.

"Well, I've told the police you were at the Capital Hilton. You better let them know I had it wrong." She sighed. "That's all we need, one more thing to make us look suspicious."

Jeff gave her shoulders a squeeze. "Like Blazevich said, I wouldn't worry too much about it. C'mon, let's get inside. You'll catch your death standing here."

"In a minute," Molly murmured. She lingered in the doorway while Jeff headed toward the kitchen.

A cool breeze whipped through her, and she shuddered. Rubbing her arms, Molly watched the cop walk down the darkened cul-de-sac to his Toyota Camry. It was parked in front of Lynette's house.

There was room for only one car in his two-car garage. Every time he opened the big, automatic door, his neighbors probably caught a glimpse of the storage unit he'd built in there. One half of his garage had been boarded up from floor to ceiling. The reinforced, unpainted thick sheets of wood created another room—accessible through a thick door that had a padlock on it.

He'd made the most of the small space, creating a maze of closets and cabinets—most of them with padlocks on the doors. In one closet, he had jumpsuits and uniforms of every kind: janitor, paramedic, cable service, pest-control service, UPS delivery, and mailman—to name a few. There was also a cabinet exclusively dedicated to holding coils of rope, and duct tape—though lately, he'd come to rely on torn-up bedsheets in lieu of rope. Watching people rip apart the sheets from their linen closets to make their own restraints had become an important part of the ritual for him.

One door, which looked as if it led to another closet,

merely opened up to a wooden wall. On the wall he'd displayed several NO OUTLET and DEAD END signs. He'd hammered nails into that wooden wall, carefully spacing them like brackets so they held up the signs. He didn't want any glue or tape compromising the integrity of his trophies. Beneath each sign, he'd written in black laundry marker the dead-end street from which he'd taken it, the cul-de-sac where he'd *cleaned a house*, as he liked to think of it. He knew it was risky to hold on to such hard evidence, but he was sentimental.

Beneath the most recent NO OUTLET sign, he'd printed in block letters: LAUREL LANE.

He didn't have a dead-end sign from Alder Court in Bellevue.

That was because he'd never set foot on Alder Court in Bellevue. He didn't kill those people. It was staged to look like one of his killings. The person who had killed Angela Dennehy, Larry Keegan, and his daughter Taylor may have slit their throats, stuffed each body into a closet, left all the lights on, and stolen the NO OUTLET sign at the end of Alder Court. But it wasn't a cul-de-sac killing. The murderer of those three people had another agenda.

Could it be he'd had a personal or professional grudge against one of his victims?

According to all the early news stories, Larry Keegan had been divorced for four years, and his ex-wife, who had since remarried, was devastated by the news. His business associates spoke very highly of him, too.

That left Angela Dennehy. He couldn't help thinking that someone wanted her dead, and then made it look like a cul-de-sac killing. Perhaps Larry and Taylor were just collateral damage.

The hinges squeaked as he closed the door to his makeshift trophy case.

As far as he could tell, the police hadn't yet figured out

that the Alder Court murders were the work of a copycat. Right now, he was the only one who knew—along with the real murderer, of course.

Frowning, he put the padlock back on the door to his trophy case. He wasn't happy someone had decided to imitate him.

He'd have to do something about that.

Chapter Seventeen

Something hit the side of her car, and Molly flinched. She was driving back from the doctor's office, and about to turn onto Willow Tree Court. *Thwack!* It happened again, this time on her car door. "Good God, what is that?" she asked no one in particular.

She almost stepped on the brake, but a BMW was on her tail, and it was sure to rear-end her. So she kept moving, turning left onto the cul-de-sac. Out of the corner of her eye, she saw some movement in the vacant lot at the corner. It was Carson and Dakota Hahn—along with Jill's son, Darren. The little brats were throwing dirt balls at passing cars. Molly wanted to roll down her window and scream at them, but she was afraid she'd end up with a mouthful of dirt. So she just kept driving.

The doctor had agreed to squeeze her in for an appointment this afternoon. She'd gone on the sly while Jeff and the kids visited Trish to make funeral plans for Angela.

The latest cul-de-sac killings had been the top news story since yesterday. So the receptionist at the doctor's office had taken pity on Molly and not charged her for missing yesterday's appointment. The doctor had recommended an ob-gyn, with whom Molly now had an appointment in a month.

That seemed like such a long time away. Molly figured she'd wait until after Angela's funeral to tell Jeff about the baby.

As she turned into her driveway, she spotted a woman at her front stoop. A pretty brunette in her mid-thirties, she held a pie in her hands. Her jeans and the clingy waffle-pattern pale blue top showed off her trim, aerobicized figure. She came down the front walkway to meet her.

Molly climbed out of the car, and shut the door.

"Are you Mrs. Dennehy?" the woman asked.

Molly nodded. "Yes."

"I'm Rachel Cross, your new neighbor."

Molly smiled. "Oh, hello, it's nice to meet you."

"What happened to your door?" she asked, nodding at the car.

Molly glanced at the dirt smudges where Lynette's and Jill's brood had hit the bull's-eye with their dirt balls. "That's the handiwork of the little darlings down the block," Molly explained. "There's a vacant lot by the intersection at the end of the cul-de-sac, and the kids sometimes throw dirt balls at passing cars."

"Sweet," Rachel said. "Well, I stand warned. I'll make sure to drive with the windows rolled up."

"Good idea," Molly said. She smiled at her. "I'm Molly, by the way. Is that pie for us?"

"Yes, it's apple," Rachel said. "I made it myself—that is, if removing it from the bakery box and covering the pie with Handi-Wrap constitutes making it."

Molly took the pie from her. "In my book, it does, definitely. This is so nice of you. I should be bringing a pie over to you, welcoming you to the neighborhood."

"Well, I heard the news about your husband's first wife, and according to the mailman, her kids live with you now. So—well, my mother always used to bring a pie over to the neighbors if there was an illness or a death in the family."

"That's sweet, thank you. And it's good to know the mailman has his finger on the pulse of what's happening around here. Too bad he can't always get the mail to the right address—which reminds me, I have something for you. . . ." Molly balanced the pie in one hand while she unlocked the door. "Would you like to come in?"

"Oh, thanks," Rachel said, shaking her head. "But I still have a ton of unpacking to do."

"Be right back." Molly scurried inside the house. She set the pie down on the kitchen counter, then grabbed the mail—rubber-banded together—that she'd gotten by mistake. There were only five pieces of mail, mostly junk; but there was something that looked like a personal letter. She left the door open as she brought it back outside to Rachel. "We got these by mistake last week. They're addressed to you."

"Well, that's mighty neighborly of you to keep them for me," Rachel said. "And about that pie, the woman at the bakery said if you heat it in a conventional oven for fifteen minutes before serving, it's incredible."

Molly nodded. "Thanks again, Rachel. I hope you'll take a rain check, and drop in any time."

Rachel gave her a nervous smile and shrugged. "I'm glad to hear you say that. I don't know a lot of people in Seattle. I moved here from Tampa, Florida. I looked at a map of the United States and figured Seattle was just about as far as I could get from Tampa—and my ex-husband."

"Sounds like an interesting story," Molly said.

She nodded. "We'll save it for some snowy night by the fire. Anyway, I dealt with this Realtor over the phone, and he sent me photos of the house over the Internet. I fell in love with it while I was still in Florida. I didn't hear about these—these cul-de-sac murders until after I bought the house." She let out a long sigh. "I'm a little nervous about being alone in a new place as it is. I feel a lot better knowing I have a nice neighbor next door."

"Well, vice versa," Molly said with a smile. "Feel free to call up if you ever get scared or you need anything."

Rachel nodded and waved to her as she started down the walkway. "Nice meeting you, Molly!"

As Molly waved back, she remembered her last conversation with Kay, in which she had promised to be Kay's Neighborhood Watch buddy.

Molly's smile waned.

Stepping inside, she closed the door and went back to the kitchen. The pie looked pretty damn good. She wondered if she should give in to her craving and have a slice. She was searching through the utensil drawer for a knife when the phone rang.

Molly snatched up the receiver. "Yes, hello?"

There was no response on the other end.

"Hello?" she repeated.

"Ask him where he really was," a woman whispered.

"What?"

The woman didn't reply. But Molly heard her breathing—like someone with asthma.

"Who is this?" Molly asked.

She heard a click on the other end of the line and then nothing.

The next afternoon, Jeff and Chris drove to Northgate Mall so Chris could get a decent suit for the funeral. The services were delayed until next week because of the autopsy.

Molly planned to work on her latest painting, still in the early stages. It was for a national soft-drink company's print ad. The client wanted an illustration with twenty people, all drinking cola at a party; but each person was from a certain period from the 1920s to the current day. It was to represent the ninety years people had been enjoying that soft drink brand. Molly thought it was a corny idea, but the money and the exposure were good.

From the basement she'd gotten Erin some watercolors and paper, so they could work together up in her studio. If the phone rang, she'd let the machine answer it.

She was still a little unhinged by yesterday's call, mostly because Angela had gotten those strange phone calls not long before she'd been murdered. Molly had told Jeff about it: " 'Ask him where he really was.' What do you suppose she meant by that?"

Jeff had seemed unfazed. "Yesterday, we got how many hang-ups and how many people calling just to hear our voices? We're in the news, and we're in the phone book, not a good combination. We're going to get some weird calls. You really need to screen them, hon."

Molly had taken his advice today. There had been several hang-ups.

She and Erin were about to head upstairs when she heard shrieking outside. It sounded like Carson and Dakota Hahn.

Molly peered out the living room window and gasped.

A man was running up the cul-de-sac with Dakota Hahn in his arms. Screaming and squirming, she was covered with blood and dirt.

"Stay here," Molly said to Erin.

She hurried outside. Next door, Rachel stepped out of the house as well.

Molly raced up the walkway. She saw Carson and Darren trailing behind the man, crying. They had blood all over their hands. Carson stumbled and fell on the pavement. He let out a loud wail.

Molly ran out to the street and scooped him up. The sleeve of his jacket was torn, and Molly could see blood. It looked like he'd skinned his arm in the fall. He was crying so hard, he couldn't seem to get a breath.

The man holding Dakota swiveled around to face her. He was about thirty, and borderline handsome, with wavy dark blond hair and a cleft in his chin. He looked panic stricken. "Are you the mother?" he asked, over the children's screams.

Breathless, Molly gaped at him—and then at Dakota, whose chubby, dirt-smudged face was lined with bloody scratches. She wouldn't stop shrieking.

"Are you the mother?" the stranger repeated, louder this time.

With Carson writhing in her arms, Molly shook her head and pointed to Lynette's house. "They live over there. What happened?"

"I don't know," the stranger yelled. "I was driving by, and I heard the screams. Then I saw the kids on that lot at the corner, and they were bleeding—"

"Ye gods, look, he's got pieces of glass in his hands!" Rachel exclaimed. Hovering over Jill's son, Darren, she held him by his wrists. The plump, brown-haired six-year-old wriggled in her grasp and cried softly—a miserable staccato moan.

Within moments, Lynette and Jill ran out of their respective houses, adding to the chorus of screams. Lynette tried to take Dakota from the Good Samaritan stranger, but when her daughter reached up to wrap a hand around her mother's neck, the glass embedded in her palm scratched her. Lynette automatically recoiled.

"God, now you're bleeding, too," the man said. "Better let me carry her inside. . . ."

Jill looked slightly crazed with her unkempt auburn hair and her too-tight black tee and purple pajama pants. She practically pushed Rachel out of the way to tend to her son. "What happened?" she demanded to know, grabbing him by the wrist. She examined his hands. "Who did this?"

"We were just playing!" Darren sobbed. "The dirt had glass in it. . . ."

Jill rushed Darren to her house at the end of the block.

Once inside Lynette's house, the stranger propped Dakota on the kitchen counter near the sink. Molly sat Carson down in a chair at the breakfast table. She carefully peeled off his jacket and checked the scrape on his arm from when he fell. It wasn't too bad. She kept telling him that he would be all right, and he calmed down a little. His jacket got the worst of it. Then she looked at his hands. Past the blood and dirt, she could see about three little pieces of glass in one hand, and two in the other. His right-hand index finger had a bad cut on it. "We'll need some tweezers, Lynette," she announced.

Running water over some paper towels, Lynette didn't seem to hear her past Dakota's incessant screams. The stranger held the little girl's arms down while Lynette cleaned off her scratched, filthy face.

Molly had a pretty good idea of what must have happened. Obviously, the kids were in the vacant lot again, scooping up dirt balls to hurl at passing cars. They must have stumbled upon a patch of dirt with broken glass scattered about.

Molly glanced over at Rachel, standing in the doorway to Lynette's kitchen, wringing her hands. "Do you need some antiseptic?" she asked, over Dakota's sobbing. "I have Neosporin at home. . . ."

Lynette didn't seem to be listening. She put down the wet paper towel and reached for her daughter. "You're scaring her," she snapped at the man. "I've got her now. There, there, sweetie . . ."

"That's Lynette's way of saying thank you," Molly murmured to the man. Lynette didn't seem to catch the remark. Molly led Carson to the sink and ran his hands under the water.

Lynette turned toward her. "Did you do this?" she hissed.

Molly frowned at her. "Of course not, my God. . . ."

"You're always complaining about the kids playing in that lot. Maybe you decided to do something about it—"

"Lynette, I wouldn't plant broken glass in there. Give me a break."

Yet Molly wouldn't have been surprised if someone whose car had been pelted by dirt balls often enough had scattered the glass in that spot—perhaps someone on the cross street. Or maybe some slob had just tossed a bunch of bottles out of a car passing by the lot.

Lynette turned to Rachel and the man. "I've got it under control, people. I'm fine. You can go now."

"Well, you're welcome, and it was awfully nice meeting you," Rachel said, with a jaunty little salute. "We'll see ourselves out."

The blond-haired stranger just looked baffled as he sheepishly followed Rachel out the door.

"Lynette, that was our new neighbor, Rachel Cross," Molly said, rinsing Carson's hands under the cold water. With her fingernails, she carefully picked out some of the bits of glass. The bleeding wasn't bad, but Carson kept squirming. "And the man was a total stranger who stopped to rescue your injured children. He got his jacket all bloody carrying your daughter around, and all you did was snap at him like he was your indentured servant. I know you're under duress, but really, a thank-you might have been nice."

"I'm pretty sure what this is all about," Lynette whispered, rocking Dakota in her arms. "Well, I'm sorry, but I felt it was my duty to talk to that police detective the other night. I wasn't looking to get you in trouble."

"You didn't get me into trouble," Molly said. "So don't worry about it." She gently dabbed Carson's hands with a paper towel. "He's going to need some antiseptic on this scrape from when he fell. . . ."

"So—you expect me to believe you're not upset?" Lynette pressed. "And you're not the one who called me?"

"What are you talking about?" Molly asked, concerned. "What call?"

Lynette quickly shook her head. "Nothing, forget it. I—I can carry on from here." She nodded toward the door. *"Thank you,* Molly."

Her tone sounded more like a *fuck you* than a *thank you.* But Molly just let it go. She needed to get home to Erin. She quickly dried off her hands and then headed for the door. Outside, she found Rachel standing at the end of the Hahns' driveway. "Are the kids okay?" Rachel asked.

Molly nodded tiredly. "Where did that man go?"

"Oh, he slinked off into the sunset with his tail between his legs." She nodded toward Lynette's house. "Well, I'm not too crazy about her. I can't believe she actually accused you of cutting up her kids. Who would do something like that? And the other one—with the chubby kid who looks like Pugsley on *The Addams Family*—she practically gave me a full body check to get at her kid. I guess I shouldn't judge them during a situation like this."

"Oh, you'll find once you really get to know them—"

"That they're both bitches?" Rachel finished for her.

Molly laughed.

"Seriously," Rachel said. "I think you're the only nice person on this block. I mean, look over there at that one." She nodded toward the Nguyens' house. "After all the screaming and commotion, it was enough to wake the dead. You'd figure any normal person would offer to help—or at least be curious about what happened. But she didn't even bother to step outside."

Molly noticed Natalie in the second-floor window. She was slouched in a rocker with one leg over the chair arm. It looked like she was reading a magazine.

He glanced in his rearview mirror at the turnoff to Willow Tree Court.

He'd known beforehand that it was a cul-de-sac. Lynette Hahn had told him—on the TV news, when she'd talked to reporters in front of her dead friend's former residence: *"We're on a cul-de-sac here. Angela moved from one cul-de-sac to another. You never think anything like this will happen to someone you know, someone you care about and love. . . ."*

The brief news clip hadn't given him a very good idea of the street's layout. It wasn't until last night, when he'd done a brief survey, that he realized most of the houses on the street were at the edge of a forest. He liked that. And the vacant lots—two of them with half-built houses—gave him so many places to hide while he studied the habits of the residents.

Of course, the house that piqued his interest the most was the Dennehys'. Angela's ex-husband seemed like the most logical suspect in the Alder Court murders. The man in the driver's seat intended to find his copycat—which meant watching the house and following around the ex-husband.

With Willow Tree Court behind him now, he studied the road ahead. It was starting to get dark. He switched on his headlights.

He glanced down at his beige jacket—at the blood on his sleeves.

Lynette Hahn's little brat had bled on him. That was what he got for being a hero. He wondered if the broken glass scattered through that lot had been planted there on purpose. Perhaps someone had a grudge against Lynette and her children. Did the same person have a grudge against Angela Dennehy?

Maybe he wasn't the only one with a score to settle on Willow Tree Court.

He rather liked the cul-de-sac. He'd already been inside the Hahns' place. He thought about coming back. Or maybe he'd find a way to get inside one of the other homes—a night visit.

He glanced at the stains on his sleeves again.

Funny, he was usually so careful when he left a cul-de-sac. He hardly ever had a speck of blood on him.

CHAPTER EIGHTEEN

He caught only fleeting glimpses of her. She was down on her knees, working in the garden on the other side of the bushes. He couldn't really tell what she looked like. In the middle of the backyard with the rake in his hand, he was too far away.

Chris was curious about her—maybe because Molly had mentioned at dinner the other night that the new neighbor was "quite a dish." She and Molly were getting to be fast friends. Molly had nothing nice to say about the other two women who moved onto the cul-de-sac over the summer: Jill Somebody and Natalie Something. Chris still hadn't met either one yet. He'd only seen Jill at a distance—or in her car. And he'd yet to lay eyes on the unfriendly jogger woman, Natalie. He figured he'd probably meet them eventually. He wasn't in any hurry.

But he was kind of intrigued by this Rachel person. Through the foliage, he could just make out that she had brown hair and fair skin.

Chris wiped the sweat off his forehead and went back to work. His dad had asked him to do something about all the leaves in the backyard. They were having people over for brunch after the funeral on Tuesday. Molly was freaking out, deep-cleaning every room in the house. Apparently, she wanted it looking immaculate, which didn't make any sense. If ever they had a good excuse for letting the place go to shit for a few days, it was now. Chris imagined telling company, *"Sorry I didn't get around to raking the backyard, but my mother died."*

It was nuts, because he just wanted to be alone to think about his mom—and maybe even have a good cry. Instead, he was running around doing all these chores for the wake tomorrow and the funeral the next day, and the reception after the funeral. They were busting their humps to make sure they were—as Molly put it—"dressed to the nines" in different outfits for each service. She needed to prepare about a dozen different dishes for the brunch, and his dad was stocking up on booze for the fifty or so guests. And the place had to look like *House Beautiful.* All these distant relatives and old friends his dad hadn't talked to in years were coming to this thing. Were they ever going to see these people again? Chris wondered if these "mourners" would have cared as much or even known about his mom dying if she hadn't been murdered.

As he raked the leaves into a big pile, it occurred to him that his mom—more than anybody—would want them to put on a first-class funeral and brunch for her. She was always big on impressing people and keeping up appearances.

He was doing this for her. Suddenly it mattered that the backyard looked nice. He felt tears in his eyes, but kept on working.

Up until last year, he'd attended only two funerals in his whole life—and both of those were for grandparents. His mother's funeral on Tuesday would be his third in six months: first Mr. Corson, then Mrs. Garvey, and now his mom. He still felt awful every time he thought about what Mr. Corson's sister and his widow had said to him. He knew it was stupid, but he couldn't help wondering if they were right. Maybe he was just a lousy guy, and his mother's murder was some kind of karmic punishment directed at him.

He wished like hell for another dull weekend in Bellevue, another night on Larry's lumpy foldout bed in the mallard shrine of a study, just one more weekend with his mom.

"Hey, how's it going over there?"

Chris glanced over toward the neighbor's yard. At a break in the bushes dividing their yards, the pretty brunette smiled at him. She wore a gray sweatshirt, jeans, and gardening gloves. "Are you Chris?" she asked.

He quickly wiped the tears from his eyes. "Hi, yeah, hi," he replied awkwardly. With the rake in his hand, he stepped over toward her.

"I'm Rachel," the woman said. "I was really sorry to hear about your mom."

He nodded. "You're the one who brought over the apple pie, right? It was really good, thanks."

"Well, you're very welcome," she said. "I got to meet Erin the other day. Now, except for your dad, I've met the whole family."

"Dad's at the office today," Chris explained. "He figured he'd catch up on stuff for a few hours while it was dead there, being Sunday and all."

Frowning, she glanced past him at the yard. "Are you burning leaves?"

He shook his head.

"Oh, I thought I smelled smoke. Well, the yard's looking good. Maybe next summer, if you've got time, you could mow the front and back here. No pressure. Knock it around and name your price. We can haggle over it later."

"That sounds good. I used to mow the lawn for Mrs. Garvey."

"Garvey?" She seemed puzzled for a moment. "Oh, of course, *Garvey*, that's the woman who used to live here—

with a teenage daughter. The Realtor told me about her. Were you close to the daughter?"

Chris shrugged. "We hung out sometimes. I haven't really seen her since she moved in with her dad and her stepmother."

Rachel blinked. "Oh, really? What happened to her mother?"

"Well, she's dead," Chris replied, matter-of-factly. Then he saw her stunned expression and immediately regretted it. "I'm sorry. Didn't you know that? There was an accident. Mrs. Garvey fell and hit her head."

Rachel stared at him. "In the house? My God, did she die in the house?"

He gulped. "I'm sorry, I figured you knew. . . ."

She shook her head. "That damn Realtor, he should have told me," she muttered. "I think he's legally obligated to inform me, the son of a . . ." She trailed off, and rubbed her forehead. "I'm sorry, Chris. Do you know what room she died in?"

He hesitated.

"No, don't tell me." She put up her gloved hand. "I don't want to know. Besides, I already have a feeling where. I'll bet it happened in the big bedroom. There's a cold spot in there, right by the door. I get chills every time I stand there."

Chris just stared at her. He couldn't believe it. From what he'd heard, that was exactly where Mrs. Garvey had fallen and bashed her head.

"I'm sorry," she said with a long sigh. "I don't mean to act like such a baby about it—especially in front of you, after what you've been through. It's still a beautiful home. I'll just hire a shaman and have the place smudged and blessed."

She made a face, wrinkling her nose. "Somebody's burning leaves, because I can smell it. Can't you?"

Chris glanced over her shoulder and saw black smoke billowing out from the other side of her screened porch. "Oh, Jesus!" he cried. "The house. . . ."

Rachel turned and let out a scream, "Oh, my God!"

Without thinking, Chris tore through the bushes and rushed past her. From working in Mrs. Garvey's yard, he knew the hose connection was by the screen-porch door. As he got closer to the house, the smoke became thicker. Every time he took in a breath, he tasted it. He heard a crackling sound. "Call nine-one-one!" he yelled.

"I don't have my cell phone with me!" Rachel replied helplessly. "Oh, God. . . ."

"Our back door's open. Use our phone!" Chris reached the outside spigot and saw the garden hose was connected to it. He quickly twisted the valve open. With a hiss, water shot out of the nozzle end. Grabbing the hose, he ran around to the other side of the screen porch, toward all the smoke. He prayed the hose was long enough and didn't snag on him.

"Chris, be careful!" he heard her call.

His eyes hurt, and he tried to hold his breath as he got the hose ready. He suddenly stopped in his tracks. The smoke wasn't coming from the house, but from Mrs. Garvey's tool-shed—about ten feet away from the screened porch. A rope of fire shot up from a pile of what looked like old newspapers by the shed's door. Little scraps of burning paper floated around the shed. Flames licked at the mossy roof, creating plumes of black smoke. But the roof hadn't caught on fire yet.

Coughing, Chris staggered back from the smoke. He directed the hose toward the shed—aiming near the roof and working his way down the line of fire. For a few moments, it didn't seem to do any good. The smoke only grew thicker. But then the flames started dying under the jet spray of water.

Chris heard Rachel clearing her throat, and he glanced over his shoulder. "It's okay," he gasped. "I think we've got it under control. Did you call nine-one-one?"

"No, I didn't want to leave you out here all alone." She fanned the air in front of her face.

Chris kept the hose on, dousing the side of the shed. The smoke started to clear. The corner of the little shed was charred black; it looked like the shadow of a ghost against the blistered wood. At the base of the door, amid a smoldering pile of soot, he could see some patches of wet newspaper that hadn't burned up.

Chris finally twisted the hose nozzle, shutting off the flow of water.

"God, thank you, Chris," Rachael said, squeezing his arm. "You're a lifesaver. I wouldn't have known what to do. Hell, I didn't have a clue! If you weren't here, I think the whole house might have burned down."

She took a step toward the shed. "What is that anyway?" she asked, pointing to the mound of refuse by the door. "That wasn't there earlier. I walked by this shed a half hour ago and didn't see any newspapers there. What's going on? Did you see anybody else out here?"

Chris just shrugged and shook his head.

"This is crazy," she muttered, a hand at the base of her throat. "They—they must have snuck back here while I was planting the annuals. I don't understand. Why would anybody do something like this?"

"I don't know," Chris said, baffled.

"Is this normal around here?" she pressed. "I mean, two days ago, those kids got cut up by all that glass in the vacant lot, and now, someone decided to set fire to my toolshed. What's going on?"

Chris glanced over at the mound of burnt debris by the shed's door.

He had no idea how to answer her.

Molly wondered where Lynette Hahn was.

Despite some residual tension after the glass-in-the-dirt

incident, Lynette had offered to co-host the funeral brunch. Bizarre as the arrangement was, it made sense to Molly that Angela's best friend play hostess in Angela's old house. Molly really didn't mind taking on the role of caterer. It kept her busy—and gave her an excuse to keep the awkward small talk with Angela's friends and relatives down to a minimum. Lynette had invited some of Larry's friends, too.

A light, misty rain had descended on the burial service in Lakeview Cemetery, where Jeff and Chris remained stoic and unshielded by the drizzle. But Erin sobbed quietly from and clung to her Aunt Trish, who held a red umbrella for both of them. Molly stood behind Trish.

Lynette's husband, Jeremy, had a sudden business thing and couldn't attend. But Lynette promised he would be at the Dennehys' in plenty of time to set up the bar and start passing out drinks to the first arrivals. She'd brought Carson and Dakota to the cemetery. They were fidgety as ever, fighting over their umbrella and picking at the Band-Aids on their hands. Courtney had her iPhone out most of the time, texting through most of the service.

Molly slipped away early to set up for the reception. She'd asked Rachel if she would like to attend. "Thanks anyway," Rachel had told her. "I didn't even know Angela. Besides, I'm giving Lynette and her kids a wide berth for a while. I can't help thinking those kids had something to do with my toolshed catching on fire. It's not that big a leap from throwing dirt balls at cars to playing with matches and setting toolsheds on fire. The cops said it was definitely arson—and sloppy arson, at that."

Just the same, Rachel had been nice enough to make a rice salad for the party—wild rice with sun-dried cranberries, smoked turkey, and green onion. Giving in to a craving, Molly had had three helpings that morning before the funeral.

She'd managed to set out all the food and plates before the first wave of guests started drifting in. Jeremy Hahn had never shown up, and Molly had played bartender for the first half hour—until Jeff had taken over, thank God.

Now she was playing hostess and fighting some morning sickness as she smiled through several Angela stories told to her by total strangers. For two hours, she made sure her guests' glasses were filled and took their empty plates. All the while, she wondered what the hell had happened to Lynette. She even asked a few people. Apparently, Lynette and the three kids had disappeared right after the burial.

Molly started to feel so sick and light-headed that she snuck upstairs to lie down. But there were about forty coats piled on Jeff's and her bed. Some woman—Molly was pretty sure she was Angela's cousin—was breast-feeding her baby in Erin's room. A man she didn't recognize was sitting on one of the twin beds in the guest room, talking on his cell phone. Chris's door was closed. She knocked and poked her head in. Chris was at his desk, and Elvis sat in the beanbag chair. They both had beers and plates of food. Chris's sweet, four-eyed portly pal gave her a goofy smile. "Hi, Mrs. Dennehy. Great rice salad!"

"Thanks, Elvis," she said weakly. She turned to Chris. "If your dad should ask, I'm not feeling well. I'm going upstairs to rest for a few minutes. And I never saw the beers."

She closed the door, and heard Elvis call out: "Thanks, Mrs. Dennehy!"

As she turned away, Molly almost bumped into Jill Emory standing at the top of the stairs. The tawny-haired forty-year-old wore a loose black pantsuit that camouflaged her plump figure. She was frowning at Molly. "Why did you leave the cemetery early?" she asked.

Molly put a hand over her mouth and suppressed a burp. "I beg your pardon, Jill?"

"You left before the burial service ended. Why?"

"To set the food out for this stupid reception," Molly shot back. She was feeling too sickly to be patient with her. "And I could have used some help from Lynette—or you. The two of you were better friends with Angela than I ever was. Where is Lynette anyway? Where's Jeremy?"

"Oh, like you don't know," Jill sneered.

"What's that supposed to mean?"

"Lynette says you've always resented her, because she was best friends with Angela. You've always been out to get her."

"I don't understand—"

"One of the reporters told Lynette that a woman phoned the police with a tip. The anonymous call came in not very long after you left the cemetery."

"What tip? What are you talking about?"

"I was just on the phone with Lynette," Jill said, clutching the post at the top of the stairs. "She's still at the police station. She said the whole thing was a frame-up. The reporters were tipped off, too. They were waiting outside the hotel when the police brought Jeremy down in the elevator with that prostitute. Are you trying to tell me you had nothing to do with it?"

Molly shook her head. She almost wanted to laugh, she was so stunned. "So Jeremy Hahn was arrested—for buying himself a hooker? Was that his 'sudden business thing'? Is that why he missed the funeral?" All she could think was, *What an asshole, he deserved to be arrested!*

At the same time, Molly wondered why the police and re-porters were treating the incident as if it were a major sting operation.

Jill didn't explain why.

Molly had to wait for an explanation from a reporter on the six o'clock news. It was a bit surreal to see the story unfold on television while two TV news vans were parked in front of Lynette's house down the block. About a dozen people loitered in front of Lynette's to see what the fuss was about.

On TV, the pretty, thirtysomething blond reporter wasn't posted outside Lynette's house. Instead, she stood in the light drizzle in front of the W Hotel, speaking into her handheld microphone: *"Seattle Police arrested local businessman Jeremy Hahn at the W Hotel this afternoon, after receiving an anonymous tip that Hahn, an executive vice president for Sea-Merit Financial, was engaged in sexual activity with a minor in one of the rooms. . . ."*

The image on the TV screen switched to show two uni-formed officers leading Lynette's handcuffed husband into a police car, parked in front of the luxury hotel. Jeremy looked angry. His casual Brooks Brothers clothes were disheveled and his thinning brown hair was uncombed so the bald spots weren't covered. Behind him, a young woman in a Catholic schoolgirl uniform was being led out of the hotel as well. But her face had been blurred digitally, which of course, made the scene appear even more lurid.

"We've protected the identity of the minor," the reporter said. *"But police sources say she is sixteen, and accepted money from Hahn in exchange for sexual favors."*

The picture switched back to the blond reporter in front of the hotel. *"I'm told the police found a substantial amount of cocaine in the hotel room—along with some child pornography. This will only add to the number of serious charges Jeremy Hahn is already facing. . . ."*

On another local newscast, they indicated that Sea-Merit Financial would be investigating if Hahn had used company funds for his sexual trysts with underage girls.

Even though she hated her guts, all Molly could think was, *Poor Lynette*.

The house was still a disaster area from the party. As she moved into the living room, Molly turned a blind eye to the dirty plates, cups, and glasses on every table. Instead, she gazed out the window at the TV news vans and the people in front of Lynette's house.

She remembered Lynette coming to her rescue, dropping by with McDonald's and her take-charge attitude the day after Angela's murder. Molly still had some food left over from the party. Taking over some dinner to the Hahns would have been the neighborly thing to do. But like Rachel, she was giving Lynette a wide berth today. After all, Lynette clearly blamed her for Jeremy's arrest—all because some woman had phoned in that tip to the police.

Molly remembered once again something Angela had told her over lunch on the last day of her life: *"Someone else is behind this, some woman. . . . Do you think it's possible somebody is trying to pit us against each other?"*

Staring out at the Hahns' house, Molly spotted a jogger in a sweat suit running up the street. It was Natalie, from down the block, out for her run—at night this time. She seemed to ignore the news vans and the onlookers outside Lynette's.

Molly recalled her doing the exact same thing last week, when the TV trucks and gawkers were there because of Angela's murder. Natalie had jogged by, barely glancing at them.

It was almost as if on both occasions Natalie knew ahead of time they'd be there.

CHAPTER NINETEEN

Molly wasn't thinking when she answered her cell phone.

Since Angela's murder, she'd been screening nearly all incoming calls on the house line. But this call had come in at eight-thirty that night, and she was dead tired. With some help from Jeff, Chris, and Elvis, she'd cleaned up most of the mess from the party.

She was trying to pay bills online in Jeff's study but kept nodding off in front of the monitor. She had her cell phone on his desk, so when it rang, it startled her. She grabbed it and switched it on: "Yes, hello?"

"Mrs. Dennehy?" It was a woman on the other end of the line. Her voice sounded raspy, almost demented in the singsong way she talked.

Molly quickly took the cell phone away from her ear and glanced at the caller ID box. The number was blocked.

"Who is this?" she asked.

"Mrs. Dennehy, ask your husband where he was when his ex-wife was murdered."

Then there was a click.

Molly stared at the phone in her hand. She knew it was the same woman who had called last week. *"Ask him where he really was,"* had been the message. This time, the woman was less cryptic.

Chances were pretty good the same woman had phoned Angela and threatened her. Maybe she'd also tipped off the police regarding Jeremy Hahn's clandestine activities, too.

The scary thing about it was this woman had known something about Lynette's husband that even Lynette didn't know. What did she have on Jeff?

Molly got to her feet and wandered into the family room. Jeff was asleep in his easy chair in front of a reality show on TV. It had been a long, grueling day for everyone, and she didn't want to wake him and grill him about where he'd been on the night of Angela's murder.

Molly remembered the mixup about which Washington, D.C., Hilton Jeff had stayed at that week. He said he hadn't been at the Capital Hilton that trip, but at another Hilton hotel.

Retreating back to Jeff's study, she went on the Internet to refresh her memory about the three other Hilton hotels in Washington, D.C. She called the Washington Hilton in Dupont Circle and got the operator.

"Hi, I'm not sure if I have the right Washington Hilton," Molly said. "But my husband was staying at a Hilton last week. He checked out Wednesday morning. He thinks he left his iPod in his room. I'm trying to track it down. Could you check if I have the right Hilton? His name is Dennehy, Jeffrey." She spelled it, and waited.

She knew the business, and hotel clerks sometimes got calls like this from wives, trying to get the goods on cheating husbands. If the clerks were smart and discreet enough, they often came back with, "We're sorry, we can't give out that kind of information." But most of the time, the hotel clerk really didn't give a damn if they were getting some cheating spouse in trouble.

"Mrs. Dennehy?" the clerk said after a minute. "I'm

sorry, but we have no record of Jeffrey Dennehy staying here last week. You might try the Capital Hilton on Sixteenth."

"I will," Molly said. "Thank you." Then she clicked off.

The Capital Hilton wasn't where Jeff had been staying. She knew that much. So Molly called the Hilton Washington Embassy Row on Massachusetts Avenue, and the Hilton Garden Inn on Fourteenth Street Northwest. She gave them the same story and got the same answer.

Jeff wasn't staying at any of the Hilton Hotels in Washington, D.C., on the night of Angela's death.

Molly kept thinking about that woman with the raspy voice.

Ask him where he really was.

She waited until morning to ask him.

Jeff had finished with his shower, and he was shaving in front of the mirror with a towel around his waist. Her arms folded, Molly stood in the bathroom doorway in her nightgown. She studied his reflection in the steamy mirror. He kept wiping it with his hand every few moments. He still had shaving cream on one side of his jaw and on his neck.

"I was at the Hilton on Dupont Circle," he said, eying her in the mirror for a moment. He worked the safety razor under his chin. "They just don't give out information like that. Jesus, Molly, I can't believe you called all the Hiltons in D.C. Why didn't you just ask me?"

"Because I think you're covering something up—something really horrible," she admitted.

His reflection gazed back at her with a raised eyebrow. "Like what? Don't tell me you think I killed Angela. . . ."

"No, but the police might think that," she replied steadily, "especially if they realize you're lying about where you were that night. Jeff, what's to keep this woman from calling the police and saying to them what she said to me?"

He nicked himself. Blood oozed from the cut along his left jaw. "Oh, crap, now look what you've made me do," he grumbled. He plucked a Kleenex from the dispenser on the counter and dabbed it on the cut. "Here we go with that whack-job woman caller again. I told you that we'd get some crank calls—"

"Jeff, Angela was getting calls the week before she was killed—from a woman, telling her that she was *going to pay for what she did.*"

"Well, what the hell is that supposed to mean?" Jeff countered, dabbing the cut again. "What exactly did Angela do? Are you telling me this crazy woman caller is somehow working with the Cul-de-sac Killer?"

Molly hesitated. She didn't know how to answer him.

"You told me yourself that Angela lied to you during that lunch. Didn't she give you some song and dance about not telling anyone about your brother?"

"Well, maybe not everything she said was a lie," Molly murmured.

He washed off his face, grabbed another Kleenex, tore off a piece, and applied it to his cut. "Listen, Molly." He sighed, pat-drying his face. "Do me a favor and screen all your calls from now on. You're letting this nutcase get to you, and I'm sorry, honey, but I don't need this shit, not now."

Molly stepped aside as he brushed past her in the bathroom doorway. He whipped off his towel and tossed it on the bed. After pulling a clean pair of boxer shorts from his dresser, he slammed the drawer shut. He stepped into the shorts and let the elastic banding go snap against his torso as he finished putting them on. "Yesterday, I buried the mother of my children, and now I have to schlep my ass to work. Can we cease and desist with all the questions? I wouldn't have told the police I was at the Hilton in D.C. if I wasn't really there. They seemed to believe me. Why the hell can't you?"

Molly opened her mouth to speak but hesitated. She retrieved her robe from the foot of their bed and put it on. "I'll go start the coffee and make sure the kids are up." She sighed. Then she headed out of the bedroom.

It was strange to see Courtney behind the wheel of her Neon without an iPhone in her hand.

Chris had been surprised to hear her car horn honking this morning. He'd figured after her father's arrest yesterday afternoon, she wouldn't be showing her face at school today. But there she was, waiting in the driveway for him.

"I know everybody will be gossiping about me," she muttered, pulling out of the cul-de-sac. "I was going to stay home for a day or two, but then I figured I might as well go to school and get it over with. Plus my mother's driving me crazy. I'm ready to kill her."

Courtney may have texted and Twittered up a storm at his mom's funeral, but her family's public humiliation had shut down all communications since yesterday afternoon. Courtney's last Facebook update had been two nights ago. She was very subdued today. She wore a black pullover sweater and jeans, and her blond hair was pulled back in a ponytail. It looked like she wasn't wearing any makeup at all. Chris kind of liked her better without it.

"I'm sorry about your dad," he said, slouching in the passenger seat. "Must have been a real shock for you. That's a raw deal."

"I wasn't too shocked," she said, eying the road ahead. "I mean, he never did anything weird with me, nothing I remember, at least. Still, I've always suspected my father had a—a thing for young girls. But it was just too creepy for me to even think about. I didn't tell anybody—except Mr. Corson." She glanced at him briefly. "Can I confess something to you? I was kind of jealous of what you and Mr. Corson had. I could have used a—a regular father figure. I was kind of hoping Mr. Corson would pay more attention to me if I dug deep and told him something really, really personal like that. Then again, I guess we all spilled our guts to him, didn't we?"

"I wouldn't mind having Mr. Corson to lean on right now," Chris said—almost under his breath.

If Courtney heard him, she didn't say anything.

They approached a stoplight. Courtney came to a stop, and she let out a long sigh. "Well, I guess between your mom getting murdered and my dad getting arrested, you and I are going to be the focus of attention at school today."

Chris smiled sadly. "You usually like being the center of attention," he remarked.

"Not this time, Chris," she replied. "Not this time."

"You can't rush genius," he said. "This is a very delicate operation."

The arrogant punk was in his late twenties and went by the name Wolf. He had short, buzz-cut black hair—except for his long bangs, which fell over one side of his face. She'd given up counting how many piercings he had besides the big hole in his stretched-out right earlobe. There were rings in his lip, his eyebrow, his nostril—and probably a lot more below the neck. He wore a ratty gray jacket that had YOU SUCK stenciled on the back.

Even if they weren't conspiring to commit murder right now, she wouldn't have wanted to be seen with him. Driving together to James Monroe High School, she'd barely tolerated his wretched body odor and his blasting heavy-metal music on her car radio. She kept reminding herself that Wolf had come highly recommended.

She made him turn off the radio once she'd parked the car near the high school's playfield. A bunch of boys in their school sweats were playing soccer. She could hear them grunting, yelling, and laughing. Every few minutes, the coach blew his whistle. Stepping out of the car, she instructed Wolf to stay put and leave the radio off. They didn't want to call attention to themselves.

By now, she'd become very skilled at maintaining a low profile. She was pretty certain no one had noticed her in the girls' locker room earlier. But she'd noticed Courtney Hahn—and the location of Courtney's locker.

Almost two weeks before, she'd managed to cut the padlock off Chris Dennehy's locker in about forty seconds. With the same pair of fourteen-inch bolt cutters, she'd had Courtney's locker door open in twenty-five seconds.

But it seemed to take Wolf forever to fulfill his part of the plan. He sat in the passenger seat of her car with a tray in his lap, working on the iPhone, which she'd removed from Courtney's purse. With the precision pliers and a tiny-head screwdriver from his tool kit, he manipulated some wires and charges, which he set inside Courtney's cell phone. He seemed to know what he was doing. Every once in a while, he'd brush the bangs away from his face and pull out one of those jeweler monocles and check on the progress of his work.

Sitting behind the wheel of the parked car, she studied the little patch of black fabric she'd cut from the bottom of Courtney's pullover. She figured Courtney wouldn't notice. And if she did, there wouldn't be much time or opportunity to tell anyone about it before she was dead—or at least, severely maimed.

She carefully folded up the cutting and slipped it inside a plastic bag. She'd already bought a little blond doll that resembled Courtney.

With a sigh, she glanced at her wristwatch. "I know I 'can't rush genius,'" she said. "But I need to return that phone to her locker in five minutes. If that doesn't happen, you don't get paid, *genius*."

He had it finished in two minutes. "Done," he said, handing her the cell phone.

She studied the phone, felt its weight in her hand. She'd

seen how tiny the charges were, and couldn't help wondering out loud. "Will there really be that much damage?"

Wolf started putting his instruments away in his little kit. He nodded distractedly. "When she presses the Talk button, I wouldn't be surprised if she blows her hand off, maybe even part of her arm. And if she's holding the phone anywhere near her head—well, let's just say, it's not going to be pretty. We're talking closed casket here."

Leaving him behind in the car, she stashed Courtney's cell in her coat pocket and started back into the sports wing of James Monroe High School. She paused at the double doors to the smaller gym, where Courtney was playing volleyball. She peeked through the windows—with crisscrossed chicken wire—in the doors.

Her blond hair pulled back in a ponytail, Courtney was looking pretty, bored, and a bit forlorn as she sat on the sidelines in her pale blue gym uniform. About a dozen other girls shared the bench with her while the two teams scrimmaged on the court. One of the girls near the net kept yelling: *"Set it up! Set it up!"*

The woman moved on, heading toward the girls' locker room. She thought about how much damage Courtney had done to her former guidance counselor with all the talking, texting and Twittering she'd done on her iPhone.

She couldn't help thinking, *Live by the sword, die by the sword.*

Courtney had only played the last five minutes of gym period, but for that brief interlude, she'd forgotten all about her father's arrest. She'd forgotten about the kids at school today, looking at her and whispering to each other.

She'd spiked two balls over the net, and her team had won.

She was still on a high about it as she headed into the locker room with the other girls. Their laughter and chatter echoed off the tiled walls. Rounding the corner to her locker row, she started to unbutton her gym uniform.

Then Courtney saw her locker and stopped dead.

Considering the day she'd had so far, she should have been expecting something like this. She should have figured some asshole might want to rip her off or just screw around with her head—now that she was feeling so vulnerable.

"Damn it," Courtney hissed, taking the broken padlock off the locker handle.

She quickly opened her locker, wondering what had been stolen. But all her clothes were there, along with her shoes and her purse. She reached inside the purse and found her iPhone—and her wallet. The money was still in the wallet.

She wondered if some narc in school administration had decided to search her locker for drugs—now that her dad was a known cocaine user. Maybe that was what had happened.

Courtney quickly shoved her wallet back in her purse. But she held on to her cell phone. She wanted to call her friend, Cindy, and tell her what happened. Maybe Cindy already knew something about this. After all, no one could keep a secret around this crummy school.

The phone suddenly vibrated in her hand, giving her a start.

The caller ID lit up: Incoming Call: Blocked Number. Courtney decided to answer it anyway. Maybe it was the asshole who had broken into her locker.

"No cell phone use in the locker room, Courtney!" chided one of her classmates. "Can't you see all the signs, stupid?"

It was that tall, obnoxious Monica Beller, thinking she was so cool with her long black hair and her big tits. Courtney couldn't stand her. Naked, Monica sauntered by on her way to the showers. Monica's friend, brown-haired and skinny Doreen Rustin, walked alongside her, wrapped in a towel.

Courtney hesitated, then threw her vibrating phone into her purse. She flipped Monica and Doreen the bird, but they didn't notice. "She's probably going to use the phone to take our pictures so she can give them to her father the pedophile," Monica was saying.

Doreen giggled.

Courtney decided not to take a shower. She'd barely broken a sweat for the few minutes she'd played volleyball. So she just applied some deodorant and got dressed. As she pulled her black sweater over her head, she noticed a small square patch cut out along the bottom. She hadn't noticed it earlier. Had her pullover come back from the cleaners like that?

"Oh, screw it," Courtney muttered. She finished dressing. Maybe she shouldn't have come to school today, after all.

In the hallway, she took out her phone again but then decided she didn't want to talk to anyone right now. She didn't even want to check if that caller with the blocked number had left a message. Shoving her phone back into her purse, she stuffed her knapsack full of gym clothes in her regular locker and then headed to Mr. Florian's world history class.

But walking down the hallway and then sitting there in that boring class, Courtney couldn't ignore so many of her classmates who stared at her, whispered to each other, and giggled. She tried to hold her head up and act above it all. But she just wanted to go home and lock herself in her room. The only good part of today had been driving to school with Chris.

He understood what it was like to be the unwilling subject of everyone's gossip. He was going through it now, the week after his mother's murder; and he'd been through it last year, after the scandal with Corson.

She remembered her mother talking last week about someone breaking into Chris's locker. She hadn't paid much attention to what her mother was saying. She hadn't been very interested at the time. But now she was.

She heard her phone vibrating against something in her purse. She involuntarily went to reach for it to see who was calling. But Mr. Florian looked over the rims of his glasses at her, and she froze. She'd let it go to message.

She really didn't want to talk to anybody right now anyway—except for maybe Chris.

Courtney waited for class to end. As soon as she stepped out to the hallway, she reached inside her purse and took out her cell. Someone in the crowded hallway bumped into her, and she almost dropped the phone. "Hey, watch it," she muttered, looking up.

She noticed Chris. He was on the other side of the busy corridor, walking away. Courtney quickly zigzagged through the crowd. "Hey, Chris!" she called.

He turned and gave her a dazed half smile. "Hey . . ."

She still had her cell phone in her hand. "I was just going to call you," she said—over all the banter and banging locker doors. "Listen, I can't stand to be here another minute. Let's get out of here. Let's ditch the rest of our classes and just go someplace where we can be alone."

Chris looked stumped for a moment. "Courtney, I'd love to, but really, I can't. I missed so many classes last week, because of my mom. I can't just take off. Plus I told Elvis I'd get together with him after school."

She pouted. "But I really need to talk to you. It's important." She handed him her cell phone. "Here, call Elvis and tell him you can't make it. He'll understand."

Chris looked at the phone in his hand and hesitated.

"C'mon," she insisted, stroking his arm. "You're the only person I want to be with right now. I absolutely hate everybody else. I really need you, Chris. . . ."

Chris's thumb hovered over the Talk button.

"Plus you owe me," she continued. "I was there for you after your Mom got killed. Remember, I came over?" She tugged at his arm. "Just call him. You can see him later tonight."

Chris glanced at the phone again. But then he shook his head and gave the phone back to her. "Tell you what," he said. "I'll meet you after school, and we can hang out. I'm seeing Elvis next period anyway. I'll tell him we can get together another time."

The phone vibrated in her hand. Courtney checked the caller ID. The blocked number again. She tossed the phone in her purse and then smiled at Chris. "Okay, then I'll just drive around until school's out, and I'll pick you up in front of the music building." It was where they used to meet after school while they'd been dating those few weeks.

She got on her tiptoes and gave him a kiss on the cheek. "Thanks, Chris."

Blushing, he gave her a shy smile and said good-bye.

After that, it was easy to ignore the people in the hallways talking behind her back. She no longer felt like a freak. Chris made her feel important again. He'd had the same effect on her last year after she'd been dumped by Shane White. Chris was so good for her ego.

She decided to kill the next two hours at Northgate Mall. According to her mom, they'd have to start pinching pennies, because her father would certainly lose his job. So—this might be her last chance to go on a shopping bender.

In her car, when she hit the first traffic light, Courtney came to a stop and fished her iPhone out of her purse. She switched the phone back to the ring setting. Then the light changed. She noticed a cop car parked on the other side of the street—near the intersection. She put the iPhone down on the passenger seat. She didn't want to get a fine for using her cell phone while driving.

For the time being, Courtney focused her attention on the road ahead. She was still in a residential area near the school—with tree-lined parkways on either side of the road. She had about five more stoplights to go until the on-ramp to Interstate 5. She picked up a little speed—and sailed through one of those lights.

Her cell phone rang.

Blindly, she reached over and grabbed it. Glancing in her rearview mirror, she didn't see any police cars. She checked the caller ID. That stupid blocked number again. "Goddamn it, leave me alone, asshole," she muttered over the ringing.

Courtney decided she'd tell them just that.

The speedometer on her dashboard read 37 MPH.

She brought the cell up toward her face and pressed the Talk button.

All at once, the phone exploded in her hand. All at once, her face was on fire.

Courtney shrieked. But she couldn't even hear her own screams. The deafening blast incinerated her right ear. In the ear that remained, she heard only a high-pitched ringing— almost like the phone.

She choked on the smoke—and the smell of her own burning flesh. Blinded, Courtney couldn't see that she was careening toward a large maple tree. The pain was so excruciating, she just wanted to die.

When the Neon slammed into the tree, Courtney didn't hear the glass shattering and metal twisting. She didn't hear the car horn blare from the impact. All she heard was that constant ringing.

The air bag deployed and hit her in the face—like a hard punch with a big pillow.

It was the last thing she felt before she lost consciousness.

In her last thought, Courtney hoped to God she would never wake up.

CHAPTER TWENTY

Her cell phone rang.

Molly put down her artist's brush and reached for her phone. Another blocked number, and another hang-up without a message. It was the fourth time in an hour. That was how long she'd been up in her attic studio working on her painting with all the partygoing cola drinkers through the ages. Her man from the fifties had an intentional resemblance to James Dean; but the woman from the twenties—in the foreground of the ensemble—looked way too much like Jean Harlow. Molly didn't want the piece to look like one of those paintings from Spencer's with Elvis, Bogart, Marilyn, and James Dean all hanging out at the drive-in. The painting was so complex, it drove her crazy. And the phone interrupting every few minutes certainly didn't help.

She kept thinking it was probably that creepy woman calling again.

Ask him where he really was.

Everything Jeff had said this morning made sense, and yet Molly still felt he was hiding something from her. Maybe all this doubt and suspicion was hormonal or something.

She went back to the painting and picked up her paintbrush once more.

The phone rang again.

"Shit," Molly muttered. She swiped up the phone and switched it on. "Yes, hello?" she said impatiently.

She heard that asthmatic breathing again.

"Listen, stop calling me," Molly growled.

"Do you know where Jeff was that night, Mrs. Dennehy?" That raspy, singsong voice sent a chill through her.

"Yes," she shot back. "He was at the Hilton in Washington, D.C. What the hell business is it of yours?"

"He wasn't in Washington, D.C., Mrs. Dennehy," the woman replied. "Check the hotel."

"I did check the hotel, and they confirmed it," Molly lied.

She heard the woman laughing quietly. Then there was a click on the other end.

Molly switched off the phone. "Goddamn it," she muttered.

The woman seemed to know she was lying. She felt so pathetic and stupid. She'd even admitted to the insane bitch that she'd doubted her husband enough to phone the hotel where he'd claimed to have stayed.

All right, she got to you, she's happy, Molly told herself. Chances were she wouldn't call again for a while.

Molly forced herself to look at the painting again, but she just shook her head. She couldn't concentrate. She quickly rinsed out her paintbrushes and retreated downstairs with her cell phone in hand. She was about to pull her sweatshirt over her head when she heard a noise in the foyer.

For a second, she froze. But then she saw the mail on the floor—below the slot. She hated that slot in the door. Whenever she was home alone, and the mail came, it always caught her off guard and gave her a start. On top of that, she sometimes thought how easy it would be for some stranger to squat down by the door, lift up that little brass lid and peek inside the house. She imagined someone doing it at night, while they were all asleep upstairs.

She went down to the foyer to check the mail—nothing but bills: Seattle City Light, Premera Blue Cross, Visa . . .

Molly let the other bills drop to the floor. The Visa bill was addressed to Jeff. She tore open the envelope. Unfolding the bill, she scanned the most recent purchases for a Hilton in Washington, D.C., or any purchases at all in D.C. There were none.

The bill didn't show any activity on his card from the period he was supposed to be at the Hilton on Dupont Circle to when he came home. The gap went from Monday, November 1 through Wednesday, November 3. There was a Shell station gas purchase in Fife, Washington, on the fourth, from when he'd taken the kids down to their Aunt Trish's house in Tacoma. And he must have bought some flowers for Trish, because a $35.10 charge that same day came from Blooms by Beth in Tacoma, Washington.

Molly checked, and she found hotel, restaurant, limo, and rental car charges in Boston and Philadelphia for his other recent business trips. So Jeff did indeed use this credit card for business. Why was there a gap for his trip to Washington, D.C.? Did he pay for everything in cash? What was he hiding?

He had an American Express card, too. Rummaging through the desk in his study, Molly found his last American Express bill. The billing period stopped in mid-October. So she phoned customer service, and after punching several numbers, she finally got a real person. Molly asked for a list of charges made between November 1 and 3, the day after Angela had been murdered.

There was nothing.

Ask him where he really was.

Frustrated, Molly started to cry. She dug a Kleenex from the pocket of her jeans and blew her nose. Maybe she just had to get out of the house for a while and leave her cell phone behind. Even if it was just for a walk around the neighborhood, she needed to go stretch her legs. It didn't matter she was wearing her sloppy painting clothes. She went to the closet and pulled out her Windbreaker.

"Get while the getting's good," she muttered to herself. "I'd just as soon be gone when that crazy bitch calls again. . . ."

She hesitated at the door. Where had she heard that before? She remembered six months ago, that night Kay had come over. She could still see Kay, sitting on her sofa with a glass of wine in her hand: *Thanks for having me over tonight. I'd just as soon not be home in case that creepy bitch calls again. . . ."*

That was just hours before her death.

Molly couldn't remember exactly what the woman had said to Kay on the phone. It was something about Kay being an unfit mother.

The house phone rang, giving her a start.

Molly marched into Jeff's study and snatched up the cordless. "What? What do you want?" she barked.

"Molly?"

She recognized Lynette's voice. "Oh, hi, Lynette," she said. "I'm sorry. I thought you were someone else. I've been getting these crank calls—"

"Molly, I need a favor," she interrupted. "I need you to pick up Carson and Dakota from school today. I already cleared it with their teachers that you'd be by. I wouldn't be asking you, but Jill can't get away from work today."

"Well, ah, sure, I guess," Molly replied, confused. "Lynette, I'm very sorry about what's happening with Jeremy. I—"

"Thanks," she said with a tremor in her voice. "But I really can't talk. Courtney's been in an accident. She wrecked her car. They took her to UW Hospital. I'm on my way there now."

"Oh, my God, I'm so sorry," Molly murmured.

"Just pick up Carson and Dakota for me, and don't tell them anything. I don't know when I'll be back. I'll call you when I find out more. Okay?"

"Of course," Molly replied numbly.

She heard Lynette start to sob. "Thank you," she said, tearfully.

Then she hung up.

Eight-year-old Carson Hahn picked up a large pebble by the entrance to the play area outside Burger King. It looked like he was about to hurl it at a car in the parking lot.

"Carson!" Molly yelled. She was sitting outside at a red and yellow plastic picnic-style table with Rachel. It had grown chilly with nightfall, and though the play area was well-lit, she'd buttoned up her coat to stay warm. She nibbled on some fries that had gotten cold while Rachel ate a salad.

Molly hadn't had any problems with Carson's and Dakota's teachers when she'd gone to pick them up. Lynette had called around 5:30 to report that Courtney's condition was critical. Chris had come to the hospital to keep her company while Courtney was in surgery. Lynette couldn't say when she'd be back to pick up the kids.

Molly had kept Carson and Dakota in line by promising to take them to Burger King. She'd had to separate Carson from Erin twice, because he liked to tease her. But the three kids had behaved themselves during their November night picnic dinner. Now they were working it off in the play area. The girls seemed to like the slide, and Carson seemed to like trouble. Molly knew—as soon as she saw him pick up that pebble.

She quickly got to her feet. "Carson, you put that down right now or you'll be very sorry!"

He sneered at her. "I don't have to listen to you!" he shot back. "And you can't hit me, because my mom will be real mad if you do!"

For a moment, Molly didn't know what to say.

Rachel threw her plastic fork into the plastic salad receptacle and stood up. "Well, I don't know your mother and I don't care if she gets mad at me. So do what Molly says before I come over there and slap your face!"

His mouth open, Carson gaped at her. He shrugged awkwardly, then tossed aside the pebble. He gave the fence around the play area a kick, and then wandered inside and plopped down on a swing.

"Thank you!" Rachel sweetly called to him. She looked at Molly and sighed. "Something tells me that's going to come back to haunt me."

Molly chuckled. "Oh, he's *so* going to tell his mother on you. But I for one thank you. I'm really glad you could come along."

"No sweat," Rachel said, picking a crouton out of her salad and nibbling it. "I think we have an easier job here than Chris does—holding Lynette's hand at the hospital, the poor guy. I'm not a big fan of hers, and I hate hospitals. My mom was in and out of hospitals for so many months. She had cancer." Rachel tilted her head to one side and squinted at Molly. "Are your parents still around?"

"My mother is," Molly admitted. "But we—well, we're kind of estranged."

"I'm sorry, that's too bad," Rachel said, fingering the straw to her vanilla shake. "My mom and I were close. She practically raised me by herself. Never mind about my dad. He's not worth going into. Anyway, they'd discovered the cancer too late. Toward the end, I moved her into my house, and took a leave of absence from my job. I was a financial forecaster for this investment firm in Tampa. The money was really good, and I had a nice house—and a gorgeous, sexy husband, an actor by the name of Owen Banner. Have you heard of him?"

Molly shrugged. "Sorry, no, I haven't."

Rachel nodded glumly. "And you never will. I basically supported him while he spent my money on booze and other women. He did three commercials and dinner theater for the geriatric crowd. Talk about a loser. He's very immature, and I guess in some warped way that appealed to my maternal side. I wanted to take care of him. But Owen didn't like having my sick mother in the house. He finally issued me an ultimatum: either my mother went or he went. So I started divorce proceedings. In the meantime, my mom died. I had no idea that I'd gotten all my financial savvy from her. Thanks to her investments, my mother left me with about nine hundred thousand bucks. When Owen got wind of this, oh, boy, did he come running back to me, ready to make amends. I know he's bad news, and that's why I moved away—as far as I could. I already had ex-sex with him about two months ago. That's one more reason I made the move here to Seattle."

Rachel slurped the last of her milk shake through the straw, then sighed. "Anyway, that brings you up to date on *moi*—motherless, jobless, divorced, and independently wealthy for the time being."

Molly shrugged. "Wow. Well, I'm glad you told me. Thanks."

Rachel reached for her purse. "Don't thank me yet, Molly. I just wanted to let you know about me and my background and my mistakes before I showed you this. . . ." She pulled an envelope from her purse, and set it on the table. "Remember, this came to your house by mistake? You gave it to me last week when we first met."

Molly remembered. It was the only piece of mail that looked like a personal letter.

Rachel pointed to the handwritten address in the corner of the envelope.

785 NW Fleischel Ave.
Portland, OR 97232

"That address is a fake," she said. "I looked it up on Google. There is no Fleischel Avenue in Portland. And see, the postmark is Kent, Washington. Somebody in Kent wants me to think they're in Portland—and they're not doing a very good job. Anyway, open it up. . . ."

Molly took out the letter. "Oh, my God," she murmured.

It was a folded photocopy—in negative—from a microfiche file of the *Chicago Tribune*'s front page, from January 30, 2007. The headline read: 3 DEAD, 5 WOUNDED IN CAMPUS SHOOTING SPREE. There was a photo beneath it, which Molly knew very well by now: a cop comforting a crying woman with blood on her blouse. They stood in front of the community college's front entrance with the crowd that had been evacuated from the school.

Someone had stuck a Post-it to the page. *You might ask your new neighbor about this,* it said.

"Isn't your maiden name Wright?" Rachel asked gently.

Molly just nodded. The piece of paper began to shake in her hand

"I didn't want to ask you about it until I knew you a little better," Rachel said. "But I looked it up. So—this Roland Charles Wright, was he related to you?"

Molly nodded again. "He was my brother. He—he had some emotional problems, obviously."

"I'm sorry," Rachel said, putting a hand on her arm. "Who would send me something like this? Do you have any idea?"

Molly just shook her head. She couldn't blame Angela anymore. The letter might have arrived at her house by mistake when Angela was still alive, but she knew Jeff's late ex-wife hadn't sent it. She couldn't blame a dead woman for those strange phone calls she was getting. Sure, Angela had lied to her at that lunch when she'd claimed not to have told anyone else about Charlie. But what if that had been her only lie?

Someone else is behind all this. . . .

This *someone* seemed to know everyone's secrets. This woman knew about Charlie—and she also had something on Jeff, concerning his whereabouts the night Angela had been murdered. When Lynette's kids were cut up by the glass in the vacant lot, Lynette had asked her, *"You're not the one who called me?"* That had been a few days before Jeremy's arrest. Had this woman hounded Lynette about Jeremy's secret the same way she was now tormenting her about Jeff? A raspy-voiced stranger's phone calls had haunted both Angela and Kay just days before they were killed. Angela was going to pay for something she'd done. And she'd asked Kay if she was a good mother or something along those lines.

"You know," Rachel said. "I think this cul-de-sac must be cursed. I mean, the woman who lived in the house before me, your friend, Kay—she fell, hit her head, and bled to death. And the mother of your stepchildren was murdered. And just in the last week, Lynette's little darlings . . ." She nodded toward the play area, where Carson was teasing Dakota and Erin. "They were cut up in that empty lot. Then my toolshed mysteriously caught on fire. Lynette's husband got arrested yesterday. And now this afternoon, Lynette's daughter gets in a freak car accident. It's like Willow Tree Court is one big bad insurance risk. I mean, please, tell me this isn't normal."

Molly's cell phone rang. She immediately thought of the crazy woman caller, but when she checked the caller ID, she saw it was Lynette. She clicked on the phone: "Hi, Lynette. How's Courtney?"

"In recovery," she answered edgily. "They sent us home. So—I'm here at your house with Chris, and I don't see my children. Where are my kids?"

"I took them out for dinner here at Burger King," Molly said. "They're fine, Lynette—"

"I need to be with my kids right now," she said, her voice cracking.

"All right, we—we'll leave now," Molly said. "Do you want me to bring you something from Burger King? Does Chris want anything?"

"I just want my kids!" Lynette cried.

"All right, we're leaving right now. Bye, Lynette." She clicked off the cell and looked at Rachel. "God, she sounds absolutely crazed."

"I could hear her," Rachel said. She put her fingers in her mouth and let out a loud whistle. "C'mon, kids," she called. "Your mom's waiting for you."

She folded up the microfiche photocopy with the Post-it attached and shoved it inside the envelope. "Do you want this?" she asked, offering the envelope to Molly. "It was addressed to me, but I think, well . . . I think it was really meant for you, Molly."

"Please, throw it away," Molly said.

She watched Rachel tear up the letter and toss it in the trash receptacle.

Chris was in his bedroom, about to change out of his clothes. He desperately needed a shower. He still smelled like the hospital.

He noticed a bright light sweep across his windows, and he heard a car.

"Thank God," he muttered. If Molly was returning with the kids, then Mrs. Hahn would be going home. He felt so horrible for her, and at the same time she'd practically sucked the life-force out of him for the last five hours at the hospital.

Chris had been waiting for Courtney outside the music building when another student asked if he'd heard about Courtney Hahn cracking up her car. A bunch of kids had seen the accident a few blocks from the school. Stunned, Chris called home to see if Molly had heard anything. She said Courtney had been taken to UW Hospital, and if he could catch a cab or a bus, Mrs. Hahn would probably appreciate having someone there with her.

But Courtney's mom was like a crazy woman—sobbing one minute, and getting so angry-bitchy at all the doctors and nurses the next. It was embarrassing to be with her. The hospital staff she abused at every turn probably thought she was his mother.

He was so busy trying to comfort Mrs. Hahn and apologizing behind her back to half the hospital staff there really wasn't much time to let it sink in about Courtney. The doctors explained that Courtney had second-degree burns on the right side of her face and neck, and third-degree burns on her right hand and arm. They said that she'd lost her right ear and two fingers from her right hand. They rattled off her various sprains, cuts, and contusions. And yet as Chris listened to them, he couldn't really think about Courtney and her pain, because Mrs. Hahn became hysterical.

"Courtney will be all right," Chris tried to tell her in the hospital corridor. "She's tough. She's going to get through this—"

"How can you even say that to me?" Mrs. Hahn screamed. "Didn't you hear him? Weren't you listening? She's not going to be all right! My beautiful little girl will never be beautiful again. . . ."

She settled down a bit after Courtney went into surgery. The doctors were hoping to save her right eye. It was only then that Chris could think about Courtney, and how pretty she was—especially this morning, without makeup. The thought of her face all burned up and mangled made him ache inside.

A nurse came out and explained to them that Courtney had made it through the surgery okay, and they were placing her in the ICU.

Mrs. Hahn had one final hissy fit, demanding to talk to a doctor. The ever-patient nurse managed to convince her that they'd know more in the morning and she should go home.

Courtney's mom had another minor meltdown when they'd gotten here and found that Molly and the kids were gone. But his dad came to the rescue and fixed her a drink. When Chris had slipped away and snuck up to his room, he'd left them standing in the kitchen with Mrs. Hahn crying in his dad's arms.

He'd only gotten as far as unbuttoning his shirt when he heard the car. Chris stepped over to the window and watched Molly's Saturn pull into the driveway.

"Call me if you need anything," he heard their neighbor, Rachel, say as she climbed out of the passenger side of the car. She headed across the yard toward her house. Carson, Dakota, and his sister piled out of the back. Molly herded them toward the house. "C'mon, kids, let's get inside," she was saying.

Chris's bedroom door was closed, and for a few minutes, he could only hear mumbling downstairs. It was hard to make out any of it.

But then there was a click, the sound of the front door opening. He went to the window again and watched Carson and Dakota amble down the driveway. Molly and Mrs. Hahn were so close to the house, he couldn't quite see their faces. He was looking down at the tops of their heads.

"Call me if you need anything, Lynette, okay?" Molly was saying.

Mrs. Hahn nodded, and started to move away. But then she stopped and turned toward Molly. "Why is this happening?" she asked.

She sounded as if she expected Molly to have an answer to that question. He could see Molly shaking her head.

"Why, Molly?" she pressed. "In just one week, my little ones were cut up, I buried my friend, then my husband was arrested, and now, this. They still don't know how it happened. One of the cops said it might have been some sort of cell phone malfunction. What does that even mean? Half of her beautiful face is burnt off. . . ."

Molly reached out to her, but Courtney's mom slapped her hand away.

"For two years, I lived here—and we were all very happy. Then you moved in," Mrs. Hahn said. "And everything changed. Two of my neighbors—my best friends—were killed within six months of each other, a freak accident and a murder. Kay had dinner with you the night she died. Angela met you for lunch just hours before she was murdered. Do you expect me to think it's all just a coincidence? I swear to God, I must have been out of my mind to leave my children in your care today. . . ."

"Lynette, you don't know what you're saying," Molly replied.

Mrs. Hahn backed away from her. "Something's truly wrong with you," she said. "Maybe you're not so different from your brother, the one who shot all those people. Deaths and accidents and tragedies—they have a way of following you around, don't they?"

"Lynette, your children are waiting for you and they're tired," Molly said in a steady voice. "Go home." She turned and headed toward the door.

Chris heard it open and shut a moment later. Downstairs, he could hear Molly's muffled crying.

He watched Courtney's mother, slump-shouldered, wander toward the street, where Carson and Dakota waited for her.

He thought about what Mrs. Hahn had said, about all the bad things that had happened after Molly came to live here. But she'd left something out, something important.

Courtney's mom must have forgotten all about Mr. Corson.

With a pair of tongs, she held the little, rubber-like blond doll over a Sterno flame. She had to be careful to burn just one side of it—so she could match how Courtney had been burned. *The whole right side of her face is toast,* wrote one of her classmates on Twitter. It might have been easier to just color half the doll's head with black Magic Marker, but that would have been cheating. Besides, it was important to her that the doll was actually burned. The slightly melted rubber face made all the difference in the world.

She hadn't a clue where Courtney would be when she pressed the Talk button on her rigged iPhone. So now she'd have to start shopping around for a little model car that looked like Courtney's Neon. The thought of smashing up the front of the model car made her smile.

She had plenty of miniature trees in her supply of dollhouse accessories. She just needed to find one that was the right proportion to the car.

The patch of fabric from Courtney's black pullover was in a plastic bag on her worktable. She would burn a bit of that, too.

She'd stopped work on the Dennehy dollhouse to create this little reenactment of Courtney's accident.

But she would get back to the Dennehy house soon enough.

CHAPTER TWENTY-ONE

With a pile of American Express and Visa bills, and her Edward Hopper wall calendar, which usually hung in the kitchen, Molly sat at Jeff's desk in his study. On the calendar, she always marked the dates for Jeff's trips and noted the city in which he was staying.

It was four-fifty in the afternoon, and she should have been up in her studio, working on her cola illustration. But Molly couldn't focus on that.

Instead, she was trying to match Jeff's travel dates and locations on the calendar with different purchases on his bills. Most of the time, he used his Visa for those business trips, and most of the time, Molly came up with a match. All the charges for his trip to Boston five weeks ago—the hotel, restaurants, taxis, a Barnes & Noble purchase, CVS Pharmacy, Logan Airport Gift Shop—were on his Visa bill.

Yet she couldn't find any expenses during his two-day trip to Denver the following week, though it was marked on her calendar. She noticed one or two gaps like that nearly every month, usually brief trips, too.

It didn't make sense. Why pay for most of his trips with this Visa card, and then sometimes not use the card at all?

Jeff must have had another credit card account, one she didn't know about. Maybe the bill was sent to his office.

Molly was about to look at his checkbook when she heard a car horn honking. She glanced out the window and saw Rachel's black Honda Accord in the driveway next door. Rachel stepped out of the car and glanced toward the house. She was wearing a sweater and jeans, and her brown hair was all windblown.

Molly went to the front door and opened it. "Hey, there," she called.

"Sorry to honk the horn," Rachel said. "I figured I'd rope you into helping me with some groceries. I went berserk in Costco. I mean, how can I pass up five pounds of snack mix? Do you have a few minutes to help a shopaholic in need?"

Molly laughed. "Sure, give me a second." Ducking back inside, she went to the basement doorway and heard the TV down there. "Erin, I'm going next door to Rachel's house for a few minutes," she called. "Okay, honey?"

" 'Kay," she answered.

Molly threw on her heavy cardigan and headed out the door.

"I have enough Charmin here to last me until the rapture," Rachel observed as they were carrying in the last of the groceries from the car. Molly followed her into the house with two light bags. She was taking it easy, because of the baby.

Except for a framed poster of the Eiffel Tower on the wall, Rachel hadn't done anything yet to Kay's old kitchen. The appliances were all white, and the breakfast nook was a little booth with built-in red leather cushioned seats. A window over the booth looked out to the wooded backyard. Rachel's phone and an old answering machine sat on the kitchen counter—near where Molly set the groceries. The message light was blinking.

"Have you heard how Courtney is doing?" Rachel asked while unloading the contents from one of the bags.

"Chris called around lunchtime," Molly said, leaning on the counter. "He talked to Lynette, and she said the doctors are very optimistic about skin grafts and a prosthetic ear. And they're pretty sure her eye's going to be all right."

"Thank God for that," Rachel said. She put two big jars of spaghetti sauce in the cupboard. "How's Lynette holding up?"

"I wouldn't know." Molly sighed. "I don't think Lynette and I are talking. Apparently, everything bad that has happened in her life lately is my fault."

"Well, I knew you were to blame for global warming, but Lynette's problems, too? My goodness . . ." Rachel began to unload a second grocery bag. "I thought I heard a heated discussion going on outside last night. It didn't have anything to do with me threatening bodily harm to her sweet little boy, did it?"

"Nope, it's all me," Molly said with a sigh. "You have a phone message."

"Someone trying to sell me something," Rachel said. "Last week, it was all those prerecorded election-related calls." Reaching past Molly, she pressed a button on the machine.

A beep sounded, and then a perky recorded voice chimed in: *"Hi, this is Claire from Comcast! Did you know you could have all the latest movies and the hottest TV shows right at your fingertips?"*

"See? What did I tell you?" Rachel said. "All I get are salespeople and charities." She went back to unloading her groceries while the recorded sales pitch went on and on. "I don't need any help putting this stuff away," Rachel said—over the recording. "This is the easy part. You don't have to stick around—unless you want to stay for a glass of wine or something."

Molly shook her head. "Thanks anyway, but Erin's home, and I don't want to leave her alone too long." She turned toward the kitchen door.

On the message machine, the Comcast pitch had finally finished. The beep sounded, and another voice came on.

"Rachel Cross?" a woman asked.

Molly stopped in her tracks. She recognized that raspy, demented singsong delivery.

"Rachel, you'll be sorry you ever moved onto that block . . . you stupid bitch."

There was a click, and then a beep.

"End of messages," announced a mechanical voice.

"What the hell?" Rachel said. "Who was that?"

"My, God, she's calling you, too," Molly murmured. A hand over her mouth, she moved toward the answering machine on the counter. "How—how long has this been going on?"

Rachel shook her head. "This is the first time. Why? Do you know this nut job?"

"No, but she's phoned me a few times—and said things."

" 'Said things'? Well, that's vague enough. What kind of things?"

Molly couldn't look at her. "Mostly stuff about my brother," she lied. She didn't want to admit this horrible woman had caught Jeff in a lie about where he'd been the night of Angela's murder.

"Well, I'm just going to star-six-nine her ass," Rachel said, reaching for the phone.

"Don't bother, the number's blocked," Molly said.

Rachel took her hand away from the phone and stared at her.

"Could you play the message back?" Molly asked. "Maybe if I hear her again, I'll recognize her voice. She's never actually left me a message. I didn't think she'd risk having her voice recorded. She must be getting bolder."

Rachel reached over and pressed a button on the answering machine. The Comcast lady came on, and Rachel quickly pushed another button to skip over it.

"Rachel Cross?"

Molly listened to that creepy voice, trying to discern if it sounded familiar. She blankly stared at the breakfast nook—until suddenly something moved past the window.

"Rachel, you'll be sorry you ever moved onto that block . . . you stupid bitch."

Molly spotted a man in a hooded sweatshirt. He seemed to have come from the woods at the edge of Rachel's backyard. It looked as if he was about to walk right up to the house.

Rachel must have spotted him, too, because she suddenly let out a shriek.

The hooded man took off—toward Molly's backyard.

Rachel frantically stabbed at the buttons on the answering machine to shut it off. "Oh, Jesus, where'd he go?" She grabbed the phone. "Did you see him? I'm calling the police!"

All Molly could think about was Erin alone in the basement, and that man heading toward her house. She ran for the front door.

"Molly, wait!" Rachel called after her. "For God's sake, don't go out there!"

She flew out the front door, and raced across the lawn. The door was unlocked. She hadn't thought there would be any need to lock it. She'd been gone such a short time. Molly flung open the door and ran up the front hallway to the kitchen.

Then she saw him. The hooded man was poised outside the family room's sliding glass door. He violently tugged at the handle. Molly could hear it rattle.

"Get out of here!" she screamed, without thinking. She spun around and fumbled for a large knife from the rack on the kitchen counter.

The rattling became louder, then stopped abruptly.

Molly swiveled around again with the knife in her shaky hand.

But the man was gone.

Natalie What's-Her-Name quietly argued with one of the cops.

They'd pulled her car over, and now her slightly battered blue Mini Cooper was parked in front of Molly's house. Everyone on the block had gathered at the end of the driveway while the police combed the area for the man with the hooded sweatshirt. Lynette had been at the hospital all day. Jill was babysitting Dakota and Carson. Both kids—along with Jill's son, Darren—had been fascinated by the police presence on their block. But now the novelty was wearing off, and they were starting to hit and poke each other. Molly held Erin's hand, while Rachel whispered to her that right now, she had sixty dollars' worth of frozen food thawing out on her kitchen counter.

Four patrol cars had shown up, and a total of six cops were checking around each home to make sure there was no sign of a break-in. The two old skeletons of half-finished homes were getting the once-over, too. Jill wanted one of the cops to accompany her back inside her house—just to double-check and be safe.

Natalie must have misunderstood, and thought they were about to do a search inside each residence. "I can't let you just barge in there!" she argued to a stocky, blond, baby-faced cop. Her voice was shrill. She wore jeans and a white top that seemed too big for her. Though pretty, she was way too thin. Standing this close to her, Molly noticed that her teeth were grayish. "I'm house-sitting for these people, and I'd need to check with the owners before I let anyone inside."

Molly wondered what the hell she was talking about. She and Jeff had joked about how Natalie should have installed a revolving door in the Nguyens' house to accommodate all the guys who dropped in—at all hours. And some of them looked rather seedy, too.

"We're just checking the grounds, ma'am," the cop assured her.

"Well, why can't I go home right now? Why are you holding me here?"

Because the police want to make sure you don't end up in one of the Nguyens' closets with your throat slit, Molly wanted to say. But she kept quiet.

"Daddy's home!" Erin declared. She started waving at Jeff's silver Lexus as it crawled up the cul-de-sac.

Molly knew he must have been alarmed to come home from work to see four police cars on the block—and most of his neighbors standing at the end of his driveway. He pulled over in front of Natalie's Mini Cooper.

"Erin, stay with Rachel for a minute," Molly said.

Rachel took her hand. "C'mon, cutie pie, keep me company."

Molly stepped around to Jeff's side of the Lexus as he opened the door. "Everyone's okay," she said under her breath. "We had a prowler. He came out of the woods into Rachel's backyard and tried to get into our place through the sliding glass doors. But I scared him off. I told Erin this is just a police drill. I didn't want to worry her."

"Oh, Jesus," he murmured, hugging her. "You sure you're okay?"

She gratefully held on to him. "Yeah, just a little shaken up."

He kissed her, and Molly kissed him back. Jeff loosened his tie and slung his arm around her, and they started toward the others.

But he suddenly stopped dead and pulled his arm away. He stared at everyone gathered at the end of the driveway. Molly realized, to Jeff, most of them were strangers. "I don't think you've met a couple of our neighbors, have you?" she said. "Jeff, this is Natalie . . . and from next door, Rachel."

Natalie looked him up and down for a moment. Then she turned to the police officer. "May I go inside my house now?" she muttered.

The cop nodded wearily, and Natalie retreated to her car.

"We haven't formally met yet either, Jeff," said Jill with a pinched smile. She put her hands on her chubby son's shoulders. "I was a friend of Angela's. I was at the funeral, but never got the opportunity to give you my condolences. And this is my son, Darren. Darren, say hello to Mr. Dennehy."

"Hello," the kid muttered.

Jeff didn't respond at all. He glanced over at Natalie's Mini Cooper as it pulled down the cul-de-sac toward the Nguyens' driveway.

Just then, Erin broke away from Rachel. She ran up to Jeff and hugged him around the legs. He patted her on the head. He gazed at Jill and her son, and nodded.

"Hi, Jeff," Rachel said, coming to him, ready to shake his hand.

He didn't reach out to her. "Excuse me," he muttered. Then he retreated toward the house—with Erin clinging to him.

"Nice to meet you!" Rachel called.

Molly was embarrassed that he'd acted so rudely—especially to Rachel, who was her friend. Jeff was like a zombie. She watched him and Erin head inside the house.

"Officer?" she heard Rachel say. "Officer, I don't know if this has anything to do with it, but right before Mrs. Dennehy and I noticed that guy in my backyard, this crazy woman left me a really weird, threatening voice mail."

Molly turned toward them.

Rachel nodded in her direction. "Mrs. Dennehy said this same woman has been harassing her, too."

The cop frowned at her. "Have you reported this, Mrs. Dennehy?"

She shook her head. "We had a lot of crank callers and hang-ups after Angela was murdered. I just figured this one was taking longer to move on than the others."

"Are the calls of an obscene nature?" the policeman asked.

"Well, she called me a bitch," Rachel chimed in. "And usually people don't call me that until they know me better."

The cop looked a bit mystified, as if he wasn't sure whether or not to laugh.

"I still have her on my answering machine," Rachel continued. "Would you like to hear?"

The cop turned to Molly. "Could you come with us, Mrs. Dennehy?"

She followed them toward Rachel's house. The cop mumbled something into a little walkie-talkie device on his shoulder. Molly glanced over at her house, wondering about Jeff and his odd behavior. He'd been so concerned when she'd told him about the attempted break-in, and within a minute or two, he'd just walked inside the house—leaving her behind.

She was reluctant to report the harassing phone calls. What if the police wanted to put a tap on the phone and listen in? Then they'd hear this woman asking where Jeff had been the night Angela was killed.

She knew Jeff couldn't have had anything to do with Angela's death. But the police didn't know that.

"Have a listen," Rachel announced, once they were in her kitchen. She pressed a button on the answering machine.

"You have no messages," the machine's mechanical voice announced.

"What? Oh, damn it!" Rachel said. "I must have pressed the wrong button and erased it when I was trying to shut it off. Of all the stupid . . ." She sighed. "Well, you can ask Mrs. Dennehy. It was this crazy-sounding woman with a scratchy voice—and a weird way of talking, almost like she was reading a nursery rhyme. She said I'd be sorry I ever moved onto this block."

The cop turned to Molly. "What kind of things has this woman said in her messages to you, Mrs. Dennehy?"

"Well, she's never actually left me a message," Molly explained. "I've only spoken with her a few times—and mostly it's just gibberish." She tried to avoid eye contact with Rachel. "She hasn't spouted anything obscene or threatening."

"One minute, please," the officer said. He retreated down the hallway—by Rachel's front door. He muttered into his shoulder walkie-talkie again.

"Molly?" Rachel whispered. "What gives? Don't you want to report this?"

"I just don't feel like getting into that whole thing about my brother again," she said under her breath. And it was partially true. In that note left in Chris's locker and the letter sent to Rachel, the telephone woman was holding that over her head as well. "I'm sorry, but right now, I'd just as soon drop it."

Rachel patted her arm. "Okay, Molly," she sighed. "But something tells me I'm not getting the whole true story here."

When she walked through the front door five minutes later, she glanced over toward Jeff's study at the stack of old credit card bills on his desk. If he asked what she'd been doing in there, she would tell him, *"I'm trying to figure out why the hell there's no record of where you were the night Angela was murdered."*

She'd just told that nice policeman it wasn't worth reporting a few strange phone calls. But she knew she couldn't ignore them much longer.

She found Jeff mixing a drink in the kitchen, while Erin

watched TV in the family room. Jeff offered her a highball.
It looked like a bourbon and water—her I-really-need-a-
drink drink of choice. "Something tells me you need this,"
he said.

She shook her head. "Thanks, anyway." She turned toward her stepdaughter. "Erin, could you go watch that down
in the basement, please?"

With a sigh, Jeff set the drink down and reached for one
he was already working on.

Oblivious to the tension in the air, Erin passed between
them and retreated down to the basement. Molly found the
remote and switched off the family-room TV. She took off
her cardigan sweater and draped it over the back of her chair
at the breakfast table. She could hear the television in the
basement starting up.

She turned to Jeff. The kitchen's island counter was between them. "Okay, so what was that all about?" she asked
him quietly. "Why were you so rude to our neighbors?"

He shrugged. "Why should you care? You hate them.
They've been awful to you."

"I don't hate Rachel. I happen to like her very much. She
went to shake your hand, and you just ignored her."

Jeff put down his drink and rubbed his eyes. "I'm sorry,
honey. I was distracted. I was worried about you and Erin
and the house. If you want, I'll send each one of them a written apology—starting with your friend . . ." He seemed to
falter for her name.

"Rachel," she said. "I've already apologized for you. But
you need to know something, Jeff. That crazy woman caller
who's been harassing me—"

"Damn it, Molly, I've told you, if you'd just screen your
calls—"

"Let me finish," she insisted. "The woman left a message
on Rachel's answering machine today. I heard it. She threatened Rachel. The same woman called Angela and Kay
shortly before they were killed. I'm beginning to think Kay's

death wasn't an accident. She could have been murdered. Have you stopped to consider all the deaths and accidents and tragedies this one little block has experienced lately? You should have heard Lynette last night accusing me of stirring up some kind of hornet's nest of bad luck for everyone here on Willow Tree Court. She even brought up Charlie in her little tirade."

"You can't take what she said seriously," Jeff pointed out. "She was half out of her mind last night."

"But the thing of it is I don't really blame Lynette for feeling that way. I've felt it too, at times. After what Charlie did, I've always worried about something horrible like that happening again to someone else I love. I've tried to prepare myself for when the other shoe might drop. Maybe that's why I became so obsessed over the cul-de-sac killings. I didn't want to tell you, but I've had some nights here when you're out of town that I've been absolutely terrified."

"But you've always acted so brave," he whispered. "Why didn't you say anything?" Setting down his drink, Jeff looked like he was about to come around the counter to hug her.

"Would it have made a difference if I said something?" she asked. "You'd have gone on your trips anyway. Am I right?"

It stopped him in his tracks.

She put her hand up. "My point is—I can't really blame Lynette for thinking bad luck follows me around. But I know it's not me or my bad luck that's making all these horrible things happen lately. I think it's the work of this demented woman on the telephone—I think she may be responsible for everything from Erin's smashed pumpkin to Courtney's car wreck. I need to tell this to the police—before someone else is hurt or killed. But one thing is holding me back, Jeff. She has something on you. You weren't in Washington, D.C., when Angela, Larry, and Taylor were killed. And yet you're sticking to that story. Well, sooner or later, the police are

going to figure out you're lying. And Jeff, God help me, I
don't want to be the one who exposes your lie. But I will. I
will, if it means I can stop this woman from hurting someone else."

Frowning, he let out an exasperated sigh. "Honey, listen . . ."

He stopped talking at the sound of someone at the front
door.

Molly heard the lock click. She peeked down the front
hallway to see Chris opening the door. He wore his school
jacket and had his backpack slung over one shoulder.

"Hey," he mumbled. "Sorry I'm late. I took the bus to the
hospital to see Courtney. But she was pretty out of it, so it
wasn't much of a visit. . . ."

Molly just nodded, then turned and walked into the
kitchen again. At the breakfast table, she grabbed her cardigan from the back of her chair. "I'm going out," she said.
"There's leftover ham in the refrigerator. Or you can order
out. I don't care. You guys are on your own for dinner."

Chris looked at Jeff—and then at her. Unlike his kid sister, he seemed to sense the tension in the room. "What's
going on?"

"Ask your father," Molly grumbled, throwing on her
sweater. She grabbed her purse. "Good luck getting a
straight answer from him. I've tried, and I can't."

She headed down the hall—and out the door.

CHAPTER TWENTY-TWO

"I heard you come in at eleven," he said.

Molly squinted at Jeff standing at the top of the attic stairs. She lay on the chaise longue in her art studio, snuggled under the comfy throw from Restoration Hardware. She realized Jeff must have snuck up there in the middle of the night and covered her with it.

He was right. She'd come home at eleven o'clock. She'd driven to Capitol Hill and gotten Thai carryout from Jamjurri. Then she'd driven to a lookout point on Fifteenth Avenue, a small park with a panoramic view of Husky Stadium, Lake Washington, and Bellevue.

Molly had sat in the car, eating her ginger chicken and gazing at the Bellevue lights in the distance. The park was across from Lakeview Cemetery, where they'd buried Angela—a fitting spot for her to admit to herself that Angela had been right all along. She didn't even want to think it, but the evidence—or lack thereof—was overwhelming. All those business trips Jeff had taken without any expense records meant he was hiding something—like an affair, or several affairs. Jeff had been with another woman the night Angela had been murdered.

The son of a bitch wasn't much better than Jeremy Hahn.
And now she was going to have his baby.

When she'd come home last night, she'd had no desire to
see him—or even sleep on the same floor as him. She'd gotten a pillow from one of the twin beds in the guest room, and
then taken it upstairs to her studio.

"I'll see the kids off to school," Jeff was saying. "You just
sleep."

"You need to make Erin's lunch," she muttered, turning
away from him.

"I'll handle it," she heard him say. "Just do me a favor. If
the phone rings today and the number's blocked, don't pick it
up. And please don't say anything to the police about those
calls. Just hold off for today. You and I will straighten this
out tonight, and then we'll both talk to the police tomorrow.
Okay?"

Molly didn't say anything.

"Maybe we can get together with that cop who's so fond
of you, that Blazevich guy."

"Yes," she said, tonelessly. "We'll have to be discreet.
When it comes out where you were that night, it'll be embarrassing for you. Am I right, Jeff?"

She heard him sigh. "We'll work this out, Molly," he said.
"I promise."

Then she listened to his footsteps retreating down the
stairs.

Molly didn't want to wait until tonight to "straighten this
out." She imagined trying to talk to Jeff about his infidelity
while his children were in the house. They were better off
having their discussion over lunch—preferably in a cafeteria-
style place, where they paid up front. So—if she wanted to
storm out of there, she could. Or maybe they'd just talk in his
office with the door closed and his assistant out to lunch.

That was where she was now, downtown on the twenty-ninth floor of the Bank of America Tower. With a trench coat on over her navy-blue blouse and black skirt, Molly stepped off the elevator and through the glass double doors to the suite of offices for Kendall Pharmaceuticals. She never much cared for the wannabe–Jackson Pollock artwork on the walls. But she liked Jeff's assistant, Peter, whose desk sat outside Jeff's office in a separate alcove. A husky, handsome, ebony-skinned man with a goatee, Peter always wore vibrant-colored shirts with dark, subdued ties. Today, the shirt was Orange Crush orange.

Usually, Molly enjoyed chatting with Peter, but this time she'd been hoping to catch Jeff with no one else around.

"Hi, Molly," Peter said, looking up from his monitor. "I'm sorry, but if you're looking for Jeff, you just missed him. He's out to lunch, I don't know where. He told me he'll be back in an hour, but you never know."

"Yeah, you never know with him," she said, working up a smile. The frosted-glass door to his office was closed; and it looked dark in there. "Well, he wasn't expecting me. I'll just go in and leave him a note."

"Go on in. Do you want some coffee or a soda?"

"No thanks, Peter." She stepped inside Jeff's office and closed the door. He had a spacious office with a bookcase on one wall, a sofa, and a large mahogany desk—on which sat a computer monitor and a framed photo of her, Chris, and Erin. One wall was a floor-to-ceiling window—with a view of the Olympics, Puget Sound, and the ferries on their way to and from the islands. Gray clouds hovered over the horizon, and not much light came into Jeff's office. Molly switched on the overhead, then went to his desk and sat down.

She was wondering about those business trips that hadn't shown up on Jeff's Visa or American Express accounts. He must have had a secret account, and the bills were either coming here or at a post office box someplace.

Molly tried his desk drawers, but all of them were locked. She wondered if he'd set up the account online. But he'd logged off his computer, and she didn't know the password. Molly tried her name, then *Chris*, then *Erin*, then *Chriserin*, and other combinations that included birthdays.

Through the door's fogged glass, she could see Peter getting up from his desk. She quickly grabbed a pen and started scribbling on a notepad.

Peter knocked, and then stepped in. "I'm headed out to lunch, Molly," he said. "I'd stick around and keep you company, but I'm meeting Mark and his mother at Ivar's. I can't keep her waiting. She already thinks I'm not good enough for her son. Anyway, take your time in here. Everything's locked up, so just turn off the lights and close the door when you leave."

Molly nodded. "Will do, thanks," she said. "And good luck with Mark's mom."

"Thanks, I'll need it," he said. Then he set some mail on Jeff's desk and headed for the door.

Molly heard the door close after him. She wasn't looking in that direction. She was staring at the mail he'd left in front of her—and the MasterCard logo in the left-hand corner of one envelope.

At this point, she didn't care if Jeff knew she'd looked at his mail. She was sick of secrets. With his letter opener, she cut open the envelope and pulled out the bill. The most recent purchase was listed on the day she'd found out about Angela's death. He'd checked out of the Chateau Granville Hotel in Vancouver, British Columbia. The day before, there were charges from BC Liquor Store, Divine Vine Florist, and Blue Water Café—all in Vancouver.

Earlier in the month, when Jeff was supposed to be in Minneapolis, he'd taken a brief trip north about sixty miles to La Conner instead. There, he stayed at the La Conner Channel Lodge, and he'd had a $122 dinner at Palmer's Restaurant, and spent $247 at Windmill Antiques & Miniatures. From all the prices, Molly could see Jeff was treating his girlfriend to the finest hotels and restaurants. He was also buying her flowers and antiques. Maybe he was in love with her.

Devastated, Molly unsteadily got to her feet. Stuffing the MasterCard bill back in the envelope, she stuck it in her purse. She turned off the overhead light and stepped out of his office. She was shaking and tried to hold back her tears as she walked through the corridor. Just outside the glass double doors, on her way to the elevators, she heard her cell phone ring.

Molly reached into her purse, and checked the caller ID: CALLER UNKNOWN.

She took a deep breath and pressed Talk. She didn't say anything. She could hear the asthmatic breathing on the other end of the line—then that voice: *"Mrs. Dennehy, do you know where your husband was when his ex-wife was murdered?"*

Molly swallowed hard. She couldn't stop shaking. "He was in Vancouver, British Columbia," she answered steadily. "And he was with you—you malignant bitch. Wasn't he? How did you like the flowers?"

She heard a click on the other end.

Jeff heard a plane soaring overhead from the airport nearby. He walked into the Marriott's bar, an all-glass and wood-beam circular dome. With the overcast skies above, the light pouring through to the bar was subdued. The place was about half full with the lunch crowd.

Jeff found her at a table with a view of the indoor pool and tropical garden area. She was dressed demurely in a white turtleneck and black slacks, and she looked nervous. She had her favorite drink, a Tom Collins, in front of her. She smiled up at him.

He plopped down in the chair across from her. "What the hell do you think you're doing?" he asked under his breath.

"I just wanted to be near you," she said.

A pretty Latino waitress approached their table. "Can I get you something from the bar?"

"Nothing, thank you," Jeff replied, turning his head away slightly.

"He'll have Wild Turkey—double, with a glass of ice on the side," the woman said.

He waited until the waitress left before he spoke again. "I'm not staying long," he frowned. "And I'm not drinking with you. I told you when we first got together six months ago that it was nothing permanent. It shouldn't have lasted even this long. I love Molly. I'm not going to let you destroy my marriage or my family." He leaned in closer to her. "Are you out of your fucking mind, setting up house right on my block?"

"But she doesn't know," argued his Willow Tree Court neighbor. "And I promise, she'll never know—not until you're ready to tell her. Have I ever tried to push you in that direction? I don't want to break up your marriage. I don't want to hurt anyone. I'm in love with you, Jeff. Like I said, I just wanted to be near you."

The waitress returned with his Wild Turkey and a glass of ice. She set a dish of pretzels between them. "Thank you," Jeff muttered, his head down.

"No worries," said the waitress, and then she headed to another table.

"I really don't get 'no worries' in lieu of 'you're welcome,' " the woman said, nibbling at a pretzel. "It just doesn't seem to be the right response to 'thank you.' It's like I wasn't worried, I was just thanking you. Know what I mean?"

He stared across the table at her. He wondered how she could act so cute right now and make lighthearted conversation. She didn't seem to comprehend the seriousness of what she'd done. "It's over," he said.

She quickly shook her head. "No, please. Listen, listen, have your drink, and—and—and we'll talk. I didn't mean to make you angry when I moved into that house. I just wanted to be close by. I'm staying out of your way, Jeff. I mean, Jesus, I've been there all this time, and you haven't even seen me—until yesterday."

He poured some of the Wild Turkey over the ice and gulped it down. "You look me in the eye and tell me that you don't want to hurt anyone, and yet you're telephoning Molly and asking if she knows where I was the night Angela was murdered."

She shook her head. "Not me, Jeff. I don't know what you're talking about. Why would I want to blow the whistle on myself? I like what I have with you. I wouldn't do anything to wreck that."

"You already have," he said.

She grabbed his hand. "Listen, if you're really that upset about the move, I'll just pack up my stuff and be gone by the end of the week. Poof, problem solved, okay?"

He had another hit of his drink and leaned back in the chair. "I'm going to tell Molly about us tonight, and I'll beg for her forgiveness. Then I'll go to the police and explain to them that someone is harassing my wife. They'll probably question you. If you're telling me the truth, and it's not you making those calls, then it's probably one of your friends. Think over which of your friends you've told about us."

"Jeff, I haven't told a soul," she whispered, tearing up.

"After today, I don't want to see you again. You'll have to move. I need you to stay away from me and my family."

"You can't mean that," she pleaded, shaking her head. "Don't be this way, Jeff. I made a dumb mistake. People in love can do dumb things sometimes. Can't you please forgive me?"

He just glanced down at the tabletop.

She sat back and kept one hand around her glass. "So— you want to break up. Do you have to be so cruel about it? Is this how you want to wrap up what we've had together? Six months, that's a pretty good run, Jeff." Her voice began to crack, but she was smiling. "Does it have to end so—so badly? Can't we hold each other one last time? C'mon, honey, you'd think I could have some closure, at least. What do you say we have one last time? Listen, if you go to the front desk and get us a room, I'll drive to the liquor store and buy us a bottle of Wild Turkey. Remember that time in Portland? It'll be just like that." Her hand came up to his face. "C'mon, baby. What do you say?"

Closing his eyes, Jeff let out a long sigh of resignation.

She parked around the corner from the liquor store's entrance, near the Dumpster, where there was less foot traffic. No one could see her at work in the car's front seat. She'd ground up ten tablets of ecstasy, and used the rolled-up liquor-store receipt to funnel it into the Wild Turkey bottle.

She'd bought the pills from Wolf, the same sleazy character who had wired Courtney's phone to blow up. She was a bit upset with him, since Courtney hadn't died. But she figured it wasn't his fault. Besides, she took a certain satisfaction in the fact that Courtney had been maimed and disfigured. No one would ever give Courtney Hahn a break or hold a door for her again just because the girl was pretty. Still, she was disappointed and had decided last night to abandon her notions of a miniature re-creation of Courtney's smash-up. After all, Courtney wasn't dead. Yet she couldn't toss out that little Courtney doll, wrapped in the material from her pullover, with half of its face blackened and slightly melted.

She sort of cherished it.

Along with the ecstasy, she'd purchased some cocaine and heroin from Wolf. It cost nine hundred dollars for a thin packet of heroin no bigger than a teabag. Wolf assured her that she was getting a terrific deal, and he even tutored her on how it should be introduced into the bloodstream for the effect she desired.

Her cell phone rang, and she saw the number on her caller ID pad. She clicked it on, and put the phone to her ear. "Hi, Jeff," she said.

"I'm in room 104, on the first floor—by the pool," he said.

"See you in about five minutes, my love," she replied. Then she clicked off.

She put the bottle of Wild Turkey back inside the long, narrow brown paper bag. Starting up the car, she pulled onto International Boulevard and thought about what Chris's guidance counselor had written in his notes regarding Jeff Dennehy:

> *He's a very nice guy, who obviously loves his son. But I believe he compartmentalizes his life. Jeff Dennehy doesn't seem to realize how his womanizing ways are spilling over from one compartment and hurting his family. With his good looks & his friendly, confident manner, I'm guessing he attracts a lot of women & it's hard for him to say no. Chris has felt very close to his dad . . . until he found out about all the cheating. But I don't know if Mr. Dennehy can stop, even with his new wife. It's as if this is how he's used to living. The guy just can't say no to a pretty woman. . . .*

As she walked down the first-floor hallway of the Marriott, she felt as if someone was following her. She kept glancing over her shoulder at the vacant corridor with its gaudy-patterned green, pink, and oatmeal carpet. She peered at the darkened doorways and alcoves but didn't see anyone. She told herself it was nothing, just her imagination.

She reached room 104 and knocked. She knew Jeff would be there waiting for her.

She knew how hard it was for him to say no.

* * *

He'd followed Angela Dennehy's ex-husband as far as the twenty-ninth Floor of the Bank of America Tower, and then to this hotel near the airport. From a table on the other side of the domed bar, he'd watched Jeff and his Willow Tree Court neighbor have their pathetic little assignation.

He'd been extra careful to make sure they hadn't noticed him. It had been a close call yesterday, when Molly had spotted him in the backyard next door. He'd barely had enough time to check out the lock on the sliding glass door to the Dennehys' house. He'd heard the police sirens while ducking back inside his car, parked on another dead-end road behind those woods. At the intersection of the other cul-de-sac, he'd watched the cop cars zoom by with their roof lights flashing and swirling. He'd counted four patrol cars. He'd felt sort of proud his presence on Willow Tree Court had prompted such a forceful response.

Jeff Dennehy's girlfriend seemed to pick up on the fact that someone was watching her in the Marriott's first-floor hallway. She kept glancing over her shoulder as she sauntered down the corridor with her big purse. He stayed hidden in the alcove with the pop and ice machines. He heard her knocking on a door and waited for the sound of the door clicking open. Then he caught a peek of her stepping inside room 104. He didn't want to listen in at the door. So he tried the window on the other side of the room and discovered that number 104 had access to the pool through a sliding glass door. Each one of the poolside rooms had one or two patio chairs outside it. An indoor mini-jungle separated the lanai area by the room entrance from the huge, star-shaped pool. So it was easy for him to wander around by those doors and not be seen.

He could hear splashing and the laughter of children as he settled down in the patio chair outside room 104. Though Dennehy and his girlfriend had shut the drapes, the edges didn't quite meet, and he could just make out their naked forms through the sheer curtain. He adjusted the chair so it was a bit closer to the glass.

"Marco . . . Polo . . . Marco . . . Polo!" some kids were yelling.

He leaned over to one side, like he'd fallen asleep in the chair. He could see into the room now. The air conditioner–radiator must have been right near that sliding door, because every once in a while that sheer curtain fluttered open—and he could see everything. He spotted a quart bottle of Wild Turkey—a little over half full—on the table near the door.

It looked like booze wasn't the only thing she'd bought to the party. Lying naked on the bed, he saw her carefully applying something that might have been cocaine to her breasts. Dennehy was naked, poised over her on all fours. She grabbed him by the hair and pulled his head down. He eagerly sniffed and licked at her nipples. Even with the door closed—and the kids screaming and carrying on in the pool, he could hear her muffled laughter.

The sheer curtain billowed and reflected against the glass, totally obscuring his view for a few moments. He wasn't sure what he missed, but as the curtain moved again, he could see her walking across the room naked. At first, he thought she was coming to the sliding glass door, but she was only retrieving the bottle of Wild Turkey.

Dennehy was sitting on the bed with his feet on the floor. He gripped the side of the mattress with his hands, and shook his head repeatedly as if having a spasm of some kind.

Perhaps it wasn't just cocaine he'd been snorting off his girlfriend's breasts, but something even stronger. Dennehy put a hand to his forehead.

She started to hand him the bottle, but he knocked it out of her hands.

All at once, Dennehy bolted up. It looked as if he was about to attack her, but he took two steps and collapsed on the floor.

The curtains began to billow again, and he couldn't see much.

It appeared as if she was just standing there with one hand on her hip, looking down at him.

The man in the patio chair kept waiting for her to help Dennehy. But she didn't move. The man thought about counting the seconds so he could time her, because she stood like that for a long, long time.

She watched Jeff Dennehy writhe on the beige-carpeted floor.

Jeff had said he wasn't into drugs. But he'd already had at three shots of Wild Turkey heavily laced with ecstasy. And she knew he couldn't say no. There was only a bit of cocaine in what he'd snorted off her breasts. Most of it was high-grade heroin.

One hand on her hip, she stared down at him. She remembered Wolf commenting that the ecstasy was quite powerful. "Two tabs, and you can fry an egg on your forehead," he'd said. She wondered if Jeff was reacting to the ecstasy or the heroin—or the combination. He was covered with sweat and gasping for air. She touched his chest with her toe, and the skin was hot. It was almost as if his body was cooking. His handsome face was crimson.

"My husband actually liked you, Jeff," she said, gazing down at him. "He didn't blame you as much as the others for what happened to us. But I do. Before Ray was even killed, I was already planning on how I'd meet you and seduce you. I knew you couldn't resist a pretty girl."

His eyes seemed to keep going in and out of focus. One moment his gaze connected with her—and the next his stare was blank. He vaguely reached out to her, but she kicked his hand away.

"My family and I went through hell for five months. My husband lost his job, our marriage was ruined, our teenage daughter ran away—all thanks to you and your meddling neighbors on Willow Tree Court," she continued. "Your children came to my husband for the guidance you couldn't give them—and then all of you turned on him. I think I aged years in those few months. But I was still pretty enough to turn your head. Less than two weeks after Ray was killed, I had you in that Jantzen Beach hotel room in Portland. Remember? That was the same night Kay died. Molly called you and got you out of bed. . . ."

Thrashing about on his back, Jeff looked like he was choking. He was like a helpless little baby who couldn't turn himself over.

Jenna Corson felt just a twinge of pity, but not enough. She stared down at him, fascinated by his suffering. "Ray and I were unofficially separated," she said. "I'd given up on us, but he hadn't. He kept coming back to me. When I discovered Ray had taken out a very expensive insurance policy, I knew something was up. It didn't take me long to figure out he was planning to kill himself—so the kids and I would be taken care of. I just didn't know how he would make his suicide look like an accident. We were spending more time apart than together, but one night while he was in the shower, I found a number on his cell phone, the number of the man he'd hired to kill him.

"I guess I could have stopped it," she admitted. "But we'd hit bottom, and there didn't seem to be any other way. Besides, I couldn't let the people who had destroyed my family go unpunished. You people on Willow Tree Court were the worst offenders. Ray took notes during his sessions with your children. Some were in his private journals, some in the school records. I stole everything he had about the kids on Willow Tree Court. So I knew all of your secrets—and all your weaknesses."

She let out a long sigh. "Even before Ray was killed, I planned to take that insurance money and whatever I'd get for selling the house—and use it to destroy you and your neighbors. That's the real reason I moved onto your block, Jeff. I didn't care about being near you. I just wanted to see the devastation closeup."

It looked as if Jeff was struggling to talk, but all he could get out was a warbled groan.

She touched him with her toe again. He was on fire. "You know, at just about the time I *accidentally* met you, Jeff, I contacted the man who killed my husband and hired him to kill Kay Garvey. He murdered Angela for me, too. He did such a thorough job on my husband, I knew he'd take care of those bitches with the same efficiency, though I suppose he could have handled Angela's death differently. . . ."

Gazing down at him, she sighed, "Oh, my God, look at you. You should see yourself."

Jeff had thrown up. Pale gray bile ran down the side of his mouth and formed a puddle under his neck. Blood oozed out of his nostrils. He stared up at her. Spasms began to rack his body.

"You know, it's funny how I've lived on that cul-de-sac for a while now, Jeff," Jenna said. "I kept wondering if you'd ever notice me. Ray used to say you people only cared about yourselves, your families, and your small circle of friends. I think he was right. I didn't go to his funeral, because I didn't want anyone from Willow Tree Court to recognize me—in case they came. I was already planning to move onto your block then. I already knew what I had to do."

Jeff's breathing became a death rattle. The crimson color began to drain from his face. He was totally still, and his eyes were listless.

"But I didn't know how I would kill you until three months ago," Jenna continued. "That's when I learned that my daughter, Tracy, had died on the street from a lethal combination of drugs and alcohol. She was only sixteen years old. My sweet little girl . . ."

Jenna began to cry, but her voice was angry and accusatory as she leaned over him. "A lethal combination of drugs and alcohol, that's when I knew how you'd die, Jeff. That's when I knew. . . ."

He stopped breathing. The room was quiet.

She could hear kids splashing and laughing in the pool outside the sliding glass door.

Naked, she walked over to the sofa and reached for her purse. Jenna took out a small pair of scissors. She picked up Jeff's T-shirt from the bed and then carefully cut a piece off the sleeve.

CHAPTER TWENTY-THREE

He'd almost lost her on Interstate 5 but managed to keep a tail on her car from the Marriott—all the way to a grimy-looking pool bar called the Side Pocket on Aurora Boulevard in North Seattle. The name was on an illuminated sign advertising Budweiser on the side of a squat one-story, gray building. BAR—POOL—GAMES—FOOD was painted in big red letters on the building. Neon signs for Rainier and Corona lit up the only window—by a red door that had ENTRANCE painted across it in white.

Pulling over on a side street, he watched her park the car and walk inside. She wore her sunglasses and a trench coat. But he could still picture her naked from forty-five minutes ago, when she'd stood over Jeff Dennehy in that poolside hotel room.

He counted until two hundred before he climbed out of his car, cut through the parking lot, and stepped inside the tavern. Peanut shells littered the floor, and Jimmy Buffett's "Come Monday" played over the speakers. The gloomy place's only good source of light was above the three pool tables, where some good old boys were racking them up. No one was playing darts or pinball at the moment. A few people hunched on their stools at the charmless bar and only one of the booths was occupied—by Dennehy's girlfriend and a lean, swarthy man with shiny black hair and a pockmarked face. It looked like she was having a Coke. The man was cracking peanuts and nursing a shot glass of something with a beer chaser.

At the bar, he ordered a Corona and paid for it. Dennehy's girlfriend and the thug she was with didn't seem to notice him wandering over to the next booth. He set his beer down on the varnished wood tabletop.

"No, let's put a hold on the Lynette Hahn hit for now," she was whispering. "She's still suffering and I want to prolong that. I may even save you the effort and take care of her myself. I've gotten a taste for it now."

"Well, if you think I'm giving back your down payment—"

"Relax, Aldo," she said, cutting him off. "You can keep your lousy down payment."

"You bet I will," he replied, a bit huffy. "I still think I should have been paid more for the Alder Court job. . . ."

Sipping his Corona, the man in the next booth listened carefully. This was what he'd wanted to hear.

"I was paid to take care of only one person, not three. And that teenage bitch bit me, too. I should get workman's compensation."

"It was just supposed to be Angela in the house that night," she replied. "I had no idea they'd canceled that field trip for her boyfriend's daughter. You're right when you say the job was only for one. But you should have aborted instead of doing all three of them."

"I think I was pretty damn creative, making it look like another cul-de-sac killing," the thug bragged. "And the cops are none the wiser."

The man in the next booth took a peanut from the basket on his table and cracked it open. So—his copycat was a hired killer named Aldo, and he was working for Jeff Dennehy's girlfriend—or former girlfriend. From the look of things back in that hotel room, he was pretty certain Jeff Dennehy was dead.

"You know"—the woman sighed—"a simple robbery-murder setup—like the one you pulled on my late husband—would have been infinitely better. Copying a high-profile murder spree only invites a more scrupulous police investigation. I think your 'creativity' there is going to turn around and bite you on the ass."

In the booth behind her, the man grinned. He kind of liked her. She was very astute.

"Well, if you're not happy with my work," Aldo was saying, "maybe you should hire someone else to handle the Dennehy woman and the two kids."

"I don't want to close the door on our relationship yet, Aldo," she replied. "But you're right about Molly and the two kids. I think I want to handle them myself. Like I said, I've developed a taste for it now."

He didn't linger. He'd heard enough to know who had imitated his work and why. Dennehy's girlfriend and Aldo didn't seem to notice him when he scooted out of the booth and ambled to the doorway.

Even with the overcast skies, it seemed bright outside compared to the gloomy bar. He returned to his car and waited there.

She stepped out—alone—ten minutes later. She put on her sunglasses and headed to her car. He watched her drive off. He didn't need to follow her. He already knew where she lived.

He stuck around for Aldo, who remained inside the Side Pocket for the next few hours. It grew darker, the streetlights went on, and the tavern's parking lot became more crowded.

Under the car seat, he kept a small hunting knife, the same one he often used when cleaning a house. He took it out and admired it several times while waiting for his prey.

At 8:20, Aldo finally came out from behind the bar's red door. He weaved a bit as he walked to his car, but he didn't seem too drunk.

The man followed Aldo's black BMW down Aurora to a Jack in the Box. Aldo used the drive-thru, and then he continued down Aurora. Eventually, he turned onto a side street and pulled into the driveway of a tall apartment complex. It was comprised of three buildings that were connected, but varied in style and color—like something out of Disneyland. A beige cedar shaker was sandwiched between two Cape Cods, one moss green and one rose colored. Aldo parked his BMW alongside the rose-colored building.

Meanwhile, the man pulled into a spot in front reserved for visitors. He waited until Aldo started down the walkway to the center building, and then he hurried out of the car. He caught the lobby door before Aldo let it swing shut behind him. "Thanks," he said, though Aldo paid no attention to him. He guessed from the size of the Jack in the Box bag in Aldo's hand that the hired killer wasn't having dinner with anyone else tonight.

He touched the knife concealed inside his jacket while Aldo checked his mailbox in the lobby. With his back to Aldo, the man pressed the button for the elevator.

It arrived a bit too soon. Aldo was still getting his mail.

The man waited, and then the elevator door started to shut. He grabbed it, stepped inside, and held it open. "Going up?" the man called to Aldo.

Mail in one hand and the Jack in the Box bag in the other, he nodded. "Yeah, hold it," he grunted, trotting toward the elevator. "Thanks," Aldo said, stepping inside. "Could you hit four?"

"That's where I'm going, too," he said, pressing the button for the fourth floor.

They rode up in silence. The man stared up at the lighted numbers above the door.

As they passed the third floor, he turned to Aldo. "Say, do you know me?" he asked.

Aldo narrowed his eyes at him. "No, why? Should I?"

He waited until the elevator door opened on the fourth floor. He nodded for Aldo to go first. "No, you shouldn't know me," he said, walking with him down the dimly lit corridor. The carpet was pale green. Somebody had a potted plant outside their door; another tenant had one of those cat-scratching poles. He and Aldo were the only ones in the hallway. He could hear a TV blaring in a nearby apartment.

"In fact," he continued, reaching inside his jacket, "you don't know me at all. So you really have no business imitating my work."

Aldo turned to stare at him. "What the fuck?"

Then he suddenly seemed to realize just who he was talking to. Aldo's eyes widened as he stared at him. He didn't appear to notice the hunting knife—not until it was too late, not until the sharp blade slashed across his throat.

Blood began to gush down his neck to his shirt. The envelopes in his hand fluttered to the floor, while his other hand crushed the Jack in the Box bag against his chest. Several fries spilled out. He slumped against the wall, and his legs started to give out from under him.

Knocking the fast-food bag out of Aldo's grasp, the man began to search his pockets while Aldo was still vertical. He wanted to make sure there was nothing on Aldo's person linking him to the woman on Willow Tree Court. He took Aldo's wallet and his cell phone.

His face a bluish-gray, Aldo numbly stared at him and blinked a few times.

Blood drops dotted the fast-food bag, the scattered envelopes, and the pale green carpet. The man was careful not
to get any on his hands. He let Aldo drop to the floor.

He didn't wait for the elevator. He took the stairs, moving
at a brisk clip. But he didn't run. On his way down to the
lobby, he thought about Jeff Dennehy's girlfriend. After listening to their conversation in the tavern, he guessed she was
finished with Aldo and no longer had any use for him. In
fact, he had a feeling he'd beaten her to the punch with Aldo.

He hoped the hired killer didn't have anything in his
apartment or in a safe deposit box that showed she'd paid
him to carry out those killings.

As far as the man was concerned, it just wouldn't do to
have the police sniffing around Willow Tree Court. No, it
just wouldn't do.

He'd made up his mind. He still had some work there.

He had a house to clean.

Molly tossed what remained of the chicken casserole into
the garbage disposer. There was still one good-sized portion
Jeff could have eaten. She'd cooked dinner for his children
tonight, and covered for him, too. She'd told Chris and Erin
that their father had an "after-work thing." Now, it was eight
o'clock, and he wasn't home. He hadn't even phoned. She'd
tried his cell several times since early this afternoon, but it
kept going to voice mail.

Let the lying, cheating son of a bitch fend for himself, she
figured, flicking on the switch for the disposer. With a loud
roar, it ground up what could have been his dinner. Then she
shut it off and went back to washing the dinner dishes. Chris
was upstairs in his room, and Erin sat at the kitchen table,
doing homework with the big TV on.

So—where was their father?

Standing over the sink, she wondered if Angela had put

up with this kind of crap. She had a whole new sympathy for Jeff's late ex-wife.

She wasn't sure what to do. Though she'd had her rough patches with Chris, she was very fond of Jeff's kids. She hated the idea of them being without a mother. And she hated the idea of her baby being without a father. After leaving Jeff's office, she'd come home and worked on her cola painting all afternoon. She'd figured she might have to start earning money to support herself—and her baby.

She was loading the dishwasher with the last of the glasses when the doorbell rang. Grabbing a dish towel, she dried off her hands and then headed to the door. She checked the peephole and saw Chet Blazevich standing on her front stoop. The last time he'd been there was the night after Angela was murdered.

Molly unlocked the door and opened it. "Well," she said.

"Hi," he said. "Is Mr. Dennehy home?" He seemed distracted by something behind her.

Molly glanced over her shoulder and saw that Chris was at the top of the stairs, staring down at them. "It's okay, Chris," she said. "I've got it. . . ."

He frowned a bit, then turned and headed back toward his room.

Molly worked up a smile for the cop. "I'm sorry, but Jeff isn't here. I'm not really sure when he'll be back—soon, I hope." She opened the door wider. "I'm sorry. Would you like to come in?"

"Thanks." He stepped inside. He wore an old tweed jacket with jeans and a loosened tie.

Erin came into the hallway from the kitchen. "Molly, can I have an ice cream sandwich?"

"Are you done with your homework?"

She nodded.

"Okay, but just one," Molly said.

Erin didn't seem interested in an introduction to Chet Blazevich. She turned and scurried back to the kitchen.

Molly led him into the living room and nodded at the easy chair. "Can I get you something? Coffee or water? An ice cream sandwich?"

"Thank you anyway," he said, with a nervous laugh. He sat down in the chair.

Molly settled at one end of the sofa. "What did you want to see my husband about?"

"Well, there's been some confusion about where he was the night the former Mrs. Dennehy was killed."

Molly didn't say anything.

"We checked with the Hilton in Washington, D.C.," Blazevich explained. "In fact, we checked with all of the Hiltons in D.C., and your husband wasn't staying at any of them."

Molly shifted on the sofa. "Is it really so important where he was?"

"It might be," Blazevich said. "We're now considering the possibility that the Alder Court murders weren't the work of the Cul-de-sac Killer. . . ."

Molly stared at him. "You mean, they think it was some sort of—copycat killing?"

He nodded. "It's looking more like that, yes."

"What makes them think so?"

He let out a wary sigh. "Without getting into too many details, Molly, the Cul-de-sac Killer is quite neat and deliberate—methodical. In the houses where he had struck, most of the blood has been inside or around the closets where the bodies were found. With these multiple slayings, it appears he ties up the victims, puts them in their respective closets—and then takes his sweet time with them, one by one."

Wincing, Molly felt gooseflesh prickling on her arms, and she nervously rubbed them. She'd read an account of the murders that indicated as much. But it was still unsettling to hear someone say it.

"From the looks of things inside the house on Alder Court," Blazevich continued, "they were all killed very quickly, almost haphazardly. I saw photos of the scene, and it was a mess. There was blood all over the kitchen. They think Taylor Keegan almost got away—or at least, she put up a good fight. Her body was stashed in the kitchen pantry. She hadn't been tied up at all." He shook his head. "That's another thing. The Cul-de-sac Killer rarely kills anyone on the first floor. The only exception—until Taylor—was Kurt Fontaine, who was murdered along with his wife in the Madrona neighborhood. They found his body in a coat closet on the first floor. But all of his other killings have taken place on the upper levels of the victims' homes. The Cul-de-sac Killer would have tied up Taylor Keegan and put her in her bedroom closet upstairs. He wouldn't have killed her in the kitchen."

"Jeff isn't a suspect, is he?" Molly whispered.

"Not really," he replied. "But—well, let's just say that he'll have to account for where he was that night—for both the police and the press."

Molly's eyes searched his, and all at once she realized something. He knew.

The police had to know Jeff was at the Chateau Granville Hotel in Vancouver the night Angela was killed. They'd obviously checked his story about having stayed at the Capital Hilton in D.C., and known it was a lie from the start. All it would have taken was a check of his credit card records—just as she'd done. The police had probably figured out a lot sooner than she had that Jeff had been wining, dining, and screwing some woman in Vancouver the night his ex-wife was butchered. Maybe Jeff had used his connections to get investigators to clam up about his little indiscretion. Or perhaps the cops had decided to do him a favor and not expose him as a lying, cheating scumbag. For a while, there was really no reason for him to get his alibi straight—as long as they knew the truth. But soon the murders of Angela, Larry, and his daughter would no longer be considered another cul-

de-sac killing—and Jeff's lying about where he was that
night would become a major issue—and an embarrassment.
The press would eat it up.

Molly locked eyes with Chet Blazevich again. She realized he was doing her a favor, bracing her for the potential
scandal. "Can I ask you something?" she whispered. "Is this
an official police visit or did you come here on your own?"

Blushing, he gave a little shrug. "I came here on my
own," he admitted. "So this visit is very *unofficial.*"

"You're looking after me, aren't you?" she asked. "You
don't want to see me get hurt."

He nodded. "I think you've been hurt enough, Molly. I
think you deserve a break. And I think that husband of yours
must have rocks in his head."

Molly reached over and put her hand on his arm. "Thank
you, Chet. Thank you, very much."

Chris stood at the railing by the top of the stairs. He
couldn't see them down in the living room. But he could
hear them pretty well—when they weren't whispering. He'd
gotten the gist of their discussion.

Molly and the cop were talking about his dad. He hadn't
been where he said he was the night of the murders. Chris
remembered something his mother had said: *"Every time he
goes out of town, it's just another opportunity for him to
screw whomever he wants. . . ."* Was that what he'd been
doing the night she was killed?

Last night, Molly had stormed out of the house, telling
them they could get their own dinner. She'd said something
to him before she left, too—something about not being able
to get a straight answer from his dad. Chris had thought at
the time that she almost sounded like his mom used to.

The cop claimed his dad wasn't really a suspect, but in all
the TV crime shows, the cops always said that about the guy

they ended up arresting. Chris knew his dad was capable of a lot of things, but not murder.

Right now, Molly and the cop were whispering back and forth. It was kind of weird the way they called each other by their first names. Their voices got a little louder, and he spotted them downstairs stepping into the foyer from the living room.

Chris quickly stepped back so they wouldn't see him. He heard the front door click open while they murmured to each other. After a few moments, the door shut, and the lock clicked. He was about to head back into his room, but he hesitated. He heard her crying down there. Chris moved to the top of the stairs. "Are you okay?" he called to her.

She quickly wiped her eyes and glanced up at him. "I'm fine, Chris."

"What did that guy want?"

"Oh, he's a policeman," she said, her voice a little shaky. "He just wanted to follow up on some stuff about the prowler I spotted in the backyard yesterday."

He couldn't help frowning at her for lying—again. His dad wasn't the only one who didn't give straight answers. The other night, Mrs. Hahn had said everyone's troubles started when Molly had moved onto the cul-de-sac. She kind of had a point.

Chris wished he could run around the track with Mr. Corson after school tomorrow. Everything in his life was falling apart again, and he missed his counselor.

He turned and headed into his bedroom, leaving the door open a crack. He wanted to hear when his dad came home.

A few minutes later, Erin stomped upstairs and got ready for bed.

While his sister was in the bathroom, he heard Molly coming up the steps. He crept to his door and saw her from behind—going down the hall toward the master bedroom. She was carrying a steak knife. She held it tight against her side—like she was trying to hide it in case he or Erin spotted her.

He watched Molly duck into the master bedroom and close the door.

At 9:05, someone gently knocked on the front door.

Molly jumped up from the sofa in the family room. By now, she was convinced something awful had happened to Jeff. She'd been waiting for the sound of his key in the door.

He wouldn't have knocked.

Hurrying down the hall, she checked the peephole. Rachel stood on the other side of the door. Molly unlocked the door and flung it open. "Hi," she said a little breathless.

"Sorry to drop by so late," she said, wincing. She wore jeans and had a cardigan over her pink T-shirt. "I saw your lights were on, and I—well, I just got another call from that freaky woman."

"Oh God, come in," Molly said, stepping aside for her.

"You must think I'm such a baby," Rachel said. "But after that creepy guy in the backyard yesterday, I'm so jumpy it's not even funny."

Molly motioned to her. "Please, come in," she said again.

Rachel stepped into the foyer. "I'm pretty sure it was the same nutcase," she said. "The phone rang, and I saw the number was blocked. But I picked it up anyway, and this raspy, weird breathing came on the other end. They didn't say anything. Like an idiot, I kept asking, 'Who is this?' Then they hung up." She rubbed her forehead. "It's silly of me to get so scared. I'm sorry to bother you. I hope I didn't wake anyone up."

Molly shook her head. "No, it's fine. Erin's in bed, reading, and I think Chris is taking a shower. In fact, I could use a friend just about now. . . ." Molly couldn't help it. She started crying.

"You poor thing, what's going on?" Rachel asked.

"Jeff still hasn't come home from work yet," she admitted. She led Rachel into the living room, where they sat down on the sofa together. "I'm so worried about him—and so mad at him! I have no idea where he is. I talked to his assistant. Jeff took off from work at noon, and he never came back. I keep calling his cell, and I keep getting his damn voice mail. . . ."

Even though she didn't give Rachel the whole story, it felt good to cry on someone's shoulder. Molly went through three Kleenexes from the pockets of her jeans. She was just wiping her eyes, when she heard Chris coming down the stairs.

"Dad?" he called. He rounded the corner and stopped at the living room entrance. "Oh, hi," he said to Rachel. "I thought you were my dad. . . ."

"Well, there's my hero," Rachel said, "the handsomest fireman in North Seattle. Chris, could you do us a huge favor, and pour Molly a great big glass of wine?" She patted her arm. "That'll help take the edge off. What do you want, white or red?"

"No, I can't," Molly said, shaking her head. "I—thanks anyway, no."

Rachel gave her a look. Then she turned and smiled at Chris. "Never mind, honey. We'll give a yell if we need you."

He nodded. "I'll be downstairs, watching TV." Then he headed toward the kitchen.

"He's a sweetie pie," Rachel said.

Molly just nodded. She heard the basement door yawn open, and then Chris's footsteps on the stairs.

Rachel took hold of her hand. "So—what's going on with the no wine?" she whispered. "Are you pregnant?"

Molly hesitated, and then nodded. "Nobody else knows yet," she said, her voice still hoarse from crying.

"Oh, that's so exciting!" Rachel whispered, giving her a quick kiss on the cheek. "And guess what?"

Molly numbly gazed at her and shrugged.

"I'm pregnant, too, Molly!" Laughing, she squeezed her hand. "I'm about eight weeks along. That's what I get for sex with the ex. But I'm keeping it. . . ."

"Well, congratulations," Molly said, with a dazed smile. But then she started to cry again. "I'm sorry. I'm happy for you, really. But I'm such a mess right now. I'm just so worried about Jeff, and so uncertain about everything. . . ."

"You're just *so hormonal*, is what's going on," Rachel said. She dug into her pocket, pulled out a tissue, and handed it to Molly. "Believe me, I know. I'm going through the exact same thing. Every day I'm on an emotional roller-coaster ride. And nauseous? Let me tell you, I've got a tiger in my tank."

Molly blew her nose, and leaned back on the sofa. She laughed.

"Don't worry," Rachel said. "I'm sure Jeff will be home soon." She leaned back on the couch so they were shoulder to shoulder. She took Molly's hand and placed it over her belly, and then she put her hand over Molly's belly. "Meanwhile, the four of us will all wait up for him."

"Rachel, thank you," Molly whispered. "I don't know what I'd do if you weren't here. . . ."

Maria was listening to "Walking on Sunshine" on her iPod, and she was in a pretty good mood that Saturday morning. The guest who had checked out of room 102 had left a five-dollar bill on the TV—along with a *Thank You!* scribbled on the notepad. Plus they'd left behind a *People* magazine, two unopened cans of Coke, and an unopened bag of Cheetos. Not a bad haul.

Wheeling her cart to the next room down the hall, she noticed there wasn't a sign on the door. Putting her iPod on pause, she plucked out her earplugs, took out her passkey, and knocked. "Housekeeping!" she called.

There was no response. Maria unlocked the door with her passkey, then propped it open with the cart. "Oh, phew," she grumbled. Every once in a while she got a really smelly room. This one was a mess, too. The bedspread and sheets had been pulled off the mattress and strewn onto the floor. On the nightstand were a glass, a tipped-over ice bucket, and some powdery substance that had to be drugs. The flickering TV was on the adult channel menu.

Maria started across the room so she could open the sliding glass door. She stepped on something lumpy beneath the white sheet. She almost tripped over it. That was when Maria noticed the blue-gray hand sticking out from that sheet.

She realized she'd just stepped on someone's arm. Then she saw the man, lying there naked on the floor. Maria screamed so loud she might have woken the dead.

But she didn't.

The clipping from Jeff's T-shirt was under the doll's right leg—just where she'd left the shirt. One of the dark-haired doll's little arms was covered with the miniature bedsheet.

She was almost finished with the hotel-room scene, which was slightly bigger than a large shoe box. It just needed a few more flourishes. She'd gotten a head start on the project. She'd been in several hotel rooms with Jeff, and they all looked alike after a while. She just needed to capture the essence of it. She was particularly proud of the tiny light that flickered in the miniature TV. It cast an interesting shadow on the nude doll when she turned off the lights in her workroom. She could imagine it was how Jeff looked last night, on the floor of the hotel room—nothing on but the TV.

And nothing on him, she thought. She was toying with the idea of drawing on the doll to make it anatomically correct and accentuate the nudity. And the thought of drawing a penis on the doll gave her a melancholy smile. She would miss him in bed. She'd have to do Jeff justice with her rendering.

Justice, she thought, gazing at the unfinished Dennehy dollhouse on her worktable.

Her cell phone rang. It was also on the worktable.

She checked the caller ID and let out an exasperated sigh. She answered it anyway. "Hi, Elaine," she said. "Now really isn't a good time."

"Well, Jenna," her sister said on the other end. "Why don't you tell that to your son? He asked me twice today when you're coming to see him."

"I'll be there next weekend, I promise," she said. "In fact, let me tell him myself. Is he there? Can you put him on?"

She heard her sister mumbling something, and then after a minute: "Hello, Mommy?"

"Hi, Todd," she said, tearing up a little. "How's my guy?"

"I just killed a bug," he said.

She smiled. "I killed one yesterday. Do you miss me?"

There was no response on the other end, and she knew he was nodding. He still did that over the phone sometimes. "When are you coming back, Mommy?" he asked, finally.

"Soon, maybe next weekend," she said. "And we'll definitely be together for Thanksgiving, don't you worry. My work here is almost done. Sweetheart, can you keep a secret?"

"Yes!" he replied eagerly.

"You can't even tell Aunt Elaine. Cross your heart. Did you cross it, honey?"

Again, silence. She knew he was nodding.

"Next time you see me, I might be bringing you a sister.

She's a little older than you, and she's very sweet. Her daddy just died yesterday. . . ."

Jenna Corson wandered back to her worktable and the Dennehy dollhouse. She put her hand on the roof. "And her brother and stepmother will be dead soon, too. She'll be all alone. So we're going to be her new family. Won't that be nice, sweetheart? Won't that be lovely?"

She listened to the silence and knew what it meant.

CHAPTER TWENTY-FOUR

She kept thinking if only she could crawl out of bed, do a few household chores—and concentrate on that for a while—then maybe she could get through the day. Maybe she'd start to feel normal again.

For the last two days, she'd been severely ill and bedridden. It had started on Friday night, while she and Rachel had been waiting for Jeff to return home. "I think you're literally worrying yourself sick," Rachel said, offering her peppermints. Rachel swore by them, but they didn't seem to help.

They'd had a false alarm when a car had come down the cul-de-sac at 10:45. But it had been another one of Natalie's gentlemen callers. By 11:30, Chris had become concerned about his dad, too. They called the police—and the hospitals. The three of them kept a vigil. But as the night wore on, Molly got sicker and sicker. She threw up four times.

Exhausted and depleted, she finally fell asleep under a blanket on the family room sofa at 3:45 that night. Chris had nodded off in his dad's easy chair while tuned in to the Syfy Channel on TV. Molly couldn't quite remember when they'd sent Rachel home.

In the morning, Molly felt so horrible she thought something might be wrong with the baby. Rachel came over and drove her to the doctor's office. Since it was Saturday, Molly's doctor wasn't there, but one of his colleagues was. Molly got in to see him, and threw up twice in his office. He ordered bed rest and prescribed over-the-counter ginger capsules to combat the morning sickness. Rachel picked up the pills for her.

She was so weak and dizzy by the time they got home that Chris and Rachel had to help her upstairs to the bedroom. When she finally got to bed, Molly didn't so much fall asleep as she passed out. She woke up to the sound of Erin screaming—the same agonizing shrieks Erin had let out when she'd learned her mother was dead.

Then Molly knew.

She was already weeping by the time Chris came to her room and told her about the call from the police. His eyes were red and his face looked blotchy from crying. When he told her they found his father dead in a hotel room at the Marriott by the airport, Molly tried to get up, but she was too frail. She reached up to Chris, and he took her hand for a few moments. She was hoping he would hug her, but he didn't. At least he held her hand.

Over the next two days, she kept telling Rachel, "I don't know what I'd do if you weren't here."

From her bed, Molly made the funeral arrangements—in the same kind of dazed sleepwalker's manner that she'd set up Charlie's service three years ago. But Rachel did most of the legwork. Rachel also looked after the kids. And Rachel backed her up when Molly tried to convince Chet Blazevich that Jeff had been murdered.

She'd phoned him on Sunday, and Chet said he'd drop by that afternoon. Rachel let him in and showed him up to the bedroom. For a moment, Molly thought about how horrible she looked and how the room must smell like vomit—and here this guy had a crush on her, or at least, he used to. But she really didn't care.

Still. Chet looked handsome in a V-neck sweater, a tie, and corduroys. He stood a few steps inside the doorway. Rachel sat down at the end of the bed.

Jeff's death wasn't his case, but Chet told her how much he knew. "Your husband checked into the hotel alone," he said somberly, looking more at the bedroom floor than at her. "But it's very possible he called someone later to join him. Unfortunately, an ice bucket spilled on his cell phone, and shorted it out. So we're going through his service provider to see if we can get a record of his calls that day. . . ."

Molly shook her head. "They'll find some number that's no longer in service or it's one of those phones you can throw away." She struggled to sit up in bed. "This woman who's doing all this, she's very careful and clever. Every time she's called me, the number's been blocked. I'm sure she was with him yesterday. It's probably the same woman he was seeing that time in Vancouver. I—I know about Vancouver. I know he wasn't in Washington, D.C., when Angela was killed. This woman was with him then. I can tell from the prices of the meals he paid for in Vancouver. Those are meals for two people. She was with Jeff then, and she was with him yesterday. She's the one who murdered him."

Chet nervously cleared his throat. "We talked to several employees at the Marriott, and nobody saw him with anyone else. It appears your husband died from ingesting a lethal combination of ecstasy-laced alcohol, cocaine, and heroin. They didn't see anything to indicate force was used in any way—though the ecstasy in the alcohol raised a few eyebrows. Not many people would take ecstasy that way, but it's not totally unheard of. And the hotel records show your husband logged in four hours on the pay-TV's adult channel."

"He was set up," Molly argued, tears in her eyes. "She thought it all out ahead of time. I know that sounds crazy and paranoid. But I also know Jeff. He didn't take drugs. This woman—she's the same one who's been causing all these accidents to people on this block—she killed Jeff. And she killed Angela, along with Larry and Taylor. I think she may have killed Kay, too."

"Mrs. Dennehy," he said. "How could she have killed those three people on Alder Court at the same time you say she was with your husband in Vancouver?"

"She—she—must have an accomplice, or someone working for her," Molly said, feeling nauseous. "She planned this all very carefully. . . ."

"You have to admit, Detective," Rachel chimed in. "In just two weeks there have been an unusual amount of accidents and deaths associated with this block. I mean, really, what are the odds? Two deaths, and a near-fatal car wreck, an arrest, and a lot of little things, too—my toolshed was set on fire last week, and three children on this block were badly cut playing in a vacant lot that just happened to be sprinkled with broken glass. I think Molly has every reason to question the notion that Jeff's death was an accidental overdose."

"Jeff didn't even smoke pot," Molly said, rubbing her forehead with a shaky hand. "So I don't think he'd be taking ecstasy and cocaine and heroin. . . ."

"Mrs. Dennehy . . . Molly," Chet said. "Please forgive me, but you say you know your husband didn't take drugs. Two weeks ago, did you know your husband was seeing other women? I mean, how well did you really know him?"

Molly began to cry. Jeff wasn't much better than Jeremy Hahn. They were both discovered in a hotel room after some illicit sexual assignation, surrounded by drugs and porn. At least Jeremy was still alive.

Couldn't the police see what was happening? How could they tally everything up and still call it a coincidence or just bad luck?

The TV news coverage of Jeff's death made him look like a sleazy character. How couldn't it? In the same broadcast, it was reported that police believed the murders of Jeff's ex-

wife, her partner, and his daughter might not have been the
work of the cul-de-sac killer, but rather a copycat. Hearing
that, people certainly had to figure Jeff was somehow involved in the slayings.

His only alibi was that he was screwing some woman in
Vancouver at the time.

Molly was sick in front of Chet Blazevich. Fortunately,
Rachel got the wastebasket to her in time. While Rachel
cleaned out the wastebasket, Molly drank a little water, but
she still didn't feel any better. "I'm sorry," she muttered fee-
bly to Chet. "It's been—it's been like an *Exorcist* marathon
here lately."

"Have you seen a doctor?" he asked gently. "You look
like you belong in the E.R."

"I'm pregnant," she admitted quietly. "I saw a doctor yesterday morning. I'm not sure how much of this is morning
sickness, and how much of it is stress. Anyway, the kids
don't know yet about the baby. Jeff didn't know, either. I
never got a chance to tell him. . . ." She started to cry again.
She couldn't help it. All her defenses were down, and she
felt so horrible.

Before leaving, Chet reminded her that Jeff's death was
still under investigation. But Molly knew he'd probably
chalked up everything she'd said as the paranoid ramblings
of a sickly, hormonal, pregnant woman—just made a widow.

She felt so frustrated and useless. Poor Chris had to drive
by himself to the coroner's office and identify his father's re-
mains. And Erin couldn't take much comfort in a stepmother
who was bedridden, groggy, and throwing up every few
hours. For both of them, more than anything, she wanted to
climb out of bed and be strong again. Rachel and Trish were
there on and off, but Molly couldn't help feeling she'd let
down Chris and Erin just when they'd needed her the most.

She wanted so much to call her mother. She missed her.
And it would have helped to know if this severe morning

sickness was something hereditary. Rachel was just about as
far along in her pregnancy, and she admitted to feeling nauseous a lot of the time. But it didn't seem to slow her down.

That Monday morning, the day before Jeff's funeral,
Molly told herself she had to get up no matter how awful she
felt. The ginger capsules didn't seem to do any good—in
fact, they only made her sicker and groggier. So Molly decided not to take any. At 6:45, before anyone else woke up,
she crawled out of bed, opened the window, and took several, deep fortifying breaths of the cold November air. Leaning on the banister, she managed to get downstairs to the
kitchen, where she found a Sprite in the refrigerator and
some deli ham. She made herself a cold ham and Swiss
sandwich and gobbled it up at the breakfast table.

Outside, it was still dark. Inside, the house was quiet. For
a few minutes, she managed to convince herself it was one
of those mornings when Jeff was on a business trip, and the
kids weren't awake yet—and she had a few quiet moments
before the morning rush to school.

To her amazement, she kept the food down. She was still
a bit frail and once again relied on the banister for her slow
ascent back up the stairs. She had every intention of making
her bed, but she crawled under the covers again for a moment—and fell asleep.

The next thing she knew, her nightstand digital clock read
11:23 A.M., and she could hear the TV on in the family room.
Molly forced herself to get up. A shower was too much of a
commitment—even with her hair limp and greasy. She
washed her face, put on a sweater and jeans, and then made
her bed.

Down the hall, she checked Erin's room to see if the bed
was made. It wasn't, and clothes were strewn on the floor.
She'd do a load of wash. It wasn't much, but she was taking
baby steps. She gathered up Erin's clothes, then paused and
sat down in Angela's rocker with Erin's dirty clothes in her

lap. Molly noticed yellow paint on the long sleeve of Erin's pink pullover. There was a yellow smudge on her jeans, too.

Molly could see the shade of yellow wasn't from Erin's limited watercolor collection. It was artists' oil paint, probably Naples Light Yellow. A six-ounce tube cost eighty-two dollars, plus tax.

She could see a few yellow stains on Erin's door, too. Molly shook her head. "Damn it," she murmured. Erin knew she wasn't allowed up in the studio by herself, and using Molly's paints was strictly verboten.

Molly got to her feet, and Erin's dirty clothes fell from her lap to the floor. She stepped over them on her way to the hall. She noticed a pale yellow paint smudge by the knob of the attic door. Molly opened the door and told herself she couldn't be mad at Erin, not now. For all she knew, maybe Erin had painted her a Get Well picture. She'd done that for her before, when she'd had the flu last January. But Erin had used her own paints then.

Molly climbed the stairs to her art studio and felt a bit dizzy by the time she reached the top. Catching her breath, she glanced around. Just past the easel and the back of her latest project—the cola ad—she spotted the tube of Naples Light Yellow. It was on the stool that usually held her water glass, soda, or coffee while she worked. The cap was off, and some of the paint had oozed out of the tube. She saw a thin paintbrush on the floor.

"Oh, Erin, for God's sake," she said under her breath. She moved toward the easel to clean up after her. That was when she saw something out of the corner of her eye. Molly swiveled around and stared at her painting of the twenty partygoers through the ages drinking cola—and the yellow X slashed across it.

"Oh, no!" she cried, a hand over her mouth. She automatically turned away—toward the bookcase. Then she realized her painting wasn't the only thing that had been destroyed up here. On one shelf, blotches of yellow paint haphazardly ran across several of the elephant figurines. A few of the glass and china ones had been smashed with a putty knife that lay on the floor among the broken shards.

"No, no, no," Molly sobbed. "God, how could she?" Some of those elephants had belonged to Charlie.

She staggered down the two flights of stairs to the family room, where Erin was in her pajamas, sprawled on the sofa, snacking on a Fruit Roll-Up and watching a cartoon on TV. "My God, Erin, why?" she asked, out of breath and half crying. "Why in the world would you do that?"

"Do what?" Erin sat up. "I didn't do anything!"

"You ruined my painting!" Molly cried. "You know how hard I've worked on that. I've spent hours and hours on it—"

"I did not!" Erin screamed. "I didn't do anything to your dumb old painting!"

"And you destroyed a whole shelf full of my elephants! Are you going to deny that, too? Why would you do something so hurtful? Are you mad at me? Is that it? You know you're not allowed up in my studio, and yet you went up there and—"

"I didn't go up there! I didn't do anything!" Tears in her eyes, Erin glared up at her.

Molly felt a wave of nausea, and she took a deep breath. She plopped down in the cushioned chair beside her. "Okay, I—I understand you're very upset," she said in a shaky voice. "And I realize you might be angry at me because I've been so sick lately—or maybe you somehow blame me for what happened to your dad. Whatever it is, we can talk about it. But first, you need to own up to what you did. Now, don't lie to me, Erin. You went up to my studio. You broke some elephants, then you took a tube of yellow paint and you painted a big X—"

"I did not!" Erin shrieked, jumping up from the sofa. She threw down her Fruit Roll-Up. "You're the liar! I didn't do

anything to your stupid painting! I hate you, I hate you!"
Crying, she ran out of the room and charged up the stairs.

"What the hell was that all about?"

Molly turned and saw Chris had come up from the basement. She heard Erin's bedroom door upstairs slam shut. She
rubbed her eyes. "Your sister decided to touch up the painting I've been working on for the last two weeks," she said. "I
guess she has some unresolved anger toward me—though I
guess she figured out a way to resolve it. Go on up and take
a look. My painting's ruined. She also destroyed about a
dozen of my elephants. Some of those I've had since I was
her age." Molly found a Kleenex in the pocket of her jeans,
and she blew her nose. "I'm sorry I've been so ill the last
two days. I can't help that. I know how you and Erin must
feel. This is a time when you've really needed me to step up
to the plate. And I've let you down. I understand if you're
angry and confused. . . ."

Half a room away, Chris shoved his hands in his pockets
and leaned against the kitchen counter. "It's okay," he said,
frowning.

She shook her head. "No, it's not okay. You're upset with
me, too. I can tell, just by looking at you. You don't even
want to come near me. Talk about unresolved anger. . . ."
She blew her nose again. The tissue started to fall apart in
her hands. "You know, I have some anger issues, too," she
admitted. "I'm so mad at your father right now. He was a
good man, and he loved you and Erin very much. But he—
he made some foolish decisions as far as women were concerned. I guess you heard enough about that from your
mother. But I can't help being mad at him for letting this
woman—whoever she is—set him up that way. I don't care
what the police say, or what you hear on the news, he was
not in that hotel room alone."

Chris nodded. "Yeah, I heard you talking to that cop yesterday, the one you seem to know so well."

"What's that supposed to mean?" she asked.

He shrugged. "Nothing, forget it." He started to turn toward the basement again.

"No, I won't forget it," Molly retorted, unsteadily getting to her feet. "And you can't just say something like that, and then leave the room. . . ."

Stopping, Chris turned around and frowned at her.

"If you're insinuating that anything at all has gone on between Detective Blazevich and me, you're way off. And if you're trying to blame me—or—or justify why your father . . ."

Molly couldn't finish. She felt sick to her stomach. She shook her head and retreated for the stairs. She made it up to the master bathroom, where she sat on the floor by the toilet until the nausea passed. Then she staggered back to bed and climbed under the covers.

She wished she'd never gotten up.

Chris stared at the big yellow X scrawled across Molly's unfinished painting. The X had finished it—for good. It was just as Molly had described it to him hours ago. Too bad, because what Molly had created so far was pretty cool, like something out of *Mad Men* with all these different characters through the century. Chris could tell she'd used a photo of him as a model for the 1940s sailor who was drinking a cola with this sexy blond woman with a peekaboo bang over one eye. She'd made him look handsome.

He glanced over at the elephants that were broken and splattered with yellow paint. It was the third shelf up—just at Erin's eye level. He'd seen the yellow splotches on Erin's door—and on her clothes. He'd talked to his kid sister after dinner tonight, and she'd denied any wrongdoing. She'd insisted she never came up here to "Molly's stupid old studio." But it reminded him of when Erin was a toddler and not totally potty-trained. She'd occasionally wet her pants and then insist that a lion had come along and splashed her with a glass of water. Why a lion, he wasn't sure. But she'd tell the lie and stick to her guns—even when the evidence was stacked up against her.

He knew she was upset, confused, and angry. He felt exactly the same way. He gazed at Molly's ruined painting and those elephants she'd had since she was a child—and his heart broke for her. Yet he kept thinking back to what Mrs. Hahn had said a few nights back, about how when Molly moved in, that was the start of all their troubles.

Every person he'd come to depend on had died within the last few months—starting with Mr. Corson, then his mom, and then his dad.

Molly had told him earlier today that she was mad at his father for getting himself killed. Chris was angry at him, too, but he also missed him. He had to remind himself this wasn't one of his dad's business trips. He wasn't coming back.

He plodded down the attic steps to the second floor. He glanced toward what was once his mom and dad's bedroom. Now it was Molly's room. The door was closed. She was probably sleeping. He knew why she was so sick and run-down lately. He'd heard her tell that cop that she was pregnant. So he was going to have another kid sister or a kid brother. He couldn't get all that excited about it, at least not right now.

Down the hall, Erin was asleep with her door open and her night-light on.

He went downstairs, where his Aunt Trish had some new age music playing on the iPod station while she prepared food for a brunch tomorrow. A medley of vegetables, bottles of olive oil and cooking wine, and packages of tofu were spread over the counter. His mother's younger sister had long, wavy gray hair, glasses, and a buxom figure she covered with loose, billowy, earth-tone clothes that always looked secondhand.

Heading toward the refrigerator, Chris worked up a smile. "Hey, Aunt Trish, what are you cooking?"

She was doing something with grape leaves. "We're making vegetable kabobs, tofu wraps, and meatless meatballs."

He didn't have the heart to tell her that most of his parents' friends probably wouldn't touch that vegan stuff. He took a Coke out of the refrigerator.

"Chris, I need to talk to you about something," she said, glancing up at him for a moment.

Sipping his Coke, he leaned against the counter. "What's up?"

His aunt started cutting the tofu in cubes. She looked down at her work while talking to him. Or maybe she just couldn't look him in the eye, he wasn't sure. "I need to make it clear to you—and Erin—that this is just for the next day or so," she said. "I can't stay here permanently—and I won't be able to look after you two. I don't know if you were thinking that or not. But I have my own life in Tacoma. I'm still planning to go to India for three months starting in February. I don't know exactly how well you and Erin get along with your stepmother. I suppose it doesn't matter much to you, because you'll be going off to college next year. But— there's Erin to consider. Have you—have you talked to Molly about her plans?"

"Not really," he murmured. He was stumped. For some reason, he'd imagined his aunt moving into the house—and Molly leaving. Part of him thought whatever bad luck Molly had brought to this house and this block might disappear along with her. He couldn't put his finger on it, but he didn't want to get close to her. Hell, she had a brother who was mentally ill—and a murderer. Was it something hereditary that could be passed on to his half sibling? And that night they'd waited up for his dad, he'd watched her smuggle a steak knife into the bedroom. What was that about?

Now, with a baby on the way, Molly would probably stay on with them. Then again, maybe she wouldn't want to stay on.

"What are you thinking?" his Aunt Trish asked.

He shrugged. "Nothing, I hadn't really considered anything past tomorrow and the funeral and all."

"Well, you need to talk to Molly, Chris," she said, blotting the tofu cubes with a paper towel.

He nodded, sipped his Coke, and wandered toward the front of the house. He stepped into his father's study. For the last few days, he couldn't set foot in this room without crying. But for the moment, his eyes were dry.

He glanced out the window and noticed a man walking his dog past the house. Chris could only see his silhouette.

He was thinking about Molly and the bad luck that followed her around. He wondered how many days would go by before someone else was hurt or killed.

He studied the Dennehy house—from the street this time, rather than from the woods in back. He had a dog on a leash, a mixed-breed stray he'd picked up yesterday. He'd let it go fend for itself again after this slow walk up and down Willow Tree Court.

He had used the dog-walking routine before to scope out different homes. It was a good ruse. People didn't worry about someone lurking in front of their home at night if the stranger had a dog on a leash. All they worried about was the dog crapping on their lawn. That older couple with the boy in college, he'd cased their Queen Anne home for six nights while walking some dog, a corgi, if he remembered right. No one ever noticed him.

He couldn't take his eyes off the Dennehy place. He already knew the entrances: front, through the garage, and a sliding glass door into the family room. A window by their breakfast table looked like the best way in. But he might end up just knocking on the front door, too. That was why he had all the different costumes in his secret room at home. Those outfits—deliveryman, cable man, paramedic—they opened doors for him. That had been how he'd gotten inside two of his homes.

The Dennehy house was perfect. There was a widow, an older boy in high school, and a little girl. Their house was a bit different from the one on Rochelle Lane—the one belonging to his widowed aunt. But it was on a cul-de-sac, and the ages of the Dennehy children were close to those of his cousins.

When he was eight, he had to stay with them at their house on Rochelle Lane in Ballard. His mother, who never married, used to dump him there for weeks at a time while she went to chase after some guy. He became the whipping boy for the family. His older cousin used to make him strip naked, and then he'd beat him up. The bratty kid sister told lies about him that would send his monster of an aunt into a tirade. As punishment, she'd lock him in a small, dark closet on the second floor—sometimes for as long as six or eight hours. He was always so grateful for the light. But that was one of the old bitch's bugaboos—when someone left a light on in a room. His cousins always blamed him whenever it happened, and he'd be locked in that upstairs closet again.

Every time his mother picked him up, he'd beg her not to send him back to live with his cousins. She told him that if he behaved better, he wouldn't get punished. She always drove him back there whenever some new man came into her life. He remembered dreading the sight of that NO OUT-LET sign at the end of their block.

Funny thing about time; it seemed those visits to his cousins went on for weeks at a time over a period of two or three years. But it was all within a year. He remembered having his ninth birthday with Warren, the stoner guy who eventually moved in with his mother. He wasn't sent to stay with his cousins again after Warren came into the picture.

In fact, he didn't set foot inside the Rochelle Lane house again—not until ten months ago, when he returned to Seattle after some jail time in St. Louis. He'd moved around a lot with his mother, and later with his mother and Warren. And he'd lived many places after he went out on his own at age seventeen. But the place that most seemed like his home had been his cousins' split-level at the end of that cul-de-sac. As much as he'd hated that place, he felt as if he'd grown up there.

Last February, he wanted to see it again. From the outside, the place hadn't changed much in twenty years. But other things were different. His bitch of an aunt had died of cancer in 2004. His older cousin, the sexual bully, had been killed in a car accident at age nineteen. He never found out what happened to his bratty younger cousin.

He stopped by the house on a Wednesday afternoon, when the winter sun was just starting to set. He had his switchblade with him. He carried it all the time. He really hadn't planned on using it that afternoon. He knocked on the door, and someone called out from the other side: "Who is it?"

"You don't know me, but I grew up in this house," he answered. "I lived here for three years with my aunt and my two cousins."

The door opened a crack—as far as the chain lock allowed. Through the chink, a handsome woman in her late sixties stared out at him. She had close-cropped silver hair with bangs and wore a lavender tracksuit.

"Sorry if I scared you," he said with a smile. "I've been away from Seattle for several years, and thought I'd take a sentimental journey. My cousins were the Coulters. I don't suppose you bought the house from them."

Eying him warily, she shook her head.

"Does the bathroom in the lower level still have those pink hexagon tiles?" he asked. "And is there still an old hand-crank pencil sharpener mounted on the wall as you walk into the furnace room? I always thought that was a strange place for a pencil sharpener."

She broke into a grin. "The tiles and the pencil sharpener are both still there."

He chuckled. "That's good to know. Well, thanks for your time . . ." He turned as if he were going to leave. He heard the chain lock rattling.

"Listen," she said. "Would you like to come in?"

He swiveled around and smiled at her. She had the door open now. "You sure it's not too much trouble?" he asked sheepishly.

"No trouble at all," she replied, opening the door wider. "You'll have to excuse the way the place looks. I wasn't expecting company. . . ."

The newspaper said her name was Irene Haskel, and she was seventy-four, a widow with two children and five grandchildren. He'd thought she was younger than that. In fact, he'd figured her to be about sixty-five, the same as his aunt would have been—had she lived.

She let him look at the upper level, and he stood outside that closet beside the bathroom. There had been a laundry hamper in there, and shelves full of sheets and towels that kept him from standing up all the way. His aunt had had another shelf with medicines, ointments, enema bottles, and a smelly old heating pad. The whole closet had smelled like that heating pad.

He noticed the bolt lock still on the outside of that door. He hadn't realized how flimsy it was until that moment.

Standing beside that woman who could have been his late aunt and stepping inside that house again brought back so much rage. He kept telling himself that she was a nice enough lady. He was still telling himself that as he grabbed her by the hair.

The Seattle Times reported that Irene Haskel had received thirty-eight stab wounds. Funny, he counted a lot—usually the seconds in order to time people and determine how long they took to do things. But he hadn't counted how many times he'd stabbed that woman with his switchblade. In fact, he barely remembered shoving her inside that tiny closet.

What he remembered most was how powerful he felt

afterward. He turned on practically every light in her house, and as he drove away, he stole the NO OUTLET sign from the end of the block.

The sense of vindication from the experience was so intoxicating that he had to do it again and again. He'd made it into a ritual now, refining every step a little more each time. The killing had almost become secondary now. The best rush was watching his victims tying each other up while he promised no one would get hurt. It gave him all the power and control. He was in charge.

Some ignorant shrink speculated in the newspaper about how *conflicted* he was. The analyst said he wanted to be discovered, so he turned on all the lights in the house. At the same time, he was ashamed, so he hid the bodies in closets. *Stupid.*

There was no conflict. He knew exactly what he was doing and how it made him feel. It made him feel exhilarated.

He slowed down as he walked past the Dennehy house again. He could see someone in one of the front windows. It was the teenage boy.

When the time came, he would save him for last.

CHAPTER TWENTY-FIVE

Exactly one week after Chris and Erin had buried their mother they were sitting in the front pew at the funeral mass for their dad.

Molly was in the same pew, but she might as well have been alone. Chris had asked Elvis to sit with him. Erin wanted nothing to do with her and clung to her Aunt Trish. Molly was the fifth wheel, seated on the aisle with Elvis at her side.

One good thing about being on the aisle—at least it was easier for her to make a hasty exit when she felt sick, even with the walk of shame down the aisle in front of everyone. Halfway through the service, she'd had to go get some fresh air. Rachel, several pews back, walked her outside, and she gave her a peppermint from her purse. It seemed to help— for a while anyway.

Molly felt a bit light-headed again as the priest gave the final blessing. She was supposed to lead the congregation out of the church, and when she did, Molly signaled to Rachel to help her. Her neighbor quickly came to her rescue, put an arm around her, and helped her down the aisle and out the church.

Outside, a few people shook her hand and gave their condolences. Molly kept thinking she just needed to lie down. But she hung in there, nodding and thanking people while Rachel kept a hand on her back. She looked around for Chris and Erin, but didn't see them on the sidewalk in front of the church.

Jill and Natalie approached her together, and each one shook her hand. It threw Molly for a loop. She hadn't noticed them among the congregation and couldn't believe Natalie, of all people, had come to Jeff's service. The reclusive neighbor gave Molly a tiny, joyless smile. "I'm sorry for your loss," she murmured.

"Thank you, Natalie," she managed to say. "And thank you for coming."

"Jenna? Jenna, is that you?"

Molly glanced over her shoulder toward the street. A thin, fortyish woman with her frizzy brown-gray hair half hidden by a bike helmet pedaled by on a bicycle. She wore a blue Windbreaker, and her bike toted a little go-cart carriage for a toddler, who was also in a bike helmet and bundled up in a jacket.

The bicyclist was looking right toward her—and her neighbors. "Jenna Corson, is that you?" she called.

Molly twisted around to look at Natalie, who suddenly glanced over her own shoulder. Molly didn't see anyone else who seemed to notice the bicyclist—or react to the name Jenna Corson.

Why would Ray Corson's widow want to come to Jeff's funeral?

Molly turned toward the woman on the bike again. With a puzzled, slightly embarrassed look, the bicyclist pedaled on—the child in the attached cart trailing behind her.

"Well, that's a little tacky," Molly heard Rachel whisper, "yelling at someone coming out of a funeral mass. Do you know this Jenna Carlson?"

"*Corson*," Molly murmured numbly. "Her husband was Chris's guidance counselor at the high school." She glanced around for Chris. If he was nearby, he might have recognized Mrs. Corson; but then Molly remembered—he'd never met her.

If anyone had a better reason not to mourn Jeff's passing it would have been Jenna Corson. *"You have a lot of nerve showing up here,"* Ray Corson's sister had growled at her and Chris at the Corson wake when they'd asked to talk to Jenna. *"Haven't you done enough damage? She's been through hell, thanks to you people."*

Why in the world would Jenna Corson attend Jeff's funeral?

Had she come to gloat?

The woman on the bicycle seemed to have been addressing one of her neighbors. Molly turned to face Natalie, but she wasn't there anymore. She'd disappeared among the mourners. "Natalie?" she called. "Natalie?"

No heads turned in the crowd. She wondered if Natalie looked like Jenna Corson.

Then it hit her. What if Natalie *was* Jenna Corson?

"Jenna!" she impulsively cried out. "Jenna Corson?"

"Molly, what are you doing?" she heard Rachel ask.

"She's been through hell, thanks to you people."

Was it Ray Corson's widow who had asked Kay the week before her death if she thought she was a good mother?

"You're going to pay for what you did," someone had told Angela.

That same someone had Angela, her boyfriend, and his daughter murdered. And that same night she'd arranged for Jeff to meet her in Vancouver. She'd known all along Jeff would have to account for his whereabouts that evening. Molly could still hear that raspy voice: *"Do you know where Jeff was that night, Mrs. Dennehy?"*

She could still see Angela in that booth in the restaurant,

a glass of wine in her hand. She'd wondered out loud: *"Maybe Jeff has found someone new, and she wants to sit back and watch us scratch each other's eyes out."*

In order to sit back and watch, she'd have had to be close by all the time. She'd have to be a neighbor.

"Jenna Corson, is that you?" the woman had called, staring directly at Molly and the women from her block. Everyone was there, except Lynette Hahn, who was at the hospital with Courtney.

Molly thought about Courtney's "accident" and Jeremy's arrest, their kids getting cut up in the vacant lot, Rachel's toolshed catching fire, Chris's locker being broken into, and the smashed pumpkins. Someone had hired a sleazy detective to look into her family history—months before Angela admitted to doing the same thing. He or she planted an anonymous note to Chris inside his locker and sent a letter to Rachel.

". . . she wants to sit back and watch . . ."

She remembered Lynette confronting her a few nights ago: *"For two years, I lived here—and we were all very happy, and then you moved in . . . and everything changed."* But Lynette wasn't quite right. Molly had lived on the block for ten months, and no had been hurt or killed. But then less than two weeks after Ray Corson's murder, Kay had had her fatal accident.

"Jenna?" Molly cried out, weaving through the crowd. "Jenna? I know you're here!" It all started to make sense, and the horrible realization made Molly's stomach turn. Ray Corson's widow was there, watching.

"Molly, for God's sake," Rachel whispered, trailing after her.

She caught a glimpse of Chris, by the church steps with Elvis. He was scowling at her as if she was crazy. His face seemed to go out of focus. The sidewalk felt wobbly. Molly's head was spinning. She reached toward Rachel just as her legs started to give out.

Then everything went black.

She could hear people downstairs, chatting quietly. Molly opened her eyes and saw Rachel sitting at her bedside. For a moment, she felt totally disoriented and thought it was morning. But then she saw the digital clock on her nightstand: 12:55 P.M.

Molly realized she was still in her dress from the funeral. She vaguely remembered riding home in the limo, and Chris and Elvis helping her upstairs to the bedroom. Trish was supposed to be hosting a brunch.

Molly tried to sit up. "Who's downstairs?" she asked groggily. "Are Jill and Natalie down there?"

Rachel shook her head. "No, the brunch was kind of a bust. People could see you weren't exactly up for entertaining. And the few that came over got one look at the booze-free, meatless vegan spread Miss Crunchy Granola had laid out, and they headed for the hills." She reached for the bottle of ginger capsules on Molly's nightstand. "It didn't even last an hour. The only ones left down there are Trish and a friend of hers, Chris and his pal, and Erin—and a ton of rabbit food no one touched." She took out a pill and offered her a tumbler of water. "Here . . ."

Molly shook her head. "No, I think those are making me even sicker."

With a shrug, Rachel put down the tumbler and set the pill beside it. "In case you change your mind." She moved over and sat at the end of the bed. "So—you kind of scared me out there in front of the church. What's the story with this Jenna person? You said she was the wife of Chris's coach?"

"She's the widow of Chris's guidance counselor," Molly

said, reaching for the tumbler on her nightstand. She gulped down some water. "Her name is Jenna Corson, and I—I think she's behind all the strange things that have been happening on this block—including Jeff's death. . . ."

Molly somehow felt stronger as she explained to Rachel about who Jenna Corson was and why she would want to hurt the people on the cul-de-sac.

"Why would this Jenna person threaten me?" Rachel asked. "I didn't have anything to do with her husband getting the ax at Chris's high school. I wasn't even living here at the time. Yet she was ready to burn my house down. I didn't want to tell you, Molly, but I got another one of those calls yesterday, and that lady is crazy. Why would she pick on me?"

"Maybe it's because you're my friend," Molly replied. She took another swig of water and sat up straighter. "I'm the one who first reported the incident with her husband and that poor student. Chris and I started it all. And look what happened. She made Chris an orphan."

"And you think she was outside the church after the funeral?" Rachel asked.

"More than that," Molly answered. "I think she was standing right in front of me when that woman rode by on the bicycle and called out to her."

Rachel stared at her. "But the only people there were Jill, Natalie, and me."

Molly nodded. She was thinking back to the day before Jeff died, when he'd come home from work, and the same group had gathered at the end of the driveway—Rachel, Jill, and Natalie. Jeff had been home so seldom that she'd had to introduce him to their neighbors. Then he'd acted so peculiar—to the point of rudeness. Was it because he already knew one of them—and he was having an affair with her?

One of the women in that group had spent the weekend with Jeff in Vancouver, British Columbia. She'd had another tryst with him in La Conner. And she'd poisoned him with drugs and alcohol in a hotel by the airport four days ago.

"So—you're saying that Natalie or Jill—*or me*—one of us is really Jenna?" Rachel let out a stunned, little laugh. "Do you need to see my birth certificate?"

Molly quickly shook her head. "No, not you," she said. "I think it's Natalie. I've always had a weird feeling about her. And just seconds after that woman called out Jenna's name, Natalie disappeared. I'd be surprised if Natalie shows her face again on this block. How much do we know about her anyway?"

At the same time, Molly couldn't totally dismiss her other neighbor, Jill. There was something very sensual and earthy about her that might have appealed to Jeff. She was just about the right age to have been Ray Corson's wife. And Molly remembered they had a young son. Was he around Darren's age? Molly wasn't sure.

She hated to even think it, but she couldn't be one hundred percent sure about Rachel, either. But then that meant Rachel had set fire to her own toolshed and left herself that threatening voice mail, and sent herself the letter with the news clipping about Charlie. And even though the bicyclist had called out Jenna's name—exposing her—there was Rachel at Molly's bedside when she'd awoken.

"Don't you think we should call the police?" she asked. "I mean, they should know about this Jenna person."

Molly smiled a tiny bit and told herself that Jenna Corson would never have made such a suggestion.

"We can't call the police, not yet." She sighed, shaking her head. "You heard me trying to explain everything to Chet Blazevich the day before yesterday. He didn't believe me—and hell, *he likes me*. No, before we go to the police, we need some solid proof that Jenna Corson is responsible for all these deaths and 'accidents.' We have to determine whether it's Natalie or Jill behind all this." Molly paused.

"Listen to me with the 'we this' and 'we that.' I didn't mean to be so presumptuous. You don't have to be involved."

Rachel reached over, took her hand. "Go ahead and presume, honey. I'm here for you. By the way, you're finally getting some color in your cheeks. I'll go see if I can find something edible for you down there. You stay put."

"Thanks," Molly said, working up a smile. She watched Rachel head for the door, and her smile waned. She had to know something. Molly waited until her new friend was in the doorway, and then she said in a quiet voice, *"Jenna?"*

Rachel stepped out to the hallway, then hesitated and glanced back at her. "Did you just say something?"

Molly quickly shook her head.

Rachel frowned at her. "Yes, you did. You said, 'Jenna.' "

"I'm so sorry," Molly replied, grimacing. "I just needed to be sure. . . ."

Rachel sighed. "Listen, I'm suddenly not feeling so well myself. I think I'll go home and lie down—"

"Please, Rachel, I'm sorry." Molly started to climb off the bed. "That was stupid of me, I—"

"I'll be sure to bring my driver's license with me next time I come over, Molly," she said. Then she turned and started down the hallway.

"Rachel, wait!" Molly heard her footsteps retreating down the stairs. She started to get up, but felt a head rush and quickly sat down on the bed again.

She heard the front door open and shut.

"Hello, you reached the Nguyens. We cannot come to the phone right now. But if you leave a message, we will be back to you."

Molly listened to Mrs. Nguyen's recorded voice. She had the Nguyens' Denver phone number in her address book by the phone in her bedroom. She sat on the edge of her bed and waited until the beep sounded.

"Hi, Dr. and Mrs. Nguyen," she said. "This is Molly Dennehy, your neighbor on Willow Tree Court. I need to ask you about Natalie, the woman who's staying in your house. It's very important. Could you call me—"

A click on the other end of the line interrupted her. "Hello?" Molly said.

"This Mrs. Nguyen," she said, in her slightly fractured English. "Molly? What you talking about with a woman in our house? There's no woman staying in our house."

Molly hesitated. "Ah, actually, Mrs. Nguyen, there is," she said. "A woman named Natalie has been staying at your house for the last two months—"

"What you mean?" Mrs. Nguyen interrupted. "No, house is empty. We have Todd to check every week. No one is living there now. We don't know any Natalie."

"Mrs. Nguyen, I've seen this woman coming and going into your house since September," Molly said. "She's a thin blonde in her late thirties—or early forties—and she goes by the name Natalie."

"No, that not right. I call Todd to find out. It's mistake. . . ."

"Is it possible someone named Jenna is staying there? Jenna Corson?"

"No! Nobody staying there!" Mrs. Nguyen declared angrily.

"Would you mind if I called your friend, Todd, and talked to him? It's very important I find out more about this woman."

"One minute, please," Mrs. Nguyen said.

"Yes, I'll wait," Molly replied. "Thank you."

While Molly stayed on the line, she thought about how she'd hurt Rachel's feelings earlier. Her only friend in the world, and she'd alienated her.

A part of her couldn't help wondering if she was a little crazy or hormonal—or just in shock over Jeff's death. This notion that Ray Corson's widow had infiltrated the block in order to invoke some kind of revenge was pretty far-fetched.

And it was all based on the fact that some woman had called out Jenna's name to a crowd of people.

Now it didn't seem so crazy. She kept thinking about the way Natalie had suddenly disappeared right after that.

Molly remembered Natalie jogging past her house when Angela's murder had drawn a crowd of newspeople and gawkers. She'd jogged past Lynette's house when Jeremy's arrest brought the spectators and news crews back to the block a week later. Though from afar Natalie had seemed uninterested, Molly wondered if her neighbor had felt compelled to be out there at that particular time. Maybe she'd wanted to witness the fruits of her labors.

"Molly?" Mrs. Nguyen said, getting back on the line.

"Yes, I'm here," she said, grabbing a pen off the nightstand.

"Have you seen this woman take anything from house?"

"No, I haven't, but then I can't be sure," Molly replied. "Do you have a phone number or e-mail for this Todd person?"

"I call him right now."

"Well, could I call him, too? Please, Mrs. Nguyen, it's important."

"His name is Todd Millikan," Mrs. Nguyen said. "425-555-8860."

Jotting it down on the front page of her address book, Molly repeated the number out loud to make sure she heard it right past Mrs. Nguyen's accent. "Is that right?" she asked.

"Yes. I call him right now."

"Thank you, Mrs. Nguyen. If you get through to him, could you call me? He might not pick up for someone he doesn't know. I'll do the same for you if I get ahold of him."

"Yes, yes, good-bye," she said abruptly. Then Molly heard a click on the other end.

She clicked off and decided to wait a few minutes before calling Todd Millikan. With the address book in her hand, Molly stood up—remembering at only the last minute to take it slow. In her stocking feet, she walked out of the bedroom and down the front stairs. She could hear water running in the kitchen and the clattering of dishes and silverware. Trish was talking to her friend, Holly, in the kitchen. From the front hallway, she saw Erin napping on the family-room sofa.

Molly quietly opened the front door. The chilly November breeze whipped against her, but she stepped outside in her black funeral dress and stocking feet. The sky was overcast, and she felt a few raindrops as she padded to the end of the walkway. Clutching the address book to her chest, Molly kept her arms folded in front of her. Down the block, the windows in the Nguyens' house were all dark. Natalie's blue Mini Cooper wasn't in the driveway.

Molly turned and headed back to the house again and found Trish in the doorway. Her friend Holly, a thin thirty-something blonde with a Joan of Arc buzz cut and glasses, hovered behind her. They both gaped at her as if she was crazy. "Molly, are you all right?" Trish asked, glancing down at her stocking feet.

"I'm fine." She nodded distractedly. "Did Chris and Elvis go out?"

"No, they're downstairs, watching TV," Trish replied. She and Holly stepped aside as Molly came into the house.

"Good. Everyone's home, everybody's safe," she murmured.

Trish closed the door behind her. "Are you sure you're okay?"

"Could I get you a plate of food?" Holly chimed in. "There's plenty left over."

Molly shook her head, and then, without thinking, she suddenly hugged Trish. "Listen, thank you so much for everything," she said. "You've both been so terrific. I'm sorry I've been ill. . . ." She pulled back. "Oh, and don't worry, I'm not contagious. Anyway, thank you." She nodded toward Jeff's study. "I need to make a call, okay?"

Trish and Holly both nodded and seemed to work up smiles for her—as if she were someone on probation from a mental institution.

Molly ducked into Jeff's study and closed the door. Rain tapped against the window, and it was dark enough that she had to turn on the lamp on his desk. Consulting the front page of her address book, she picked up the cordless phone and punched in Todd Millikan's number. She counted four rings until a message clicked on.

"Hi, it's Todd," the recording said. *"You've missed me, but you got my voice mail. You know what to do. Talk after the beep. Ciao for now."*

Beep.

"Hi, Todd," she said into the phone. "My name is Molly Dennehy, and I live down the block from the Nguyens' house on Willow Tree Court. I can't get ahold of Natalie, and I'm kind of concerned about something. Could you please call me as soon as possible?"

Molly left her phone number, and then clicked off.

She gazed at Jeff's computer monitor for a moment, and then reached for the mouse. She went to Google, typed in Jenna Corson, and clicked Images.

The response came back, "Did you mean Jenna Carlson?" And there were dozens of pictures of Jenna Carlsons, but not one picture of a Jenna Corson. Molly tried Facebook, and came up with a nineteen-year-old Jenna Corson at Marquette University in Milwaukee, and a fifty-two-year-old mother of five in Oakmont, Pennsylvania.

She glanced out the rain-beaded window at Rachel's house next door. She needed to apologize to her—and she wanted to tell her about Natalie. But reaching for the phone, Molly hesitated. Instead of making the call, she went back to the computer keyboard and tried a new entry on Google Image: Rachel Cross.

Most of the results were for a singer/songwriter named Rachel Cross, and there were a lot of photos of purses called

Rachel Cross Body Bags. Molly went through eleven pages
with twenty Rachel Cross pictures per page, and she didn't
see her neighbor in any of the photos. She'd really hoped to
find something, too. She still wanted to call her, but right
now, she couldn't afford to trust anyone.

She tried Jill Emory. After six pages of the wrong Jill
Emory, pictures of Jill St. John started coming up. Molly re-
fined the search, and typed in Jill Emory, Seattle Art Institute. At the bottom of the first page was a small photo of
someone who looked very much like Darren's mom, posing
with another woman—at some formal occasion. Molly
clicked on the image. *Stepping Out in Style! Friends of the
Arts Gala Fundraiser Nets $50,000 at Seattle Art Institute*
was the headline of the story—from 2007. Scrolling down
past about twenty photos, Molly found the one with her
neighbor, looking slightly slimmer in a black dress with a
red satin jacket. All smiles, she posed with a pretty blond
woman. *The Art Institute's Jill Emory chats with Keynote
Speaker, Barbara Campbell,* said the caption.

That cleared Jill.

She wished she knew Natalie's last name—so she could
try looking up her image. She kept glancing over at the
phone, waiting for it to ring. She started sketching on the
desk notepad—a cartoon of a woman. It looked a little like
Natalie.

Molly suddenly put down the pen and opened the side
drawer to Jeff's desk, where she'd stashed the bill from his
secret MasterCard account. She glanced at the charges for
the La Conner Channel Lodge, the Palmer Restaurant, and
Windmill Antiques & Miniatures.

La Conner was a little over an hour away by car.

Molly glanced at the crude cartoon she'd drawn on the
notepad. Getting to her feet, she hurried up to her attic studio. She was a bit winded reaching the top step. She still
hadn't put away the yellow paint or cleaned up the mess.
Molly ignored all the destruction as she retrieved her sketch

pad and charcoals. She didn't want to work up here. She needed to be in the front of the house, where she could keep an eye out for Natalie's Mini Cooper should it come down the block. And she wanted to be near the phone in case it rang.

She brought the pad and charcoals down to Jeff's study. Molly sat down and started to draw from memory a portrait of her neighbor, the woman who called herself Natalie.

As she worked on the drawing, Molly lost track of the time. She was trying to capture on paper Natalie's fine, limp dark blond hair when she glanced up at the window. The rain was coming down harder, and it had turned dark out. She clicked the mouse on Jeff's computer and checked the time: 4:11 P.M.

It had been three hours since she'd called the Nguyens and left that message for Todd Millikan. She phoned the Nguyens again. It rang twice before Mrs. Nguyen answered: "Hello?"

"Hi, Mrs. Nguyen, it's Molly Dennehy calling again. I was just wondering if you were able to get ahold of Todd yet."

"Oh, yes, I talk to him," Mrs. Nguyen said. "You mistaken. He come by a few times to check on the house with friend, Natalie. But no one staying there. House is empty, he said. You mistaken."

"Mrs. Nguyen, that's just not true. How well do you know this Todd person? He isn't being honest with you. He—"

"Todd is friend of my son for fifteen years!" she interrupted impatiently. "I trust him. He looking after house while we are away for two years now. You mistaken."

Molly said nothing. All she could think was that Natalie— or *Jenna*—must have somehow gotten to this Todd person. He'd put her up in the Nguyens' house and now he was covering for her. Maybe she was paying him or having sex with him. Or maybe she was blackmailing the guy. It didn't really matter how she'd gotten him to work for her.

What mattered most was that Todd knew someone had caught on to the deception. And even if Mrs. Nguyen hadn't said anything, Todd could be sure it was the Willow Tree Court neighbor who had left him a voice mail: Molly Dennehy at 206-555-2755.

So Natalie—or Jenna—or whatever she called herself when she was screwing Jeff—certainly had to know by now that she'd been found out.

"Mrs. Nguyen," Molly said finally. "Todd's lying to you. But I guess you'll have to find that out for yourself. Thanks for your time."

She hung up, clicked on the phone again, and dialed Rachel's number. It rang four times and then the message clicked on. It was one of those impersonal automated greetings. Molly waited for the beep. "Hi, Rachel," she said. "I don't know if you can hear this, but call me as soon as you can. I need to apologize. And I have to tell you something about our neighbor down the block. Please call me back, okay?"

Molly clicked off the phone, then went to the window and looked at Rachel's house. Rain pelted the car, still in the driveway, and there were some lights on inside the house.

She thought back to the last time she'd seen a light on in that house and no one had picked up the phone.

She knew Rachel was upset with her, and that was probably why she didn't answer the phone. Still, Rachel had been getting those threatening calls—just as Kay and Angela had been getting. And now that Natalie—or Jenna whatever her name was—knew she'd been found out, all bets were off. All hell could break loose.

Molly reached for the phone again, but a knock on the front door stopped her. She hurried into the foyer and checked the peephole. Someone was holding a driver's license up to the other side of the viewer. Molly couldn't make out whose license it was. The photo and the writing were slightly blurred.

"Molly, is someone at the door?" Trish called from upstairs.

She hesitated, but then opened the door.

Rachel was on the front stoop, with a hooded Windbreaker on to protect her from the rain. She was holding up her driver's license. "This is my Florida license," she said. Then she showed her a piece of paper with her picture on it. "And this is my temporary license for Washington state, and here's my Macy's card. . . ."

"Molly, who is it?" Trish called.

"It's Rachel for me!" she called back. She smiled at her. "Get in here."

Stepping inside, Rachel put the cards in her pocket and pulled back the hood to her Windbreaker. "I heard you apologize to my machine," she announced. "And I decided to forgive you since you're recently widowed and knocked up and all. I'm glad to see you're out of bed."

Molly nodded and quickly pulled her into the study. She closed the door.

Rachel unzipped her Windbreaker. She glanced down at the sketch pad on Jeff's desk. "That's Natalie, isn't it?"

Molly nodded. "It's her name around here, at least. Tomorrow, I'm taking that sketch up to La Conner, and I'm hitting the spots where Jeff wined, dined, and had sex with that bitch. Someone's bound to recognize her."

"So—you think she's really this Jenna person?" Rachel asked, a tiny bit skeptical.

"The owners of that house down the block, the Nguyens, they have no idea she's living there," Molly whispered. "I just talked to Mrs. Nguyen. Their house sitter, some guy named Todd, has them convinced the place is empty. And I have a feeling from today on, it will be. She's not going to stick around now that she's been found out. . . ."

Rachel stared at her and didn't say anything. Her light brown hair was a bit wet, and some raindrops slid down the sides of her face. For a moment, Molly wondered if she really believed her—or if maybe she'd just been trying to placate her earlier.

Molly remembered the pitying look Chet Blazevich had given her when she'd tried to convince him that Jeff had been murdered. She thought about the way just three hours ago, Trish and Holly gazed at her as if she were a mental patient. Was Rachel like them? Did she think all of this was in her mind—some paranoid conspiracy scenario from an unbalanced woman who was "recently widowed and knocked up and all?"

"I'm not making this up, you know," Molly insisted. "I was just on the phone with Mrs. Nguyen fifteen minutes ago. I'm not sure why, but this Todd person lied and told them the place is empty. He's been covering for this woman. And now she knows she's been found out. But I don't think she'll quietly disappear, either. I think she'll wreak as much havoc and take as many lives as she can before she vanishes."

Rachel didn't say anything. She just kept looking at her with a bewildered expression.

"You don't believe me, do you?" Molly asked, tears in her eyes.

"I do believe you, honey," Rachel whispered, nodding. She grabbed her hand and squeezed it. "I believe you, and I'm scared. I'm scared for all of us."

The rumbling of the clothes dryer seemed to drown out her crying.

After five days, Chris and Erin were headed back to school tomorrow—and they didn't have any clean clothes. Neither did Molly, for that matter. Still in her black funeral dress, she'd gone down to the basement after dinner to do some wash. She'd gathered a load of whites and found several of Jeff's V-neck T-shirts. The shirts still smelled like him. He would never wear them again. She pressed one of the T-shirts to her face and started sobbing.

She didn't hear anybody coming down the basement steps. But Molly glimpsed a shadow sweeping across the utility room wall. She swiveled around to see Chris standing in the doorway of the recreation room. "Oh, Jesus," she gasped, a hand over her heart.

"Sorry, I didn't mean to scare you," he said sheepishly. He was wearing sweatpants and a *Futurama* T-shirt.

"That's okay," she said in a scratchy voice. "I just didn't hear you—for a change." Usually it sounded like a stampede when he was going up or down stairs. Molly set the T-shirt on top of the dryer. She tore off a sheet of paper towel from a roll above the laundry sink and blew her nose.

"You wanted Elvis to call and let us know once he got home all right," Chris said. "He just called my cell. You can relax. He's home, and he's fine."

"Thanks," Molly said.

Chris and Elvis had stared at her as if she was crazy when she insisted Elvis phone them when he got home. She'd gotten a similarly perplexed look from Trish and Holly when she'd asked them to do the same thing as they'd left this afternoon. They'd called before dinner, saying they'd made it back to Tacoma okay.

"I know you think I'm being way overcautious," she said. "But I have a good reason to be."

"Why is that?" he asked, raising an eyebrow. "You still think some lady killed my dad and mom—along with Larry and Taylor and Mrs. Garvey?"

"I forgot that you heard me talking to Detective Blazevich on Sunday." Frowning, Molly nodded. "Yes, I think this woman is the one behind Courtney's accident, and Mr. Hahn's arrest, and Rachel's toolshed catching on fire. I think she broke into your locker, too. Your mother even talked about it with me that last day—"

"The day she was killed," Chris said.

Molly nodded. "Over lunch, your mother asked me, 'Do

you think some woman is trying to pit us against each other?' And I believe your mother was right."

Chris didn't say anything. He folded his arms and leaned against a support beam.

"Let me ask you," Molly said. "Do you really believe your father was alone in that hotel room when he overdosed? You know he didn't do drugs, Chris. Don't you think he might have been tricked into taking them?"

"Maybe," he muttered, shrugging. "I used to think I knew my dad really well, but things changed. I'm not so sure anymore."

Molly studied his hurt, confused expression as he glanced down at the floor. She realized she couldn't tell him that Jenna Corson could have orchestrated all the recent killings and tragedies—not until she knew for certain. If he knew the scandal with Mr. Corson had caused his parents' deaths, Chris wouldn't be able to live with the guilt.

"I believe Natalie, the woman staying in the Nguyens' house, might be responsible for everything that's going on," Molly said.

"That's the jogger lady you don't like," Chris said. "Is she the one you were yelling at in front of the church today? I couldn't make out what you were saying. . . ."

Molly nodded. "I think she's very dangerous. She knows she's been found out, so I doubt she'll be coming back to the Nguyens' house. If she has any unfinished business, she's going to wrap it up very soon. We have to be on our guard. If you see her, Chris, you need to let me know."

Reaching up with one hand, Chris tugged at the clothesline. "Well, I really don't know what she looks like, so that'll be kind of tough."

Molly could tell he wasn't taking her very seriously. She opened the dryer, took out a pile of warm towels, and started folding them. "I'm just trying to tell you to be very careful and cautious for the next day or two. As soon as I can gather some more information about this woman, I'm going to the police."

"Why don't you go to the police now?" he asked.

"Because—like you, they don't believe me," Molly replied edgily. "They think I'm paranoid—and irrational and maybe crazy."

"I was talking to Elvis, and he said ladies can get that way when they're pregnant."

Molly put down an unfolded hand towel. "So—you know?"

"Yeah, like I told you, I heard you talking to that cop."

"And how do you feel about becoming a big brother again?" she asked nervously.

He gave an uneasy shrug. "To be honest, I'm not really sure. Are you keeping it?"

She scowled at him. "Of course I'm keeping it! What kind of question is that?"

"Well, you said you were mad at Dad. I wasn't sure how you felt about having his baby."

"Chris, I loved your father," she said. "I want very much to have this baby. I know you and Erin have had your problems adjusting to me as your stepmother. You'd probably prefer to go live with Aunt Trish, or have her move here. But—"

"Aunt Trish doesn't want us," he interrupted. "She told me last night. She's got her own life, and she's going to India in a few months. So you're it. Nobody else wants to take us."

Molly let out a stunned laugh. "Well, I don't have anybody else but you guys. So I guess we're stuck with each other. Are you okay with that, Chris?"

"Sure, I guess," he murmured.

She smiled at him and then uncertainly put her arms out. Chris shuffled over and awkwardly hugged her.

She patted his back. "I really wish you were happier about this—and about the baby."

"Give me a little time, Molly, okay?" he whispered. "Just a little more time."

He went to bed at 11:20. Molly stayed up late, getting MapQuest directions from the Internet for the places she needed to visit in La Conner tomorrow. She got an e-mail from Rachel at 12:55 A.M:

> I'm locking up and going to bed. I can see your study
> light is still on. Get some sleep. You don't want to get
> sick again! See you tomorrow ☺

But Molly didn't go up to bed. She got a blanket and slept on the living room sofa. If Natalie's car came down the street, she wanted to hear it. And if someone tried to break into the house, she wanted to hear that, too.

She had her family to protect.

CHAPTER TWENTY-SIX

"Hi, it's Todd. You've missed me, but you got my voice mail. You know what to do. Talk after the beep. Ciao for now."

Standing in the driveway, Molly held the cell phone to her ear. At this point, she really didn't expect him to pick up or call her back.

With a sigh, she clicked off her phone and shoved it in her purse. She already had a supply of peppermints to ward off morning sickness in there. She set the purse on the front passenger seat of her Saturn. Also on the seat were MapQuest directions to various spots in La Conner, and her sketch of Natalie. A bottle of water was in the cup holder.

She'd put Erin on the school bus, and her stepdaughter had actually hugged her good-bye—the first demonstration of affection since the yellow-paint incident. Chris had taken his dad's Lexus to school. He and Elvis had picked it up at some police holding lot on Monday. Molly figured the cops had taken it from the hotel so they could search it for drugs.

Before leaving the house, she'd called Rachel to make sure she was all right. "Not really," her neighbor had replied, sounding groggy. "I didn't sleep well last night, and I'm feeling a little baby barfy right now. Call me when you get back from La Conner, okay?"

Molly hadn't slept too well herself. She'd kept listening for a car on the block but never heard anything. She'd finally dozed off at around three in the morning. Without her usual two cups of Starbucks Breakfast Blend, she still felt sluggish. But at least she wasn't sick.

It was chilly and overcast out. She had on a black sweater, jeans, and a pea jacket. Before ducking behind the wheel, she glanced once more down the block at the Nguyens' house. The windows were dark, and Natalie's car wasn't in the driveway.

As far as Molly knew, Natalie hadn't come back since the funeral yesterday. If that woman shouting, *"Jenna!"* at her hadn't sent her scurrying, an obvious bulletin from Todd about her precarious living arrangement certainly had. That meant her things were still there—maybe even some personal items like an appointment book or a journal.

Molly made sure her car doors were locked; then she hiked up the collar of her pea jacket and started down the street toward the Nguyens' house. Lynette's car wasn't in the driveway, and it hadn't been there yesterday, either. Next door, Jill's Toyota was parked in front of her garage.

Heading up the Nguyens' walkway, Molly glanced over to Jill's house to make sure no one was watching her. She rang the Nguyens' bell twice and then tried the door. *Locked.* After a cautious glance over her shoulder, she crept behind some bushes alongside the house to the first window. The curtains were open, and she studied the formal dining room— with a chandelier over the table for six. She saw a sweater, some magazines, and what looked like a pile of mail on the table. Over on the side table, there was a boom box.

Molly had been inside the Nguyens' house twice—once for a party, and another time to pick up donations for a charity drive. She remembered a beautiful silver service on that side table. A silver bowl with two silver candelabras had been in the center of the dining table. Molly wondered if the Nguyens packed up all that stuff and put it in storage whenever they went to Denver.

"Have you seen this woman take anything from house?" Mrs. Nguyen had asked.

Perhaps Natalie—or whatever name she used with the pawnbroker—had sold a few household items for some quick cash.

Molly skulked out from behind the bushes and crept around to the back of the house. She tried the kitchen door. It was locked, too. The kitchen window was open a crack, but she couldn't reach it. By the garbage cans, she noticed an empty square plastic crate to collect recycling. Grabbing the crate, Molly threaded her way through some bushes by the house. She found a bare spot beneath the kitchen window, set the plastic box upside down, and stepped up on it. The crate didn't feel too sturdy. She nervously clung to the windowsill. She was terrified of falling and possibly harming the baby.

Past the screen window, she peered into the Nguyens' kitchen. It was a mess. When Molly had last seen the place, Mrs. Nguyen had the kitchen looking spotless, and on the counter had been a collection of top-of-the-line cooking aids—a Mixmaster, rice cooker, blender, and toaster oven. None of those things was there anymore. But the counter was cluttered with dirty plates and glasses, empty bottles and cans, Styrofoam containers, and fast-food bags.

To get inside, she'd need a screwdriver or something to pry the screen off the window. And even then, she couldn't boost herself up past the sill to climb in—not from this vantage point. She needed a ladder and someone to spot her.

Molly stepped down from the crate. She crept along the side of the house, stopping at every basement window, and then getting down on all fours to see if any of them were unlocked. She rounded the corner and was about to test the fourth basement window when she heard a twig snap behind her.

Molly turned and saw someone standing a few feet away, staring down at her.

"Oh, Jill, God, you scared me," she said.

"What are you doing?" her neighbor asked.

Molly straightened up and then stepped around the shrubs. "Oh, I—I was looking for Erin's pet ferret, Fergie. She—she got out, and I chased her down the block to the backyard here. You haven't seen her, have you?"

With a baffled look, Jill shook her head.

Molly glanced toward the Nguyens' house. "I hope I didn't disturb Natalie."

"I don't think she's home," Jill said. "I haven't seen her since the funeral yesterday. How are you holding up?"

Molly shrugged. "I'm a little better than yesterday. Thanks for asking."

"Listen, if Natalie doesn't come back tonight, you and Rachel will have the cul-de-sac to yourselves," Jill said. "Lynette and the kids are staying at her sister's, because she's closer to the hospital. And Darren's sleeping over at a friend's tonight, so I'm going to our cabin on Anderson Island."

"Well, have a good time," Molly said.

"That detective mentioned at that block-watch meeting that we should let neighbors know if we won't be home, so I figure what the heck. Anyway, I should get cracking if I want to catch the next ferry." She turned and started toward her house. "I hope you find your ferret!" she called over her shoulder.

"I'll weed her out!" Molly replied.

Five minutes later when she got back to her car, Molly dug the cell phone out of her purse and dialed Rachel again. She still sounded sleepy when she picked up. "Hello?"

"I'm sorry to bother you again, but could you do me a big favor?" Molly asked.

"What is it?" Rachel asked, yawning.

"Just make sure if Natalie comes back, that she doesn't leave again. I don't want her clearing out the house and then disappearing. Could you keep a lookout while I'm in La Conner?"

"I'll set up a roadblock should she return," Rachel said. "Seriously, I might go to the mini-mart for a few minutes, but I won't linger. I promise."

"Thanks," Molly said. "When I get back this afternoon, we'll have the entire block to ourselves. Everyone else will be gone. If Natalie left anything behind in the house, this is our chance to sneak in there and take a look. How would you like to help me get inside the Nguyens' later today?"

"You mean like breaking and entering?"

"Well, you'd hold a ladder while I pry a screen off the kitchen window and climb inside. So—yes, breaking and entering."

"Sounds like fun. Sign me up. Listen, I'm still not feeling a hundred percent right now. But I should rally by the time you get back. I'll call your cell if Nat makes an appearance."

"Thanks, Rachel," she said. "Feel better. And be careful. Watch your back, okay?"

"I will. Good luck up in La Conner."

Molly heard her hang up on the other end. She clicked off and set the phone down on the passenger seat.

Biting her lip, she started up the car and pulled out of the driveway. She glanced over at Rachel's house. She wondered if her neighbor really took her seriously. Did she have any idea just how dangerous Natalie could be? Rachel was the only friend she had right now, and she didn't want to lose her.

As she pulled out of the cul-de-sac, Molly was still worried about Rachel.

She didn't notice the NO OUTLET sign at the end of the block was missing.

Chris didn't take his father's Lexus to school.

He drove it to the Marriott by the airport. He parked in the same tiered lot his father had probably used five days ago. He'd brought along a photo of his dad. He wasn't sure how much he believed Molly's rants about a woman causing all these recent deaths and accidents; but he knew she was right about something. His dad wouldn't have been in that hotel room alone.

He decided to try the coffee house off the lobby first. It looked like they were finishing up the last of the breakfast rush crowd. He ordered a bowl of Rice Krispies and an orange juice, which cost him $13.50. He showed his dad's photo to the waitress, and she didn't recognize him. The busboy who filled his water glass didn't recognize his dad, either. And the photo didn't look familiar to two waitresses Chris stopped on his way out of the restaurant.

Wandering around the hallways, he stopped three maids and showed them his father's picture. None of them had seen his dad on Friday.

In the lobby, he stopped to talk to a uniformed guy who was holding doors and hauling suitcases. He was a good-looking Latino not much older than him. His Marriott name tag said FELIX. Chris showed him the photo of his dad. "Did you happen to see this man here on Friday?"

Felix popped three Tic Tacs in his mouth and immediately started munching them. "He looks just like you," he said, studying the photo. "Who is he?"

"My—my uncle," Chris lied. "He overdosed in one of the rooms."

"Oh, shit, man, that's the guy the police were asking about," Felix said. "He's your uncle?"

Chris nodded. "I want to find out if he was alone or not."

Felix glanced past Chris's shoulder. "C'mon, step out with me. The desk clerk is looking at us. Goddamn weasel is always on my case. . . ."

Chris went through the lobby doors with him to the covered atrium, where there was a baggage cart for pushing suitcases and a valet station. He zipped up his school jacket. "Anything you heard, anything you could tell me would be really helpful," he said.

"Well, I hear he had himself a real party there in 104," Felix said. "If you gotta go, that's the way to go. Wait here. . . ." He took the photo over to a tall, blond guy at the valet station.

Shoving his hands in his jacket pockets, Chris stood by the door. He watched Felix show the photo to his pal. He whispered something to the blond guy, and they both chuckled. Chris had a bad feeling about this. His eyes started to tear up.

Felix came back, fanning himself with the photo. "Yeah, I didn't see him myself, but my buddy and I know the girl who waited on him in the bar. The police didn't talk to her. But I can track her down for you for . . . twenty bucks."

"Twenty bucks," Chris repeated. He held out his hand. "Can I have the photo back?"

Felix gave it to him.

Pocketing the photo, Chris backed toward the lobby door. "Thanks," he said. "And fuck you. I'm going to have a talk with your pal, the desk clerk, and then I'll tell the police you were holding out on them."

"Hey, now, wait a minute, wait a minute," Felix said. "First off, hot shot, dry your eyes. That wasn't your uncle in the picture, was it? He looked too much like you. He was your dad, wasn't he?"

Chris quickly wiped the tears away. "Are you going to help me or not?"

Felix nodded. "A friend of mine, Roseann, she's a part-timer here, and she uses her sister's green card. She'd be in a shitload of trouble if the hotel or the cops got wind of that. So her sister is covering for her, and saying she worked Friday. She's saying she saw nothing and they're sticking to that. But between you and me, your old man came into the bar, and Roseann waited on him. Rosie remembered, because they found him dead and his picture was on TV the next day. Anyway, Rosie said he was with a woman."

"How can I get ahold of this Roseann?" Chris asked.

"You can't. And you aren't repeating what I just told you to anybody, because if you do, I'll kick the shit out of you."

"Please," Chris whispered. "I think this woman might have killed my father. I need to know if your friend heard anything or if she can describe her. I promise I won't use your friend's name or say where I found out. Please, I'll pay you. . . ."

"Jesus, don't start crying on me again, man," Felix whispered. He glanced over at a Lincoln Town Car approaching the drive-thru. "And I don't want your stinking money anymore, either. . . ."

Chris stood by while Felix opened the back door of the Lincoln Town Car. His smile and his enthusiastic, "good morning" were ignored by the rich-looking middle-aged woman who emerged from the back of the car. He hurried to get the lobby door for her, and she walked through without glancing at him. Then Felix retreated to the back of the Town Car, where the driver had popped the trunk. He collected two big bags and brushed past Chris as he loaded them onto the baggage caddy. "Roseann's working her other job today, selling dried flowers at Pike Street Market," he whispered. "She has the first dried-flower stand down from where they throw the fish."

"Thanks," Chris said. "Thanks a lot."

Felix nodded. With a grunt, he pushed the baggage cart toward the door.

She started to slow down for the turn to Willow Tree Court up ahead. She could see the black Honda Accord pull out from the cul-de-sac. It was Rachel Cross's car, and it passed her going in the other direction.

In the rearview mirror, she took one last glance at Rachel's Honda Accord, growing tinier with the distance. Then she turned onto the dead end. She'd borrowed a beat-up old station wagon from a friend. She had a lot of packing to do today, and the Mini Cooper couldn't have handled the load.

Her days of free room and board at the Nguyens' were a thing of the past. It had been a sweet setup for nine weeks. She'd had a good run, but it wasn't quite over yet.

She studied the Dennehys' house as she drove by. The widow's car wasn't in the driveway. It didn't look like anyone was home at Lynette's or Jill's either. So her timing was pretty close to perfect.

She pulled into the Nguyens' driveway, then quickly jumped out of the car and let herself inside the house. She hurried through to the garage entrance, where she pushed the button for the automatic garage door. Once it was open, she pressed the LOCK button. Running back to the station wagon, she climbed inside, started it up, and pulled into the garage. In less than a minute, she pressed the OPERATE button, and the garage door closed again.

It took a half hour to load up the station wagon with all of her stuff—along with a few things that the Nguyens wouldn't miss. Hell, the things they'd really miss—the valuable items—she'd already sold at the hock shop weeks ago. All that remained were some DVDs and some fancy scarves and clothes belonging to the wife.

She glanced out the front window at the other houses on the cul-de-sac. There still weren't cars in any of the driveways. She was wearing a fatigue jacket, a black tee, and jeans, perfect camouflage clothes.

The November wind whipped at her long, dark blond hair as she stepped outside. She cut around back and made her way along the edge of the woods—into the Dennehys' backyard. She crept up to the sliding glass doors and peered into the family room. A fancy floral arrangement was on the table by the sofa—no doubt, condolence flowers from some family friend.

She realized her nose was fogging up the glass. She gave the door handle a tug, but it didn't give. She glanced around for a flowerpot under which a key might be hidden. But there wasn't one. She felt along the top of the frame to the sliding glass door, but again, no luck.

Undaunted, she moved onto the next yard and the next house. It took her only five minutes to find a key underneath one of the flowerpots by Rachel Cross's screen porch. She tried it on the back door and felt the lock turn. She held her breath for a few seconds as she opened the door and waited for an alarm to sound. But it stayed quiet.

The house smelled like cinnamon toast. The kitchen was pretty spotless—except for a near-empty glass of milk by the sink. She didn't linger. She moved toward the front of the house and started up the stairs.

She wanted to see the bedroom.

The windmill in front of Windmill Antiques & Miniatures stood about ten feet high. The store itself looked like a slightly decayed antebellum mansion—with white pillars, a porch, and a porch swing. Posted along the front lawn was a collection of novelty wind toys: a man rowing in a boat, a woman swimming, a sailor with flags, and a British bobby directing traffic, among others.

Molly hoped she would have better luck in the antique store than she'd had at the La Conner Channel Lodge. In the chalet-style lobby, she'd questioned two bellhops. Neither one of them recognized Jeff's photograph—or the sketch of Natalie. She'd tried the fiftysomething woman at the registration desk, giving her the dates Jeff checked in and checked out. She showed her Jeff's photo and asked if she remembered whether or not he'd checked in alone. Molly got a very haughty, "I'm sorry, ma'am, we're not allowed to give out that kind of information. The privacy of our guests is very important to us."

Molly wanted to tell her: *Well, what—and who—my husband was doing in your hotel is very important to me.* But she didn't think of that comeback until after she'd nodded politely to the woman and ducked out the front door.

The antique store was three blocks away. As she stepped inside, a little bell on the door rang. It had a slightly musty smell, like an old attic. There was a grand staircase right in front of her—with dozens of clocks and ornately framed paintings and old photographs on the wall. To her right was a parlor, with wall shelves full of vases, lamps, and desk clocks. An elaborate toy train set—complete with a bridge, two crossing gates, and a town full of stores, houses, and foliage—was on a big table in the middle of the room. To Molly's left was a room with a dozen different dollhouses. Miniature furniture, lamps, knickknacks, and tiny dolls—including dolls of pets—lined the shelves of the big room.

She didn't see any other customers on this floor, but she could hear some footsteps above her.

Farther back from the stairs, at the sales counter was a ruggedly handsome, balding man of about fifty. He wore a tight-fitting yellow polo shirt that showed off his buffed physique. He smiled at her. "Let me know if I can help you find anything."

"Actually," she said, approaching the counter, "I'm hoping you might answer a few questions about something my husband bought here last month." She took out the Master-Card bill and Jeff's photo. "It was a charge for $247.90 on October seventh. This is his picture. I don't know if you'd remember—"

"Oh, yeah, I remember him," the man said, with a chuckle. "My coworker, Sheila, she was instantly smitten. She was all over him as soon as he walked in the store. Me, I helped the woman. . . ." He hesitated. "Um, I mean, the—the next customer who came in after him, it was a woman."

Molly showed him the sketch of Natalie. "Did the woman look anything like this?"

Nervously drumming his fingers on the countertop, he looked at the picture and gave an uneasy shrug. "I—um, you know, I'm not sure."

"It's okay," Molly said. "I know he was here in La Conner with another woman."

"Listen, your husband seemed like a nice enough guy. I don't want to get anybody in trouble."

"You can't possibly get him into any more trouble than he's already in," Molly said. "He died last week."

"Oh, God, I'm so sorry," the man murmured.

"Thanks," Molly said. She showed him the charcoal drawing again. "I'd really like to know about this woman he was with—to give me some closure. This is just a rough sketch. But does it look anything like the woman you waited on? She's got blond hair. . . ."

He frowned. "It could be her. But she had her hair up and she was wearing sunglasses. If I remember right, her hair was closer to brown. I'm sorry, I can't say for sure."

"Her hair is almost brown. It's a darker shade of blond. Was she very thin?"

He shrugged. "I couldn't tell, really. She had a coat on the whole time."

"Do you remember if he called her by name—or anything they said to each other? Anything at all?"

"Not really." He scratched his bald head. "He came in first, by himself. Sheila started helping him, and about a minute later, the woman came in. She asked for my help while Sheila and your husband went into another room. She told him, 'I'm getting you a surprise for later down the line,' and she made sure he didn't see what she picked up. I thought that was kind of weird."

"Why was it weird?" Molly asked.

"Well, she said it was for him," he replied. "But all she bought was dollhouse furniture."

The woman in Molly's sketch went through Rachel's bedroom dresser and pocketed several pieces of jewelry—including a diamond ring and pearl necklace that together were probably worth at least two thousand bucks.

If someone had told her last year that she'd be breaking into people's homes and ripping them off, she never would have believed it. But then a lot had changed in the last year, and she had no idea how desperate she'd become.

She checked the closet for shoes, and wasn't impressed. There was nothing in the bathroom medicine cabinet worth taking, no prescriptions.

She headed downstairs, where she found sixty dollars in cash, a Macy's card, and a checkbook in a kitchen drawer. She took the card, the cash, and three checks from the middle of the book. She noticed a door off the kitchen and opened it. The basement—it was worth a peek, at least. The wood staircase had a nonslip, gridded rubber runner and led down to a big room with a beige carpet. There was a treadmill plugged into the wall with a boom box and several CDs scattered beside it. About a dozen boxes were stacked against one wall. She opened one up: just books. Another box was full of old LPs.

She gave up and tried a door to the next room. It led to a small corridor with an empty clothes closet on one side and a bathroom on the other. The bathroom had gaudy black and silver striped wallpaper and a shower stall with a fogged glass door. Straight ahead was the laundry room, which had an alcove with a workbench. Some tools—a hammer, crowbar, pliers, screwdriver, boxes of nails and screws—had been unpacked, but a box sat on the table with WORK STUFF—TOOLS & HARDWARE scribbled on it. There was a room off the work area with a latch and a padlock on the door.

All she could think was that Rachel must have something pretty valuable locked up in there.

She reached toward the workbench for the crowbar.

Her trip to the mini-mart seven blocks away took longer than she'd expected. She'd gotten there to find a BE BACK IN 5 MINUTES sign on the door. She'd waited close to fifteen minutes before finally giving up. She'd climbed out of the car, walked up to the store's door, and spat on the handle.

Irked and feeling a bit stupid for spitting on the door handle, she'd driven to Safeway for the emergency toilet paper—as well as a six-pack of ginger ale to combat her morning sickness.

Actually, she was feeling a lot better since she'd talked with Molly this morning. At the wheel of her Honda Accord, she watched the road ahead and chuckled at the notion of breaking and entering into the Nguyens' house with Molly tonight.

She'd promised Molly she'd keep a lookout for Natalie and wouldn't linger at the mini-mart. But now it had been nearly an hour since she'd left for the store. She put on her turn signal and slowed down as she approached Willow Tree

Court. She turned into the cul-de-sac and tapped the brake so she could get a long look at the Nguyens' house down the block. No car was in the driveway—and from what she could tell there were no lights on in the house.

She'd promised Molly that she would make certain that if Natalie came back, she wouldn't let her leave again. And it looked like Natalie hadn't come back—not yet, at least.

"Good," she whispered to herself. Then she pulled into her driveway.

"The woman bought practically two hundred and fifty dollars worth of dollhouse furniture?" Molly asked. "And then she had my husband pay for it?"

The man behind the counter at the antique store shrugged. "Well, your husband paid for her purchases, but he bought something, too. I didn't see what it was. Sheila boxed it up for shipping. I was helping the woman with her dollhouse stuff. But I took it into UPS the next day."

"He had it sent someplace?" Molly said.

"Yeah, I can look it up by the date. We save all our receipts here for up to a year. You said it was October . . ."

"October seventh," Molly said. She watched him duck into an office under the top of the stairs. He poked around in there for about two minutes, and then emerged with two handwritten receipts and a copy of a UPS waybill.

"Here we are," he said, setting the paperwork down on the counter in front of Molly.

She was hoping to see the name and address of his mistress. But the shipment went to his office in the Bank of America Tower. Molly glanced at one of the receipts, and all it said was Jade Antique + 25.57 shipping & tax = $148.60. She felt a brief surge of anger that Jeff had spent that much on the bitch who probably ended up killing him. One of the first things she'd look for when she searched the Nguyens' house tonight would be a jade vase or brooch.

"You mentioned you don't know what he bought exactly," Molly said. "Do you think Sheila might remember? Is she around?"

"She's traveling through Europe right now," the man said, shaking his head. "And I really don't know how to get in touch with her. She's one of the few people in the world who doesn't own a cell phone. I can tell you what the woman purchased—if you're interested."

Molly glanced down at the other receipt. It said: Dollhouse figures, and had a list of codes for four items that totaled with tax to $99.30. She started to shake her head, but then hesitated. "Sure, why not?" she said. "If it's not too much trouble—that would be great. By the way, you've been very nice, thank you."

"No problem." He picked up the receipt and came around the counter. "I—I'm really sorry about your husband, Mrs. Dennehy. The dollhouse accessories are over here. . . ."

She followed him into the parlor, where the different dollhouses were on display. He checked the receipt. "The first thing on here is a doll," he said, reaching for an item on a wall hook. He took down a see-through plastic container with cardboard backing and a brown-haired man-doll inside.

"The dad," Molly said.

"Actually, it says on here, 'Teenage Son,' " the man corrected her. He read the back of the container. "They're very specific about these things. Next we have something in the dining room section. . . ." He glanced at the receipt again as he moved to a glass case, where miniature furniture pieces were displayed. He pointed to a tiny round table with four curved-back chairs. The set reminded Molly a bit of her own breakfast table—or rather, Angela's.

"And she got a living-room piece as well," he said, showing her to another glass case. "There it is—number four-hundred-twenty-nine . . ." He pointed to a miniature grandfather clock.

Molly stared at the dollhouse clock. It was just like the one in her family room that didn't work.

"And finally . . ." The store clerk checked the receipt again and led her back to the doll display. "She got another member of the dollhouse family." He plucked a blond doll from the hook, glanced at it for a moment, and then showed it to Molly.

She stared at it, and slowly shook her head.

"Isn't that the damnedest thing?" she heard the man say. "That doll looks just like you, Mrs. Dennehy."

And he was right.

"Hey, hey, hey, hey!" he heard someone yelling over a chorus of cheers.

Threading his way through the crowded market, Chris could tell he was getting close to the fish place. For one thing, he could smell the fish—and he saw the crowd of people ahead, most of them tourists, no doubt. "Coho Salmon!" someone yelled. "Hey, hey, hey!" For a second, the crowd parted and Chris caught a glimpse of one of the merchants. The guy—with thick suspenders holding up yellow wading trousers—grabbed a big fish from a bed of ice and hurled it through the air at one of the guys behind the counter. The crowd whistled and clapped.

Chris noticed among them a dad with his toddler son on his shoulders. The little boy wore a Mariners hat and was clapping with delight.

Watching them, Chris felt an awful pang in his gut, and tears clouded his eyes. His head down, he looped around the onlookers by the fish market and continued past the stores and the vendors. People bumped him and brushed past him, but he didn't look up—not until he found a Kleenex in his pocket and blew his nose. He wiped his eyes with the cuff of his school jacket, the same cuff someone had cut a piece from when they'd broken into his locker. It was all frayed now.

He heard the crowd behind him, cheering on the fish-throwers. Some sidewalk musician nearby played "Moon River" on a harmonica. He started looking for the flower vendors. Felix had said it was the first dried-flowers stand by the fish place. Chris saw a stand with all sorts of fresh flowers in tin buckets. A thin Asian girl with a boy's short haircut was at the register. Chris approached her. "Are you Roseann?"

She gazed at him curiously, and then nodded. "Yes, yes, we have roses."

"No, I was asking if your name is Roseann," he said loudly—to compete with another round of shouts and applause from the fish market fans. "I'm looking for Roseann!"

"I'm Roseann," he heard someone say.

Chris turned and saw a display table of dried flower bouquets—in baskets and vases and wrapped in cellophane. The prices were posted beneath each arrangement. Sitting at the end of the table, a pretty Latino woman with big eyes and long black hair was busy at work. She wore pale blue rubber gloves while she strung together dried flowers into an arrangement. "Who are you?" she asked, giving him a wary look.

Chris could barely hear her over all the people. He sheepishly approached her, and then glanced around to make sure no one heard him. "Felix over at the Marriott said you might be able to help me," he explained. "He said you waited on my father and some woman at the bar there on Friday."

She frowned. "Yeah? Well, Felix has a big mouth, and I don't know your father from a hole in the wall. So do me a favor and get lost." She looked down at her work again.

After what Felix had told him about her being an illegal

immigrant, Chris hadn't expected her to speak English so well. "Um, my father's the guy they found dead in one of the rooms on Saturday morning," he said. "Felix told me you remembered him. I promise, I won't cause any trouble for you. Felix already told me he'd kick the shit out of me if I went to the police or anything."

She studied him for a few moments, and finally nodded. "I see it now," she murmured. "You look a lot like your father. He was a very handsome guy. He drank a Wild Turkey with rocks on the side. I have a memory for these things. The woman, she had a Tom Collins. Your father paid—in cash, and he was a good tipper. What else do you want to know?"

He was at a loss for a second. "Well, the woman he was with, what did she look like?"

Roseann let out a little laugh. "Like trouble. I could see he was mad at her about something. They were arguing. Your father kept talking in a low voice. And I heard her say to him—like twice, 'I just wanted to be close to you.' Then she started crying, but I could tell she was faking the tears."

"How could you tell?"

She shrugged. "With some women, you can just see when they're working a guy. And this one was a real hustler."

"So do you think she might have drugged my father or did something to make him overdose?"

Roseann shrugged. "I only saw them in the bar together. She left first, then your father paid the tab. But I wouldn't be surprised if she talked him into meeting her in that room later."

"Could you describe her—the way she looked?"

"Light brown hair, cute face, good figure," Roseann said.

"Did my dad ever call her by name?" Chris asked. "Maybe *Natalie*?"

Frowning, she shook her head. "No, I don't think I heard him call her anything. But you know, I just thought of something else. She ordered a Tom Collins, but hardly drank any of it. That's the mark of a true hustler. She'll get a guy drunk, while she just pretends to drink. That way, she keeps a clear head so she can work him later. Anyway, that's my take on that lady. But don't quote me, okay? I can't get involved with any police. Felix wasn't kidding. He'll beat the shit out of you if you go to the cops with any of this. I'll make sure he does, too. I don't care how cute you are." She sighed. "I hope you're able to track down that bitch. But you can't expect any more help from me. Understand?"

Chris just nodded.

Roseann put down the bouquet she was working on, then got to her feet and plucked an $11.99 dried flower bouquet from a vase. She wrapped some cellophane around it. "Take this—*para su padre*, for your father's grave."

Chris took the dried flowers. "Thank you," he whispered. "Thank you very much."

Sitting down again, Roseann solemnly went back to her work. "No worries," she said.

Standing by her car, parked in front of Windmill Antiques & Miniatures, Molly spoke into her cell phone. "Yes, thanks, Peter, I'm feeling much better than I did yesterday," she said to Jeff's assistant. Her hair fluttered in the chilly, seaside breeze. "Anyway, the reason I'm calling is about a month ago, Jeff had something delivered to the office from an antique store in La Conner. I was wondering if you remember him forwarding it to someone else. . . ."

"Let me check," he said. "Just a sec, Molly. Can you hold on?"

"Sure, thanks, Pete." While she waited, Molly glanced at her wristwatch: 11:55. She hadn't heard from Rachel yet. It made her nervous to think Rachel was the only person home on the cul-de-sac.

"Molly?" Peter got back on the line.

"Yes, I'm here," she said anxiously.

"There's a UPS package in the closet in his office. Windmill Antiques and Miniatures, is that the one?"

"Yes," she said. "Could you—could you set it aside for me? I'd like to pick it up this afternoon."

"They've got me running around all over the place today. So I'll leave the package with the receptionist—just in case you miss me. And by the way, we should get together early next week so you can go through Jeff's office. Jeff has a lot of his personal things here."

"Of course," she said. "Thanks, Pete."

"Well, if I don't catch you this afternoon, Molly, I know I told you this before, but I—I really liked working for Jeff." His voice had a tremor in it. "I'm going to miss him. . . ."

"Thanks, Pete," she said again. "Don't make me cry, okay? And don't you start crying, either."

She heard him blow his nose. "Too late," he murmured. "Take care, Molly."

When she clicked off the line, she reached into her purse for some Kleenex. She wiped her eyes and blew her nose. The bag from the antique store slipped out of her hand.

After having put that poor salesman through the paces, she couldn't walk away without buying something. So she'd bought one of the same miniatures Jeff's mistress had purchased.

The doll that looked like her had spilled out of the bag. Swiping it off the pavement, Molly stuffed it back in the bag, opened her car door, and set the bag on the passenger seat. It was strange the woman had bought dolls of her and Chris. And clearly, she picked the miniature grandfather clock and breakfast table set after the ones in the family room. That meant this woman had been inside the house.

Molly shuddered and buttoned the top of her pea jacket. Then she took out her cell phone and made another call, this time to Rachel.

But it rang and rang—until the machine clicked on.

Molly impatiently listened to the greeting and waited for the beep.

"Rachel, are you there?" she said. "It's me, Molly. Can you pick up? I thought for sure you'd be home. Now, I'm kind of worried. Rachel? Are you there?"

She opened the front door and heard Molly leaving a message on the answering machine. But there was another sound that stopped her just past the threshold. A strange, splintering noise came from down in the basement.

Molly was still talking, asking if she was home.

She quietly set her groceries down in the front hallway, and then crept toward the kitchen. She noticed the back door was ajar—and a few drawers had been left open. She went to the cabinet, and from behind a box of Frosted Flakes, she took out a handgun.

At last, Molly shut up and clicked off the line. The message machine let out a beep, signifying the message had been recorded. The splintering noise continued downstairs, and then she heard a snap, and something clattered. It sounded like a metal piece hitting the floor.

She edged toward the open basement door and saw the light on down there.

She set the gun on the counter and pried off her shoes. She wasn't sure what to expect. Picking up the gun again, she started to tiptoe down the basement steps.

For a minute, Natalie had thought she'd heard the front door. But it must have been some background noise from wherever Molly Dennehy was leaving her message. Natalie paused for a few seconds, listened carefully, and then went back to manipulating the padlock with the crowbar.

She knew she was pushing her luck. Rachel could be back at any minute. It was risky to stay here. She'd gotten enough with the jewelry and the blank checks. And yet, she just had to see if there was something really valuable behind this basement door.

People on crystal meth could be pretty reckless at times.

She couldn't help it. This was an addiction, a disease. It wasn't her fault. She'd started out trying it to lose weight—and for a bit of a thrill. And now she'd gone through all her money, lost her job, and gotten kicked out of her apartment.

Todd hadn't known her situation when she'd gone with him on one of the few occasions he actually checked the Nguyens' house for them. They'd walked around the house, made sure no one had tried to break in, watered the house-plants, and cleaned up the yard a little. For months and months, he'd been giving the key to one friend or another and having them check the place for him. Natalie couldn't believe none of the guys had ever ripped off the Nguyens. She'd volunteered to check the house for Todd every week on a semi-permanent basis. Then she'd had her own copy of the house key made. The stupid slacker, Todd, he didn't even realize she'd moved in.

It had been a perfect setup. The house had been full of so many things she hocked for drug money. Her dealer stayed with her there for a while, and she even turned some tricks there—all on this squeaky-clean *family* block.

But the funny thing was that two of her neighbors' hus-bands had gotten caught with drugs in hotel rooms, where they'd had illicit sexual trysts.

Natalie had kept to herself—mostly to discourage neigh-bors from dropping by. But yesterday, she'd let Jill from next door talk her into attending the Dennehy funeral. It had gone on and on, and after shaking Molly's hand, she couldn't wait to get the hell out of there. She'd driven up to Everett to party for the evening. Then she got the call from Todd.

He was wise to her now. That bitch Molly must have said something, because she'd left him a message at just about the same time Mrs. Nguyen had phoned, asking if a woman was living in her house.

So her plan for today had been to return to the Nguyens, quickly pack up her stuff, and then disappear. She was taking a big chance lingering here in Rachel's. But she almost had the lock pried off the door. It was so loose that she could feel the screws wobbling. A crack in the wood had formed under the latch. With a grimace, she gave it one more forceful tug.

The latch mechanism suddenly flew off the edge of the door. It hit the basement floor with a clatter. Gasping, Natalie staggered back and laughed. The door creaked as she opened it. Setting the crowbar on the worktable, she stepped into the dark room and felt around by the door for a light switch. She found it and flicked it on. The bright, fluorescent overhead sputtered for a second, and then went on. It hummed quietly.

Natalie stared into the windowless room at what looked like a Ping-Pong table—covered with a huge white sheet. There seemed to be several different-sized boxes stacked and spaced about a foot from each other beneath the coverlet. Natalie carefully pulled off the sheet and gaped at a replica of Willow Tree Court, all made up of dollhouses and fake trees and foliage. The Nguyens' house and Jill's place were a bit smaller and not quite up to scale with the others. Walking around the table, she could see those two houses were just hollow facades—like the mock-ups of the unfinished houses on the cul-de-sac.

But this house, the Dennehys' place, and the Hahns' were all detailed and had certain rooms completely furnished. In the duplication of Rachel's bedroom, a little blond doll about the size of a finger lay on a pale yellow carpet. A piece of lavender fabric was wrapped around it. A few globs of what looked like red nail polish were on the doll's head, and it spilled over into the blond hair and onto the yellow carpet.

From earlier, when she'd peered through the glass doors at the Dennehys' house, she knew the model accurately copied their family room—right down to the big-screen TV, sofa, coffee table, and grandfather clock. Two dolls—a brown-haired man and a blond woman—were leaning against a round breakfast table for four. It was almost as if they'd been set there temporarily—until Rachel found a better spot for them.

Natalie thought she heard something—a stair step or a floorboard creaking. She stood perfectly still and listened for a few moments. Nothing.

She moved over to yet another dollhouse, a two-story Colonial, set on a smaller table beside a bookcase against the wall. She didn't recognize the house. But two bedrooms on the second floor, the kitchen, and the pantry were painstakingly furnished. There was a man doll in the open closet of the bigger bedroom and a woman doll in the closet of the smaller bedroom. Each one had been dotted with that same crimson color polish. A third doll—it looked like it was supposed to be a girl—was on the pantry floor. It too was marked with red nail polish. Natalie couldn't help thinking it looked like a replication of a cul-de-sac-killing crime scene. "This is weird as shit," she murmured to herself.

On the bookcase, along with stacks of dollhouse furniture in their cartons, there was another little model. It looked like a mock-up some set designer might have created in preparation for a play. It resembled a hotel room with a queen bed, TV, table, and chairs—and another little doll on the floor. This one was of a man, and he was naked.

Natalie picked it up and studied it.

"Put that down," someone whispered.

Startled, she swiveled around and saw Rachel standing in the doorway. She had a gun pointed at her.

A hand over her heart, Natalie stared at her. She started to say something, but when she opened her mouth to talk, the words wouldn't come out. She just shook her head.

"I thought you were a prowler," Rachel said. She took a step back, and then set the gun down on the worktable. "Are you deaf or something? I told you to put down the doll."

"What is it?" Natalie asked.

"It's for a special project. Put the doll back where you found it. How many times do I have to tell you?"

"Okay, okay, Jesus . . ." Natalie set the doll back inside the little replica of a hotel room.

Rachel was still standing on the other side of the doorway. "Now, get away from my models. I don't want them ruined. . . ." She nodded toward the other corner of the room, where there was a tall cabinet.

Frowning, Natalie did what she was told. "I had no intention of ruining your stupid dollhouses," she grumbled. "Now, just let me out of here, and I'll—"

"But they would have been ruined," Rachel interrupted. She reached back for something on the workbench behind her. "Your blood would have gotten all over them."

"What?" Natalie murmured.

All at once, Rachel rushed toward her, raising the crowbar in the air.

Screaming, Natalie backed into the cabinet. The door opened and several small bottles of model paint fell out. They hit her shoulders and then clattered onto the cement floor. Rachel was practically on top of her. Natalie put her arm out, but it was too late. She felt the crowbar slam against her skull—just above her left eye.

She let out a frail cry and reeled back against the cabinet. More paint bottles fell out and crashed to the floor. She felt her legs giving out under her.

"This is just more work for me," Rachel grumbled. "Now I have to make a doll for you."

Natalie stared at her—until blood oozed into her eye.

She thought of that red nail polish.

She caught a glimpse of Rachel raising the crowbar in the air again. But then everything went out of focus. Natalie tried to hold herself up by leaning against the cabinet. Somehow, she still thought she could make it out of that room if she just kept standing.

But she heard Rachel grunt—and then a loud pop.

It was the sound of her skull cracking.

CHAPTER TWENTY-SEVEN

She thanked God the receptionist was a temp. If it was Juliet, the usual receptionist, then she would have to hear her condolences and explain that she was feeling better—and saner—than she'd been yesterday at the funeral. She probably would have gotten emotional and cried. And Juliet would have called this coworker or that coworker of Jeff's so they could give their condolences, and the whole damn thing would have gone on for an hour.

All she wanted to do was pick up the package Jeff had bought for his mistress, and then sneak out of there.

At the reception desk just inside the glass double doors to Kendall Pharmaceuticals, the temp explained that Peter had to run an errand. But yes, indeed, he'd left a package for her. She reached under the desk and then pulled out a large UPS box—about two by two feet. She set it on the desktop. "It's not too heavy," she said. "But if you'd like some help carrying it out, I can get someone. . . ."

Molly carefully lifted the box to get a feel for the weight. It was bulky, but weighed only about five pounds. "No, that's all right," she said. "Thank you."

"I heard about your husband, Mrs. Dennehy," the receptionist said, getting to her feet. She opened one of the glass doors for Molly. "I'm very sorry for your loss."

"Thank you," she said again, working up a smile as she peered at her over the top of the box. She made her way to the elevator, and managed to press the Down button. The package felt a bit heavier and more awkward as she waited for the elevator to arrive. She couldn't help remembering the last time she was here, when Jeff's mistress had called to taunt her—just hours before his death.

The elevator finally arrived, and she stepped aboard. It was crowded and stopped five times before she finally made it down to the lobby. As she walked to the garage elevators, Molly was sweating, and she felt a little dizzy. Some woman on a cell phone bumped into her and almost knocked the box out of her hands. Molly wanted to scream at her to watch where she was going, but she said nothing. The woman moved on without even looking at her, not a break in her conversation.

By the time Molly stepped off at Parking Level D (for *Dalmatian*, the sign said, with a photo of the spotted dog), she was so upset and sick that she just wanted to drop the box on the floor and kick it all the way to her car. But even though her arms ached, she carried the package to her car. She heard her own footsteps on the concrete, echoing in the dark, winding garage. In the distance—perhaps a level or two levels up—someone's tires squealed as they turned the corners from one ramp to another.

Molly set the box down on the hood of her Saturn and caught her breath.

She couldn't wait until she got home. She had to see what Jeff had secretly picked up while antique shopping with his mistress in La Conner last month. Molly took her keys out of her purse and ran one across the box's taped top flaps.

But she heard something that made her stop. It seemed to come from the elevator alcove, but an SUV parked in the next row blocked her view. She heard a woman snickering. The laugh was kind of husky and scratchy.

Molly froze and listened to that voice—and the set of footsteps. All she could think about was that crazy woman on the phone, and how she seemed to know everything. Did she somehow know that Molly would be picking up this package today—*her* package? Had she somehow orchestrated it?

Molly heard the snickering again.

"Who's there?" she called. Her heart was racing. The footsteps came closer.

"Oh, you have a dirty mind," she heard the woman whisper. Then Molly saw her come around the corner and down the ramp. It was another woman on a cell phone. She snickered again. "I mean it, stop," she said into the phone. "Now you're just being gross. . . ."

Watching the woman climb inside her VW, Molly slouched against her car for a few moments. Her heartbeat finally started to slow down. She felt so stupid—and vulnerable, and angry. Taking a deep breath, she turned and tore open the top of the UPS box. It was full of Styrofoam peanuts. They stuck to the lower sleeve of her pea jacket as she clawed her way to another box within the box. Some Styrofoam peanuts fell out as she pulled out the smaller parcel. It was about half the size of the outside box. She used her key to cut away at the tape sealing it up.

Molly found an item wrapped in tissue paper. It felt heavy in her hands. As she tore away at the thin paper, she could discern the jade green color.

Then she saw the tusk.

She knew the jade piece wasn't for his mistress. It was an elephant for her collection, and it was beautiful. Molly broke down. Hugging the figurine, she leaned against her car and sobbed.

For a few minutes, she didn't feel sick or stupid or angry

or scared. For those few minutes, she just missed her husband.

In only her bra and panties, the woman who called herself Rachel Cross mopped up the trail of blood on the basement floor. The crimson streak went from the corner of her secret workroom through the laundry room and into the bathroom. Natalie's body was behind the fogged glass door of the shower stall, curled up on the floor. The drain now caught all the blood.

Jenna had gotten blood on her sweater and her jeans. She'd thrown them in the washing machine. The clothes were churning through the spin cycle now. She'd already rinsed the spattering of blood off her hands, face, and hair.

She'd changed her mind about making a doll for Natalie. There just wasn't any time. For the last twenty minutes, she'd contemplated chopping up the body. She'd even gone through the box of tools on the workbench and took out two different saws, wondering if they could cut through bone. She imagined taking sections of the body outside in lawn bags, and then burying them in the forest in back.

But she decided it was best to leave the body in the house. From what Molly had told her, Natalie wasn't supposed to be staying at the Nguyens'. According to the driver's license Jenna had found in the wallet inside her fatigue jacket pocket, Natalie's most recent address was on Mercer Street on Capitol Hill in Seattle. In that same pocket, Jenna had also found her own engagement ring, the pearl necklace Ray gave her on their tenth anniversary, some cash, and several of her blank checks. So—in addition to trespassing, Natalie was a thief. Jenna had met enough of her daughter's street friends at Tracy's shoddy little memorial service to recognize a crystal meth addict when she saw one.

Natalie's mysterious presence on the block had actually

bought Jenna some time yesterday and today. When after the funeral, her old friend, Laurie Bauer, rode by the church on her bike and called to her, Jenna had thought it was all over. But then Molly assumed Natalie was Jenna Corson. She thought Natalie was responsible for all the recent deaths, accidents, and tragedies on Willow Tree Court. Natalie was the perfect suspect.

But Jenna knew it was only a matter of time before Molly figured her out. She'd already suspected her. How long before Molly realized the peppermints she'd given her—along with those ginger capsules she'd picked up for her—only made her sicker, more sleepy, and a bit delirious? Molly had already stopped taking them.

And yesterday, when Molly uttered her name as she was leaving the bedroom, it was all Jenna could do to keep from reacting. She'd stifled the same natural instinct to react an hour before when Laurie had called to her in front of the church. She'd gone to a lot of lengths to become Rachel Cross—with forged driver's licenses from Florida and Washington, a birth certificate, and other documents. Once she met up with Aldo, the killer-for-hire connected her to all sorts of criminals, who in turn provided her with so many illegal services. She'd had a computer hacker create an exceptional credit history for Rachel Cross. She'd already started getting junk mail for Rachel Cross before even moving into Kay's old house.

She'd also sent herself that anonymous note and slipped it in Molly's mailbox just minutes after the mailman had delivered the mail one day last month. Several pieces of her junk mail had made their way into the Dennehys' mailbox with no help from her. Mail mixups just happened when people lived next door to each other. It somehow forced neighbors to look out for one another and get closer.

That had been why Kay was the first to die. Jenna wanted the house.

But she couldn't stay. Laurie almost outing her wasn't the

only reason why Jenna had to wrap things up. Someone had murdered Aldo. They'd slit his throat the same day she'd killed Jeff. Of course, getting murdered was probably a professional risk in Aldo's business. But if the police dug deep enough, they might find evidence linking Aldo to her and her late husband. After all, Ray and she had both employed his services.

Jenna had to finish everything tonight. After she killed Molly and Chris, she would set fire to all the houses on Willow Tree Court, including this one. She'd already reported a possible arson to the police a little over a week ago. Of course, no one knew she'd set her own toolshed on fire. She'd worked out the delay. She'd left a lit cigarette inside a pack of matches on a stack of old newspapers, half-soaked with gasoline. She'd been talking with Chris Dennehy for over ten minutes before he smelled the smoke.

So it was in police records that Willow Tree Court had a potential firebug.

Standing in the doorway to her workroom, she hated the idea of having to torch all her dollhouses. But she couldn't afford to be sentimental. And it would be appropriate to start the fire in this room with the model of the cul-de-sac.

They'd expect Jill's, the Hahns', and the Nguyens' houses to be empty.

Jenna fiddled with her bra strap as she sauntered back to the bathroom. She stared at the corpse behind the fogged glass door of the shower stall.

They would be expecting to find a body in this house. And they would find one. It might take a day or two before they realized it wasn't Rachel Cross, and that Rachel Cross didn't exist. By that time, Jenna, her son, and her new stepdaughter, Erin, would be far, far away.

Natalie was buying her some more time—again.

Jenna glanced at her wristwatch. She had to go pick up Erin from school and then buy gasoline.

* * *

Chris looked at the lighted numbers above the door.

He stood alone in the elevator with the bouquet of dried flowers in his hand. This was his third time in the building, and he still didn't know his way around. But he was pretty sure he was headed to the right place.

He couldn't think of anywhere else to go—or anyone else he could talk to.

Roseann had confirmed for him that Molly was right. His dad had been set up by some woman, and she'd most likely left him dead in that hotel room. Was Molly right about the rest of it, too? Had the same woman, this Natalie person, arranged his mother's murder—along with Larry's and Taylor's? Had she murdered Mrs. Garvey, too—and made it look like an accident? Then that meant the same woman had rigged Courtney's cell phone to explode. She'd broken into his locker and left him that note about Molly's brother. She'd set fire to their next-door neighbor's toolshed. And she'd seen to it that the police and reporters knew where and when to find Mr. Hahn with a teenage prostitute and a stash of drugs and porn.

Why was she doing all these things? What did she have against his family and his neighbors on Willow Tree Court?

He couldn't go to the police without getting Roseann in trouble. So he'd come here. On the way, he'd driven past the Arboretum, where Mr. Corson was murdered. Chris kept thinking how much he could have used Mr. Corson's guidance right now.

The elevator stopped and the doors opened on the fourth floor. Chris started down the hospital corridor toward the Intensive Care Unit.

Courtney was the only one he could think of who might have some answers. She'd survived an attempt on her life. If nothing else, at least they could commiserate with each other over what had happened to their fathers. He hated comparing his dad with Mr. Hahn, who was pretty damn perverted—and pompous. But his dad and Mr. Hahn had both been exposed in similar sleazy situations.

As he turned the corner for the ICU, he heard someone's cell phone go off.

"Mrs. Hahn," he heard a woman say. "I'm sorry, but you're not allowed to use cell phones in here."

"Oh, leave me alone. Don't you have anything better to do?" Mrs. Hahn replied, all huffy-sounding. And then her voice took on a sweet tone. "Hello?"

Chris almost bumped into a nurse, who was emerging from the ICU visitors' lounge. She was shaking her head. "Arrogant bitch," she muttered.

He saw Mrs. Hahn, sitting alone on one of the two tan, cushioned love seats in the small lounge area. A TV bracketed high on the wall was muted and tuned in to some afternoon talk show. The coffee and end tables all had magazines and boxes of Kleenex on them. The window looked out to the parking lot.

Mrs. Hahn had her cell phone to her ear. She suddenly stood up. Her purse dropped off the edge of the love seat and fell to the floor. "Goddamn you!" she yelled. "Who are you? Why are you doing this? Goddamn it!" She hurled the cell phone against the wall, and it smashed into several pieces that scattered on the carpet.

His mouth open, Chris stopped at the edge of the lounge area. Mrs. Hahn turned and flopped down on the love seat. She buried her face in her hands and sobbed.

"Mrs. Hahn, are you okay?" Chris asked, gently. He put down the dried flowers, picked up a Kleenex box, and offered it to her.

Without looking at him, she plucked a tissue from the box, wiped her eyes, and blew her nose.

"What was that about?" he asked.

"It's this awful woman," Mrs. Hahn said, her voice strained. "She hasn't called since Jeremy—since before Mr. Hahn was arrested. I couldn't tell anybody about the calls, because she kept saying Jeremy was . . ." She took a deep breath. "Well, she said all these filthy things about him that I didn't think were true at the time. I still don't think it's true—despite what everyone says."

His brow furrowed, Chris gazed at her. "You mean, she told you ahead of time that he was involved with—"

"Yes," she interrupted impatiently. " *'Lynette, did you know your husband likes to fuck teenage girls?'* " she said in a scratchy, singsong, mocking voice. "I thought the calls started because some nut had seen me on TV when your mother was killed. But this woman kept calling. For a while there, I thought it was Molly. I couldn't go to the police, because of what she was saying about my husband. He still hasn't gone to trial. So I still can't go to the police, and she knows it, goddamn it."

"Molly was getting phone calls, too—about my dad," Chris pointed out. He sat down on the arm of the love seat across from her. "Molly said my mom was getting harassed, too—by the same woman."

"I knew about the calls to your mother," Mrs. Hahn muttered, wiping her eyes. "But I didn't know Molly was getting them, too."

"You said it stopped for a while?"

She nodded. "After Mr. Hahn was arrested. This is the first one since then."

"Can I ask what she said?"

"She said, *'So, Lynette—'* " Mrs. Hahn took on that crawly, mocking voice again. " *'How does it feel to have everything taken away from you?'* "

Chris frowned. "That's it?"

"No," Mrs. Hahn whispered. "And then she said, *'Now you know what you did to me.'* "

"What does she mean by that?" Chris asked numbly.

"I have no idea."

Chris got up and started collecting the broken parts to her

cell phone. The battery had fallen out, and he put it back inside. The screen was cracked and the casing was in shards. He set everything on the coffee table in front of her. Then he picked up the flowers. "Is it okay if I see Courtney?" he asked.

Slouched in the love seat, Mrs. Hahn wiped her eyes again and nodded. "She was asleep earlier, but she should be up now."

Chris walked down the corridor toward Courtney's room. He wondered what the woman caller meant when she'd told Mrs. Hahn, *"Now you know what you did to me."* Had Mrs. Hahn gotten this woman's husband arrested in some kind of sex scandal? Did this woman have a daughter who was disfigured, maimed, or almost killed?

The last time he'd seen Courtney had been the afternoon before his dad had died. She'd been totally out of it, pumped full of drugs and painkillers. Her face had been so red and swollen that it had seemed almost twice its normal size. He'd barely recognized her.

The drapes in her room were closed now, but the TV was on—a *Friends* rerun. The light from the television flickered across her bed, which was raised near the headboard. Courtney was sitting halfway up. A bandage covered her right eye, but the other one was open. The swelling had gone down. Past the staples in her face and the shiny red skin, Chris could see a little bit of the old Courtney. But her blond hair had been shorn off, exposing a dark hole and pink scars where her right ear used to be. A tube was stuck in her nose, and she had another one in her arm. A third tube ran out from under the covers. That explained why one of the three bags hanging on a contraption at her bedside was full of urine.

Courtney's uncovered eye seemed to catch sight of him, and a tiny smile flickered across her chapped, blistered lips. Her right hand rested on her stomach. The bandage didn't quite camouflage the fact that her first two fingers were missing. The other hand worked the volume on the TV control. She put it on mute.

"Oh, crap, don't look at me, Chris," she murmured. She blocked his view of her face with her good hand. "I'm like something out of *Night of the Living Dead*."

Chris tried to smile. "Actually, you look better than you did the other day when I was here. The swelling's gone down."

"You were here?"

He nodded. "You were pretty well medicated."

"Are those dead flowers for me?" she asked warily.

"Yeah, they're *dried*, not dead." He set them down on the dresser across from her bed. He noticed a big card with a cartoon nurse on the cover leaning against a vase of flowers.

"Actually, they're very pretty, thanks," Courtney said. She finally took her hand down. "I got a card there from Madison. Can you believe it?"

Chris picked up the card and opened it. Inside, Madison had written: *Get well soon! I really miss you! XOX—Madison.* He carefully put the card back. "So—are you in a lot of pain?"

"It's not as bad as it was," she muttered. "They have me on a ton of drugs. I'm going to be a Vicodin addict when I get out of here—and I'll be a circus freak, too."

"Don't say that," Chris whispered.

The uncovered eye glanced toward the drapes. "Why not? It's true."

"Do you know if they're any closer to figuring out who did this to you?"

"Nope," she said, her ravaged face still turned away from him. "All they know is someone broke into my gym locker and rigged my cell phone. They think it might have been another student, pulling a prank that went too far. They're not really sure."

Chris hadn't heard that about the locker. So on two separate occasions, someone had broken into both Courtney's and his lockers.

She finally turned toward him again. "I heard about your father. I'm really sorry."

"It was a lot like what happened with your dad," Chris said. "They found him in a hotel room—with drugs and porn. Some woman set him up to overdose."

"Only difference is your dad's dead, and mine's out on bail, living in a Best Western in Lynnwood." Courtney sighed. "I'm not sure which one is better off."

"Remember the morning you had your accident, when you were driving me to school?" Chris asked. "You said that you told Mr. Corson about your dad. You said we all spilled our guts to him. And you were right. He knew my dad had screwed around on my mom."

"Yeah, Corson was wise to all our family secrets," she said.

"Did he know about Madison's mom and her drinking problem?"

"Sure," Courtney said, with a weak nod.

"It's kind of like he came back to haunt us," Chris heard himself say. "Every secret we told Mr. Corson has been exposed. Our parents are getting killed or thrown in jail. It's like his ghost has come back to get even with every one of us on Willow Tree Court who did him wrong."

Courtney sighed. "I guess you blame me more than anyone else for getting him fired."

Chris didn't say anything. But he was thinking, *Yes, you and your iPhone.*

And that was what had exploded in her face.

He stepped up to her bed. "Mr. Corson used to scribble down notes when I was talking to him in his office for those formal sessions. Did he do the same thing with you?"

"Yeah, sure, he used to take a lot of notes," Courtney said.

"He probably collected some juicy stuff there, too. Who do you think has those notes now? The school?"

Chris remembered, and he slowly shook his head. "No," he replied. "Not anymore."

"Hi, Molly, it's Rachel calling at around three-thirty. . . ."
Molly stood in her kitchen with the big UPS box on the counter. She hovered near the answering machine, listening to the voice mail.

"I got your message earlier," Rachel went on. *"I'm fine. Don't panic when you see my car isn't in the driveway. You asked me to make sure if Natalie comes back that she doesn't leave again. And I've done that. But I really need to go to the store. I know you'll be home soon, because Erin's bus drops her off at a quarter to four. I'll be back before then, okay? I really don't think you're going to see Natalie again. But you'll see me—very soon. Okay? Bye."*

Rachel knew her very well by now. When Molly had driven up the cul-de-sac and noticed there wasn't a car in her driveway, she'd thought for certain something was wrong. But now that she'd listened to Rachel's message, Molly felt better. It was 3:35, so she must have just missed her. Natalie couldn't have come back, packed up, and left again in that short a time.

Molly still had some Styrofoam peanuts stuck to the sleeve of her pea jacket when she took it off. More peanuts fell out of the UPS box and onto the kitchen counter as she dug out the smaller parcel again. She took out the jade elephant and carried it up to her attic studio. She was going to clear a space on her shelf for it. But thanks to Erin, there were some recent vacancies.

Setting down Jeff's elephant, Molly stopped and stared at her cola ad painting with all the characters through the ages—and the big, yellow *X* slashed across it. She hadn't really assessed the damage yet. Nor had she cleaned up the mess Erin had made. She figured it might take a day or two, but she could fix the painting. As for the yellow paint on several of her elephants, a little turpentine could get that out.

Molly carefully put the cap back on the tube of Naples Yellow Light and returned it to the drawer with the other paints. She set the brush in some paint thinner. Then she bent over and picked up the putty knife Erin used to break three of the more fragile elephants. Molly put the knife back in the jar, where she kept it with a couple of old brushes and a sponge brush—on the second to top shelf of her supplies cabinet.

Before closing the cabinet door, Molly hesitated, and then glanced around.

She stored a stepladder in the other corner of the room, and it was there now. The stool was near the easel, where she usually kept it. And there was a chair against the wall in another corner of the room, where it always was. None of those things had been moved close to the cabinet.

Frowning, Molly glanced up at the putty knife in that jar—on a shelf that was almost six feet high.

Erin was only about three and a half feet tall.

Despite the November chill, she kept the window of her Honda Accord rolled down. It smelled like gasoline in the car. Two full five-quart canisters sat on the floor of the backseat. She had a grocery bag back there, too—with juice for Erin. She also had a blanket on the seat, in case Erin got cold.

Drumming her fingers on the steering wheel, she watched the children file out the main doors of the two-story elementary school. One set of windows in the front had pictures of turkeys, pumpkins, and Pilgrims for Thanksgiving.

Along with several other mothers, Jenna was parked in

the line of cars behind three buses in the school's loading zone. As the mob of kids moved closer to the bus, Jenna stepped out of the car and started looking for Erin.

"Aunt Rachel?" she heard someone say.

She'd persuaded Erin to start calling her that a few days ago. And she was pleased to hear it now.

Lugging her book bag, Erin broke away from the crowd of youngsters and ran to her.

Jenna squatted down, kissed Erin on the cheek, and then zipped up her open jacket. "I've come here to pick you up," she whispered. "Molly wants me to take care of you this afternoon. She—well, she just doesn't want to see you. I don't understand her sometimes, I really don't."

Her big eyes staring, Erin gave her a sort of puzzled, wounded look.

Jenna shrugged. "Let's not think about Molly. She's so awful. It's like I was telling you the other day, the only reason I'm Molly's friend is to make sure she doesn't try to hurt you. I'm never going to let that happen, honey." She took the book bag from her.

"Erin?"

Jenna glanced up and saw a stocky, pale woman of about forty waddling toward them. She had short hair, studded earrings, and wore a trench coat. Jenna smiled at the woman. "Hi, I'm Rachel Cross," she said, holding out her hand.

The woman eyed her warily, but shook her hand anyway. "I'm Shauna Farrell, vice principal."

"Molly said she'd call the school," Jenna whispered. "Something tells me she didn't. The poor thing, she's going through a lot right now. She wanted me to take Erin for the afternoon." She put a hand on Erin's shoulder. "Honey, could you introduce me to Ms. Farrell?"

Erin spoke past a finger crooked on her lower lip. "This is Aunt Rachel from next door," she announced. Then she reached over and tugged at Jenna's sleeve.

"If you'd like, I can call Molly," Jenna offered. "Only I think she's resting."

The vice principal's expression softened. She smiled and shook her head. "That won't be necessary. Please give Mrs. Dennehy my condolences."

"I'll do that," Jenna said. "Thank you." She took Erin's hand and walked her to the car.

She made sure Erin was buckled in the front passenger seat. Then she reached back, took out a box of Juicy Juice from the bag, and offered it to her.

Erin took it, but then frowned at the box with the straw in it. "It's already open."

Nodding, Jenna started up the car. "Yes, I opened it for you, honey."

"I want one I can open up myself," Erin said.

"Don't be silly," Jenna said. "Now, drink up. . . ."

"But I want one I can open—"

"Goddamn it, don't be such a little brat," she growled.

Erin gazed at her. She looked a bit scared.

Jenna shook her head, and clicked her tongue against her teeth. "You know, that's what Molly's always saying. She says you're a very bad girl, and that's why God made your mommy and daddy die. Isn't that a horrible thing for her to say? I don't believe that for one second. She's just being mean. I think you're wonderful, Erin. I wish you were my daughter." She reached over and stroked her hair. "You have pretty blond hair, honey. But sometime soon, we should change your hair. In fact, we'll both change our hair. I could use a different style and different color—nothing permanent, mind you. We could both be redheads for a week or so. Wouldn't that be fun?"

Erin shrugged. "I guess. . . ." She still eyed her juice container suspiciously.

"Of course it would be fun," Jenna said firmly. She pulled into traffic. "Now, drink up. It's your favorite. . . ."

Fifteen minutes later, no one noticed the black Honda Accord parked in back of a strip mall, where half the stores were shut down. There, by the Dumpsters, no one saw Jenna take something wrapped in a blanket from the front seat of the car. She carefully transferred it to the trunk.

Then she ducked back inside the car and drove away.

He didn't have the address anymore. It had been nearly eight months since he'd gone there by cab that one time. He remembered it was in Kent on Forty-second Avenue, one of those boring-looking new apartment complexes.

As Chris drove his father's Lexus through rush hour traffic on Interstate 5, he kept thinking about that call to Mrs. Hahn. *"How does it feel to have everything taken away from you?"* the woman had asked. *"Now you know what you did to me."*

Mrs. Corson's husband lost his job and his family because of a sex scandal. Mrs. Corson had lost her daughter, too. Tracy Corson had run away and didn't even come back for Mr. Corson's funeral. *"Because of you,"* Mrs. Corson had told him, *"our lives were destroyed."*

He and Molly had started it all when they'd reported to the principal about Mr. Corson hugging Ian in the varsity locker room after hours. The whole thing might have blown over, but his dad and mom had both become so worked up over the incident. Then Mrs. Hahn and Mrs. Garvey got involved. And between Courtney and Madison, it was suddenly all over the Internet, Twitter, and Facebook about Mr. Corson and Ian.

In a matter of eight months, all of the people responsible for Mr. Corson's firing had had their lives snuffed out or destroyed.

Mrs. Hahn was wrong. The rash of deaths, accidents, and tragedies on Willow Tree Court didn't start when Molly had

moved onto the block. The devastation began shortly after
Mr. Corson was murdered. And his death was still unsolved.

Chris gripped the steering wheel so tight that his knuck-
les turned white. He anxiously watched for the Kent exit and
saw it was in the left lane of the Interstate. A car horn blared
as he switched lanes to make it over in time. His stomach
was in knots. He wished he had an exact address. He only
had a vague recollection of how the taxi had taken him to
Mrs. Corson's apartment complex.

But he remembered Mrs. Corson very well, and that part
didn't quite make sense. She was kind of dumpy with frizzy
brown hair and a birthmark on her cheek. Plus she looked
older than Mr. Corson. According to Roseann, the woman
with his dad at the hotel bar on Friday had been cute, with a
good figure. Maybe Mrs. Corson had toned up, but most
birthmarks couldn't be removed.

The other thing that didn't seem right was the toolshed
catching on fire next door at Rachel's house. She hadn't even
been living on Willow Tree Court at the time of Mr. Corson's
firing or his death. Why would Mrs. Corson pick on her?

Hunched close to the wheel, Chris watched for the street
signs. He was pretty sure this was the same road that led to
her apartment complex. He'd just passed Forty-seventh Avenue Southeast, and he could see a forest just beyond the
new townhouses and apartment buildings. *Just five more
blocks,* he told himself.

Another thing that didn't quite make sense to him had
been how his mother had been murdered—along with Larry
and Taylor. Those two had nothing to do with Mr. Corson.
Why did they have to die? Had they just been in the wrong
place at the wrong time? He remembered how he'd planned
to spend that night at Larry's with his mother. Larry and Taylor had been scheduled to go on some overnight trip to
Olympia, only it had gotten canceled at the last minute. Had
the killer been planning to find his mother alone in that
house?

Wrong place, wrong time.

He saw the street sign for Forty-third Avenue, and the layout was beginning to look familiar. Chris turned left onto
Forty-second and noticed the NO OUTLET sign. He could see
the gate ahead—and the four identical beige buildings beyond that. He remembered Mrs. Corson lived in the second
building on the second floor, but he had no idea what apartment number it was.

Parking in an alcove near the entrance, he climbed out of
the car and checked the directory by the pedestrian gate. It
was one of those phone intercom-directories. The instructions on how to use it were embossed on the steel plate that
had the touch keys and phone cradle. He hated these damn
things. He pressed *99, and then selected 2 for the ABC list-
ings. It was hard to see the names past the glare reflecting off
the dirty glass to the display window. With the pound sign,
he scrolled down the tenant roster to the *C*'s. But he didn't
see *Corson* listed there.

Was Molly right? Had Jenna Corson moved onto their
block? Was she calling herself Natalie now? He'd never seen
Natalie. She'd probably been avoiding him, knowing he'd
recognize her.

He heard a car approaching. He still had the phone in his
hand, and pretended to talk into it as a woman in a station
wagon pulled up to the entrance. He noticed her reach for
something on her sun visor. With a click and a mechanical
hum, the gate slid open. Chris watched her drive through and
head toward the first building. He waited until she was far
enough away; then he quickly hung up the phone and snuck
through the entrance just as the gate started to close again.

Second building, second floor, he told himself. Maybe the
current tenant knew where Mrs. Corson had gone.

The wind kicked up, and he hiked up the collar to his
school jacket as he made his way to the second building. He
glanced up at the overcast sky. It would be getting dark soon,
he could tell.

Chris was pretty sure it was the second alcove with a stairway that had a sign: UNITS E–H. He climbed up only one flight, but he was short of breath as he stopped in front of apartment 2-F. Under the doorbell, he noticed a piece of white tape with *Yeager* scribbled on it. But he could see there was another piece of tape beneath that. Chris carefully peeled it back, and saw the handwritten *J. Corson.*

He rang the bell. He could hear movement on the other side of the door. He waited a few moments, then rang the bell again and knocked. The door opened as far as the chain lock allowed. Peering out at him was a slightly chubby woman with brown bangs in her eyes and a thumb-sucking toddler in her arms.

"Hi," Chris said. "Sorry to bother you, but I'm trying to find the woman who used to live here, Jenna Corson."

The woman shook her head. "She didn't leave a forwarding address. I can't help you." She shut the door.

Chris felt a huge letdown. Slump-shouldered, he stood by that door for another moment.

Suddenly, it opened again. "Hey," the woman said, peeking out at him. She bounced the toddler in her arms. "Try Monica Ballitore in three-G, one flight up. She was a friend of hers. She might know where you can find her."

"Thanks a lot," Chris said. Then he hurried up the stairs to apartment 3-G and knocked on the door. He heard footsteps, and then someone's voice on the other side. "Yeah, who's there?" she called.

"I'm looking for Monica Ballitore!" Chris replied loudly.

The door swung open. "That's me," she said. "Who are you?"

Chris stared at the fortysomething woman. She had frizzy brown hair and a birthmark on her cheek. An unlit cigarette was in her hand.

"Your name's Monica Ballitore?" he asked.

She nodded. "Have we met?"

"Yes," Chris said steadily. "Jenna Corson sort of introduced us. Do you know where she is?"

"I don't have a clue. I haven't heard from her since she
moved. You look really familiar. Just where did Jenna *sort of*
introduce us?"

"In her apartment," Chris replied. "You pretended to be
her."

Her mouth dropped open. "Oh, Christ, you're the little
shit who caused all that trouble for her husband."

Chris remembered calling Mrs. Corson from his cell
phone. In order to get in and see her, he'd said he was a floral delivery guy. But he'd been uncertain whether or not
she'd figured out his ruse. With a little help from caller ID,
she'd have found him out.

Obviously she had. He never met Jenna Corson. He'd met
her friend.

"Why did Mrs. Corson make you pretend to be her?" he
asked.

Monica Ballitore sneered at him. "I don't have to answer
any questions from you."

"She didn't come to her husband's funeral," Chris said.
"Is it because she didn't want anyone to know what she
looked like? Did she already have some sort of plan to get
even with us? Was she making sure she could move onto our
block, and no one would figure out who she really was?"

"I don't know what the hell you're talking about," she
replied, frowning. "You're gonna have to leave now."

"Please, listen to me," he begged her. "I need to know
where Mrs. Corson is. It's urgent."

"Well, good luck," she said. "A while back, I asked the
apartment building management company if they had a forwarding address or contact information for her, and they've
got nothing, nada, zilch."

"You still haven't told me why you pretended to be her
that day," he said.

"Because, Jenna asked me," Monica Ballitore replied edgily. "She didn't want to see you—"

"All that stuff you said to me about how I destroyed your family, and how you didn't want to see me again—did she tell you to say that?"

She nodded. "Yeah, and considering what you put her through, you have some nerve coming back here, sniffing around."

Chris glared at her. "My parents were both murdered, and your friend Jenna Corson is the one who had them killed. That's why I'm 'sniffing around' here. I need some help finding her. You owe me at least that much. Do you have a picture of her?"

The woman let out a defiant laugh. She put the cigarette in her mouth and stepped back to close the door. "Fuck off," she muttered.

"Don't you tell me that," Chris growled. "Don't you dare tell me that. . . ." He shoved the door open.

The woman staggered back. The cigarette fell out of her mouth, and she screamed. "Get out of here! Get out right now, you son of a bitch!" She reeled back and slapped him across the face.

It stung. Chris stopped himself. He realized he'd barged into the front part of her apartment. It smelled like stale cigarette smoke. His hands were clenched in fists at his sides. He took a deep breath and backed out of the doorway. "I won't ask you any more questions, lady," he said evenly. "But the police sure as hell will."

He turned away and the door slammed shut behind him.

His heart racing, Chris started down the stairs. He had tears in his eyes. As he reached the bottom of the stairwell, his cell phone went off. He didn't realize how much he was shaking until he pulled out the phone and checked the caller number. It was home. He clicked on the cell. "Molly?" he said, out of breath.

"Hi, Chris, I'm glad I caught you." She sounded tense. "Listen, did you—did you decide to pick up Erin from school?"

"What do you mean?" he asked.

"I just came back from the bus stop," Molly said. "I was going to meet her. But the bus just zoomed on by. I figured maybe you'd picked her up at school."

"No," he said numbly. "No, I didn't."

"Damn, I was hoping she'd be with you," Molly said. "I suppose she's still angry at me. Did she say anything to you? Maybe she went home with a friend. . . ."

"She didn't mention it to me."

"Okay, well, then I—I'll call the school," she said in a shaky voice.

Chris felt a pang of dread in his gut. "Let me know as soon as you hear anything."

"I will. Listen, Chris, I'd feel a lot better if you were here. Come home as soon as you can, okay?"

"I might be a while," he said. "I'm way down in Kent."

"What are you doing there?"

"I was looking for Mrs. Corson," he admitted.

There was a silence on the other end for a few seconds. "Why are you looking for her?" Molly asked finally.

"You know why, Molly. I think you've been right all along. I'll be home soon, okay?"

"Good," she said. Then she hung up.

CHAPTER TWENTY-EIGHT

"She was wearing a navy-blue jumper with a pink long-sleeved turtleneck," Molly said into the phone.

She stood at Jeff's desk, looking out the window at the street. She kept hoping someone would come by and drop off Erin—or maybe Rachel would return. But Molly hadn't seen a single car drive by since she'd come home. All the other houses on the cul-de-sac were empty. It was 4:25 and getting dark out.

Erin should have been on that bus forty minutes ago. Since then, Molly had called Chris and the moms of several of Erin's friends to make sure she hadn't gone home with someone else. Erin had hugged her good-bye this morning, but that had been the first and only sign in a few days that her stepdaughter didn't absolutely loathe her.

Now, Molly wondered if Erin didn't have a damn good reason for hating her—and for running away this afternoon. Perhaps Erin had been unjustly accused of destroying her painting and that shelf full of elephants.

Erin would have had to use a stool, chair, or stepladder to reach that putty knife on the second to top shelf of the cabinet. And if she'd used something to boost herself up to that shelf, why would she bother putting it back exactly where it had been? The putty knife had been left on the floor, and the tube of paint had been left out with the cap off. Why move the chair, stool, or stepladder back where it belonged?

Yet Molly had found yellow paint smears in Erin's room and on her clothes. Had somebody set her up? Chris wouldn't have framed his kid sister and let her take the heat for something he'd done. It just didn't make sense. But the only other people in the house had been Rachel and Trish.

If Erin had indeed been innocent of the sabotage, then who could blame her for wanting to run away from home—and her crazy, wicked stepmother? Maybe she was sulking in a playground somewhere between the school and here. Molly couldn't help feeling conflicted about phoning the school and possibly sending out an Amber Alert.

But Jenna Corson was out there, and in all probability, she'd killed Erin's parents. From Molly's brief conversation with Chris, it seemed he'd figured that out, too—on his own.

So what was to keep Jenna Corson from abducting Erin and possibly murdering her?

"She was wearing white kneesocks and Keds saddle shoes," Molly told the school secretary on the phone. She paced within the small confines of Jeff's study. "And—and she had her hair down. She has blond hair. . . ."

"Yes, blond hair, we have that here from the description you gave us," the woman said. "I'm putting you on hold for just a minute, Mrs. Dennehy, okay?"

Molly didn't get a chance to respond before she heard a click on the other end. It sounded more like she'd been disconnected than put on hold, but she stayed on the line anyway. Biting her lip, she glanced out the window again.

The two streetlights on Willow Tree Court had gone on. It was officially dark out. If Erin had indeed run away, she would have headed home by now.

"Mrs. Dennehy?" It wasn't the secretary's voice. "Hi, this is Shauna Farrell, the vice principal. Your neighbor picked

up Erin when the children were getting out of school. She
said you asked her to take care of Erin this afternoon."

"What?" Molly said, panic stricken. All she could think
of was Natalie driving off with Erin. "I—I did no such thing.
How could you just . . ." She paused and took a deep breath.
"Did you see my neighbor's car? Was it a blue Mini
Cooper?"

"No, I'm sorry, I didn't see the car, Mrs. Dennehy," the
woman answered. "But I figured it was all right, because
Erin called her Aunt Rachel, and she was holding her hand."

"It was Rachel?" Molly asked. She could feel her heart
still pounding.

"Yes, your neighbor, Rachel Cross," the vice principal
said. "She is your neighbor, isn't she?"

"Yes," Molly replied, still not certain what to think. She
glanced out the window at Rachel's house and the bare
driveway. In her message, Rachel had said she would be
back by 3:45, and that had been almost an hour ago.

"Mrs. Dennehy, are you still there?"

"Ah, yes. Rachel told you that I'd asked her to look after
Erin today?"

"That's right. She said you must have forgotten to call the
school. Erin seemed very happy to see her. In fact, she broke
away from the other children and ran over to her. . . ."

Molly figured Erin would never do that with Natalie. She
barely knew the Nguyens' uninvited houseguest. It must
have been Rachel. But it didn't make sense. Molly hadn't
asked her to look after Erin this afternoon. Or had she?
Sometimes lately, she thought she might be losing her mind.

"Mrs. Dennehy, here at the school, we're always very
careful to look out for the children's safety," the woman said.

"Yes, of course," Molly murmured. "There must have
been some miscommunication. I'll call Rachel right now.
Will somebody be there in case I need to get in touch with
you?"

"Yes, I'll be here for the next hour. In fact, I'd appreciate it if you got back to me, and let me know that everything's all right. And I'm sure it will be, Mrs. Dennehy."

"Thank you," Molly said.

As soon as she clicked off with the school, she called Rachel's cell and anxiously counted the rings. She winced when the voice mail greeting came on. "Hi, Rachel," she said, after the beep. "It's Molly, and I'm wondering where you are. Erin wasn't on the school bus. I just got off the phone with the school. They said you came and picked her up. To tell you the truth, I'm kind of confused. You should have said something. Anyway, call me as soon as you can."

Molly hung up, and then she glanced out the window again. Nothing. On her way to the kitchen, she turned on the front outside lights and the hallway light. She played back Rachel's earlier message on the answering machine: *"Don't panic when you see my car isn't in the driveway. You asked me to make sure if Natalie comes back that she doesn't leave again. And I've done that. But I really need to go to the store. I know you'll be home soon, because Erin's bus drops her off at a quarter to four. I'll be back before then, okay? I really don't think you're going to see Natalie again. But you'll see me—very soon. . . ."*

Not once did Rachel mention that she was going to pick up Erin. If she'd impulsively decided to do that, why wouldn't she call her and let her know? Rachel didn't quite sound like herself in the message. What was so important at the store that she couldn't have stuck around here for another half hour? Obviously, she hadn't gone to the store. She'd gone to Erin's school.

Molly suddenly imagined Jenna/Natalie holding a gun to Rachel's head while she'd left that message. Had she been waiting in Rachel's car—with a gun aimed at her—while Rachel picked up Erin for her? The vice principal hadn't seen the car, so she wouldn't have noticed another woman waiting in there. That crazy, raspy-voiced woman on the phone had warned Rachel that she would be sorry she'd moved onto the block.

Molly couldn't help picturing Rachel lying dead in a ditch somewhere, while Jenna/Natalie drove off with Erin.

She heard a car.

Molly ran to the front of the house and flung open the door. She saw Rachel's Honda Accord pull into the driveway next door. But it looked like Rachel was alone in the car. Molly's heart sank. She moved toward Rachel's driveway.

Rachel climbed out of the front seat. "I just listened to your message at the stoplight on Gleason Street," she said hurriedly. "You can relax. Erin's fine, but I'm not." She pointed to her own house. "I need to hit the bathroom. I'm peeing for two now. Go back inside and wait for me. I'll be right over."

"But where's Erin?" Molly asked.

With her keys in her hand, Rachel hurried to her front door. "Molly, she's fine. She's happy. Go back inside before you catch your death out here. I'll be over in five minutes to explain everything."

Molly watched her unlock the door, open it, and duck inside the house. She felt the chill, and rubbed her arms. Rachel had just said Erin was fine. She'd said it twice. But Molly was still worried. She stood there another few moments, and then retreated inside the house. She left the door open a crack, went back to Jeff's study, and stared out the window.

"Damn it," she whispered, after waiting nearly five more minutes. She thought about calling the school to tell them Erin was okay, but first she wanted to hear what Rachel had to say. Frowning, Molly glanced at her watch. It was almost 5:15, and dark as midnight out. She couldn't believe Rachel had picked up Erin without telling her.

Finally, she heard Rachel's door open and shut. She saw

her neighbor cut across the driveways to the front of the house. She'd changed into a loose-fitting, dark, poncho-type of sweatshirt with big pockets in front. She already looked very pregnant. Molly came around and met her in the doorway.

"Sorry to leave you hanging," Rachel muttered, stepping inside. "My system's all out of whack, because of the baby. I know you're upset about Erin. I couldn't call you. Do you have a Sprite or ginger ale or something carbonated to help my heartburn?"

Molly closed the door after her, and then led the way to the kitchen. "I've been climbing the walls with worry for the last ninety minutes, Rachel," she said edgily. "I thought for sure Natalie-Jenna-Whatever-Her-Name-Is had abducted Erin. In fact, I called the school. I was ready to call the police. What the hell happened? I can't believe you picked up Erin at school without telling me. You just left me hanging. . . ."

"Mea culpa, mea culpa," Rachel said with a sigh. "You're not going to like it any better when I explain what happened."

Molly dug a can of 7UP out of the refrigerator and wordlessly handed it to her.

Rachel opened the can and sipped her soda.

"I'm waiting," Molly said, crossing her arms.

Rachel frowned. "Well, Erin called me from school. Apparently one of her little friends actually has a cell phone. I didn't even know Erin had my number. Did you give it to her?"

Molly shook her head.

"Well, she knows it, because she called me and asked me to pick her up after school. She said she didn't want to come home. . . ." Rachel paused, and then sipped her 7UP again. She glanced down at the kitchen floor. "Erin said it didn't feel right at home anymore, because her real parents weren't here. She said she didn't want to see you or be around you. I'm sorry, Molly. There's no way to sugarcoat that."

Molly felt like she'd just been kicked in the stomach. She told herself those were the sentiments of an upset and confused six-year-old. But it still hurt. She walked around the kitchen counter and sat down at the breakfast table. "Where is she?"

"You might not like this, either," Rachel warned. "Lynette's sister, who lives near the UW Hospital, is looking after Lynette's kids. Erin's with them. I dropped her off. I figured after an hour with Carson and Dakota Hahn, you and home will start looking pretty good to her."

Molly knew she was expected to laugh, but she couldn't.

"I tried calling you as soon as I dropped Erin off," Rachel said. "But my cell phone started acting up on me. I couldn't call out, but I got your message all right. Modern technology, you go figure. Anyway, please don't be mad at me, Molly. Erin made me promise I wouldn't tell you, and this is the first time she's asked me for something. I didn't want her to think she couldn't trust me."

Molly frowned at her. "Well, I'm not sure *I* can trust you. On top of that, you made me look like a major idiot with the vice principal at Erin's school. You told her that I must have *forgotten* to call the school about you picking up Erin. And there I was on the phone with them asking which neighbor picked up my stepdaughter. God, I must have come off as a total flake. What were you thinking?"

"I'm really sorry," Rachel murmured, shrugging. "I guess I shouldn't have gotten involved. Maybe—maybe you ought to call the school, and tell them everything's okay."

Molly stood up. "Yes, we don't want to worry the people at Erin's school," she grumbled. "God, with everything that's been going on lately, I can't believe you'd . . ." She shook her head and left the room. She reminded herself that Rachel had been a good friend to her. Without Rachel, she never would have made it through the last week.

In Jeff's study, she picked up the phone and hesitated before dialing the school. "I'm done venting!" she announced loudly. "I know you were just trying to do Erin and me a favor. You meant well. . . ."

"I figured you couldn't be mad at me too long," Rachel called. Molly could hear her filling a glass with ice. "You need my help breaking into the Nguyens' house tonight."

Molly frowned at Rachel's light tone. It didn't seem right. She wanted to get inside that house to look for clues to her husband's murder—and the deaths of several others. Rachel made it sound as if they were planning to pull off some kind of high school prank.

Of course, Molly still felt confused and a bit stung by what went on with Erin. It was hard getting past that.

She phoned the school and got Vice Principal Farrell on the line. She explained that Erin was fine, and it was just a misunderstanding. "I'd asked my neighbor to pick up Erin *next* Wednesday, not today," she said, making Rachel the flaky one.

When Molly came back to the kitchen, she found Rachel sitting at the table with a second can of 7UP—and a tall glass of ice—in front of the chair beside her. "I figured you could use a drink," she said, pouring the 7UP in the glass. "And under the pregnant circumstances, I guess this is about as wild as it gets for us."

Molly worked up a smile and sat down next to her.

"Are we all squared with Erin's school?" Rachel asked.

Molly nodded. "It's all straightened out."

Rachel raised her can of soda to toast her. "So—forgive me?"

Molly took the glass of 7UP and clicked it against Rachel's soda can. "All's forgiven."

Rachel sipped hers. "Well, come on, drink up. The toast doesn't count unless you drink, too."

Molly started to raise the glass to her lips, but then she set it down again. "Oh, I almost forgot about Chris." She got to her feet. "I called him when Erin didn't get off the bus. He's on his way here, probably going crazy with the rush-hour traffic. He was down in Kent, chasing down a lead about Jenna Corson."

"Really?" Rachel murmured. "What kind of lead?"

"I don't know. But he put it together himself that she's the one behind all the horrible things that have been going on around here lately—no coaching from me." Molly grabbed a pencil and a piece of paper from the basket in the corner of the kitchen counter. "Do you have Lynette's sister's address? I'll tell Chris to swing by and pick up Erin."

Rachel looked stumped for a moment. "Oh, I—I left it in my coat in the house. I can pick her up later. Maybe we can send Chris in an hour or so, and then we'll use that time to do a little breaking and entering at the Nguyens'."

Molly leaned back against the counter and folded her arms. "You don't seem to take that idea about searching their house very seriously."

Rachel laughed. "Are you kidding me? I'm nervous as hell about it. In fact, sit down." She pointed to Molly's glass. "Wet your whistle and tell me your plan."

"I need to call Chris first," Molly said. "He's probably going out of his mind with worry." Again, she found herself retreating to Jeff's study to use the phone—rather than talk on the kitchen extension in front of Rachel. She dialed Chris's cell number.

He picked up on the second ring: "Hi, Molly, what's going on?"

"Erin's okay," she said. "She's at Lynette's sister's house—with Carson and Dakota. I guess she still hates me and doesn't want to be around me. So she called Rachel from school and asked to be picked up. Rachel dropped her off at Lynette's sister's place."

There was silence on the other end. Molly wondered if she'd lost the connection. "Chris? Are you still there?"

"Yeah, I'm just trying to wrap my head around that story, because it sounds pretty screwed up."

"Sounds screwed up to me, too, but that's what happened," Molly said. "Anyway, I just wanted to let you know that Erin's all right. I'm here with Rachel. I'm guessing traffic has been heinous."

"Yeah, but I should be there soon," Chris said. "By the way, Molly, you slept downstairs, so you didn't hear it. But Erin had a nightmare last night, and she woke me up. She was extra scared because you weren't in your bed. She'd gone to you first, Molly. She's crazy about you. She was really happy when I told her that you were staying and taking care of us. So that story about Erin hating you? It's bullshit."

Dazed, Molly didn't say anything. Suddenly she was worried about Erin again.

"I gotta go," she heard Chris say. "There's a cop one lane over, and I shouldn't be driving and talking on the cell at the same time. See you soon." He clicked off.

Molly hung up the phone, then went to the window and stared out at the darkness. She saw part of her own reflection in the glass—and then someone stepping up behind her.

She swiveled around. Rachel smiled and offered her the tall glass of 7UP. "Did you get ahold of Chris?"

Molly nodded and took the glass. "Yes, he's on his way."

"Good." Rachel sat on the edge of Jeff's desk.

Molly looked down at her 7UP, but didn't taste it. "You know, when I first realized Erin wasn't on the bus, I thought Chris might have picked her up. I had this notion that they both hated me, so he was taking his kid sister and running away. He assured me just now that Erin likes me very much." Molly paused to let it sink in. "That was nice to hear, but it doesn't quite gel with the story you told me, does it?"

Rachel shrugged. "Well, maybe Chris was just trying to make you feel better, Molly."

She shook her head. "I don't think so. Chris is a nice kid, but he's never gone out of his way to spare my feelings. I usually know where I stand with him."

Rachel let out a tiny laugh. "Just like his father."

Molly stared at her and said nothing.

Rachel laughed nervously, and then flicked her hair back. "Or—so I gather, I mean, from what you've told me about Jeff."

Molly's eyes kept searching hers. The ice clinked in her glass, and she realized her hand was shaking. She set the glass down on Jeff's desk. She was thirsty, but hadn't even sipped any of the 7UP, because Rachel had poured it. On some unconscious level, she knew it might make her sick—like the peppermints and the ginger capsules Rachel had given her.

Now she knew who had slashed a yellow X across her painting and set it up to look as if Erin had been the culprit.

Now she knew the woman standing in front of her had seduced and murdered Jeff.

Molly heard a car, but she didn't turn to look out the window behind her. She didn't want to turn her back on this woman.

She listened to the car pulling into the driveway and watched the headlight beams sweep across Jenna Corson's face.

Chris turned off the ignition to his father's Lexus. Straight ahead, in the window to his dad's study, he noticed Molly standing and talking to their neighbor, Rachel.

Rachel's story about picking up Erin at school sounded wrong in so many ways. At the last stoplight on the way home, Chris had tried to phone Mrs. Hahn to confirm that her sister had Erin. But he'd gotten some weird tone pattern, and then a recording: *"The person you are trying to reach is not accepting calls at this time. Please try your call later. . . ."* Then as the recording had lapsed into Spanish, he'd remembered Mrs. Hahn had broken her cell phone.

Even with Mrs. Hahn's broken phone, he didn't understand why his sister would call Rachel—to be taken to Mrs. Hahn's sister's house. How did she even know Rachel's number? He sure as hell didn't know it. If Erin wanted to be picked up, she would have phoned him before calling the lady next door. And she wasn't mad at Molly anymore, so it just didn't make any damn sense.

He climbed out of the car and hurried to the front door. It was strange that neither Molly nor Rachel had come to let him in when they were only a few feet away in his dad's study. He had to unlock the door with his key.

As he stepped inside, Rachel turned and smiled at him. "Well, hi, Chris."

"Hi," he said tentatively. Taking off his school jacket, he hung it on the newel post at the bottom of the stairs.

"Molly said you were in Kent, following a lead," she said.

Bewildered, he glanced past her—at Molly, who stood by his dad's desk with her arms folded. He could feel an awful tension in that small room—as if he'd just walked in on them at the brink of an argument.

"She wants to know if you talked to anybody about Jenna Corson," Molly said steadily. "She wants to know who you talked to, and what they told you. But I have a few questions for you, *Rachel*. For example, why would Jenna Corson set fire to your toolshed and threaten you on the phone when you had absolutely nothing to do with her husband's firing or his murder?"

Rachel scratched the back of her neck, and laughed. "I'm not sure I know what you're getting at, Molly. But we agreed that it's probably because I'm your friend. Remember?"

"It threw me off for a while, that's for sure," Molly said. "I was actually worried for you."

"What's going on here?" Chris murmured, glancing back and forth at the two of them.

"I remember the first day we met," Molly continued. "I gave you that letter you must have addressed to yourself and slipped in our mailbox. I told you about Lynette's kids throwing dirt balls at cars. The very next day, her kids got all cut up,

because someone had scattered broken glass in that vacant
lot. I always thought that was too much of a coincidence."

Rachel smirked a tiny bit. "You said they'd been doing
that for a while. They probably pissed off a lot of people. It
was bound to catch up with them eventually. Sounds to me
like they had it coming. *'Time wounds all heels,'* I like to
say."

Chris stared at their new neighbor: light brown hair, cute
face, and even with that poncho she was wearing, he knew
she had a nice body. She perfectly fit Roseann's description
of the "hustler" who had been with his father at the hotel on
Friday, the woman who had killed him.

He remembered what Mr. Corson had said to him on
what would be the very last time they'd ever see each
other—at that running trail by Lake Union: *"Your neighbors
on Willow Tree Court and the ones like them, they'll have to
pay. . . . It reminds me of this saying my wife has. 'Time
wounds all heels.' "*

Stunned, Chris kept staring at her.

With an exasperated little laugh, she shoved her hands in
the pockets of her poncho.

"You're Mrs. Corson," Chris heard himself say. "You
killed my parents. . . ." His fists clenched, he took a step toward her. "Where's Erin? She's got nothing to do with what
happened to Mr. Corson. What the hell have you done with
my sister?"

All at once, Jenna Corson grabbed Molly by the hair and
pulled a gun from the pocket of her poncho. She pressed the
barrel to Molly's head. Chris froze. Jenna Corson didn't say
anything. Yet Chris knew if he took one more step toward
them, she'd shoot his stepmother in the head.

Molly shrieked and desperately tried to push her away.
But Mrs. Corson slammed the butt end of the gun against
her temple. It made a terrible, hard-thump sound, and Molly
groaned. She seemed stunned—and dazed into submission.

Her eyes rolled back as she slouched against Mr. Corson's widow.

"Get the blinds!" Mrs. Corson barked at him. She nodded toward the study window. "Do it!"

Glaring at her, Chris moved to the window and lowered the blinds. "Where's Erin?" he asked again.

"Your sister's fine, Chris," she said, backing away and dragging Molly into the front hall. She jabbed the gun barrel against Molly's temple. "I've got Erin. She'll be all right. I don't blame her for what happened to Ray. You're the ones who started it. That's why I saved you two for last. . . ."

Hesitating, Chris began to follow them down the hall toward the family room.

She tugged at Molly's hair, yanking her head back. "Molly, you were under a tremendous strain. They'll say you snapped, poor thing." She let out a tiny laugh. "You shot your stepson, and then set fire to every house on the block. And then you shot yourself. They'll find you both in this room. Everyone will say insanity must run in your family, Molly. They'll say you were unbalanced, just like your crazy, murdering brother. I paid good money to a private detective in Chicago to find out about Crazy Charlie. . . ."

Molly just moaned in protest. She seemed too disoriented to struggle. Blood oozed from the corner of her forehead where Jenna had hit her with the gun.

Jenna knocked over a standing lamp as she backed into the family room. It hit the floor with a crash but didn't break. She didn't even glance at it. She still held Molly up by her hair. "By the way, this gun is registered in Jeff's name. They'll think it was his. I got Jeff to buy it for me two months ago. All the paperwork has his name and this address on it. I told Jeff there were some break-ins in my neighborhood, and I needed a gun. Wasn't that sweet of him to make sure I was protected?"

Standing in the hallway, uncertain what to do, Chris heard a noise outside. It sounded like a car door opening and closing. But Mrs. Corson didn't seem to hear it over Molly's anguished moaning, which only got louder.

"After tonight, I'm going to disappear—with Erin," she announced. "Erin's still innocent—and young enough to become my own. The Dennehy family owes me a daughter, goddamn it." Though she had tears in her eyes, she smiled. Her lips brushed against Molly's ear. "I'll leave here with more than one child of Jeff's. The baby I'm carrying, Molly, it's his. . . ."

Chris shook his head. He couldn't believe what she was saying.

All at once, someone rapped against the front door.

Molly tried to scream out, but Mrs. Corson slapped a hand over her mouth.

"Seattle Police!" the muffled voice called from the other side of the door. The man knocked again, and then he rang the bell. "Is anyone home?"

Wide-eyed, Mrs. Corson glared at Chris. "Get rid of him!" she whispered, dragging Molly into the kitchen area. She kept the gun barrel pressed against her head.

At the front door, Chris glanced out the peephole, and saw a cop carrying something wrapped in an old blanket. It took Chris a moment to realize the guy was holding Erin. Her head was pressed to the policeman's shoulder. Chris flung open the door.

"This little girl was locked in the trunk of the car next door," the cop said angrily. "Do you know what's going on here?"

Erin stirred and let out a feeble, sleepy cry. A piece of duct tape dangled from her cheek. Chris guessed the cop must have peeled it back from where it had been covering her mouth.

"That's my sister," he murmured. He opened the door wider.

The cop stepped inside and carried Erin into the living room. Chris shot a look over his shoulder toward the kitchen. He didn't hear anything. He followed the policeman into the living room. The guy was about thirty, with wavy dark blond hair and a cleft in his chin. He carefully set Erin on her side on the sofa, and then pulled back the blanket. Someone had tied Erin's feet together, and her hands were bound behind her with rope.

"Oh, Jesus," Chris murmured.

"I was patrolling the neighborhood," the cop said. Hovering over Erin, he patted her head, and then tugged at the rope around her wrists. It looked too taut to loosen by hand. "I heard whimpering coming from the Honda Accord in the driveway next door. Do you know who's responsible for this?"

The policeman wasn't looking at him. Chris had to tap him on the shoulder. The cop glanced back at him. Chris tried to mouth the words, *Get some help.*

The man squinted at him. "What?"

Chris nodded in the direction of the kitchen. "Get help," he said under his breath. "We're not alone here. . . ."

Molly heard Chris talking to the policeman in the living room. Chris's voice dropped to a whisper. She couldn't make out what he was saying, but obviously he was trying to tell the cop they were in trouble. Obviously, Jenna could hear Chris whispering, too.

"What does he think he's doing?" she muttered. She started to drag Molly closer to the hallway.

With all her might, Molly elbowed her in the ribs. Jenna let out a gasp and doubled over. The gun flew out of her hand. It toppled onto the hallway floor and slid for a few inches across the hardwood.

Screaming, Molly pushed Jenna aside and ran for the living room.

"What the hell's going on?" she heard the cop yell. He came out of the living room, drawing his gun. "Hold it right there!"

Molly stopped in her tracks. "She was going to kill us and

take my daughter," Molly explained, gasping for air. She pointed back at Jenna, behind her. "She's killed several people—including my husband. . . ."

"It's true," Chris said. "She's the one who did this to my sister."

Molly noticed Erin on the sofa, her feet tied and her wrists bound behind her. "Oh, my God," she whispered. She started to move, but the cop was pointing the gun at her. Molly hesitated.

Chris turned to the cop. "That's my stepmother, she's okay. It's the other one. . . ."

The cop still had the gun trained on her—and Jenna. He nodded at Molly. "Kick that gun over here."

"Goddamn it," Jenna growled. But she stayed perfectly still.

Molly still couldn't quite get her breath. She felt a bit dizzy, and her heart was pounding furiously. She obeyed the cop. The gun glided across the hardwood floor and stopped nearly right in front of him.

Chris went to his sister on the sofa and started to untie the rope around her wrists. Her eyes closed, she was crying softly—almost as if she were having a nightmare.

With a hand on her bleeding forehead, Molly stared at the cop. He retrieved the gun, did something to the safety, and then stuck it in his belt. He looked a bit familiar. He nodded gratefully at her. "That's good, ma'am."

But he still had his gun pointed at her and Jenna. He glanced over his shoulder at Chris. "Stop doing that. Don't untie her. Get away from her."

Baffled, Chris gazed up at him. "Why? What do you mean?"

The cop smiled a tiny bit. "Because," he said. "You'll just have to tie her up again—for me."

That was when Molly noticed for the first time that his blue policeman's uniform looked shoddy and fake. That was when she recognized the man who had carried a screaming Dakota Hahn down the block after the children had cut themselves. He'd obviously been hanging around the cul-de-sac, studying the layout.

"Oh, Jesus, no," she whispered.

He stepped back into the living room. "Over there with the ladies," he told Chris, nodding toward the hallway. He pointed the gun at Erin now.

Chris stared at him, half scared, half defiant. He didn't budge.

"Do as I say," the man said patiently. "Don't try to do anything brave, because that's just going to get someone killed."

Chris finally looped around him and came over to Molly's side. He held on to her arm. She could feel his hand was shaking.

Jenna sighed. "Just because her husband worked for a drug company, it doesn't mean there are any drugs in the house. You're going to be disappointed."

"We'll see about that," the man replied, the gun still trained on Erin.

Molly said nothing. She knew he hadn't come there to rob them.

"You, *stepmom*," he said, nodding toward the light switch on the wall. "Is that for the lights outside and down here in the hall?"

She nodded. "Yes, both."

"Turn them off, please. I don't want anyone to see me working down here."

Molly reached over and switched off the lights. The upstairs hallway light and a lamp in Jeff's study were still on. She stood in the shadows with Chris at her side—and Jenna Corson behind them. Molly knew he planned to turn on all the lights in the house—once his work was done.

"I don't want to hurt anybody," he said in a calm voice. "Just do as I say, and I'll be out of here in a half hour. Now, I'll need all of you upstairs. . . ."

* * *

For twenty minutes, they sat on the floor of the upstairs hallway: he, Molly, and Mrs. Corson. Just a few feet away, the man sat near the top of the stairs with his arm around Erin, occasionally tickling her ear with the barrel of his gun. She'd come out of her stupor, and seemed to realize what was happening. Tears streamed down her cheeks and she was trembling.

For long stretches of time, no one uttered a word. Erin whimpered behind the duct tape he'd pressed over her mouth again. The only other sound was the tearing of sheets. He'd had Molly pull some bedding from the linen closet, and they'd started ripping them into wide strips for their own restraints. Chris felt like one of those people in the horror movies, forced to dig their own grave. He couldn't help thinking this was more than just a robbery.

Every few minutes, Mrs. Corson broke the silence and tried to bargain with the bogus cop—killer to killer. "Listen, there are four other houses on this block, all empty, all ripe for the picking," she'd said. "I can tell you which houses offer the best merchandise. I don't give a shit about these people. You can take what you want, and do whatever you want. Just don't tie me up. Tie up the others. Leave them here with me, and I'll make sure you get away with a good haul. I'll make sure there are no witnesses."

"Keep tearing those sheets, honey," he'd replied. "And be quiet. Otherwise, I'll have to tape up your mouth—like the little one here."

That had been a few minutes ago, and Jenna Corson hadn't uttered a word since.

Now the man had the gun pointed at Chris. "I don't want to hurt anybody," he said again. "It's up to you to make sure no one tries anything foolish. Starting with your houseguest here, I want you to tie up her legs at the ankles. . . ."

With several strips of the linen in his grasp, Chris obediently crawled over to Mrs. Corson. His hands shook as he tied her ankles together.

"No, don't," she murmured under her breath, squirming.

"Now roll her over on her stomach and tie her hands be-hind her," the man commanded. "Make it good and tight, be-cause I'm going to test it. Let's see if you learned anything in the Boy Scouts about tying knots."

"I wasn't in the Boy Scouts," Chris muttered. Glancing over his shoulder, he saw the man had the gun pressed against Erin's head once more. Chris knew his sister would be dead if he tried to lunge at the guy.

As he turned Mrs. Corson over on her stomach, she re-sisted and let out a pathetic cry. He struggled to tie her hands together. "No, no, no, no," she whispered.

When he finally finished, Chris was out of breath. He glanced up at the stranger.

"Now, it's your stepmom's turn," the man said, brushing the gun barrel against Erin's nose. Trying to turn her head away, she whimpered in protest.

"Tie her up the same way you did the other one," he said. "The quicker you do it, the quicker I'll be out of here, and you folks can go back to doing whatever it was you were doing."

Molly handed Chris some strips of linen as he crawled over to her. She rolled over on her stomach without any prompting. Chris tied her legs first, leaving a little slack. If she was able to pry her shoes off, she stood a good chance of slipping her feet out of the binds. Then he tied up her wrists. Chris couldn't stop trembling. He was so scared he kept thinking he might throw up. He let out a grunt as he finished tying the knot—acting as if it was as tight as he could make it. But the linen restraints around her wrists were loose enough for Molly to wriggle her hands free—with a little effort.

He glanced over at the man again, who stood up. He held the gun down over the top of Erin's head. He smiled at Chris. "Okay, your turn," he said. "Tie yourself up at the ankles. . . ."

On the other side of Molly, Chris started tying his own ankles with the strips of bedsheets. He figured the man would pay particular attention to the work he did on himself, so he made the restraints fairly tight.

When Chris looked up again, the man had Erin wiggling facedown on the floor. "Okay, roll over on your stomach," he said to Chris. "Put your hands behind you."

Chris was obedient. He kept thinking it was too late to take his chances and pounce on the guy. He should have done that before his ankles were bound. But the son of a bitch had had a gun on Erin the whole time. With the side of his face pressed against the carpeted floor, Chris could only see him from the waist down as he stepped over Mrs. Corson, and gave the sheets on her wrists a tug. "Good," he murmured. "Nice job." Then he tested the restraints on Molly's wrists. "This could have been a little tighter. . . ."

"I thought it was pretty tight. I—"

Chris didn't finish. He felt a powerful blow to his side that knocked the wind out of him. He couldn't even cry out with pain. It took him a few moments to get a breath—and realize the man had kicked him. Doubled up in agony, he gasped for air. Suddenly the man was on top of him. His knee dug into Chris's back as he pulled his hands together and tied up his wrists with the strips of linen. He made the restraints so tight, it almost cut off the circulation in Chris's hands.

He stepped over to Molly and wrapped another linen strip around her hands. She winced as he tied up the knot.

"Now, not a peep out of anyone," he announced, standing over them now. "I'm going to split you up. If you stay quiet and do what I tell you, no one will get hurt. You, you're first. . . ."

Chris glanced over and watched him put his gun in his police holster. Then he grabbed Mrs. Corson by the shoulders. "You're the guest," he said, hoisting her to her feet. "So you belong in the guest room. . . ."

"Oh, God, no, please. . . ." Jenna Corson cried.

But he had her by the arm and led her into the guest room. With her ankles bound, she was forced to take tiny hops.

"Here we go, here we go," he cooed, holding her up.

"Thattagirl . . ." Once they were inside the guest room, he shut the door.

"Oh, Jesus, not the closet," Mrs. Corson cried out. "You're him, you're him. . . ."

Chris suddenly realized—along with Mrs. Corson—that this man was the Cul-de-sac Killer. He heard Jenna Corson's muffled whimpering in the next room and wondered if the man was stabbing her in there right now.

"Chris, listen to me," Molly whispered. He turned toward her so they were facing each other. He lifted his head off the carpet. "If he puts you in your bedroom closet, there's a small knife in one of your brown shoes—the pair you never wear. I left it in there a few days ago. If he sticks you and your dad's and my closet, I hid a knife just to the left of the door—underneath one of my slippers. . . ."

Chris remembered seeing Molly on Friday night with a steak knife in her hand as she'd come upstairs. That had been the night before they'd found out his dad was dead. He'd heard that cop tell Molly about how the Cul-de-sac Killer stashed his victims in closets and then killed them one by one.

Dazed, he just stared at Molly and blinked.

"If you can cut yourself loose," she said, "grab your sister and get out of here. Don't stop for me. I'll take care of myself. Just keep running. Don't try going to one of the neighbors, because no one else is home."

Chris heard Mrs. Corson sobbing. A door slammed shut from within the guest room—and then there was silence. It must have been the closet door. He thought perhaps Mrs. Corson was dead, but he heard a pounding noise—like she was kicking at the door. It was just like the cop had said.

With a click, the guest room door opened, and the man strode out to the hallway. "Okay, your turn, kid," he announced. Chris felt the killer grab him under the arms and lift him off the floor. He caught a glimpse of Molly, who shot him a look of encouragement and nodded.

Chris grimaced in pain as the man pulled up his bound hands in back and pushed him toward his room. He thought the guy was going to break both his arms. He frantically hopped down the corridor, and it was all he could do to keep from stumbling.

"See how you like it in here, shit head," the man grumbled, steering him toward the closet. "Teach you to fuck with me." He swung open the door, and then shoved Chris into the closet.

Chris knocked several hangers askew. Clothes fell on top of him and dropped to the closet floor. He helplessly stumbled onto the floor as well. Desperately glancing around, he caught sight of his brown shoes—just as the door slammed shut.

Then darkness swallowed him up.

Molly's heart broke at the sound of Erin's stifled screams. The killer carried her to her bedroom. "There, there, now, sweetie," he murmured. "Be a good girl. . . ."

His sweet, gentle manner was somehow even crueler than if he'd been rough with her. At least, it felt that way to Molly. He seemed so icy calm and deliberate. She was terrified that he'd kill Erin before he came back for her, before she even had a chance to help the kids escape.

Alone in the hallway, Molly rolled over on the carpet—two complete revolutions—until she was lying at the top of the stairs.

She could still hear Erin's muffled crying as the man emerged from her bedroom. Molly turned on her side and gazed up at him. "Please, don't hurt my little boy down in the basement," she whispered. "He's only six."

His cold eyes narrowed at her. A tiny smile tugged at the corner of his mouth. "Are you trying to tell me I missed one, stepmom?"

Molly twisted around until she was almost sitting up.

"Bobby!" she screamed. "Bobby, honey, get out of the house! Run!"

He turned toward the stairs, his back to her for a moment. Molly leaned back, and then she kicked the backs of his legs with all her might.

He let out a loud yell and toppled down several steps. But he managed to grab hold of the banister halfway down. Wincing, he rubbed his elbow. "Goddamn bitch," he muttered, shaking his head.

But then after a few moments, he chuckled and gazed up at her.

Reaching for the cuff of his navy blue trousers, he pulled it up to reveal a leather sheath strapped to his leg. He took a hunting knife out of that sheath.

Molly struggled to loosen the restraints on her wrists, but she knew it was in vain.

She watched him. He seemed to stare right into her. With the knife in his hand, he slowly came up the stairs.

"Nice try, bitch," Chris heard the man growl.

He'd thought for sure Molly had kicked him down the stairs. Her ruse had been very convincing. If Chris hadn't known better, he'd have thought for sure there was another kid in the house.

Now, he heard what sounded like a slap, and then a dull thud. Molly groaned in pain. Chris swallowed hard, and another wave of panic swept through him. He prayed to God that the guy hadn't kicked her in the stomach. She was pregnant. Maybe she would live through this, but would the baby?

For some reason, it suddenly mattered to him very much that Molly was carrying his little brother or sister.

For the last few minutes, he'd blindly felt around behind his back for the shoe with the knife in it. At last he'd found it. But it took him several contortions to angle the knife correctly. He nicked his finger, and then the palm of his hand, and finally his wrist. With each little slice into his flesh, he grimaced. Tears rolled down his cheeks. The sheet strips around his wrists became damp with his blood—and even harder to cut.

He could hear Molly moaning in pain. "C'mon, step-mom," the man grunted. "It's your turn. Something tells me you know what's coming up. . . ."

There was a strange shuffling sound, which began to fade. Chris knew the killer was leading Molly to the master bed-room—and into the closet there. He heard him chuckling, and then silence.

Frantically, Chris kept pressing the knife blade against the blood-soaked restraint and poking the sharp end through the wet fabric. "Please, God," he whispered. "C'mon. . . ." He maneuvered the knife some more, and heard a tiny rip-ping sound. Finally, he tore through the tattered restraints and rubbed his sore wrists.

His shoulders ached, and the little cuts on his hands stung, but Chris didn't care. Working in the dark, he quickly hacked through the linen strips around his ankles. He could hear a knocking sound. It might have been Mrs. Corson banging against the guest room closet, but he wasn't sure.

He struggled to his feet and opened the closet door. It creaked on the hinges. His legs were a little wobbly, and his side ached from when the man had kicked him. Clutching the small steak knife, he glanced around his bedroom for something else he could use to defend himself. He was going up against a guy with two handguns. And if the news-paper stories were correct, the man carried a knife, too. Most of the Cul-de-sac Killer's victims had been stabbed to death or strangled.

Chris spotted his Louisville Slugger in the corner of his bedroom. He slipped the knife in his pocket, and then grabbed the baseball bat. He crept toward his doorway.

Peering down the empty hall, he noticed the light on in

the master bedroom. The killer was in there with Molly, but Chris couldn't see them—only their shadows crawling across the bedroom wall.

With the bat resting on his shoulder, he quickly crept into Erin's room. He took a deep breath, and braced himself for what he might find behind the closed closet door. He opened it, and let out a sigh. Curled up on the floor amid her shoes, Erin helplessly glanced at him. She tried to talk past the duct tape covering her mouth.

"You have to be quiet, and keep still, okay, peanut?" Chris said, under his breath. Taking the knife from his pocket, he cut the restraints around her ankles and wrists. The rope Mrs. Corson had used was harder to cut than the sheets, and it seemed to take forever. It was no help that Erin kept squirming, and he was afraid of nicking her. All the while, he could hear Mrs. Corson next door, banging at the closet door.

Finally, he cut through the ropes. "Leave the tape over your mouth for now, okay?" he whispered to his little sister. "It'll hurt if I rip it off, and I don't want you crying. We have to be really quiet. Now, let me give you a piggyback ride. C'mon, all aboard. . . ."

Erin was trembling as she grabbed him by the shoulders and climbed on his back. Chris quietly moved to her door and checked the empty hallway.

"I'm saving you for last, bitch," he heard the man say. His voice came from the master bedroom. "I want you to know how it feels to stay in there for a while. And then I'm going to take my sweet time with you."

Chris crept across the hallway to the stairs. With her arms around his neck, Erin clung so tightly she was almost choking him. The steps creaked as he hurried down them, but Mrs. Corson was still kicking against the closet door—and that was louder. She started to scream and cry. At the bottom of the stairs, Chris leaned the bat against the wall. With his free hand, he reached inside the pocket of his jacket, which hung on the newel post. He took out his cell phone and shoved it into his pocket with the knife. Skulking to the front door, he opened it, then went back and retrieved his bat.

The chilly night air felt good as he ducked outside. He closed the door, but made sure the lock didn't click. He would be going back in there.

Chris carried his sister to the end of the driveway, and then lowered her down. He glanced up at the windows in the front of the house, but didn't see any movement. He squatted down again to whisper to Erin. "I want you to run to the Hahns'. No one's home, so you'll have to hide in the playhouse in their backyard. Don't come out until you hear the police sirens, and even then, make sure they're here in front of the house before you let anyone see you. Okay?"

She touched the duct tape over her mouth, and nodded.

He gave his sister a kiss, and then tugged at the corner of the duct tape. "If you tear this off really fast, it might not hurt so much. But it's still going to hurt, and you might cry—so wait until you're in the playhouse. Be brave. You're doing great so far, Erin. Now, go. . . ." He turned her toward the Hahns' house.

Chris watched his sister scurry toward Courtney's place. The empty house was dark—except for one light on in the living-room window. He kept staring at Erin until she disappeared in the shadows.

He took out the cell phone and dialed 9-1-1. Waiting for an answer, he turned back toward the house. Molly and Mrs. Corson were still inside there with that maniac. He glanced up at the second-floor window and didn't see anything.

Then he heard a loud, piercing scream.

"God, no, don't!" Jenna Corson cried out behind the closed door of the guest room. "Please, no, wait . . . wait . . ."

A knife clutched in her hand, Molly paused in the hall-way. Her head throbbed, and blood was smeared around her mouth. She had a cut lip from where he'd hit her.

While stashed in the darkened bedroom closet, she'd managed to find the knife she'd hidden and cut herself free. She'd heard him in the guest room, talking with Jenna Corson. She'd been unable to make out the words, but from their tone, it had sounded like they were having a normal conversation.

Once Molly had crept out of the master bedroom, the murmurings in the guest room next door had become clearer. Jenna Corson had been talking: ". . . so actually, see, you're doing me a favor. Just let me take the little girl, and I'll go quietly. I won't do a thing to stop you. In fact, you can take as long as you want with the other two. I'm in no position to contact the police—ever. Don't you see what a wonderful opportunity this is for you to demonstrate your power? By letting me live, you show that you're not a monster. You're in total control. You're calling the shots. We're a lot alike, you and me. . . ."

Molly had checked both Chris and Erin's rooms and found the closets empty. She'd felt such relief, she'd almost cried. While in Erin's room, she'd heard the man muttering something in response to Jenna's proposition. For a few moments, she'd wondered what he'd said.

But now as she stood outside the guest room, Molly knew his answer.

She heard Jenna Corson screaming: "God, please, no! Wait . . ."

Molly saw her chance to escape. But she couldn't. Despite everything Jenna had done, Molly couldn't just leave her there with that killer. In the next room, Jenna was shrieking. And in all probability, the soft, punching noise was the sound of his knife penetrating her skin.

Molly opened the door, and for a few seconds, she was so horror-struck she couldn't move. Only the closet light was on, but it was enough for her discern the grisly scene in front of her. Jenna was squirming on the floor as he stabbed her. Her hands still tied in back of her, she writhed and screamed.

Her poncho was covered with blood. Bent over her, the Cul-de-sac Killer was so enrapt in his work he didn't seem to notice the hallway light. He didn't seem to notice someone else had come into the room.

Molly suddenly snapped to. Rushing toward him with the knife, she thrust it in his back—just below his left shoulder blade. He let out a howl and twisted around so quickly the knife handle snapped off. The blade was only halfway inside him.

Wide-eyed, he glared at her. Dropping his bloodstained hunting knife, he turned on Molly. All at once, his hands were around her throat. She fought him off as best she could. She couldn't breathe or scream out. He almost lifted her off her feet as he pushed against the wall. Molly struggled, clawing at his hands and face. But he was relentless. His stranglehold only became tighter until he was crushing her windpipe. She started to black out.

Suddenly Chris burst into the room with a baseball bat. The man let go of Molly and reached for his gun.

She fell down on the floor and gasped for air.

Chris swung the bat at him, slamming it against his arm. Molly heard something crack. The killer let out another howl. He swiveled around, and she glimpsed the blood on his pale blue shirt—trailing down from the blade sticking out of his back. His hand fumbled for the gun in his holster, but the way his arm dangled at his side, it looked broken. He backed toward the wall.

"Son of a bitch," Chris cried, swinging the bat at him again.

The killer dodged it, and fell back against the wall. All at once, he froze. His eyes locked on Chris. A gasp came from his open mouth—along with a little stream of blood. He coughed, and more blood spilled over his lips.

In the distance, Molly heard a police siren. She was still too weak to stand and trying to get a breath. She rubbed her sore neck.

Her attacker listed forward. She could see the blood dripping on the wall behind him. As he turned his back to her, she noticed the blade was completely buried beneath his shoulder blade now. It must have been pushed in all the way when he'd fallen against the wall.

The baseball bat still in his grasp, Chris moved away from him.

The man braced himself against the wall as he slowly, painfully made his way toward the door. "You're both dead anyway," he wheezed, his back to them. He started to laugh, but he choked and coughed up blood again. It spattered on the wall. He turned slightly. With a smile on his crimson-smeared mouth, he reached for the switch by the door and flicked on the light.

Then his legs seemed to give out beneath him, and he fell over dead.

With the room lit, Molly realized what he'd meant when he'd said, *"You're both dead anyway."* She realized Jenna Corson wasn't there anymore.

Jenna had managed to slip away unnoticed. She'd left the torn linen restraints in a tangled heap on the bloodstained carpet. But the hunting knife the killer had dropped was gone.

Chris shuddered as he stared down at the corpse. "Erin's safe," he murmured. "Those—those sirens, I think that's the police on their way. I called them. Are you okay?"

"Chris, she's out there," Molly whispered with a nod toward the door. "She has his knife."

He glanced over at the door, then down at the carpet. He seemed to notice the drops of blood that marked a trail from Jenna's shredded restraints to the guest room doorway.

The light had been on in the hallway earlier, but now it was off.

Molly crawled over to the dead man and pried the gun out of his holster. As she started to get to her feet, Chris came over and helped her up. He still held the bat in his other hand. Outside, the sirens were getting louder, and in the window, Molly could see the shadows of headlights and swirling red strobes. She patted Chris on the shoulder and then started toward the doorway.

"Jenna?" she called out, trying to keep her voice from quivering. "The police are outside, and you're badly hurt. You'll bleed to death if you don't get some help. You can't possibly get away...."

Before Molly realized what was happening, Chris brushed past her and stepped out to the darkened hall. She reached out to stop him, but it was too late. With the bat poised on his shoulder, he moved down the hallway and then hesitated. Molly hovered behind him.

Even with the blaring sirens, she could hear Jenna's labored gasps, like a death rattle. Down the shadowy hallway, Jenna sat on the floor near the top of the stairs with her back against the railing. She appeared half dead.

"Mrs. Corson?" Chris said with uncertainty. "I've—I've wanted to tell you ever since Mr. Corson died that I'm sorry. Not a day goes by that I don't think of him and regret—what—what happened. I miss him, Mrs. Corson. I'm sorry I ever doubted him."

Jenna gazed at him. Her head was tipped to one side as she struggled for a breath. Bloodstains covered the front of her poncho, but she still clutched the killer's hunting knife in her hand.

"But you doubted him, too, Mrs. Corson," Chris continued in a shaky voice. "You left him when things got bad. You were separated from him at the time he was killed. I think you feel as guilty as I do—maybe even worse. I think that's why you killed so many people you felt had wronged him. You needed to prove something—that you weren't like the rest of us. But you gave up on him, Mrs. Corson. And even with all the people you killed or hurt—including my parents—it doesn't change that. You still doubted him, too."

She raised her head slightly. Tears welled up in her eyes.

"Ray—he liked you so much," she murmured. "He—he used to say you were a very smart young man. And he was right."

Then Jenna Corson started to cry.

Molly could hear the police at the front door. She moved to the top of the stairs. "We're up here," she called down to them. "We're out of danger, but there's a woman stabbed up here. She—she's pregnant. She needs a doctor right away. . . ."

She saw three policemen in the foyer, all with their guns ready. From the sound of it, there were more outside, too. She noticed one of them mumbling into a little microphone device on his shoulder.

She glanced over at Chris, standing over Jenna. His head down, he leaned the baseball bat against the wall. Molly couldn't hear Jenna sobbing anymore. She wasn't moving.

Molly set the gun on the post at the top of the stairs. "Is my little girl out there?" she called down to them. "Is she all right?"

"Yes, ma'am," one of the cops said as he started up the stairs.

"Erin?" she called loudly.

Past all the noise outside—the engines purring, policemen muttering to each other, someone issuing instructions through a haze of static on a police radio—she heard Erin calling out. "Molly, are you okay? Is Chris okay?"

Chris glanced over his shoulder and gave her a sad, weary smile.

Molly sank down to the floor, and sat on the top step. "We're all right, honey!" she called back. She felt her eyes tearing up as she smiled at Chris. Her voice dropped to a whisper. "We're going to be all right. . . ."

EPILOGUE

Chris tried not to stare, but Courtney's face was still a mess. Nearly a month had gone by since Mrs. Corson's attempt at murder had left Courtney maimed and disfigured. Her blond hair—coming in brown now—was growing back, but it still didn't cover the hole and red scars where her right ear had been. She hadn't gotten her prosthetic ear yet. The patch was off her eye, but she had a painful-looking scar that ran from the outside corner of her eyelid down to the side of her cheek. She wore a bandage over her nose—to cover some recent work on the scar tissue there.

Chris strolled down the hospital corridor with her. Cheesy-looking Christmas decorations festooned the hallways. In some of the rooms, Chris noticed pint-sized trees with lights and ornaments. For this visit, he'd dressed up in khakis and a blue argyle sweater his mom had bought him last year.

With her mangled hand, Courtney pushed along the wheeled contraption that held her IV bag. She wore a beautiful pale pink silk robe over silvery-looking pajamas. It was odd to see her so elegantly dressed in nightclothes while her face was ravaged.

She'd transferred to a different hospital two weeks before. It was closer to the city—and a bit grimier. "My mother tells people we switched because they have the best plastic surgeons here," Courtney said—over the squeaking wheels of her IV holder. "But the truth is, this hospital's cheaper than the other place. Since my dad got the ax, his insurance won't cover any of this. We're majorly screwed. My mother's putting the house on the market after the first of the year."

They passed an old woman in a hospital gown, slumped over to one side in a wheelchair. "God, this place is so gross." Courtney sighed. "Anyway, I don't think my mother's going to have many bidders on the house. I mean, after everything that's happened on the block, who in their right mind would want to live there? God, talk about creepy. I can't believe they found that crystal meth jogger woman all chopped up in the basement shower stall next door to you."

"Actually, Mrs. Corson didn't cut her up," Chris said. "But I guess she thought about it. That's what you probably read. It was part of her confession."

"That's so bizarre about her drug-addict daughter following you around."

Chris just nodded.

"And then those dollhouses they found in her secret room down there," Courtney went on. "I hear she had dolls of you and your stepmother—and of your mom and dad. Did you see any of them? Did the police show you?"

Frowning, Chris shook his head. "No, I really didn't want to see them."

She sighed. "I guess if I were you, I wouldn't have wanted to see them, either."

They walked in silence for a few moments. Chris thought of all the other discoveries the police were making. They'd arrested a twenty-seven-year-old hood named Mark "Wolf" Blanco, who had sold Mrs. Corson the drugs that had killed his dad. The cops said the same guy had wired Courtney's cell phone to explode.

Mrs. Corson had given the police a full confession and named names of all her accomplices—from Wolf Blanco to some forgery expert, and from a computer hacker to a dead hit man named Aldo Mooney, who had killed Mr. Corson, Mrs. Garvey, Chris's mom, Larry and Taylor, and apparently several others.

Of course, the most notorious discovery the police had made was the identity of the Cul-de-sac Killer, a thirty-two-year-old drifter, sometime seaman named Earl Richard Schreiber. In a special room he'd built in the garage of his Crown Hill rental home, the police found an assortment of knives, guns, and ropes; several costumes—from cop to courier; diagrams of the houses he'd struck; and DEAD END and NO OUTLET signs from the cul-de-sacs he'd visited. According to one article Chris read online, the police also uncovered in his secret room scores of S&M magazines, most of them dealing with bondage. Police in Portland, Sacramento, and St. Louis were now linking Schreiber to several unsolved murders in those cities.

He'd stabbed Mrs. Corson four times before Molly had stopped him.

Now, three weeks later, she was still in critical condition. They had her under police guard in a private room—in the same hospital where Courtney was staying. In fact, Mrs. Corson had been at this facility when Courtney transferred here.

"Couldn't your mother have put you in another hospital?" Chris asked her, wincing a bit. He knew it was a tactless question, but he had to ask it. "I mean, I know Mrs. Corson is in a different wing—and she's under armed guard and too weak to do anything. But I'd feel weird here under the same roof as her. I'd want to stay somewhere else—*anywhere* else."

"Like I said, this is the cheapest place where my mother could still tell people that we moved here for the specialists." Courtney gently touched the scar tissue where her ear used to be. "Mom has to keep up appearances. That's why she still pretends to stand right alongside my stupid father and support him. It doesn't make sense sometimes why my mother thinks she has to lie. She even lies to herself. She's an expert at it."

Up ahead, Chris noticed a handsome, blond-haired college guy strutting down the corridor, wearing a sports jacket, denim shirt, and an expensive-looking scarf. A gawky version of him, probably a kid brother going through puberty, tagged alongside him. Mr. Handsome College Guy was carrying a small poinsettia plant. His eyes seemed to lock on Courtney for a moment, and he grimaced a little before averting his gaze.

After they passed by, Chris could hear the kid brother whisper: "God, did you see her face?"

Courtney kept walking a few more paces. In the silence, Chris listened once more to the squeaking wheels of her IV holder. Then Courtney stopped. "I think that's enough exercise for one day," she murmured. "I'd like to go back to my room."

"Sure," Chris said, putting his hand on her back.

"What were we talking about anyway?"

"Mrs. Corson," he muttered.

She nodded. "You were asking if it upset me to have Mrs. Corson so close—after everything she did to me."

"We don't have to talk about it."

"I don't mind." Courtney gave a blasé shrug. "It won't be for much longer. I hear they're transferring her to a prison hospital by the end of the week. And besides, I really don't think about her all that much."

Chris could tell she was lying. He wasn't sure why.

Maybe it was just something she'd picked up from her mother.

There was a Picasso print in her ob-gyn's ultrasound examining room—right above a magazine bin that hung on the wall. An issue of *Vanity Fair* was face out at the front of the stack. Lying on the table, Molly stared at the cover photo of Cate Blanchett while Dr. Lantz applied the cold gel to her lower abdomen. The magazine reminded her that in three months, the *Vanity Fair* Hollywood issue would be released—featuring a two-page cola ad with her party illustration. She'd been able to fix the painting. She'd seen the ad mock-up, too, and been impressed: *Quenching Thirsts for 90 Years!* Molly was already fielding a slew of other job offers.

By the time that issue of *Vanity Fair* hit the stands, she'd be five months along—if all went well. Right now, she really didn't look pregnant—just a bit overweight in the midriff. Molly hated this dumpy stage. She couldn't wait to be really *showing*, without-a-doubt-pregnant. Then maybe she'd stop worrying and feel more confident about the baby's health.

"I've got news for you," Dr. Lantz had told her. "From now on, even after the baby's born, you'll never stop worrying."

She'd just had an ultrasound three weeks before, immediately following Jenna Corson's capture. Molly had wanted to make sure the awful pills and peppermints Jenna had given her hadn't hurt the baby. Lantz had said from the sonogram and his examination, everything looked fine.

But Molly needed to be reassured again. She'd asked for another ultrasound. Lantz had agreed to squeeze her in for an appointment. She'd also asked about Jenna's baby, if there was any chance it had survived. There had been no mention of Jenna's pregnancy in any of the articles Molly had read.

None of the cops or reporters she'd spoken with knew about it. That was Jeff's child Jenna had been carrying. Molly needed to know what had happened to it. So she'd asked Dr. Lantz if he could find out for her.

Molly liked Dr. Lantz. In fact, with his light brown hair, brown eyes, and boy-next-door looks, he reminded her of Chris O'Donnell, whom she'd been crazy about in high school. Dr. Lantz was happily married with three daughters, so Molly figured it was safe to have a harmless little crush on him. They couldn't possibly get involved.

She wasn't ready to get involved with anyone. Chet Blazevich had paid her another unofficial visit at home last week. *"Just checking in,"* he'd said. Molly had appreciated knowing he was looking out for her. And she liked him a hell of a lot.

But when he'd asked to take her out for dinner sometime, Molly had told the handsome cop it was just too soon.

"I can wait," he'd told her.

"Well, that's the true test," she'd replied. "Will you still like me when I'm not fat and hormonal and pregnant with someone else's baby?"

"I'll still like you," he'd promised. He'd also promised to check in on her and the kids from time to time—if she didn't mind.

Molly didn't mind one bit.

Moving the ultrasound scanner over her gel-smeared, slightly expanded lower abdomen, Dr. Lantz studied the sonogram and announced, "We're looking good here, Molly. Everything is as normal as normal can be."

Molly studied the sonogram monitor and the little oblong cloud that was supposed to be her child. It still didn't seem real.

"By the way," Dr. Lantz said. "This is strictly off the record, but I talked to Jenna Corson's doctor for you a few days ago. Mrs. Corson wasn't pregnant. She thought she was—and refused to believe she wasn't. Anyway, sounds like a hysterical pregnancy."

Molly actually found herself pitying Jenna—until she thought about all the tainted pills and peppermints Jenna had given her.

"Are you sure everything looks okay with the baby?" Molly pressed.

Dr. Lantz nodded, and moved the scanner a bit. "Do you want to know the sex?"

Molly hesitated. She hadn't wanted to before, but somehow it mattered now. She didn't want to think of this baby as *it* anymore. She nodded. "Tell me. . . ."

"It's a boy," he said.

Molly gazed at the cloud on the sonogram, and smiled. She was looking at her son. "Are you—are you sure he's okay?" she asked. "I mean, after all, he's been through a lot. . . ."

"So have you," the doctor said. "But I guess he's a real survivor, just like his mom."

Molly kept staring at the screen. She couldn't take her eyes off him.

"I hate these stinking lights," Chris announced.

He'd assembled the fake Christmas tree in the family room and carefully arranged three of the four white light strings on the branches. But one string in the middle had just gone out. Now he was testing each bulb to find which son-of-a-bitch light was screwing up the whole son-of-a-bitch string.

He didn't even want Christmas this year, but he was putting up the tree to make Molly and Erin happy. They were in the kitchen, baking Christmas cookies for Erin's class tomorrow. Erin sat on a step stool on the other side of the counter, frosting the cookies. The sweet, homey smell filled the house—as did the sound of Johnny Mathis singing "Winter Wonderland" on Molly's iPod Christmas mix.

"I want to put the star on top of the tree!" Erin declared.

"You did it last year," Chris said. "It's Molly's turn. She hasn't had a chance to put the star up yet."

"But I want to," Erin whined.

"Oh, it really doesn't matter that much to me," Molly sighed.

She'd said the same thing last year when his dad had suggested she do the tree-topping honors. Erin had wanted to do it then, too. And Molly—obviously still trying to win them over—had insisted that Erin have her way. But Chris remembered his dad hadn't been pleased. He'd told them later that it would have been a nice gesture to let Molly put the star on the tree—to acknowledge she was part of the family.

That was last year. Chris really didn't have time for all this Christmas tradition now. He still had schoolwork to catch up on from the two weeks he'd missed when first his mom and then his dad had been killed. He also had to start looking for colleges that might offer swimming scholarships. It was the kind of thing his dad might have helped him with.

His dad would have been putting up the tree, too.

Chris missed him. He missed both of them so much.

Maybe another reason he didn't really feel like Christmas was because it would be his last one in this house. Molly wanted to move in the spring. After what had happened in the guest room, she didn't feel like converting it into a nursery. Chris didn't blame her a bit. He didn't even like going in there. Though they'd replaced the carpet in that room and in the hallway, he could still picture where the bloodstains had been.

As much as he hated to leave this house, where he'd once been happy with his parents, all of that had changed. He understood Molly's need to have a place that was hers, where no one dead had a hold over them.

"Just for the record, I'm not having fun here," Chris said, still trying to locate the defective light. "I hate these lights, and I hate this tree."

"Well, take a break," Molly said, putting on a pair of oven mitts. "I can do that later. There's no rush. We still have two weeks until Christmas." She opened the oven and took out a sheet of cookies.

He shook another little bulb, and suddenly, all the lights on the faulty string went on.

"Yippee!" Erin cried, a smudge of frosting on her cheek.

Chris glanced over at her and Molly. He worked up a smile.

But Molly put a hand over her mouth, and her color suddenly didn't look so good. "Excuse me," she muttered, rushing out of the kitchen.

He heard her footsteps racing up the stairs, and a few moments later, a door slammed. He scratched his head. "I don't get why she always goes all the way upstairs to barf when there's a bathroom down here."

Erin shrugged. "I think she likes barfing upstairs." She went back to frosting the cookies.

She didn't seem to understand why Chris was chuckling. He'd have to share his kid sister's little pearl of wisdom with Molly when she came downstairs again. In the meantime, he finished arranging the last of the Christmas lights. The tree was actually starting to look pretty.

He began to wonder if Molly was all right. Usually, she was back downstairs and feeling better a few minutes after praying to the porcelain god.

He went to the foot of the stairs. "Molly?" he called. "Are you okay?"

No answer.

He started up the stairs. In the second-floor hallway, he

saw the stairwell door to her attic studio was open. He heard murmuring up there. It sounded like she was on the phone.

Chris knew it wasn't any of his business, but he crept to the doorway.

"It's all right, Mother," she was saying. "I understand why you couldn't come to the funeral. You didn't even know him. But I want you to think about coming here for Christmas or New Year's. I miss you, Mom. Most of all, I think it's time you met my kids. Chris and Erin are really pretty great. . . ."

Smiling, Chris quietly walked toward the stairs. He would go down to the kitchen and talk to his sister. He'd get her to agree. They'd ask Molly to put up the star.

Visitors needed to be cleared in advance. He saw a note attached to the clipboard with the sign-in sheet that the patient's sister, Elaine Lawles, would be coming by at six-thirty.

In the hospital hallway, the uniformed police guard sat outside Jenna Corson's door. He was tired, and desperately trying to stay awake. Last night, he'd pulled an eight-hour shift working security on his second job at Westlake Mall. The thirty-four-year-old had wavy red hair, a mustache, and—at the moment—dark circles under his blue eyes.

He sat at a desk outside room 404. In front of him was a small poinsettia plant, a bottle of Evian water, a *Sports Illustrated*, the clipboard with the sign-in sheet for visitors, and a phone he wasn't supposed to use except on official business. The ringer was turned down low.

He barely heard it ring when the call came through at 6:25. It was the front desk, telling him that they'd issued a visitor's pass to Elaine Lawles, and she was on her way up. He thanked them, hung up the phone, and got to his feet.

The door to 404 was open. Nurses and doctors had been in and out of there all day. He peeked in on the patient. She was snoozing. She had a pasty complexion, and her limp brown hair needed washing. The hospital gown was hardly flattering. Still, she looked like she might have been kind of pretty—when not borderline comatose with a tube in her nose. They had Jenna Corson hooked up to an IV drip. Her heartbeat was monitored on a small screen at her bedside. There were no flowers or Christmas decorations in the room. Elaine Lawles was her first family visitor.

When she didn't show up by six-forty, the guard started to wonder if Jenna's sister had gotten lost. That was easy to do in this maze of a hospital. He sat down, and was about to call the front desk when he saw someone approaching. She wore her visitor's badge on the lapel of her trench coat. In one hand, she carried a little Christmas evergreen plant with tiny red and gold ribbon bows on it. He gaped at her.

"I'm Elaine Lawles, and I'm here to see my sister, Jenna Corson." she said. Then she frowned at him. "It's impolite to stare."

He cleared his throat. "Um, sorry," he muttered, reaching for the clipboard. "Could you sign in, please? And I'll need to hold on to your purse while you're in there."

Putting down the Christmas plant, she surrendered her bag, and then scrawled her name on the form. It was barely legible. "I'd like to talk to my sister in private. May I close the door?"

He didn't see anything wrong with it. There was a window in the door. He wanted to warn her that it wouldn't be much of a conversation. Jenna Corson was still very weak, and they'd pumped her full of painkillers and antidepressants. So far, he'd chalked up about fifty hours of guard duty here in the last three weeks, and he'd heard the patient mutter about twenty words—tops.

He watched the woman stroll into Jenna Corson's room. "Hey, sis," she said. "It's me, Elaine. Are you awake? You don't look so bad. . . ."

Then she closed the door behind her.

The guard could hear murmuring. He started reading his *Sports Illustrated*.

After a while, he heard a muffled, high-pitched hum.

At that very moment in another wing on that same floor, Elaine Lawles was passed out in the last of three stalls in the women's room. Someone had stolen her trench coat, her purse, her shoes, and her visitor's pass. A syringe—with just a trace of propofol left in it—was on the gray-tiled floor between her and the toilet.

Anyone resourceful enough could have figured out how to get their hands on a syringe and the sleep drug if they'd been around the hospital for two weeks.

Elaine had come empty-handed to visit her sister—no flowers, magazines, or candy.

The Christmas plant now on the nightstand table in room 404 had been a gift for another patient in the hospital, a teenage girl who was in there for a series of skin grafts.

The guard outside Jenna Corson's room got to his feet. Moving closer to the door, he heard the incessant high-pitched drone more clearly now. The guard looked in the window—at the woman standing at Jenna Corson's bedside. She was holding a pillow over Jenna's face.

That sound came from the cardio monitor. It accompanied the flatline on the screen.

He heard a stampede of footsteps, and a doctor hurriedly issuing instructions. A crew of doctors and nurses were racing up the hallway toward room 404. The guard counted seven of them. Two were pushing a resuscitation cart.

They would be in there working on her for the next thirty minutes—with one of them periodically yelling, "Clear!" But the line on that monitor graph would remain flat.

The woman they pulled off Jenna Corson had a hospital gown under the trench coat. For someone who was so scarred up, she was awfully strong. She would later tell the police that suffocating Jenna Corson hadn't been too difficult.

The hard part had been giving Jenna's sister the shot of propofol. "You try working a syringe when you don't have all your fingers," she told them.

Still, somehow, Courtney had managed to do it.

More Nail-Biting Suspense From Your Favorite Thriller Authors

The Night Caller by John Lutz	0-7860-1284-6	**$6.99US/$8.99CAN**
The Night Watcher by John Lutz	0-7860-1515-2	**$6.99US/$9.99CAN**
The Night Spider by John Lutz	0-7860-1516-0	**$6.99US/$9.99CAN**
Only Son by Kevin O'Brien	1-57566-211-6	**$5.99US/$7.50CAN**
The Next to Die by Kevin O'Brien	0-7860-1237-4	**$6.99US/$8.99CAN**
Make Them Cry by Kevin O'Brien	0-7860-1451-2	**$6.99US/$9.99CAN**
Watch Them Die by Kevin O'Brien	0-7860-1452-0	**$6.99US/$9.99CAN**

Available Wherever Books Are Sold!

Visit our website at **www.kensingtonbooks.com**